A DANGEROUS MAN

Jack pulled her around to face him and then backed her slowly against the wall of the stable. Her face paled and her eyes became wide, but she went. She didn't fight him. That's what could get her killed; she didn't fight, didn't see danger when it had its hands around her waist and was pressing against the long fall of her skirts.

He was danger. He shouldn't be anywhere near her, couldn't she see that? Hell, the whole town saw it, but not her. She just kept looking up at him, her eyes blue and soft and trusting. She'd get herself killed without any trouble at all, just the way she'd get herself kissed, just by looking at him. Just by relaxing into his hands when she should have been tensing in outrage. Just by raising her face, her lips parted, her breath sweet when she should have been cussing him out. She probably didn't know how to cuss. Trouble was, she knew how to kiss.

CLAUDIA DAIN

A KISS TO DIE FOR

LEISURE BOOKS NEW YORK CITY

In memory of my mother,
who taught me everything.

A LEISURE BOOK®

December 2008

Published by

Dorchester Publishing Co., Inc.
200 Madison Avenue
New York, NY 10016

ISBN 10: 0-8439-5059-5
ISBN 13: 978-0-8439-5059-5

The name "Leisure Books" and the stylized "L" with design are trademarks of Dorchester Publishing Co., Inc.

Printed in the United States of America.

10 9 8 7 6 5 4 3 2 1

Visit us on the web at www.dorchesterpub.com.

A KISS
TO DIE FOR

Prologue

The Texas wind was blowing hard and cold, but he didn't care. All he cared about was that little girl in his sights; she was a woman full grown, but slight, like a girl, with red hair the color of ripe pumpkins hanging down her back. The wind blew her hair hard, making strands of it whip around her head like straw in a cyclone. She kept pulling at it, tugging those wild strings of hair down with her white hands until she held them like a bouquet.

Only one reason for a woman to wear her hair loose on a day of such wind; she wanted to catch a man's eye.

She'd caught his.

He'd seen her before. This game she was playing with him was an old one and he let her lead him around in it, knowing it built her confidence to have him chase after her. Knowing it made her sure of herself. Knowing that soon she'd do something reckless. And he'd be right there when she did.

He'd give her what she was asking for.

Maybe even today.

He got hard thinking of it, thinking of her under his

hands, soft and willing. Her mouth telling him yes when he wrapped his arms around her and asked her to marry him.

That's what she was wanting from him, a proposal of marriage, and that's what he'd give her. That, and a few dozen kisses. But she'd be getting more than kisses from him. A whole lot more.

He knew exactly what she wanted. Same thing they all wanted. And he was more than happy to oblige.

He was nothing if not accommodating.

She was a pretty little thing, her hair so bright against the milk white of her hands. She had a spray of freckles across her knuckles that about matched the color of her hair. She was smiling at him, her eyes blue and round with excitement. He'd arranged this meeting with her yesterday, as she was walking out of church with her folks. He'd whispered to her as she'd passed, her head down as she walked behind her ma, and she hadn't answered. But here she was.

Her folks didn't know about him, not yet. They'd know soon enough. Once she agreed to marry him, they'd know it all.

"You're a pretty little girl," he said, closing the distance between them.

"I'm not a little girl," she huffed, letting loose of her hair. It rose up in the air and twisted, writhing and hot against the blue of the sky.

"Is that why you came today? To prove to me you aren't so little?"

"Is that why you asked me out here? To make sport of me?"

She turned her back on him in a sulk that begged to be petted out of her. He accommodated her, giving her just what she wanted from him. He knew everything about this game they were playing.

He stroked down the wild tangle of her hair, holding

2

the length of it in his fist. It was cool and smooth across the back of his hand.

"Your hair's like slick fire," he said, pressing up against her. "Is your mouth the same?"

She turned in his arms, her hair wrapping around her throat and breasts like a red silk cord. She wanted to give in, but couldn't. He was moving too fast.

"You gonna make me beg for it?" he said on a whisper.

"Would you?" she asked back, raising her eyes to his.

"Nah"—he grinned, lifting up her face—"I'm gonna make you beg. More fun that way."

He kissed her then, liking the smallness of her pressed against him. Her mouth was like fire, after he had tutored her some.

It was her first kiss.

She acted as if she liked it fine. She was pressed up against him, her breasts small and hard and high, and her arms wrapped around him. She was holding nothing back, which was just how he liked it.

"You beggin' yet?" he breathed against her throat. That red hair of hers was still wrapped around her, so hot against the white of her throat.

"No, you'd better," she breathed roughly, "you'd better—"

He cut off her air with a kiss that had her hanging on to his belt for balance. When he was done, she laid her forehead against his chest and gulped in air, her fingers still wedged in his belt.

"Are you playing with me?" she whispered, hiding her face from him.

He wrapped his arms around her with a huge smile. This was it. Time to give her what she'd come all the way out of town to get.

"Hell, no, darlin'. I'm not playing with you. I want to marry you."

"You do?" She looked up at him. She had the most powerful blue eyes.

"I do," he said. "Will you?"

She bloomed like a flower, right there in his arms. "Yes!"

He kissed her again, sealing the pledge they'd just made between them. She sure seemed to like his kisses.

"I've got a little something for you," he said softly as he ended the kiss. His eyes were gentle as he looked down at her; this was the moment, the perfect moment.

"You don't need to give me a thing," she protested but she reached out her hand for whatever the gift was that he had brought her. "I'm just so happy right now, I don't need another thing to make it perfect."

Women said things like that. They didn't mean them. He knew that.

He kissed her once more, in parting, while he gave her the gift he'd brought just for her. Just like a flower, she was, just like a flower that bloomed bright and fresh with the sun on it and then was blown down by the first cold wind.

When she collapsed on the ground, her throat crushed like a broken stem, the wind blew hard at her unbound hair; it flew up and twirled against the sky, glistening red against deep blue. No one now to hold it down, to keep it off her face and out of her eyes. It didn't much matter anymore. He studied her for a minute, that pretty hair flying wild in the wind, and then left her.

She'd got what she came for.

Chapter One

The train pulled into the Abilene station with a chug and a lurch that rocked his body forward in stiff synchronism. He held himself erect and kept his balance, keeping his eyes on the town coming into view through the dusty windows of the westbound train. Abilene had grown some since he'd last been through—more houses and a wooden church—but had shrunk some, too. The Drovers Cottage hotel was gone, moved to Ellsworth a few years back since the cow trail had moved west. The dance house he'd used was gone and the town looked light a few saloons. Abilene didn't look like the wild cattle town it had been right after the war. Still, it would have a jail and that's where the man in the seat in front of him was headed.

With a final wet hiss, the train gave its last lurch and was still.

"Get up, Jessup," he mumbled. "This is where you get off."

"Name's not Jessup. I tell ya, ya got the wrong man."

"Get up anyway," he said, tired of the whole conversation. Twenty miles of the same bull was wearing his patience thin.

Jessup got up slowly, stretching as he stood, rubbing a hand through his hair, examining his fingernails, stamping his feet in his boots.

"You look fine enough to hit jail," Jack said.

He helped him along with a poke in the back that propelled Jessup reluctantly down the aisle toward the open door of the car. The other passengers, the three of them, watched only to break the monotony; they'd heard enough of the same for the past twenty miles to make them eager only for Jessup's removal from their car.

The sun was bright after the dark interior of the car, hitting the dirt and bouncing around in the air as if off a mirror. Jack blinked and Jessup took his chance.

He threw his weight against Jack and smashed him into a seat. He banged his tailbone on the hard wooden edge; pain flared and then dulled. Fed up, he caught Jessup at the open door and lowered his fist like a sledge hammer, not caring if he cracked the man's skull and let out the sawdust. Jessup fell all the way out and down and landed on the platform. And stayed put.

Until a woman knelt beside him to help him up.

It was then that he noticed he'd drawn a crowd. Not a one of them looked happy. He'd remembered Abilene as a happier place, but that may have been because he'd spent his time here drunk.

Abilene had changed, all right.

Looking more carefully at her, the little Samaritan, he felt drunk again. Lust slammed against him hard, leaving him short of breath. She was fair skinned, dark haired, and blue eyed. Full bust covered in lace and ruffle and a rounded bottom draped with a length of blue ribbon trailing down, she was staring at him with accusation in her prairie sky eyes.

If that wasn't enough, she looked as proper as a

preacher's wife. If he wanted to get out of town without a fight, he'd need to keep his distance, no matter that he could hear the blood pounding in his ears . . . and elsewhere. Best thing would be to get away from her right quick and then keep clear of her until he left town. Women like her didn't mess with men like him, he'd learned that often enough to get it straight in his head.

"Get up, Jessup, and move your sorry hide," he snarled, keeping his eyes away from the Samaritan. Jessup, the fight mashed out of him, cooperated. Which was too damn bad, now that Jack thought about it, since he was suddenly in the mood to kick some tail. He left all thoughts of tail by the train with the blue-eyed girl and marched his man toward the center of town.

The snarls of the good citizens of Abilene followed him, not that he cared.

"Brutality. Nothing but blatant and unrepentant brutality," Esther Morris concluded as she watched the bounty hunter and his poor abused prisoner walk away.

"What else? He's a bounty hunter. Nothing lower on God's green earth than a bounty hunter." Isaiah Hill spat, his tobacco juice leaving a brown, wet smear on the wooden platform. Esther backed up to widen the range between them.

"Yeah, but he's more than just a bounty hunter. He's Jack Skull," said John Campbell. As the stationmaster, he knew more about strangers coming in on the train than almost anyone, since he was there more than anyone, even Anne, though just by a hair.

"*That* was Jack Skull?" Isaiah asked, almost swallowing when he meant to spit. "Thought he'd be bigger."

"Big enough," John snorted.

"Jack Skull?" Anne edged in. "I didn't think he was real. . . . I mean, I thought folks just sort of made him up."

"He's real enough and you saw how mean he was."

"Well, but he may have had cause," Anne said slowly.

7

"It isn't as if a bounty hunter would bring in a man who wasn't wanted for something. The law—"

"The law makes use of bounty hunters, but don't like them, and you know that's the truth, Anne. Now, don't go making more of the man than there is. He's no good. You saw for yourself," John insisted.

"The whole world knows about Jack Skull and what kind of man he is," Isaiah put in.

"I know it didn't look good, his knocking the man down like that for no apparent reason, but I'm sure that he must have been provoked," Anne said softly.

"A brutal man requires no provocation, Anne," Esther said, her tone severe. "You're too soft, Anne; you mustn't look for excuses when there are none."

"Yes, ma'am." Esther was good friends with her grandmother and it wouldn't do her a bit of good if this story got back to Miss Daphne.

"Course she's right," John said. "Well, he's in Abilene now; the best we can hope for is that he jumps back on the train and heads out. It's a quiet town we've got here now and we don't need his kind."

Isaiah spat in agreement.

"Yeah, I'd bet he'll be gone before dark. It don't take no time atall to get a feller locked up."

The sheriff slammed the door shut on the outlaw and threw the keys on top of his desk. They skidded to a stop next to a battered lamp. The tracks on his desk showed that this was his usual way of storing his keys. Jack smiled as he tore up the handbill on Jacob Jessup, no longer at large, but safely tucked away. His eyes scanned the wall where the wanted posters were nailed in twisted rows. John Jacobs, Brazos, Texas Al, Big Nose Pete, Kid Walker; he knew them all, by face and name. There were no new men offered up for hunting.

"Want a drink?" the sheriff offered.

Jack looked up at the man and took his measure. Not many lawmen wanted to spend time with a bounty hunter. Why would this one be any different?

"Sure," he answered and remained standing, waiting. He wasn't going to horn in anywhere unless personally invited.

The sheriff smiled and said, "Have a seat."

Jack sat back in a wooden chair that wobbled unevenly and was scuffed in the seat. The townsfolk of Abilene didn't seem to want to put much municipal money into the sheriff's office.

"Rye?"

"Rye's fine," he answered.

"Name's Lane, Charles Lane."

"Jack Scullard," he said, taking a swallow and enjoying the burn of it as it slid down.

"Scullard?"

"Yeah. Scullard."

"Different version of your name going around these parts," Lane said mildly.

"Yeah, I heard."

Sheriff Lane leaned back in his chair until it hit the wall and balanced. "You know how you came by it?"

"Maybe," Jack said, finishing off his drink. "You want to tell me?"

Sheriff Lane shrugged and upended his own cup. "Talk is that you prefer bringing in the heads, the skulls, to live men; make the same money and a lot easier to tote."

"Makes sense," Jack commented, his eyes on the sheriff's face.

"Yeah." Lane nodded. "Makes sense. Only that's no skull sitting in my cell."

"It takes an experienced lawman to notice the details like that," Jack said wryly.

Lane nodded and smiled slowly. "Yeah, well, they didn't hire me for my smile."

9

Jack smiled back and set his cup on the stained desk, waiting.

Lane picked up the slack. "How'd you come by Jessup? He's been wanted near on a year."

Jack shrugged as he answered, "Played cards with him last night in a hole just east of here. He fit the description."

"That all?"

"He cheats," Jack said casually. "But, yeah, that's all."

"You didn't think you might have the wrong man? Plenty can match his description; hell, I'm not that far off."

"You think I got the wrong man?"

Lane smiled and poured himself another shot, the front legs of his chair hitting the floor hard as he reached for the bottle. He silently offered his guest another shot; Jack waved him off.

"No, you got the right man, all right. I know Jessup from Ogallala, it just seems like it would have been easy to make a mistake."

Jack's blue eyes studied the sheriff without rancor. He knew he hadn't made a mistake in Jessup. He knew he couldn't explain how he had known Jessup was wanted to a man who didn't hunt men for money. He also knew that Sheriff Charles Lane wasn't liquoring him up to talk about Jessup.

"He fit the description," he repeated, rolling the cup between the palms of his hands, waiting.

Lane nodded and played with his own glass. He didn't drink from it.

"You been collecting bounty long?"

"Long enough."

The two men sat in the shadowed interior of the rough jailhouse, the slanted morning light catching the points of the splinters on the walls and warming the wood to amber. They waited each other out, each comfortable in

10

the deliberate silence, each feeling for the measure of the man in the opposite chair.

"You got me figured out yet?" Lane asked.

"Enough for me to keep sitting here," Jack said easily. "You want something. You going to tell me what it is or do I got to figure that out, too?"

Lane smiled and slapped his drink down on the table. Everything the man did, he did hard.

"There's been some killings out around here. You heard anything about it?"

Jack kept his face blank and his hands easy. "No."

"Women," Lane spat out in disgust. "It's been women that's getting killed."

"What kind of women?"

"Not that kind. Nice women. Unmarried women."

"How many?" He said it very calmly, almost softly.

The sheriff looked him in the eye and wiped his hand across his mouth. "Three."

"That's a lot of killing," Jack said. "Since when?"

"First one was a year ago, then four months after that, then just last month. All nice girls."

"In town?"

"No, but in the area, maybe thirty square miles."

"That's a lot of ground to cover."

"Yeah, but with the railroad hooking everybody up . . . makes it easier."

"Yeah," Jack whispered, his eyes on the splinters in the walls, now nearly invisible since the light had shifted. But he'd feel them if he banged up against that wall.

"We've been working hard to keep things quiet; don't want the people to get in a hanging fever. The U.S. Marshal's been working on it, but it's a big area and he—"

"You want me to nose around."

"Yeah."

Jack sat and studied the sheriff's silence. He was a big man, black of hair and eye, with a crooked nose and high cheekbones. He didn't look comfortable asking favors.

"These women," Jack said, "they bloodied up, beaten, anything like that?"

"No, clean as Sunday."

"Pretty gals?"

"A mother's dream."

Jack paused and could feel a line of sweat make its way down the side of his neck just as his next question made its way up into his throat.

"Strangled?"

The silence between them was heavy. The heat of the day was building, but it was nothing against that silence.

"Yeah."

Jack could read the sheriff's thoughts easily enough, especially since he didn't think Lane was making much effort to hide them. He was a stranger, he was a man given to violence, and he knew a lot about something that was being kept secret; it was a lot to add up and it added up pretty quick. Jack gave the man credit for not throwing a noose around his neck right then.

"There've been a couple of murders down around Red River Station that sound about the same," Jack offered. "Nice girls, marrying age, strangled and left. I've been following the trail left by the killer. It's one of the reasons I came north."

"Trail led you here? To Abilene?"

"Yeah, seemed to. I hadn't heard about any more murders, but with the marshal keeping them quiet, I guess I wouldn't have."

Lane poured himself another shot and poured one for Jack without asking permission. They both needed a drink.

"You followed him up from Texas," Charles Lane said as he sipped his drink. "He seems to have settled himself in Kansas for a spell."

Jack took a long swallow, emptied his glass, and set it

down softly on the scarred desk. He studied his dusty boots for a long moment before turning his gaze on the sheriff.

"Looks like I'll be stayin' awhile."

Chapter Two

Anne left the train station only after everyone who was getting off had gotten off; that included the bounty hunter. The way he had looked at her sent her stomach rolling into the middle of her knees. Bill sure didn't make her feel that way.

Not that he should. No one should. It was completely unacceptable and highly improper. Miss Daphne would have a fainting, screaming fit if she found out that a bounty hunter had looked at her as if she were the last meal for a hundred miles.

Miss Daphne would not hear about it from her.

But she might hear about it from Esther Morris.

They thought she had defended Jack Skull's actions because she was softhearted, but they were wrong; that wasn't it. At least not all of it. It was worse than that. She was taken with Jack Skull.

She'd never looked at a man and had such a jolt of feeling fire through her. She knew without asking how wrong that was. But knowing that what she was feeling was forbidden, that the man himself was forbidden, didn't

14

seem to be helping her any. He was the most blatantly compelling man she'd ever seen and, rough as he looked, she'd wanted to walk right up to him and tuck herself under his arm.

That was bad.

The way he'd looked at her, it didn't seem that he'd have minded much. It was a look that had made her forget to breathe.

That was real bad.

No man had the right to kick the breath out of her; that he was a bounty hunter didn't make it worse or better. He was a man and that was bad enough.

Anne allowed herself a soft sigh as she walked up the path to her house, that is, Miss Daphne's house. Sarah met her as she opened the door.

"Anybody interesting this time?"

"Let her be, Sarah," Nell, Anne's mother, said as she hurried forward for her share of the news. "Who would get off that would be of any interest to us?"

Sarah shot her sister a look, but held her tongue on that issue.

"No one much," Anne said as she untied the strings to her bonnet and hung it on a stand near the door. "I spoke a bit with John Campbell, just pleasantries and such." Telling her mother, aunt, and grandmother about the prisoner falling at her feet and the bounty hunter looking her over was not on her list of open topics.

"Esther Morris came by, just briefly," Miss Daphne said from the kitchen.

Anne's heart sank. Esther must have come at a dead run if she had made it to the house before Anne did; she had raised a bit of dust herself hurrying home.

"Did she?" Anne answered her grandmother sweetly.

"Yes," Miss Daphne said calmly, wiping flour from her hands.

Sarah gave Anne a look and moved out of the line of

15

fire; she had tried to give Anne a chance to come out with it herself. It would only be worse now because she had tried to hide something.

"She said there was an altercation involving an outlaw and a bounty hunter and that you were right in the middle of it," her grandmother said, displeasure shining from her brown eyes.

Anne knew better than to point out that Esther must also have been in the middle of it, as well as Isaiah and John. Miss Daphne didn't concern herself with what they did; they weren't family.

"Now, Mother, Anne can't be responsible for the behavior of that bounty hunter," Nell said valiantly.

"Anne can certainly be responsible for her whereabouts, her company, and her deportment," Daphne said coldly.

"Speaking of deportment," Sarah cut in, "what did he look like? Handsome man or rough as a post?"

Anne held her breath, uncertain of her next step in this rocky conversation. She knew Sarah's purpose was to shake Miss Daphne loose on the issue of the fight, but she didn't see how an honest answer would help her. Still, they'd find out eventually. Esther Morris likely hadn't died on her way home.

"Well, I wouldn't exactly say he was handsome."

"Then what exactly is he?" Sarah prodded.

Anne chewed the inside of her lower lip as she chose her words. "He's dusty, unshaven, clean-featured, lean, and taller than John Campbell."

"What color are his eyes?"

"Blue." It was out before she could stop it. She looked at her mama and her aunt and then closed her eyes before she could see what look her grandmother was giving her. She shouldn't have been looking closely enough to have noticed the color of his eyes. Even she knew that. She didn't need a lecture on it.

"Blue? Why, he sounds like a good-looking man, Anne." Sarah chuckled. "You best keep your guard up while he's in Abilene or you'll have two beaus to manage."

"Don't be ridiculous, Sarah," Nell snapped. "Anne has more sense than to spend time with a bounty hunter and risk offending Bill besides."

"Offending Bill?" Sarah snapped back. "A woman is allowed to have more than one man courting her and Bill should remember that."

"She can only marry one," Miss Daphne said.

That closed the subject since no one would willingly marry a bounty hunter. And she did have Bill, after a fashion. It was an ideal courtship to her mind. He wasn't around much, he was presentable and well thought of in town, and he satisfied her family's need for her to have a "prospect." Yes, Bill was the ideal beau. When he was in town, he courted her prettily enough. He was handsome, too. Eleanor Parker almost regretted marrying Clyde Barton after she had seen Bill.

But then, Eleanor hadn't seen the bounty hunter yet.

"Anne," her grandmother said, the chill in her voice cooling the room, "I trust that, in future, you will keep the proper distance between yourself and that bounty hunter. God willing, he will be out of town by nightfall. In the meantime, remember who you are and what is expected of you."

Sarah and Nell, as daughters of Daphne Perkins Todd, said nothing to alleviate the burden of respectable responsibility deposited upon Anne's shoulders. They had been taught the futility of revolt decades ago.

"Yes, ma'am," Anne answered, her head lowered, her eyes lowered. Her spirits lowered to a back-burner simmer.

Miss Daphne looked all three of them over once, sharply, and then said, "Come, Nell, I need your hands with the baking."

Claudia Dain

Nell followed her mother into the kitchen after giving Anne a quick smile. As soon as Daphne was behind the closed kitchen door, Sarah grabbed Anne by the hand and led her out onto the front porch. They sank down onto two straight-backed wooden chairs and Anne let out a breath of relief.

"You may only marry once, but you should at least have the fun of a hectic courtship," Sarah said without preamble. "Tell me what you really think about this bounty hunter."

"I don't think anything," Anne said, refusing the invitation to think about the bounty hunter. "I didn't even speak to him."

"But you saw him?"

"As did Esther and John and Isaiah."

"I don't care if they saw him," Sarah said, "and I don't care what they thought of him. What did you think?"

"I didn't think anything then and I don't think anything now." It would be true because she would make it true. There was no room for a man, that man, in her thoughts.

Sarah sat back in her chair with a grunt. "That's too bad, Anne." Folding her slender arms across her chest, she looked up at the porch ceiling and said casually, "Because I was thinking that it wouldn't be such a bad thing for you to have two beaus, and if you thought this bounty hunter was nice to look at, you could use him to set a fire under Bill."

When Anne sat up stiffly at that, Sarah continued, "Bill's been slow to ask you to marry. He's a fine prospect, if he is a bit shy in his courting. He'll get you out of this town as well as any man and that's what you want, isn't it?"

No, it wasn't what she wanted, but she wasn't going to fight about it with her aunt, or anyone else in her family for that matter. She did want to leave Abilene, see a bit

18

of the world beyond a dying town in the middle of the prairie, but she didn't need a man to get it done. Of course, Sarah didn't see it that way and her grandmother would want to skin her raw if she even suspected that she was thinking of "running off." That's how they saw it, each one of them. A woman who left home without a husband at her side was running off to God knew where. Perdition, most like.

But she wasn't going to get married. Ever. Of course, they didn't have to know that. Why fight that fight? Let them think that she was in a marrying frame of mind; her trouble was in keeping Bill off balance. If he was slow in his courting, that was all to the good, but he was building up steam for something; she could feel that coming like wind sliding off the prairie. What she needed was some way to slow him down. Could be a bounty hunter would do that better than she.

Two men on a lead rope would make Aunt Sarah happy. Bill being one of them would keep her mama and grandmama happy. Keeping both men tussling with each other and not with her would keep her happy.

Maybe having that bounty hunter around wasn't such a bad thing. All she had to do was get him to come loping around her. Judging by how he'd stared at her, that didn't look to be a problem.

But it wouldn't do to give in too quick. They all thought she had her heart tossed into Bill's hands. It would only help her if they kept thinking it.

"I thought you all liked Bill," Anne said.

Sarah shook her head and patted Anne on the hand with sympathetic condescension. "I don't dislike Bill. I don't care about Bill, or the bounty hunter either. I care about you and I don't want to see you end up like me and your mama twenty years from now. I'm doing for you what I wish someone had done for me when I was your age. I married the first man who asked, hoping he'd take

19

me away from my mama when all he did was bed me and leave me. What I want for you is the chance to get out of Abilene; die somewhere other than this dying place. Now, don't you want the same?"

"Of course I do. You know that," Anne said. But without the burden of a man. She wasn't going to hitch herself to any man.

"Then cinch yourself up and pick the man who can get it done for you," Sarah said, her blue eyes bright and hot. "Miss Daphne would flay me red if she knew I was talking to you this way, but when Esther came by and spit out all she knew about that bounty hunter and the way he looked at you, something just popped. You take your chance, Anne, and don't you wait on any man."

Bounty hunters never stayed any place long. If she was going to use him to nudge Bill off, she'd have to move quick. He could leave on the next train.

The bounty hunter *had* seemed to like the look of her and by his manner, didn't seem the sort to dawdle in a courtship. No, he seemed most . . . direct. That was a polite sort of word for what he was. Anne fought the shiver that wrapped itself around her spine when she remembered how he had looked. And how he had looked at her. She didn't want him for that. She just needed someone to shake Bill off a bit. Nothing more to it than that.

"What's it going to be?" Sarah asked. "You going to wait on Bill, hoping he'll do the right thing, or are you going to use that bounty hunter the way the good Lord meant for a man to be used? Use him to light a fire under Bill."

Anne didn't say a word, that shiver had her good and hard, but she got up off the porch and headed toward town.

Chapter Three

"I need a horse."

The hostler lowered his pipe and looked him over. Suspicion was written on his features like a sign. Jack stepped in out of the bright morning sun and walked down the row of horses, leaving the hostler and his suspicions behind him.

"This black looks good. How much?"

"My name's Powell," the man answered, not answering. "I own this place and most every horse in it."

"Congratulations," Jack said, watching Powell rise to his feet and come toward him. "How much for the black?"

"The black's not available," he said around his pipe stem.

"Fine," said Jack, tipping the brim of his hat. "What about the sorrel? Available?"

"Nope," he said. "Belongs to Mrs. Halloway."

"Mrs. Halloway owns a fine animal."

"You're Skull, ain'tcha?" Powell asked, digging his thumb in the bowl of his pipe. "When you leaving town?"

"Soon as I get a horse," Jack said, turning away. "What

21

about the dun? Looks a bit old, but fit. Mrs. Halloway own this one, too?"

"Nah," Powell said, looking down at his pipe and then blowing through it to check his draw. "But it's—"

"—not available."

"That's right. Seems to me—" He stopped to draw on his pipe again. "Seems to me that a man in your line would be real hard on horseflesh. I'd be losing money on any horse I let you take."

Jack smiled slightly and fingered the brim of his hat. "I haven't killed a horse yet."

"Could be you're lucky."

"Could be," he said softly. "How about you sell me a horse? That way, whatever happens, it's between me and the horse."

"Well, I don't know," Powell drawled, putting his pipe back in his mouth. "I'm not too sure about that either." Putting his hands in his pockets, he said pointedly, "I saw the way you pushed that man off the train. Don't figure any horse of mine would fare better."

Jack pulled off his hat and struck it a few times against his leg as he walked to the end of the stable and back to face the owner of his only way out of Abilene.

"Anybody else want to sell me a horse?"

"Well . . ." Powell hesitated, clearly debating with his conscience. "There's Emma Walton. Her man died and she's got a wagon load of kids to tend. Seems she'd need the money more than the horse."

"That's fine. Now, where can I find Mrs. Walton?"

That question apparently caused another internal debate within Powell's straining conscience; he turned a bit red, clamped down on his pipe stem as if it were the lifeline to heaven, and said with obvious reluctance, "Down the street, toward the Demorest Restaurant, past the church, and on the right. Kids all over the place. You'll find it."

"I'll find it," Jack said, adjusting his hat. "Thanks."

"Nothing," Powell said cheerfully in parting.

"You got that right," mumbled Jack as he left the stable.

He was still mumbling under his breath when he passed the Demorest Restaurant. The two men sitting on the bench outside the place stopped talking and eyed him as he passed while a woman and a man sitting at a table near the window stopped eating to glare at him as he walked by. He was as welcome in this town as a porcupine in a bedroll. He ignored them when he understood that they'd do nothing more than glare and stare.

Powell was right, the Walton place was an easy hit. The front porch was yawning with kids. A baby was sitting in the dirt of the front yard eating . . . dirt. Jack shrugged. Dirt never killed anybody. One or two of the kids ran in, slamming the door behind them; he could hear their muffled yells. Mrs. Walton came out directly, calling her kids to her as she did, picking up the baby and resting him on her hip. That baby grabbed a fistful of his mama and held tight.

They faced him and it was a crowd. No one spoke, so he guessed it was up to him.

"Morning, ma'am." He tipped the brim of his hat. "Fine day."

She didn't answer right off, just pulled one of the kids back from the edge of the porch to shove him behind her. There wasn't room enough behind her to hide them all.

"Mr. Powell sent me this way. . . ." She looked alarmed and like maybe she'd skin Powell when she saw him again. "Thought you might have a horse to sell."

"Don't have nothing here you'd want."

"But, Ma, what about—"

The girl didn't get any further; her ma shoved her into the house and slammed the door.

"Ma'am?" Jack proceeded. "I need a horse. I'll pay good money."

She considered, he could feel it, and continued to keep her eye on him. He stood stock-still and let her take his measure. He needed that horse. And she needed the money.

"Ain't he the one?" one of the kids whispered.

"Pushed him right off," another whispered in the shrill tones of a child who has no idea how to whisper. "Made him fall down."

"He's mean."

"You little kids stay back or he'll push you off, too!" one of the older girls hissed. They shuffled back like penned cattle.

"Lillian, bring Joe around," Emma Walton said, her eyes not leaving his.

He hoped Joe wasn't one of her kids.

Lillian sprang to the job and came around the side of the house tugging on a frayed rope. Joe followed. Joe was a brown gelding. At fifteen hands, he was a good-looking animal and didn't look to be more than ten years old.

Lillian ran up on the porch and held on to Joe from there.

"He's a fine-looking animal, Mrs. Walton. I'll pay seventy-five dollars for him and the tack that goes with him." It was a fair offer.

With a nod of acceptance, Emma Walton sent Maureen in to fetch a pen and paper. She drew up a bill of sale as she balanced the baby on her hip while he got the bridle and saddle on Joe. Lillian brought him an old brown saddle blanket after another nod from her mother. It was all over in a matter of minutes. Pocketing the bill of sale and leading Joe out of the yard, Jack could feel the eyes of the Walton clan on his back. They were clearly still nervous about him.

And he hadn't pushed even one of those kids off the porch.

His walk back through the center of Abilene was about what he expected. He was more and more certain he felt the weight of that bill of sale with each step he took, and more and more thankful for it. If any man stood to be named a horse thief, it was he.

"Isn't that Emma Walton's horse?"

"You know it is."

"Didn't *he* come in on the train? Isn't he leaving the same way he came in?"

"I heard Powell wouldn't sell him spit."

"Powell always was smart as March wind."

Jack ignored them and kept walking. At least Joe wasn't giving him any trouble.

"Where'd you get the horse?" one of the onlookers asked him. He looked up; she was the first one to talk to him directly. She was a spry woman with a mass of dark hair and bright blue eyes, sort of reminded him of the little Samaritan.

"Bought it," he answered without breaking stride. "And Mrs. Walton's got the same number of kids now as she did when I got there."

One of the kids hanging around in front of the mercantile ran off down the street, back toward the Waltons'. His word obviously wasn't good enough. It figured.

The dark-haired woman with blue eyes kept looking him over as he tied up Joe at the sheriff's. She seemed to be sizing him up for purchase, though that was a crazy thought. Jack walked into the sheriff's office through the open door. Lane was sitting behind his desk, eyeing the horse he had tied to the rail.

"If anybody asks, I bought this horse from Mrs. Walton for seventy-five dollars. I have a bill of sale."

Lane smiled and draped his legs over the corner of his desk. "If anybody asks, I'll tell 'em."

*   *   *

Anne stood and watched the westbound train depart. The steam curled around the wheels before rising to stain the sky. Car after car lumbered past, heavy, almost reluctant in their initial momentum, they eventually would have to be forced to a stop at the next station, farther down the line: Solomon City, then Ellsworth, Russell, Hays City, Trego, Buffalo Station to the northwest or Great Bend, Larned, Kinsley, and Dodge City to the southwest. Due south lay Council Grove, Emporia, Newton, and Wichita, while due east lay many more options, the grandest being Kansas City. She knew them all, each stop, each station, on the web of lines that connected Abilene to the world, but she had been nowhere. Abilene was all she'd ever remembered seeing. She'd seen enough of it to last a lifetime.

"He didn't get on, did he?"

Anne turned and looked into her aunt's blue eyes. Sarah knew something.

"He didn't," she answered. "I thought he'd be out on the first train."

"Is that why you're here?" Sarah said. "Looking for him?"

"I'm not looking for anyone," Anne sniffed. "Why, did you find him?"

"Whole town's found him," Sarah said on a laugh, "even though you're the one who's supposed to be looking for him. You'd starve as a bounty hunter, Anne."

"What's he doing that the whole town is watching?"

"He bought himself a horse." Sarah grinned.

Anne couldn't see that buying a horse would be much to look at, even in Abilene.

"Tried to hire one from Powell first," Sarah said with a smile, remembering the story as she'd heard it from Susanne. "Powell wouldn't hear of it. Then he tried to buy one and didn't get any further."

"That's ridiculous. How is Mr. Powell going to make a profit if he refuses to let out his stock?"

"Said he figured that Jack Skull would kill any animal he sat on."

"Ridiculous."

"Wait, it gets better," Sarah said. "Skull practically had to beat it out of Powell to get the name of anyone in Abilene who'd sell him a horse. Powell eventually coughed up Emma Walton."

"He hit Mr. Powell?" She needed him for her plan, but she didn't want to hitch up with anyone as violent as that. Not even for a day or two. No matter how he looked.

"Emma hid her kids on the porch as if the Apache had come to visit," Sarah went on, not to be derailed in what was a fine story, no matter how much truth there was to it, "and when Jack Skull looked ready to throw a couple of them off the porch just for sport, she agreed to sell him Joe, tack and all."

"I can't believe that he would tangle with a child," Anne murmured.

"Then he parades that horse down through the center of town like the governor himself, not a trace of guilt to the tips of his fingers, and holes up with Charles Lane. And speaking of his fingertips," Sarah said, turning to face Anne fully, "you didn't say what a handsome man he was, Anne. He's a sight. Why'd you let a man like that walk clean away without a tussle from you?"

A man like that? According to Aunt Sarah, he had beaten Mr. Powell, threatened to throw innocent children around, intimidated Emma Walton, and was unconcerned about the whole matter. So he was handsome. Lots of men were handsome. Bill was handsome, though in a different way. Jack Skull was rougher, though his features were finer, more cleanly cut, and his eyes the soft blue of a hazy summer sky. And the way he'd looked at her, as if she were the only person in the world he wanted

27

to be looking at, as if he'd come to Abilene just to find her.

Anne shook herself mentally. He was rough. His hair was long and tangled, his clothes dusty, and his expression forbidding. That's what he looked like and his manners were made to match. Tangled. Dusty. Frightening.

He was not the sort to stay in Abilene, which made him just about perfect.

"So he's still in town?" Anne asked as she and Sarah left the platform.

"For now," Sarah said with a knowing look. "But he's bought a horse; that must mean he plans to use it."

"He might have checked into the hotel, though."

"He might have."

Sarah couldn't shake the smile that shadowed her lips and gave up trying after a while; there was little enough to smile about in her life. She might as well enjoy the sensation. If Anne was taken with the good-looking bounty hunter, it wouldn't do her any harm; besides, he didn't seem as ornery as folks made him out. And he was such a pretty man. Why, if she wasn't an old woman, she might try to corral him herself.

"It was kind of him to give Emma money for her horse; she surely needs it," Anne said as she casually looked up and down the street.

"Well, he bought the horse, Anne; it wasn't a donation."

"Still . . ." Anne looked into the window of the Demorest Restaurant. He wasn't there.

"Still?"

"It's just that . . . he can't be as bad as people say. No one could be that mean. People just like to talk."

"You're the one who saw him push that man from the train. I only saw him lead a horse he'd just bought. And that was bad enough."

A Kiss to Die For

"Was he cruel to the horse?" Anne asked, stopping to look at Sarah.

"No, there's just something about the man, beyond his pretty face, that makes you pause. Still"—Sarah took a deep breath to feed her resolve—"he's a comely man and sure to leave town. You could do worse. And to tell you the truth, I think half of what they're saying about him is empty talk to pass long hours. I looked him over good and proper; he don't have the look of a killer. Just don't think he's more than he is and you'll save yourself some hurt."

"I won't," Anne promised absently, resuming her stride.

The Cattlemen's Hotel was the only hotel left in Abilene; it was also on the edge of town, as far away from the grumbling humanity of Abilene as he could get and still stay in Abilene. The exterior was shingled and painted, the porch shady and well swept, the glass dusty. The interior was worn but respectable with red carpet and one tufted chair in the small lobby. He'd seen a dozen hotels just like it. His reception was exactly what he was learning to expect.

"And you wish to stay how long?"

"As long as it takes," Jack said, his throat hoarse.

It was clearly not an answer that pleased the proprietor.

"I will require some information as to the duration of your stay. You are not our only patron."

Jack looked around. He couldn't hear another person. The lobby was empty. The porch was empty. Jack looked at the man behind the counter and kept his silence. The man behind the counter developed a twitch underneath his left eye.

"Here's a week in advance. I'll let you know if I'm staying longer."

The proprietor held his tongue. It was a good thing.

Claudia Dain

Jack had just about had it with Abilene and her prickly residents.

He climbed the angled stairs that led to the second floor; the sixth one creaked. He would remember that. His room was on the north side of the building, facing the street. There were two windows, a bed, a washstand, and a rack for his clothes. It was a respectable room; the bedding looked clean and, better yet, smelled fresh. He turned around and locked the door and headed back out to buy supplies for his trip onto the prairie. He'd be leaving in an hour at worst. He was eager to go; there was no point in dawdling around in an unfriendly town when all the excitement was happening elsewhere.

He had a murderer to catch.

He crashed into the little Samaritan on the stairs first.

It was on the sixth stair, the one that creaked. His arms wrapped around her torso, steadying them both. Her hair, as dark as prairie earth, got in his mouth. She smelled like flowers.

It all rolled over him in the space of a breath and then he let her go, holding on to her elbows just long enough to be sure that she was firmly on her feet. He let go and backed up, up to the seventh stair, the one that didn't creak. He had to back up from her because all he wanted to do was keep pressing her down until her back was to the floor and her skirts were over her head. He'd never wanted a girl like that, so hard and so fast, not in his whole life. He didn't want to feel that way now. He didn't want to feel that way ever.

"Excuse me, ma'am," he growled, tipping his hat, using the brim to cover his eyes.

"No, I . . . excuse *me*," she said, her voice as soft as rainwater.

Her bosom rose as she spoke and he couldn't help watching the rise and fall. Then he felt like hell because he couldn't leave her alone, even with his eyes. She blocked him on the stair; if she didn't move aside, he'd have to brush against her to get down and out of the hotel. And he had to get out. He had to get away from her before he kissed her to the soles of her feet without even knowing her name.

"Ma'am?" he mumbled, urging her to get out of his way.

"Hmmm?"

She was staring at him, he could feel it, though she remained unmoving except for her breast, rising and falling. The urge to touch her was mounting in him and he felt a twinge of panic that he hadn't felt in twenty years. He couldn't have her. She was proper. Off his range.

He looked up and saw what he knew he'd see. She was looking at him, her light blue eyes unblinking, her mouth soft and open, the pulse in her throat beating visibly.

She stared at him, her gaze moving all over his face, taking in his untamed hair, his two-day growth of beard, his hungry eyes. She took it all in and stood there, looking softer by the second.

It was the chilly cough of the proprietor of the Cattlemen's Hotel that broke the moment. Jack was thankful for the intrusion. She turned toward the sound and he bolted down the stairs and out the door. He left her behind on the sixth stair.

Chapter Four

She was so pretty. Small and slight, her hair the black of river mud, smooth and slick. He was watching her and he knew she could feel his eyes on her. Knew that she was flattered by it. Knew that she wouldn't fight it when he made his first move. He knew how to make it so a woman wouldn't fight, not until the last breath. Not until it was too late for fighting.

But that time wasn't now. He was just getting started with her.

He'd been watching her for weeks, building her trust in him. That was important to a woman. She needed to trust. That was the hard part. What made it easy was that she wanted to trust a man. Any man. As long as she believed the man could be her man.

Which made it just perfect, because he wanted to be the man she chose, the man she gave herself to. The man she trusted. The man she'd marry.

That was what he needed.

And he knew just how to get it.

With a smile, he tipped his hat, and rode out of town.

He'd be back. And she'd be waiting for him, just to win another smile from him. Not much longer now. Not much longer before he kissed her.

He'd been out of Abilene for a day and felt measurably better, away from the blatant hostility of the town, away from *her*. Jack squinted into the late afternoon sun and pulled his hat lower. He was still a bit thrown by his reaction to her. It didn't happen much, feeling a woman's pull that way; made him feel like a calf being roped and tied up. He didn't like the feeling.

Trouble was, he liked the feel of her.

Jack pulled off his hat and slapped it a couple of times against his leg, pulling his thoughts back into line. Adjusting his hat down over his tangled hair, he considered the site of the last murder.

McPherson was a remote spot just west of the old Abilene Trail and east of the old Ellsworth Trail; in the middle of nothing and on the route to nowhere. Good spot for a murder. The cabin was a scant mile from the town proper, isolated and abandoned, the boards shrunken and wind scraped, the roof just able to keep out water. There was a bed frame, stark and wooden, and a shelf in the corner; that was the extent of the furniture.

There was no blood.

There was no sign of life.

There was nothing to see, nothing to learn. It was just an old shack in the middle of nothing. The place where a girl recently turned woman had died.

The sun slanted low through the small square of a window in the western wall of the cabin; it was getting late, time to make camp. Jack took a last turn, his eyes scanning the space, looking for evidence. There was none. There never was.

He left the cabin on quick feet; he wanted to make camp before dark and there was no way he was going to bed down in there. Grabbing Joe, he mounted and rode north, toward Abilene. He'd not make Abilene before dark and didn't care to. A night in the open was more welcome than the reception he'd get in that town. He'd rarely been in a town that had more quills than Abilene had set against him. Only the sheriff and that Samaritan gal had shown him any sign of welcome, and he understood the sheriff's reasons. Why the Samaritan hadn't clawed her way out of his range, he couldn't figure. If she understood men at all, she'd light out, leaving a trail he couldn't follow.

The rise and fall of her breasts and the smell of her hair came to his mind again with the unexpected force of a hot wind running before a prairie fire. She should have run then, that minute, instead of standing so still, caught in the trap of his arms. But he'd been the one to do the running.

Jack stroked Joe's neck and urged him northward, running again from the image of the dark-haired girl and the soft rhythm of her breathing. He'd bed down on the prairie, just south of the Smoky Hill River, halfway between the cabin and Abilene; it was an easy ride and, though he was running, he was in no mood to push himself hard.

He got his fire going and his bedroll spread just as the sun touched the rim of the earth, heating the sky with color just before the long fade to indigo. He laid his horsehair rope around his bedroll in a loose loop. The sound of the darkness changed suddenly and he faded back into the growing shadows, leaving the golden firelight to warm an empty camp.

The newcomer edged into the light slowly, carefully, taking his time with each step. Jack watched from just beyond the man's range of sight. He, too, was careful.

"Coffee's ready," the man said, using a folded rag resting on a rock to lift the boiling pot off the fire.

"Help yourself," Jack answered before moving a few feet

to his right, not willing for the man to use his voice to find range.

"Thanks," the man answered, pouring a cup. "You?"

"Only one cup. It's all yours."

"Thanks again."

The man's hands were both blatantly occupied. Jack had circled his own camp and could detect no other men waiting for him in the dark. He moved into the light of his fire, approaching the man head-on, his hands coiling a length of rope, occupied.

"Name's Foster. I'm a U.S. Marshal."

Jack had heard of him; this man fit the description. "Scullard."

"Haven't seen you around; you new to the country?"

Marshal Foster kept sipping at his coffee. Jack kept playing with his length of rope. Both men edged around each other with caution born of experience.

"Yeah," Jack said, his hat masking his features in heavy shadow so that only his stubbled jaw was clear in the firelight. "Up from Texas. Huntin' bounty."

The marshal nodded and threw the gritty remains of his cup onto the hard soil of Kansas. "Figured you for a bounty hunter. Who you hunting up here?"

Foster refilled the cup and held it out to him, but he kept his distance. A lot could happen when a man got too close.

"Been some murders down around Red River Station, track led north; heard from Sheriff Lane in Abilene that you've had some of the same up here."

The marshal set the full cup down on a flat rock and moved back from it; he stayed in the fire's glow, but he put some distance between himself and Jack. Jack appreciated the effort.

"You heard right. It's damn ugly when men take to killin' women." The marshal spat in disgust.

Jack nodded. The memory of a woman lying in the dirt,

her blood running away from her life in a torrent, flashed like lightning in his mind. "It's rare enough, thank God." He set the rope down and picked up the coffee, glad for something to rinse his mouth with.

"You seen it before?" the marshal asked, reading Jack's face too clearly.

"A few times, mostly with the Comanche. Never pretty."

The marshal brought his horse into the light and hobbled him, showing Jack the level of his trust. Jack pushed back the hat from his face, allowing the marshal to see him clearly, returning the trust he had been given.

"Comanche? You with the Rangers down there?"

Jack took a long swallow, ignoring the coffee grounds that he felt on his tongue and between his teeth. "Yeah, used to be."

"Good outfit."

"Hard service."

"That why you quit?"

Jack raised his blue eyes to the marshal's brown ones and allowed himself a smile. "You think I quit? Maybe they threw me out."

The marshal looked back, eye to eye, and smiled slowly. "No, they didn't throw you out."

"You're right, they didn't. But they might have. Too many rules for me."

Foster chuckled and got out his own cup, filling it with coffee. "That I can believe. You don't strike me as a man who sticks to the trail."

"You're making a lot of quick decisions about me," Jack said, drinking again and watching the marshal on the other side of the fire.

"Some, I'll admit."

"Any you won't admit?"

The marshal didn't answer, not with his mouth, but his eyes were sharp and he was keeping Jack in his line of fire.

"Tell me about those killings down at Red River Station."

Volumes were spoken of trust and suspicion in that one command. The U.S. Marshal was no fool.

"Three women in all," he began, his voice even and low, "and all went the same way. Strangled."

"You know that's how it's been up here."

"Yeah, Lane told me as much." Jack looked up into the sky, black now and filled with stars beyond measure, so distant and so bright. So familiar and so cold. "Three women, one of them south toward Fort Worth, one just west of the Station, and the last just north of Caldwell."

"I know those towns," Foster murmured.

"Yeah, anyone who ever rode herd on cows knows those towns."

The marshal studied Jack in the flickering light of the fire, so small a light against the myriad stars. Jack let him look his fill.

"There's been one down off the Arkansas River, not far from Wichita. Three days ago."

"Does Lane know?"

"Not yet."

"Same way?"

"The same," the marshal growled.

The silence lengthened. The fire popped, sending sparks skyward. A shooting star flared across the sky, a strong, smooth arc that dwarfed the light of the stars held motionless by an invisible hand. Jack made a wish for luck; the way the marshal was looking at him, he'd need it.

"When did you hit Abilene?" Marshal Foster asked.

"Yesterday," Jack answered.

Foster nodded, accepting it.

"About those towns . . ." the marshal began.

"Yeah, all on the trail."

"You rode the trail?"

"In my day," Jack said. "Not many didn't."

"True, the Chisholm Trail saw a lot of cows a few years back."

"And a lot of riders."

"So he's following the Chisholm Trail—"

"At least until Wichita," Jack interrupted. "Now he's on the Abilene Trail."

"That how you see it?"

Jack threw away what was left of his coffee and scoured the cup with sand. "More coffee?"

"No. Thanks." The marshal watched him intently.

"I don't see it any way at all," Jack said, sitting on his bedroll. "I've been following a trail up from Texas and the killings are staying tight to the trail I followed as a hand."

"Abilene's the end of the trail," Foster said, considering Jack again across the fire. Jack was in Abilene.

"Yeah," Jack murmured, lying down on his blanket, facing the stars.

"You going to be in Abilene awhile?"

Jack heard the suspicion in the man's voice and couldn't fault him. He saw again the bodies of the women, broken and bloated, their beauty and youth taken with the tightening of a cord. He buried the image and made sure his rope was securely in place around his own bed, a barrier to snakes that might come crawling in for comfort during the night.

He thought again of the dark-haired girl who had smelled of wildflowers in his arms. He remembered the sheer magnetism of watching her breathe. She lived in Abilene.

Putting his hat over his face, blocking out the stars, Jack answered the marshal's question.

"Yeah. I'll be there."

Chapter Five

Jack and the marshal had parted company that morning. They had no more information to give each other regarding the murders; the marshal was going to stay in the area surrounding the Abilene Trail north of Wichita. Jack was going back to Abilene.

He rode into town just about noon; he could almost hear the town groan in disgust. The Demorest Restaurant window was full of faces, all looking at him. Powell at the livery clamped down on his pipe and shook his head, probably figuring he was a stupid cuss for heading back into Abilene when he'd made it safely out. Well, Jack had never made any claim to being smart.

Lane wasn't in his office, so Jack made his way on down to his hotel. The desk clerk didn't look any happier to see him than anyone else in town had. One thing he was learning about this new Abilene; it was consistent. The old Abilene, the cattle town he remembered, had been a whole lot more fun. This Abilene was as dead as the trail that led to it. As dead as the women who now lined it as grisly signposts pointing north.

It was with that image in his head that he faced the clerk.

"Get me a bath."

The man sniffed and then said, "The bathhouse is under repair and not open for business. We do not provide private bathing arrangements until after eight P.M."

That was a load of bull and Jack knew it. "I want a bath and a cake of soap and a towel in my room in fifteen minutes. I also want you to see to it that my clothes are washed and back in my room by eight P.M. Understood?"

Fortunately for the clerk, he was quick to agree. Jack was in a mood to blow a fly off the wall for buzzing.

"Good," he snarled and then went up the stairs two at a time, skipping that memorable sixth step.

A gang of three boys was waiting in the hall in front of his room. Upon seeing him, they began whispering and pointing, leaning toward the tallest of them to share instant insights. Jack looked more closely. The tallest kid looked like a Walton. He, obviously, was the exhibit.

"Hey, kid, how's your ma?"

The tallest kid straightened and hissed to his friends, "I *told* you I knew him!"

Jack kept a straight face and opened his room door. The kids were about to tumble in behind him, so he turned and blocked the doorway, looking down at the three of them. They blanched just a bit and gazed down at the floor.

"You worried about Joe? He's fine and fit, not a bruise on him," Jack offered.

"No, we . . ." the kid stammered, "I just wanted to see if you was really back in town. Some folks was talking—"

"Kid, folks always talk. You show sense to check it out for yourself."

"I do?" He puffed a bit. "Thanks, Mr. Skull."

"The name's Scullard, Jack Scullard. Which Walton are you?"

"Tom, Mr. Skul—Scullard."

"Well, Tom, I'm about to take a bath, so you run on and tell your ma that Joe is doing well with the man she sold him to."

"Sh . . . sure, I sure will," he stammered. He was clearly the spokesman for the group.

The bathwater was delivered just as the boys were shuffling off down the hall. They stared at that water as if it were blood. Didn't they think he took a bath? Glancing at himself briefly in the small mirror that hung above the pitcher, he found he couldn't blame them if they didn't. He hadn't cleaned up in two weeks. He looked it.

Stripping down and leaving his dirty clothes out in the hall for someone to pick up, Jack had one foot in the water when there was a knock on the door. He knew enough about boys to know that they wouldn't have the guts to come back that quick. Wrapping himself in the towel and palming his revolver, he answered the door.

"You won't need the gun. I won't fight you for the water."

Jack grunted and hefted his gun, as if considering, then put it down on the washstand near the tub and faced Sheriff Lane. The steam was rising with angry energy, taking the heat with it.

"You talk. I'll wash," he said, dropping the towel and getting in. He was a big man; water sloshed over the rim. At least the clerk hadn't stinted on the water.

"Find anything?"

"Nothing except that there's been another murder down near Wichita," he said, rubbing the soap over his arms and chest.

Sheriff Lane eyed the gun sitting next to him, measuring its distance to Jack's soapy hand.

"I met up with Marshal Foster," Jack continued, trying

to ignore Lane's reaction and the logic of it. "Happened three, four days ago. Talking it over, it seems that the killer is sticking to the old trail."

Jack rubbed his face and the tops of his shoulders, the tips of his hair wicking up the soapy water. "That trail ends in Abilene."

"So you're here."

"I'm here."

"And the marshal?"

"He'll be in touch from time to time, but he wants to stay farther out. So far, none of the murders seem to have actually taken place in a town of any size, just in the vicinity."

Charles considered Jack as he washed the dirt of days from himself. He wasn't a man to leave the best part of the hunt to someone else.

"You think he'll strike here, don't you? You think the next gal will be in Abilene?"

Jack reached for his razor and scraped at his throat. "I think Abilene is the end of the trail."

"And?"

"And he's sticking to the trail."

The sheriff chewed on that while Jack finished shaving. The water was murky brown by the time he was clean.

"But these murders happen with months in between. If there was one just four days ago, there shouldn't be another in at least a month or more."

"I'll have a lot of time to kill, that's true, but I'm not leaving Abilene, at least not for long," Jack said, closing the subject.

"You'll need money."

"I've got enough."

Jack stood and toweled off, leaving faint brown smears on the white cloth. He went to his bags and pulled out a pair of fawn-colored pants and a dark blue shirt and began dressing.

"What are you going to do after you finish dressing? Sit around the hotel lobby for a month?"

Jack kept buttoning up his shirt, but his blue eyes met the sheriff's. "You got something in mind?"

"There's talk of a horse thief running around down near Hutchinson; thought maybe you could use some quick and easy money."

Jack strapped on his gun belt of plain and unworked leather; it bore the stain of sweat that only years of hard use could leave. "No money is easy and it's hardly ever quick."

"Not even for a bounty hunter?" the sheriff asked.

"Not even." Jack smiled in return. "Still, I'll head down there and check it out. Now's the best time. I reckon Abilene will be quiet for a while yet."

"Especially with you gone." Lane chuckled.

"You can get out anytime."

The sheriff left, chuckling.

There was nothing to keep Jack in the room after he'd put on his scuffed brown boots, so after straightening up his bed and repacking his gear, he grabbed a handful of his dirty clothes and dumped them outside the door to land with the rest.

The sleeve of a sweaty shirt fell across the Samaritan's toes.

She didn't even jump, she just stared at him.

He stared right back.

Her eyes were the light blue of a winter sky, her hair so dark a brown as to be almost black, her skin was pale as heavy cream. She had faint freckles across her nose.

"You *are* back," she said, her voice as soft as a sigh.

She had been looking for him? That was bad. He didn't need her hanging around, messing with his pulse the way she did. She was too pretty, too town-proper, too off-limits for his kind. If he didn't get away from her soon, he'd back her up against the wall and show her just how different he was from her Saturday night beau.

"Excuse me, ma'am." He edged past her. It went well; the hall was wide.

"Oh, please," she said, keeping pace with him. He didn't look at her, he just kept his eyes on the end of the hall and the freedom the staircase would offer. "I came to apologize."

"For what?" He didn't look at her. He kept moving, but his feet had slowed.

"For . . . for interfering with the man on the train. I'm certain you were only doing what was needed. I seem to have gotten in your way."

That stopped him cold.

"You're apologizing for standing there and having a man fall at your feet? Whad'ja do, run over and try to catch him?"

"No, of course not."

"Then why are you apologizing?" If he didn't get his feet moving again he'd be apologizing to her for pressing her up against the wall and kissing her blind.

"Well, I . . ."

She had the most incredible eyes he'd ever seen, soft blue with black lashes that spiked and curled. If he kissed her, would her lashes brush against his cheek?

"Excuse me again, ma'am, but I've got to go," he mumbled and all but tumbled down the stairs in his hurry to get away from her.

She tumbled down after him, like a dog on a leash.

"But I . . . I was going to ask you about the man on the train. Is he very dangerous?"

He looked back at her from the doorway to the hotel, his shadow casting long smudges over the dust tracks on the floor. She was poised on the last stair, one hand holding the rail as if to steady herself, or like a dog chained in the yard when the master is walking away, straining to follow.

44

Was Jessup dangerous? Not compared to him. If he didn't get some hard distance between them, she'd find that out damn quick.

"He had a price, I brought him in, I got paid. Nothing more to know than that."

He tipped his hat and took two steps onto the boardwalk.

She said it soft, but he heard it.

"Good-bye."

"Anne," the hotel proprietor snapped, "I never thought to see you linger when the train from Ellsworth is due in. You know they always see a lot of passengers."

"Oh, yes, I'd forgotten. Thank you for reminding me. But, do you know if Mr. Skull will be leaving soon?"

"I have not asked him his travel plans," he said curtly. "Anne, your train."

"Oh, of course, excuse me."

Her quick step could be heard on the walk as she made for the train station. Mr. Webster allowed himself a small smile of satisfaction.

Jack just about had the saloon to himself. There was an old man asleep in a shadowed corner, but since he didn't talk much, the saloonkeeper had to rely on his other customer for conversation. The man was a talkative sort and quiet seemed to weigh on him like a stone. Jack wasn't a free talker, but he understood the man's need to talk. He'd had a trail partner once who'd been much the same and it was from him he'd learned the peace of long listening. It wasn't a habit he was going to break for a bartender in Abilene. Though maybe he should think himself lucky that anyone in Abilene would talk to him at all.

"Heard about the train, of course," the man was saying.

Jack nodded and sipped his beer.

"Guess he had it coming?"

"Matter of opinion, I guess," Jack said.

"Well, now, that's the truth. Been some who's said that no man deserves to be roughed-up, no matter the crime. The law's the law and that's the end of it. Then again, some say that you might have been provoked and that he had it coming."

"Yeah?" Jack said with a tight smile. "And who said that?"

"Well." The bartender flushed. "It's just a manner of speaking. There could be any number of reasons for that feller to land on his tail in the dust. Any number."

"Umm-hmm." Jack kept drinking.

"So, heard you're up from Texas."

Jack finished his beer.

"I've never been down there, but my sister married a man who settled about ten miles east of San Antonio. Heard it's pretty country, pretty country. Been meaning to go and see for myself, but never seem to get the chance. You like Texas?"

"Well enough." Jack slapped his glass down and the bartender refilled it.

"Your people in Texas?"

Jack took a long, smooth swallow and set his glass down softly. The wood was dark and scarred, but heavily waxed. There was a burn mark just three inches from his water ring.

People? He didn't have any people.

"No," he said softly.

The sharp click of women's shoes could be heard outside and they both turned to it. The little Samaritan was scooting past, all in a hurry, the ruffle on her bustle bouncing.

"Who is she?" he asked the bartender, turning when the man didn't speak up immediately.

For the first time, the bartender had nothing to say.

More than anything he could have said, the man's silence roused Jack's curiosity.

"She got someone to look after, is that where she's going?"

"Where she goes ain't none of my business," the bartender said, moving off down the bar to check his stock of bottles.

He hadn't said it was none of Jack's business, but it was in the air between them all the same. Damn, but he was getting tired of stepping so light in this town.

"Simple question," Jack smiled, walking toward the window to catch another glimpse of her. "Hard to answer?"

"I don't make it a point to discuss ladies in my saloon," the man grumbled, rubbing his hand over his thick mustache.

"Fair enough." Jack smiled in momentary surrender. He was watching her, swaying that bustle off down the street, until she turned out of sight.

Whoever she was, he was sure to find out.

"Hello, Anne, it sure is good to see you again and so nice to have such a warm welcome back home. You seen Rob around? He was supposed to pick me up in the buggy since I've got all these trunks, but I suppose he got busy and forgot all about me. Again. I swear, if I didn't have my sister to visit in Ellsworth, I don't know if a body would know if I lived or died. Oh, there he is now, covered in dust, wouldn't you know, and now he'll get me all dusty on the way home and me in my new velvet jacket. Did you notice my new jacket? A gift from my sister. You know she has more clothes than she has time to wear, so when I remarked on how bottle green was just the perfect color for me and made her look sallow, well, she up and let me have it. Wasn't that kind? Listen, I'll wear it to church on Sunday and then you can really look at it and tell me what you think. I swear, I think it makes me look so stylish, and a lady on the train said it makes me look five years younger. Of course, I had to tell her how old I am, but she assured me that she would never have guessed."

"You ready, Sue Ann?"

"Coming, Rob! Did you get the little brown—"

"Yes, I got the little brown trunk. It's under the boot. Now let's get along. Good day to you, Miss Anne."

"So long, Anne. I'll see you on Sunday."

"Good-bye, Sue Ann. Good-bye, Rob," Anne said as she stood on the platform, deserted now that Sue Ann and Rob Weaver had driven off.

It was a short stop. Even as the Weavers were driving off, the train was steaming up to head farther east. She turned and watched as it built up steam and then churned away, leaving a gray cloud to mark itself; just like God leading the Israelites out of Egypt with a cloud to guide them. And just like the Israelites, she longed to follow that cloud of smoke that led further and further from all she could remember knowing.

Anne sighed, full of restlessness mixed with a dollop of melancholy, and turned for home.

The bounty hunter, Jack Skull, was nowhere in sight. She looked, and then sighed again with restlessness.

Her house appeared much too soon to suit her restless frame of mind and she stifled another sigh. Her grandfather had built the house and he had built it to impress. And it had, then. It was one of the first frame dwellings built in Abilene and had large windows and a nice porch. There was even some wedding cake trim under the eaves. It was still one of the biggest houses in town; she thought her grandfather would like knowing that. Miss Daphne, left alone with her daughters, had done her best to keep it up, but it was a lot of house for a bunch of women and it took a lot of money to maintain. They didn't have a lot of money. Not anymore.

"Anyone interesting on the Ellsworth train?" her grand-mother asked.

Anne started a bit in surprise. Her grandmother was on her knees in the dirt, weeding the flowers bordering the front walk, and Anne hadn't seen her.

"Oh, Sue Ann and Rob Weaver. Sue Ann was visiting her sister in Ellsworth and Rob came to pick her up."

Miss Daphne nodded but kept her eyes and hands busy with her weeding.

"Then there was Mr. Dodd from the mercantile. I didn't speak to him, but I heard he had gone to Ellsworth to pick up some dress goods."

"They should have sent Mrs. Rivers for the dress goods. Chris Dodd doesn't know scarlet from violet."

"Yes, ma'am."

Anne edged up the walk, eager to get inside. She had duly reported her activities and conversations and was ready for a fortifying glass of buttermilk.

"You didn't see that bounty hunter again?"

Miss Daphne said it calmly enough and kept her eyes on the dirt at her fingertips, but the weeds were flying furiously.

"No, ma'am," she answered, a little sad that it was the truth.

Miss Daphne was not through with her yet.

"Now when is that beau of yours coming round? He's been gone awhile now."

"You know he said he'd be back at the end of the week, Grandma. He has business to tend down toward Wichita. He told us all when he was here to dinner last week." She did not want to be blamed for Bill's absence when he had announced his intentions to them all; she had done noth-ing to drive him off, except quietly hold him at arm's length. "He's not my official beau anyway," she argued softly, still trying to get up the path. Was it her imagina-tion or was her grandmother scooting out into the walk-

49

way a little more with every weed pulled? "There's no formal agreement between us, you know." There'd be no agreement with any man, no matter his courting skills. She wasn't falling into that trap.

"Oh, yes, I know," her grandmother said, sitting back on her heels and forgetting the weeds hanging from her fingers. "But he's a better prospect than that shiftless bounty hunter, miss. Don't think I don't know that he's set your petticoats fluttering. It was in your eyes from the moment you came home today and I can read that sort of look as well as anyone and maybe a darned sight better."

She didn't know what was in her to make her answer back the way she did. Maybe it was the restlessness that seemed to grow with every breath, restlessness that had blossomed since she'd first locked eyes with Jack Skull. Whatever it was, she did it.

"Grandma," she said softly, "I don't think he's shiftless. He appears to be both busy and successful at his job."

Miss Daphne's brown eyes narrowed and her lips thinned. The lifeless weeds fell from her stiffened fingers.

"Are you contradicting me, Anne? Are you taking a contrary position merely to irritate me? Is this how you respect your elders and after I've taken care of you and your mama and, yes, even your aunt, for all these years? You know full well that Bill is a sight more man than any bounty hunter could ever hope to be. You know that Bill has been seriously courting you for over a month. You know that Bill has been welcomed into this home, my home, which is something that bounty hunter will never be."

"Yes, ma'am," Anne murmured, her eyes downcast, sorry she had said anything at all. What did it matter anyway? She wasn't getting married, though it made Miss Daphne happy to think she was. Any plan that kept Miss Daphne happy was a good plan.

"You agree that you are being contrary? You know that the good Lord never meant for a child to be so obstinate with her elders. Now you do what's right, Anne."

"Yes, ma'am." Doing what was right was all that mattered, really, and her grandmother was certain she knew what was right better than anybody.

"Very well," Miss Daphne sniffed, satisfied for the moment. "I could use your hands to help with these weeds. I don't want my spring flower show to be anything less than what folks have come to expect."

There was nothing Anne could say, nothing she could do without acting the ungrateful, unrepentant child she had been accused of being. It wasn't worth the fight. Anne fell to her knees and kept her head bent to her assigned task.

"Yes, ma'am."

"I think she should look to that bounty hunter and I told her so myself."

Nell gazed at her sister in horror, her mouth dropping open and staying that way, even though her mama had scolded her about that particular bad habit for thirty years.

"You didn't!"

Sarah was enough of Daphne Perkins Todd's daughter to flush, but she stuck to her guns.

"I certainly did."

Nell watched as Sarah rolled out the dough, sprinkling flour over the loaf before working it some more. Sarah was ignoring her. Nell made a conscious effort to close her mouth and then turned back to her shelling.

"Well, I can't imagine why. Bill Tucker is her steady beau and he's over here every chance he can get. It'll only be a matter of time."

"Humph," Sarah said, pummeling the dough.

"Besides, what would Anne want with a bounty hunter when she has Bill?"

Sarah looked up, her blue eyes fierce and her hands wrist deep in bread dough.

"Has Bill? She doesn't *have* Bill. And Bill isn't all that regular in his attentions besides."

"A man has to work—"

"He isn't working that hard on Anne."

Nell couldn't withstand her sister's fierce expression any longer and looked down at her shelling. The pile of pecans was building nicely.

"Nell, have you *seen* that bounty hunter?"

"No, I have not." Her tone shouted that she could hardly have been prouder of that fact.

"Well, go take a look," Sarah said with a smile. "He's a man to see. Don't see many like him in a lifetime."

"Are you saying he's good looking?"

Sarah grinned. "That's what I'm saying."

Nell sniffed. "That hardly makes him fit for Anne. Sarah, he's a bounty hunter! What would he want with a nice girl like Anne?"

Sarah's grin expanded up to her eyes and she shrugged.

"Listen, Nell, haven't you even once thought that Bill was just a little too cocksure of Anne? Why, he just expects her to be sitting here waiting for him whenever he happens to roll into Abilene. A man gets a real sudden thirst when water gets scarce."

"But, Sarah, Bill is so . . . nice."

"And he's got a light foot now. How long do you figure he'll stick around if he and Anne do wed? One week in four?"

"But Jack Skull—"

"I've seen him, Nell"—Sarah smiled—"and I've seen how Anne reacts to the mention of him. Let them dance around each other a bit, and hope Bill sees it. Anne needs to have more than one man caught in her bustle before she settles down and Bill needs to know that Anne's not his for the taking. He should fight for her. She'll need the joy of that memory later, when life wears her down."

"But Bill has been so sweet in his courting," Sarah argued, eating a pecan in her confusion. When she realized it, she fought the urge to spit it out. Mama never would tolerate eating the food whilst cooking it. "And he and Anne have an understanding."

"What understanding is that?" Sarah mocked. "That she'll sit like a hound and wait for him at the window?"

"I don't think it's like that, but a woman should be faithful. And patient."

Sarah abandoned the dough and stood in front of her sister.

"Is that so? And what did being faithful get you, Nell? What did it get me?"

Nell had no answer. She ate another pecan.

"You love me?"

He whispered it, his voice a caress against her throat, his hands gentle on her ribs, rising to feel the weight of her breasts.

The moon was dim, the gray clouds scattered across its face, and the air held the bite of an early spring night. But it was spring and that was what she felt in his arms; like a flower opening, earth warming, life erupting. All this she felt when she was with him. He bathed her in desire, showering it upon her, effusive in his love words and in his courting.

She had never felt such things before.

"Yes, I love you."

She did. It exploded in her with the force of birth.

"You want me, as I am?"

Did she want him? Oh, yes, it was all she could think.

She wanted him, his laughter, his gentleness, his desire. She wanted him, all of him, forever.

"Yes." She said it against his mouth and it was a plea. He kissed her and she leaned into him, loving his strength.

"Then marry me," he begged, his hands cupping her, his whisper sending chills over her skin.

"Of course." She laughed. It was perfect. He was perfect. This moment of her life she would remember forever, for the rest of her life, and she would tell her daughter just how her daddy had proposed. "Of course, yes, I'll marry you."

"You'll make a home for us?"

"A beautiful home with fresh bread every day and clean sheets once a week—" She was laughing and sobbing against his chest, rubbing her face against the strength of him, learning his smell, so happy that she hurt.

"You'll take my name? Have my kids? I want lots of kids."

"So do I."

She pulled away to look into his face. He was so earnest, even the light of such a dim moon could show her that. Such sweetness in a man, to be so earnest. Take his name? Nothing meant more to her. She had lived her whole life to take his name and bear his children.

"So do I," she repeated. "As many as we can and—"

She never got to say more because he kissed her then. Such a kiss, a kiss to rock the world, a kiss to begin a new life with a new name.

A kiss to die for.

A moment of confusion followed by frantic fear was all she had time for. Her forever ended then, on that cool spring night.

She died silently to fall at his feet in a swish of fabric. He sprayed his seed over her as she hit the ground, the worn fabric of her skirt instantly dusted in dirt. He did not look at her again, but the moon pushed aside the clouds for just an instant to light the body of the woman as she lay alone in the vast dark of the prairie.

Chapter Six

He found her just southeast of Abilene, near Council Grove. Horse tracks led right to the spot, tracks not more than a day old. A single horse had brought her to the place of her death.

There was nothing around for miles except the survey markers; the railroad was set to lay track through Council Grove, but there was nothing here now. She looked about as alone as a murdered woman can look. She lay on her back, her arms open wide, as if she were trying to hug the sky and coming up with only an armload of air. But that was a mistaken image. She hadn't died alone. Someone had done this to her and stayed with her until it had been finished.

Boot tracks, man-sized, mixed with her smaller footprints. His stride was long, the depth of his boot track deep; a big man and tall. Her boots were scuffed and the soles thin; well worn. His prints led off to the east and then disappeared where he had mounted and ridden off. The tracks were something. He'd come upon this one so quick that the tracks hadn't been washed out by weather.

Jack bent down and looked close at the dirt that was his only clue. The horse's gait was off, the right rear hoof leaving a heavy print in the hard soil of Kansas. Maybe it was bad shoeing, maybe it was the horse, but it was something. Something to work with. Something to find.

Only one set of horse prints; she'd ridden with him to her death. The horse had continued on with his rider, the tracks showing the lighter load he carried going north. Abilene was north.

Another one; he hadn't thought there'd be another one so quick. It didn't fit the pattern and anything that didn't fit the pattern made him sweat. He was sweating now and the sun wasn't high enough or strong enough to be the reason.

He crouched down, studying her in the strong light. Her throat was badly bruised, the skin chalk white everywhere else, showing off the purple and black of her neck like a bold necklace. But it was no necklace. It was the mark of her death.

He bent closer, studying the mark, wanting it to tell him something about just how the girl had died. He'd seen enough death wounds in his life to have the knack of knowing how it had happened, what kind of round had shattered bone or the length of the knife that had pierced the lung. Or just what it had been that choked off air until air didn't matter anymore.

The wound around her neck was heaviest in the front; the pressure had come from the back, pulled tight against her wind until she'd run out of air. The mark was even and smooth, not the raw burn of rope, except that there was an oval of uneven bruising and in the middle of that oval, a pair of parallel lines. Deep bruises they were, dark and bold. The pressure had been strong there. But what would leave a mark like that? Not a whip, not a wire, unless barbed wire? But the wound wasn't punctured . . . it was just like all those others. He'd never seen death wounds like this until finding that first gal, Abbie, down in Texas, and he'd not known what he was looking at then. He still didn't know. And another girl was dead.

He couldn't just leave her. He didn't know her people, so he couldn't bring her to them. Standing, Jack slapped his hat against his leg and Joe still remained easy. He was learning Jack's ways and knew that the flying, slapping hat was no threat.

There was nothing for it; he would have to take her into Abilene, hoping Lane could identify her and get her folks told and her body in the ground. He couldn't just leave her, not out in the open with her eyes looking up at the sun without blinking and her arms stretched out and empty. He wouldn't leave her. And that meant the end of the secret, at least in Abilene.

Jack approached her politely, almost wanting to ask her pardon for the way he had to touch her. Smoothing down her skirts, he lifted her by her outstretched arms, holding her for a moment in a stiff embrace until he could get her body positioned over Joe. Joe made no complaint. There was no blood smell.

He covered her with his bedroll spread out, but skeins of her black hair fell down to almost brush against the ground. She was a pretty girl. But then, they were all pretty girls.

Another one dead, and so soon.

Jack mounted carefully, not wanting to disturb her. He'd come looking for a horse thief and found a body. Jack pulled down on his hat until his face was in full shadow. Another death; he should have known. He'd seen a comet just last night. Comets were omens of disaster.

It was as still as death in Abilene that afternoon when he rode in, almost as still as the girl lying over his saddle. Her hair swung in tempo with Joe's gait. It was the only thing about her that moved; there was no life left in her. Nothing but that dark fall of swinging hair.

The folks in Abilene were no more happy to see her than they were to see him.

"This time he's killed one. And a woman, too."

"No shame, that's what. He'd do anything for money."

"No pride either."

Jack ignored them and tied up at the sheriff's. Joe, at least, wasn't giving him any trouble. He left the girl and checked the office. Lane was out. Given the mood of the growing crowd, that was bad.

"What could she have done that he'd have to kill her?"

Jack turned and walked back to his horse, scanning the onlookers as he did. There were about twenty of them, not counting the kids, and more coming from down the street. Lane wasn't among them. Lane would have looked like a haloed angel about then.

"What was she wanted for?" someone asked. Jack searched the crowd and pinned the voice to the face. It was Powell, the man who wouldn't let his horses out of the stable.

"She wasn't wanted for anything, least that I know of," Jack said.

"Does that mean he just killed her for the fun of it?" a child asked his ma, only to be pulled behind her skirts and held there.

"I didn't kill her. I found her and brought her in. Can anyone here identify her?"

"You mean he killed her and doesn't even know who she is?"

Jack heard an angry whisper and a muffled slap; poor kid probably got a quick one on the tail.

"Don't you normally know the names of the folks you hunt?" asked a man in a well-pressed coat. He didn't seem to be carrying, but that could be misleading. There was always room in a pocket for a small pistol.

59

"Yes, I do," Jack said, keeping his voice level and calm. "I don't know who this woman is. I'd like to find out."

"Now, folks, let's get this woman off that horse and give her a respectful burial before anything else," a man said.

Jack studied him. He was a bear of a man, barrel-chested and dark bearded, his brown eyes ringed with heavy brows and lashes so that he resembled a huge raccoon.

"Now, Reverend, that's fine but we've got a woman here who's been kilt and the man who did it is standing plain as a stump for all to see."

"Mr. Hill, that's an assumption and a man doesn't deserve to hang on an assumption. Besides, we don't even know how she died."

"We know she's dead and he's a man who wouldn't take much pushing to get it done," another citizen said, his florid complexion flushing with emotion.

"Don't forget, Reverend, he pushed a man off of a moving train!"

"Sue Ann, that's not the way I heard it," Reverend Holt admonished.

"That's not the way it happened."

Jack turned at that voice. He knew her voice, knew the feel of her breath on his face and the scent of her skin. He turned and saw her at the rim of the crowd that had formed around him. Jack willed her to keep her distance and stay out of the trouble he could see galloping toward him like a herd of mavericks.

"No, it ain't," Jack said, cutting her off as she took a breath to continue, silencing her. "And that has nothing to do with this. This girl was out on the prairie, alone, and she deserves a name to go with her burial."

"I agree," said a familiar voice.

Jack allowed himself a deep breath. Sheriff Lane moved through the crowd, the folks making way for him. Lane might think him just as guilty of murder as the others, but he wouldn't be leading the way to the scaffold. Not without a trial, anyway. Lane was a cautious man who didn't jump too quick to a spot until he was certain the spot would hold his weight.

Lane lifted the blanket and took a gentle hold of the girl's dark hair. The bruise on her neck stood out boldly in the strong afternoon light, purple and red and black, and her face was dark red and puffy with congealed blood. Even with all that, she had been a pretty gal and young.

"Lord God, he strangled her!"

Sheriff Lane lowered her head and dropped the blanket down to cover her. They shared a look then and Lane heaved a sigh. The killings would no longer be a secret, a secret kept to protect the quiet lives of the people of Abilene.

"Who is she?" Jack asked in an undertone.

"I don't know, not from here," Lane answered softly.

"What are you waiting for, Sheriff? Lock him up!"

Sheriff Lane looked at Isaiah Hill, owner of the boot shop, and made himself chuckle. "What'd you think, Isaiah? You think this man killed this gal out on the prairie and then dragged her in here just so he could get arrested?" Lane looked Jack up and down, smiling as he did. "You think he'd bring in his own victim, just to find out her name?"

"He would if he was smart and wanted to throw us off," Hill mumbled, sticking to his theory.

"Do I look smart?" Jack said with a small smile.

There were a few titters at that and the crowd started to break up, with the help of both Reverend Holt and Sheriff Lane. It was painfully obvious that the people of Abilene didn't think he looked too smart. At the moment, he didn't think it was a good idea to get insulted about it.

"I'll be ready to do the service whenever she's ready,"

Holt said. "Thank you, Mr. Skull, for bringing her to us. We'll see she gets a good burial."

"The name's Scullard, Reverend, and thanks for your help."

The reverend looked surprised at the name and then nodded and went on down the street toward the church. There were a few hangers-on, mostly kids, and the Samaritan. Her blue eyes were huge and her freckles stood out against the white of her skin; Jack looked askance at the girl draped over his saddle and then back at the Samaritan. She looked ready to faint.

"Where'd you find her?" Lane asked.

Jack could hardly hear him; he could only stare at the girl who stood so still in the face of ugly death. She shouldn't have to see something like that, something so brutal, so final. Wasn't there anyone to take her home?

"Go on, ma'am," he said, his voice hardly above a whisper.

She looked at him then and he watched her take a shaky breath that made her bosom rise underneath all that ruffled lace. She looked at him as if he were the last horse for fifty miles of hard walking, as if she wanted him to grab her and take her away from Abilene and the dead girl who lay across his horse.

Yeah, as if any decent woman would mess with him. Not unless she was either desperate for a man or a half-wit, and even then she'd have to be drunk. This gal wasn't any of that.

"Go on," he urged.

She slowly left then, one step at a time, until she was walking away from the death he had brought with him. She never should have seen anything like it, not in her life. Death and murder, those were his companions, and he worked real hard to keep honest folk away from such filth, even if it did leave him shoved to the edge of polite society. An outcast, by choice and disposition. Jack heaved a sigh and turned to face Lane.

"The gals in that family are a potion," Lane smiled.

"There's more than one?"

"Her ma and her aunt; her grandma you can leave out."

"I'll leave them all out."

Lane nodded in easy agreement. It wouldn't do to have a bounty hunter running after Anne; she was too innocent for his kind and too sweet for them all.

"Out on the prairie you said?" he asked, getting back to it.

"Yeah, out toward Council Grove, near the railroad markers. There was a trail this time, but it played out after a mile or two. Wind kicked up."

The two men carefully untied the girl from her perch, Joe waiting patiently to be relieved of his burden. Keeping the blanket arranged around her, they carried her into the sheriff's office. The dark was soothing after the harsh light on the street.

"That's north of the last one," the sheriff said, laying the girl down on an empty bunk in an empty cell. Jessup watched from behind his bars and said nothing.

"Yeah," Jack said. He took the blanket and arranged it around the girl with all the consideration of a lover until she was well covered and insured of her privacy.

"How far south do you make Council Grove from Abilene?"

Jack left the girl in her cell and walked back to the sheriff's desk. He sat down on his chair and waited for Lane to pour him a drink. When his glass was full, he drained it, without waiting for Lane. Lane was not offended.

"About twenty-five miles."

Death was twenty-five miles from Abilene, and coming.

Chapter Seven

Doc Carr came before anyone had to go hunting for him. He'd heard all about the murder from at least three sources and was slipping on his coat by the time the third walked through his door. Walking to the sheriff's, he heard it again a few more times, once from a child of six who lisped it out with ghoulish delight.

Jack Skull was universally deemed responsible. Malcolm Carr was not disposed to disagree. He'd known more bounty hunters than he wished to and found them all disreputable and violent to a man. Jack Skull had the worst reputation by far. He had no desire to stand face-to-face with Jack Skull. No decent man would.

What he thought was clear when he opened the door to Lane's office and raked Jack with a gaze as sharp as any scalpel. Lane swallowed a smile. Jack lowered his hat brim and leaned against the rough wood wall of the jail-house. It didn't matter to him if the doc liked him or not; he was here because of the girl. If anyone might know who she was, it would be the only doctor for fifty square miles.

Doc Carr flipped back the blanket and got down on his knees to get a closer look. Black hair swept out from the confines of the blanket to tangle on the floor; a rope of hair had wound itself around her throat and across her breasts like a fancy necklace. The doctor eased the strands away from the wound that had killed her.

He rubbed his hands over her head, down her arms, around her ribs.

"No sign of any other injury; no breaks that I can tell." Carr stood to face Lane. "You don't need me to tell you how she died. It's plain enough."

"Yeah. Looks like he used a cord of some kind, doesn't it?" Lane asked. "You make it out to be rope or something smoother, like leather?"

The doctor got back on his knees and studied the raw bruise on the slender throat. "Too even for rope. Leather. Maybe a driving whip; too slender for a bullwhip. I don't know," he sighed, getting to his feet. "Could be lots of things. I've never seen a wound quite like it. The double line of bruising, I don't know what to make of that. Not many men would kill a woman this way." He looked at Jack as he said it. It was as plain a statement as an indictment.

Jack didn't answer the look. What the doc thought didn't much matter.

"You know her?" Jack asked.

"I know her," Carr answered, looking hard at Jack and then shifting his gaze to Lane. "She's part Cherokee, from her grandmother. Lives with her aunt out on Lyons Creek; not much out there."

"Wouldn't her aunt be hunting her? She's been gone awhile," Lane said.

"Probably not. Spends most hours drunk as she can get. That's how I know about her, the girl had to fetch me to tend her aunt's broken arm when she got tripped up in her skirts."

"That how you know her? As 'girl'?" Jack was angry, his anger pressed down and squeezing out like apples being pressed for cider. The girl deserved the dignity of her name.

Doc Carr looked at him briefly and then back down at the dark-haired girl; he covered her with the blanket as he answered.

"Her name's Mary. Mary Hyde."

"We'll see Reverend Holt gets her well buried," Lane said, urging them out of the room.

They went gladly enough; only Jessup was left to keep her company in the darkness of her death. Jessup would have been happier if they had taken her with them. He was of no mind to keep company with a dead woman. But Jessup had no say in the matter.

"How does she compare with the others you've seen?" Lane asked Jack. That brought Carr up short and he looked hard at Jack.

"The same," Jack said. "Just the same."

"Yeah, that's what I was wondering."

"Others?" Carr cut in. "What others?"

"There's a trail of bodies from here to Texas," Jack said.

"We've had our share of murders around here, Malcolm, and the marshal and I decided it would be best if we kept it quiet, so as not to alarm folks needlessly."

"It's hardly needless if people are dying!"

"You don't understand, Malcolm," Lane said, "these killings are spread all over the country, months apart."

"And all women?" the doctor asked.

"All young women," Jack supplied.

Malcolm Carr studied Jack coldly for a moment before asking, "You're from Texas, aren't you?"

"Sometimes," Jack answered, returning the look without blinking.

"Now, Malcolm," Lane said, "Jack's been hunting this man longer than I have. The killings started in Texas, best we can figure. We're all working to find the man responsible for this."

"You don't seem to be succeeding," Malcolm said, glancing across the floor to the bunk that supported Mary Hyde.

"Take me to her place so I can talk to her aunt," Jack said. "Maybe she'll have something to tell us. I've been chasing empty clues for months and need to talk to someone who can maybe give me a description."

"It's not difficult to find," the doctor bit out, clearly wanting to avoid such close and extended proximity with Jack Skull. "East bank of Lyon Creek, just below West Branch."

"I need someone who can introduce me to the aunt, someone she trusts, so that she'll talk."

Carr found it hard to argue against that; no one would willingly talk to Jack Skull. They made plans to leave ten minutes later; the doc wanted to close his office and Jack wanted to get a drink.

He went to the same saloon, the Mustang, and ordered a beer from the same man. He was still talkative.

"Heard about the girl, of course."

"Of course," Jack said before he took a long swallow of the brew.

"Pretty thing, by all accounts, and hair as black as coal. Shame a poor girl like that had to end up dead out on the prairie."

"Her name's Mary," Jack said, wiping his mouth with the back of his sun-browned hand. "Mary Hyde."

"Pretty name, too. Lots of Marys in these parts. Popular name, being from the Bible and all. My mother's name is Martha. Funny, when you think about it, Mary and Martha? You know the story, Martha always working at her house and Mary sitting around, idle. Just like my ma, never still, always sweeping or washing or ironing or canning or sewing, but never still. And now this Mary—"

"Yeah." Jack cut him off. Mary Hyde was about as still as a woman could be. "You know Mary Hyde?"

"Nah," the bartender said easily, "don't leave town much and she's not from around here."

"How do you know?"

"Bob Walton mentioned it, after he brushed coattails with Doc Carr. Heard she's from Lyon Creek way."

If there was one thing Jack had figured out, it was that there were no secrets in Abilene.

"You ever been down there?" Jack asked. Anyone could have done it, especially a man with a mother who was so busy tending to her house that she'd have little time left to pour on her son.

"If you're going to accuse me, you might as well know my name. It's Shaughn O'Shaughnessy and no, I've never been to Lyon Creek. Never been to much of anywhere. Too busy running the bar."

He didn't seem offended by the unspoken accusation. Jack smiled and took another long swallow. A man couldn't afford to be touchy when he owned a saloon; he'd have to learn to get along with all kinds.

"As long as we're exchanging names, mine's Jack. Scullard."

It may have been the first time Jack had told Shaughn something he didn't already know.

"Scullard?"

"Yeah. Pass that around, if you've a mind."

"Jack Scullard. Seems familiar," Shaughn mused.

"Glad to hear it," Jack said, letting himself smile a bit. Maybe he was making a bit of progress in this town.

"What part of Texas claims you again?"

Jack finished off his beer before answering, "The big part."

O'Shaughnessy licked the edges of his drooping mustache and pondered, quiet for a time. The saloon was quiet; even the old man in the corner had stopped mumbling in his sleep. The first flies of the season buzzed with angry spring energy through the dark room, searching for a place to light.

The Mustang was not a large saloon, the floors were wide plank, the walls sanded board planks, and the bar dark stained pine; the heavy woodiness of the place was relieved only by a beveled mirror behind the bar. It was a fine mirror, framed in gilt wood, carved and ornate, and over four feet long. Jack could see himself clearly in that mirror. He could just about see the whole room. There was a single large window on line with the bar and two glass doors, open now, since the weather was so friendly. It was through those open doors that he saw her walk by, bustle as busy as ever.

A train whistle blew high and long and a long curl of dark hair flew back over her shoulder as she picked up her pace.

"What is it with that gal and trains?" he muttered.

O'Shaughnessy's tongue snapped back inside his mouth to hide behind his teeth. Seemed the man would talk about anything, anything except the little Samaritan who smelled of wildflowers.

"She got a name?" Jack asked, pushing his glass away from him. "I don't think there's any warrant out on her; this isn't business," Jack joked lightly.

"Then it'd be personal? You don't need to know nothing personal about that gal."

Shaughn O'Shaughnessy clearly had his limits and that gal was one of them.

"Then let's make it business," Jack said, sick of the dodge and wanting a simple answer. "She ever leave town? Ever take that train she's always meeting?"

Shaughn blanched a bit, the red running away from his cheeks to bury itself in his neck. Jack Skull with a burr in his boot was no fun to mess with.

"She stays put, like me, even more. Never left Abilene

that I've ever heard." Jack just stared at him, considering, waiting, until Shaughn said, "She's a good girl of good family and all her family's here, in Abilene."

"Her name?"

"Anne. Anne Ross."

Jack smiled and pulled his hat down low. "No, no bounty on an Anne Ross. Thanks for your help."

Shaughn didn't answer, he just threw his rag down on the bar hard enough to make it slap and then wiped so hard he got a splinter in his palm.

Doc Carr stuck his head in the door just then and Jack walked out to meet him. Their horses were hitched in front of the sheriff's, Joe looking eager enough for all that he'd already been ridden a distance that morning. Carr looked nowhere near as eager as Joe did. They all knew why.

Lane stood chuckling on the boardwalk in front of his office as they rode off; Jack ignored him. Malcolm Carr turned in his saddle to scowl. Neither one had any effect on Lane's good humor.

Jack turned once to look back toward the train. Anne Ross stood there, trim and straight, a pillar of immovable expectation in the midst of arrivals and departures. Jack shook his head at the sight she made and then turned his face south, toward Lyons Creek.

They found the place late that afternoon, when the dipping sun cast their mounts in long shadow. Carr led in, since his was the familiar face and they didn't want a bullet shot into the dust to be the first howdy they heard in that isolated place.

But no shot rang out. No one answered the doc's call of greeting. No sound came from inside the squat sod house that hunkered down within sound of Lyons Creek's babble. A few scrawny chickens scratched in the raw dirt around the gaping door; there was no dog to give warning. All was quiet in that late, slanting afternoon light; a house was never meant to be so quiet. Jack felt the muscles in his stomach clench at the heavy quiet of the place and he licked his lips to cover the rolling beginnings of nausea. He never could stand the heavy press of quiet when there should be the sounds of living. Jack fingered his gun, stroking the heft of his grip, finding comfort. Carr led in, but Jack pulled his six-gun free of the holster, ready to shoot anything that didn't look exactly right.

The first thing that hit him was the smell. Wool socks gone wet, a horse blanket that hadn't been shaken in a month, a hat changed color from sweat; those were the flashes he had of what could make that smell. And it was dark. The only light came from the open door and that was a yellow bolt across a black dirt floor, lighting only itself and not casting the room in anything but heavy shadow. It took a few seconds for his eyes to adjust and when they did, he saw her. Sprawled in the dirt next to what passed for a bed. She lay on her face, her skirts hiked up to her knees. She was snoring.

"There she is," the doc informed him with a pointed finger.

"She seems real broken up that her niece's gone missing," Jack mumbled.

"She cares more for the bottle than she ever did for that poor girl," Malcolm said, turning the woman over.

Jack studied her for a moment. She had the look of a drunkard, the bloating and the gauntness and the ashen color. And the filth.

"There's blood," he said, bending down, touching his fingers to it to make sure.

Carr hoisted the woman onto the bed and examined her. "She's broken off a tooth, probably when she fell on her face. There's some blood on her lip."

Jack looked around and found the tooth embedded in the side slat of the bed. "Here it is. Don't guess she'll miss

71

it since she drinks her meals." He threw the broken tooth in the cold ash of the fireplace.

"Mary," the doc called. "Wake up."

"Her name's Mary, too?" Jack asked. "Not much of a family legacy."

The doc slapped drunken Mary on the cheeks lightly as he said, "She had a daughter once, named her Mary." Mary was not responding. Doc Carr dripped some cool water from the bucket onto her throat; that started her stirring. "Died in childbed."

Jack made up his mind right there that if he ever had a daughter, he wouldn't be naming her Mary.

Mary groaned a bit and then coughed. A new smell was added to the mix: sour whiskey. Jack waited while Carr got her full awake and then he moved out of the shadows to stand in the yellow bolt of sun, longer now than it had been. Mary was still too drunk to care that there were two men in her home when before there'd been none, and one of those men a hard-looking stranger.

"We've come about your girl, Mary," the doc said.

A few blinks and another wet cough was her chief response.

"Mary's gone."

"Gone where?" she rasped out, her voice hoarse with disuse.

"Gone dead," Jack said, pulling her gaze to him.

"Dead how?"

"Dead murdered," Jack answered, more than a little disgusted at her reaction. He'd seen people show more emotion at the news of a missing cat than this woman showed for blood kin.

"Hmmm." She scratched herself. "Drink?"

Doc Carr handed her a ladleful of water. She rinsed her mouth and spat. The water lay in a puddle on her floor before sinking in to leave a dark brown spot just shy of the block of sunlight. This woman liked her chosen place in the dark.

"How long has your niece been gone?" Jack asked, stepping through the light until he stood next to her bed.

"I dunno," she said, scratching her head, the sound of it rough under her nails. "Where'd you find her? Not here?"

Doc Carr got up from the edge of the bed and walked slowly to the open doorway. It looked like he had just about had his fill of Aunt Mary and her devoted care of her niece. Jack had seen and heard worse, though rarely from family.

"She was out on the prairie, north and west of here. She wasn't alone," Jack said. "She been keeping company with anyone?"

Mary slouched against the wall behind her bed, chewing on a dirty fingernail. Finally she shrugged. "She bragged on havin' a beau and couldn't stop telling me how sweet lookin' he was. She was far gone on him."

"Who was he?"

Another shrug. "I didn't ask. She's of an age to find her own man."

Jack studied her with a ripple of revulsion. Blood kin and she didn't even have a care as to the girl's welfare.

"Did you ever see him? Could you describe him?"

Mary smiled, the hole where her tooth had been a newly opened cave in a crooked smile. "Sure I saw him. Little Mary couldn't stand not having me see the man who was courtin' her. Course, it was a fair distance and it wasn't a clean look, but I saw him."

Doc Carr turned back into the room, listening.

"What did he look like?"

"Why, he was sweet lookin' right enough." She licked her thin, cracked lips and gave him a slow wink. "Like you, honey."

Chapter Eight

"If she was saying that the man looks like me, it's not a lot to go on," Jack said the next morning to Sheriff Lane.

Doc Carr, who'd been talking to Lane when Jack showed up, didn't say a word. No, his expression said it clear enough. *Unless the man is you.*

Charles Lane smiled at the doctor and lit a slim cigar. He took a quick pull and studied Jack Skull through the curling gray smoke. He was a good-looking man, hard but well favored. Tall and lean, like all who spent their days in the saddle, he was burned golden brown by months in the relentless sun. Longish brown hair hung down to his collar. Jack's features were refined, precise, and were only kept from being pretty by the deeply etched lines bracketing his mouth and the hard stare of his clear blue eyes. Jack was wrong; it was something to go on. Not many men had his look.

"If you'll excuse me," Doc Carr said. "Could we get together for breakfast later, say around eight?"

"Sure." Lane nodded. "Eight at the Demorest."

The doctor left without taking his leave of Jack. Jack didn't bother to get upset about it.

"When he asks, tell him I didn't do it."

"When he asks, I'll tell him," Lane said, sitting down behind his desk and motioning for Jack to help himself to a chair.

"What makes you so sure I didn't?"

Lane drew some smoke into his lungs and watched it curl out of his mouth before answering. He'd been thinking about it since first meeting Jack and then thought about it some more when Jack had told him about the string of murders along the Abilene Trail. He was as sure of his answer as a man could be.

"You're not the type." He flicked ash to land on the floor. "Too surly."

Jack lowered his hat to shadow his eyes and tipped his chair back on two legs.

"Thanks."

"Every killer I've ever known, and I've known a few, had twenty friends who'd swear he'd give his life for a stray dog." Lane tipped his own chair back. "You like dogs?"

"Not much."

"See?" Lane smiled, taking another drag. "Not the type."

They balanced in comfortable silence while Lane worked on his cigar. A buckboard passed by the open door pulled by an old gray and driven by a weathered farmer. There were the sharp clicks of a woman in high-heeled boots walking past; Jack didn't turn. The steps didn't have the right sound for Anne Ross. And there wasn't a train due in.

"You know any men who like dogs and look something like me?" he finally asked.

"Maybe." Lane scowled, thinking.

"I'd like to meet a man who'd give his life to save a dog," Jack said, fingering his six-gun.

* * *

Claudia Dain

The dog had wiggled itself into the shape of a doughnut by the time Nell answered the door and then hurled itself forward with the excitement of a posse to wedge open the crack she created. Bill was greeted by a wet black nose before Nell could even get the door all the way open to give a proper greeting herself. She knew who it had to be. Only one person got such a greeting.

"Hello, Bill. Did you have a nice trip?"

"Hello, Nell." He grinned widely, his smile wide and even. "You're looking well, as lovely as ever, and yes, it was a good trip. I just left my gear at Powell's, didn't even unpack, though I don't think Powell will notice, not the way he keeps the place."

Bill Tucker edged past the dog, still squirming in delight, ears back and tongue out, to stand in the foyer. A big house by Abilene standards, it was sparsely furnished and scrupulously clean. The woodwork showed its sophistication by being painted ivory and the floors were polished with wax and dark with use. A moss-green damask love seat in the front parlor was positioned between the two front windows hung with fine lace and faced a single rose velvet upholstered chair. Two wooden chairs with carved roses on their backs were placed on either side of the fireplace. The piano had been sold and the place it occupied had been partially filled with plants that couldn't survive Kansas winters outdoors. The Easter lily sported two cream-white blooms.

"Hello, Bill," Sarah said, coming down the stairs, smiling a crooked half smile. "You want to stand around talking about your trip?"

"Good morning, Sarah." He beamed up at her, flashing his perfect smile like a well-used weapon. "No," he said almost bashfully, "I came to see Anne. She's home, isn't she?"

"Why, Bill, you ought to know Anne's schedule by now," Sarah said, coming down the rest of the way. "The eight-fifteen's coming in from Dodge, and just when did you get back in town, by the way?"

Nell coughed her embarrassment but Bill ignored the oblique rudeness of the query.

"I didn't take the train this time. I rode in not an hour ago. Just stopped to wash up and change."

"Good morning, Bill. I didn't know you had a horse."

"Good morning, Miss Daphne." He aimed a subtle bow in her direction. "I bought this one a few days ago, south of here. A real bargain. I'm sorry to disturb you by coming to call so early, but I was hoping to catch Anne—"

"She's down to the train, as you've no doubt been told. Would you care to have a bite of breakfast? We've finished an hour since, but I'd be happy to fix you something solid."

"No, thank you, ma'am." He bowed again. "Though I appreciate the kindness. I'll just go on to the station now, if you'll excuse me."

"Of course, Bill. And welcome back," Miss Daphne said with all the grace of a sovereign granting a boon.

The three women stood in the foyer for an instant, watching him go. The dog he had to wrestle to keep from following him.

"Dammit! Sit still!" Sarah barked.

Dammit curled down a bit, chagrined for the moment, long enough for Bill to get the door closed, and then leaped to the parlor window to watch until Bill was out of sight. His tail swung wildly long after Bill had disappeared, his look hopeful and trusting. Expectant and patient.

For an instant, Sarah was put in mind of Anne.

It was not a happy association.

It was in that moment that Sarah decided to scout out Jack Skull for herself. She'd take his measure, eye to eye, and trust her own appraisal of the man the whole town was talking about. She was certain that he would do just fine. She wasn't going to wait one minute longer for Anne to stumble over the man on her walks to the depot. She wasn't going to wait and hope that Jack Skull would give Anne some attention and thereby give Bill Tucker some competition. No, she was going to introduce herself to Jack Skull and see where that led her. Bill Tucker was entirely too cocksure of Anne. Anne needed another beau, even if he was a bounty hunter.

She wasn't fool enough to think that she owned the train platform, but it was hardly fitting for him to keep looking at her that way. There wasn't much around, but she couldn't be the only woman he'd ever seen in Kansas.

He was looking at her as if she were. The worst of it was, she didn't mind one bit.

Anne moved a small half step away from Jack Skull. His feet didn't follow her. His eyes did.

"Good day, Anne. How's Miss Daphne today?"

"She's just fine, Mrs. Rivers. What were you doing on the train?"

Jane Rivers smiled and adjusted her hat. She ignored the bounty hunter standing not three feet from her. He didn't seem to mind. Anne couldn't understand how Jane did it; *she* couldn't seem to ignore Jack Skull for the space of a breath.

"Sally Monahan took one look at the fabric Chris Dodd picked out and sent me straight off to buy some of the right color. Tom was getting an earful when I left. I don't think he'll be sending Chris out again, at least not while Sally's breathing."

Which was just what her grandmother had predicted. Anne heaved a sigh. Miss Daphne seemed to be right about everything and wasn't shy about saying so. Was she right about Jack Skull?

Anne risked a sideways glance, using Jane's body as a shield. It didn't work. The sight of him, staring at her, sent shivers right down to her feet. She didn't need that kind of response; she simply needed him to pursue her just a bit to cool Bill down. She didn't need to get all heated up by a pair of cold blue eyes.

"Anne? You all right?" Jane asked, casting a look of grim censure over her shoulder at the obvious cause of the problem.

"Yes," she started, dragging her eyes back to where they ought to be, fixed on a calm and respectable matron, not a wild, lean, hard-looking man. She was getting as bad as he was at keeping her eyes where they belonged. She had more control than that.

"You sure?"

"Of course." Anne smiled, acutely aware that Jack would see her smile and wondering how he would respond to it.

He lowered his hat over his eyes and turned to look at the train. She was more than a little disappointed.

Jane left slowly, a mumbled farewell the best she was going to get from Anne. Anne looked away from Jack, studying the train, which was sitting perfectly still and doing nothing even remotely interesting. Still, she stayed put. And looked.

A wind kicked up and shifted the weight of fabric that made up her bustle. She eased a hand back and smoothed things into place.

Jack Skull took off his hat and slapped it against his leg. The same wind ruffled his long brown hair, curling the ends as they brushed against his shoulders.

Their eyes met in that instant. She looked quickly away, studying the immobile train. By the way her skin was tingling, she guessed that he wasn't looking at the train. Mercy, but she needed to get better at this.

"You like trains."

He said it as a statement, not a question. She didn't know how to reply. If she heeded her grandmother, she shouldn't reply at all, but just hustle herself on home.

She didn't move.

"You prefer the Kansas Pacific or the Atchison, Topeka, and Santa Fe line?"

She liked the Kansas Pacific; engine number 119 had strawberry-red wheels and a canary-yellow cowcatcher, but what did any of that matter when he was standing so close and looking at her as if she were candy? She should say something to encourage him; he'd been standoffish up till now and she wanted to pull him in closer.

"Ever been on the Kansas City, Lawrence, and Southern Railroad? Smoothest ride in Kansas."

She'd never been on a train that she could remember. She only watched them. He took a step nearer, putting his hat firmly on his head, brushing the hair away from his face. All thought fled, pushed off by the nearness of him.

"Course, a bumpy ride has its own charm."

The hair stood up on her arms and she crossed her arms over her chest. Her next breath was a shaky one. But she didn't move. She wasn't going to take a step away from that kind of flirting, even if it did brand her the most wanton fool west of Kansas City. She really did need to get better at this.

"I've never been on a train," she said finally, keeping her eyes on the train. Mama had told her she had a becoming profile.

"There's one waiting." He gestured, taking another step nearer. His boot touched the hem of her flounced skirt. "All it takes is a ticket."

His voice was low, gentle, and she could feel his restraint. Was he attracted to her and fighting to keep it polite or was his restraint against the violence they all said was part and parcel of the man? She didn't know. All she knew was that he was compelling. And she wasn't afraid of him. She was that big a fool.

A Kiss to Die For

"Where would you go?" he said softly.

Where would she go? She would just go. She would just run, run out of Abilene before she died here, run to another place, to set her eyes on something new before life collapsed on her. No one, ever, had asked her where she would go. The going had been the goal, no other destination beyond that.

She looked into his eyes then, stunned by the question. His eyes were so blue, so clearly and flawlessly blue. His features were perfect, chiseled and fine, with a starburst of lines radiating from the corners of his eyes that only served to make his eyes seem bigger and warmer. Smile lines. Even bounty hunters must have cause to smile sometimes. He wasn't smiling now. His look was focused, penetrating; the kind of look that should have made her squirm. She stood stock-still, strangely aware of every breath, almost willing herself to breathe under the intensity of his stare.

Where would she go? The answer whispered inside her, shocking her: *Wherever you would take me.*

No, that was the wrong answer. Had to be. She was smarter than that.

"Anne!"

She jerked at the sound and then tried to cover the insult of her reaction by turning at his voice and smiling widely in greeting.

"Bill. You're back."

His smile faded a bit at her response. Wrong. She had done it wrong. Bill needed more warmth than that, but she couldn't forget Jack standing within the circle of her skirts and she couldn't ignore the feel of his eyes on her. It was very difficult to manage two men.

"Just this morning," Bill said, his eyes on the bounty hunter who stood too close to the girl he was courting. Anne took a step away. Jack let her maintain that distance. But he was still too close.

Bill took her hand and drew her to him for a very acceptable public kiss on the cheek and then tucked her arm in his and took another step away from Jack. She was now a full five feet from the bounty hunter and in the firm possession of Bill Tucker. They faced him, their two to his one, while Jack continued to look into her eyes. When several seconds had passed, he slowly moved his gaze to Bill's face, making it very clear by his leisurely deliberation that Bill's maneuvering in no way controlled him. She felt Bill stiffen and mindlessly patted his arm to calm him down. Jack took note of her touch and then looked into her eyes. For some peculiar reason, she was embarrassed. Which was ridiculous.

"Morning," Bill said stiffly. "Name's Tucker. You in town long?"

Jack smiled and shifted his hat back on his head. "Just long enough to settle some business."

"What kind of business?"

"Bill, I—"

They both ignored her.

Jack just looked, this time at Bill.

"You hunting somebody in these parts?" Bill asked.

"I am." It was said bluntly, with no apology or explanation.

Anne could feel Bill back up, though he never took a step, reassessing the man who stood so immovable in the thin spring sun. The bounty hunter had been disliked and distrusted on sight, urged out of town with every word and every look, yet here he was, as comfortable in his own skin as a turtle in his shell. She wondered how he managed it. It was a skill beyond her ability, certainly. He seemed profoundly untroubled by the turbulence he caused with his very presence, uncaring that Bill, for one, was eyeing him like a rabid wolf. He had no one's approval and didn't appear to need it.

A Kiss to Die For

"Whoever it is, you've got no call to be bothering Miss Ross."

Jack smiled, a smile as cold as January air, and turned his gaze to Anne. "Was I bothering you, Miss Ross?"

The words "A bumpy ride has its own charm" repeated themselves in her head and she blushed. She wasn't so sheltered that she didn't know what he'd meant by that; they had a dog, after all. The worst part was that it hadn't bothered her a bit.

"No," she mumbled, not quite able to meet his eyes with Bill pressed against her side. "I wasn't bothered." That should keep Jack coming at her and upend Bill. Too bad it was the truth.

"Don't lie for him, Anne. A man like that couldn't help but bother you just by breathing," Bill said, his chest puffed out like a rooster. When Jack Skull lost his smile and took a step toward him, however, Bill took a step back. And took Anne with him.

"Why would you call the lady a liar? She's got no call to lie and doesn't look the sort to lie even if pushed to it."

"That's not what . . . I don't have to defend myself to you, Skull. What goes on between me and Anne is personal and private."

"The name's Scullard, Bill," Jack said, his tone easy though his features weren't, "and I'll ask you again not to call the lady a liar."

"It's all right," Anne said, trying to loosen Bill's grip on her upper arm. In his angry frustration, he was squeezing her so hard her fingers were going numb. "I don't mind."

That hadn't been exactly what she'd meant to say, the expression on Bill's face told her that.

"Anne! Let me handle this!" Bill scolded, jerking her backward slightly as he tried to put some distance between them and the most dangerous man this side of the law.

83

"Is he bothering you, Miss Ross?" Jack asked sweetly, his hand dropping down near his gun belt.

"No! I'm fine, everything's fine," she said quickly. This was getting out of hand, like a prairie fire spreading from a single spark. She hadn't planned for this. Trouble was, Jack Skull messed up her thinking and he wasn't too kind on her breathing either. "Bill, I'm heading home and you're welcome to join me. Mr. Skul—Scullard—" She dipped her head in dismissal and walked as gracefully away as she could with Bill clutching her arm like a limp club. Jack stayed on the platform, watching them leave; she didn't turn around to check, she just knew that he was watching her by the trembling that gripped her insides.

"What were you doing with him?" Bill asked as soon as they were out of earshot.

Anne looked at Bill out of the corner of her eye. He still looked angry.

"I wasn't with him," she said calmly. "I was watching the train and talking with Jane Rivers and he just happened to be standing there and then he just sort of started talking to me."

"But you didn't talk to him."

When she didn't say anything, but gave a delicate snort to indicate he didn't have the right to tell her whom she could talk to, Bill said, "I should have known. You're too sweet to want to tangle with his sort."

Naturally, he misread her, managing to think what he wanted to about her. He wouldn't want to believe that she'd willingly talk to another man, so he'd arranged the facts to suit his wants. Men were good at that. Sure made the world a comfortable place for them.

She smiled at him, aware that they had almost reached her house and Miss Daphne might be looking. He wasn't hard to smile at; he was darkly good looking with black hair, thick black eyelashes, and soft blue eyes. He was the most handsome man she had ever seen. Until Jack Skull had come to Abilene.

"I don't know why *you* were tangling with him." He had forced her into the role of peacemaker between two blowing bulls. She wasn't happy about that.

"Pure jealousy, honey," he said, leaning into her as they walked. "The only man I want to see you with is me."

Anne smiled in response. Bill sure did try to get her settled down when she was feeling ruffled, which wasn't all that often. She hated fuss of any kind and most especially hated to be in the middle of it. Bill had known her long enough to know that. Which was why it was so irritating that he had charged in with Jack that way, dragging her along with him. Let him fight it out with Jack alone. She didn't need to be a party to it.

"You understand, honey? Here I was, hurrying to find you, missing you so bad it felt like I hadn't breathed one solid breath in a week, and I find you standing toe-to-toe with another man. I was shocked, Anne, just plain shocked."

Guilt flooded her and she tucked her head down, ashamed of herself in that instant. He was right. He was her beau and he had been looking for her and she had been standing very close to another man. Enjoying it. Enjoying Jack. She even enjoyed that Bill was jealous. She was using Bill and using Jack against Bill and she felt sick about it. But she wasn't going to stop. She needed them both too badly to stop.

"So you found her," her grandmother said from the front porch. Anne raised her head and took a breath to steady herself. She wasn't going to look ashamed in front of her grandmother, no matter how guilty she was. She didn't need to get scolded twice. She prayed Bill wasn't going to say whom he had found her with.

"Yes, ma'am." He smiled, looking well satisfied. "Now I

feel like I really am back in Abilene, with Anne on my arm."

"How sweet," Nell murmured, holding the door for them as they passed through.

"Adorable," Sarah murmured in sarcastic agreement.

Sarah watched them, Daphne making sure Bill had a strong cup of coffee, Nell bringing in a plate of gingerbread for him to devour, Anne sitting quietly at his side on the divan. Dammit pressed against his leg in silent ecstasy. Bill had it easy and took it easy, accepting it all with buoyant good humor, expecting nothing less.

"Excuse me, please," Sarah said suddenly, tying on her hat. "I just remembered something I need in town."

Chapter Nine

"Morning, Charles."

"Good morning, Sarah," Sheriff Lane said, rising to his feet. He looked discreetly behind her.

"I'm alone," Sarah said with a crooked grin.

"I see. Nell busy at home?"

Sarah moved into the room and sat down in the chair facing the desk; Lane moved back around the desk to face her.

"Charles, I didn't come to talk about Nell and if you're not man enough to arrange your own love life, you don't deserve one."

Lane coughed a bit into his fist and then faced down this unexpected adversary. "You're getting more like Miss Daphne every day, Sarah."

"Bite your tongue, Charles," she snapped good-naturedly.

He smiled and eased into his seat. "So, why did you come?"

"I'm looking for Jack Skull and I know he spends considerable time with you, when he's in town. Do you know where he is?"

"Now, Sarah, don't go after him with that tongue of yours. He's not as dangerous as everyone thinks and I'd like it if people in this town would give him a little room."

"What could I do to him?" She shrugged dramatically. "He's bigger and tougher than I am; I wouldn't hurt him. Tell me where he is."

"Why?"

It was a standoff. Sheriff Charles Lane could be as easygoing as a well-fed dog, but there were times when he dug in his heels and refused to move an inch. This was one of those times.

"Anne's not as old as you are and needs a little help arranging her love life," Sarah finally said.

"So?"

When Sarah said nothing further, raising an eyebrow that clearly said she thought he had more under his saddle, Charles leaned forward in his chair, comprehension dawning.

"Is Jack the help you have in mind?" he asked, laughter rolling up to bubble in his mouth as he spoke.

When Sarah didn't laugh, didn't smile, and didn't answer, his laugh ended on an abrupt choke.

"He's not the sort for Anne," he said sternly, speaking with all the force of the sheriff of Abilene, Kansas.

Sarah wasn't impressed or intimidated. "Thought you said he wasn't dangerous?"

"That's not exactly what I said," he said, sitting straight up.

"Close enough," she said, meeting his eye and maintaining her own strict posture.

"What are you planning?"

Sarah relaxed enough to grin. "Nothing fatal."

"I'm relieved to hear it, ma'am," Jack said from the doorway.

Lane visibly relaxed in his seat, glad to transfer the problem of Sarah Todd Davies to another man. Sarah relaxed, glad to have Jack Skull in her sights. Jack was the only one in the room who wasn't relaxed. What did this woman of middling years want with him?

"Introduce us, Charles," she said in a near perfect imitation of Miss Daphne's most commanding voice.

"Yes, ma'am," he said with a smile. "Mrs. Sarah Davies, Mr. Jack Scullard. Jack, this is Mrs. Davies."

"Pleased, ma'am." Jack tipped his hat in her direction.

"My pleasure, Mr. Scullard. Scullard? French, isn't it?"

"Yes, ma'am."

"From Texas, I think it's rumored?"

"By way of Louisiana, ma'am."

They studied each other, the polite and serious measuring of another person who might become ally or foe. Jack did it daily, hourly; it was a simple technique of survival that had taken years to perfect. Sarah did it naturally, as a woman does, and had done it well from the cradle.

"Mr. Scullard, do they have apples as far south as Louisiana?"

"Yes, ma'am, they do."

"And do you have a taste for apple pie?"

"Yes, ma'am."

"As do I." She smiled. "Would you be so kind as to escort me to the Demorest Restaurant? They serve a lovely apple pie and I'd like you to share the pleasure with me."

"Now, ma'am, I don't think—"

"I've got a hunger to taste some apple pie. Miss Daphne doesn't allow apples in the house since they trouble her digestion. I would rather not eat alone." There was nothing pathetic about Sarah Davies, but she sounded almost pathetic now.

"Ma'am," Jack said, giving in, "I'd be pleased to escort you to the Demorest." He didn't smile, not with his mouth, but his eyes showed his amusement. This woman wanted something from him—what he couldn't imagine—but at least according to her, it wouldn't be fatal.

The looks they got when he escorted her to a window table in the Demorest almost were.

"Just ignore her," Sarah Davies said out of the side of her mouth. "Emmie Winslow looks at all cowboys that way."

"I'm not a cowboy," he said as he drew out her chair for her.

"You have the look of one. Were one once, I'd guess."

"Yes, ma'am," he said, sliding into his own chair with a lift of his leg. "What'd a cowboy ever do to get her so riled?"

"Drove a few beeves through this very window. It took almost six months to get it fixed proper."

Jack smiled slightly. "Spirits run high at the end of a drive."

Sarah studied him briefly before calling out, "Two apple pies, two coffees, Emmie."

"Now, ma'am . . ."

"My invitation, my treat," she countered swiftly, closing the subject.

Jack let her have the last word, knowing how women liked that, but he wasn't going to have any woman paying for his feed.

"You ever run a trail into Abilene?" she asked.

He didn't know where this was going, but couldn't see any harm in talking with her. Maybe she was the town eccentric.

"In sixty-eight."

"We saw a lot of cows that year. And a lot of cowboys."

Jack smiled at her as Emmie set down the plates of pie and the mugs of coffee.

"They do tend to run together, ma'am."

"That they do," Sarah said softly. "I miss those days sometimes. Town had more life to it back then."

"It sure did."

Sarah looked up at him at that and smiled her first

genuine smile at the soft twang of wistfulness she heard in his voice.

It was in seeing her smile that he knew who she was; she was kin to Anne Ross somehow. No two women could have that smile and not be related.

It was like watching shutters folding over his eyes, the way he withdrew and pulled in. Sarah couldn't help smiling again.

"I would guess that you've met my niece, Anne."

"Wouldn't say I'd met her," he said softly.

"Seen her then? Folks say there's a likeness between us. I take it as a compliment."

"You should."

"I'll say 'thank you' for us both to that." Sarah took a bite of her pie, tart and crisp, savoring the flavor and the texture before washing it down with coffee. Powell from the livery walked by, teeth clamped on his pipe, shaking his head. Sarah ignored him. "There's ways I don't want her to be like me, though."

"How's that?" He'd stopped eating his pie after two bites and wasn't nursing his half-full coffee. Had to keep his gun hand free, she supposed.

"I've got no man. Neither does Anne."

Anne had no man. Sweet words to hear when he spent too much time thinking about the look of her, the smell of her, and that brief feel when he'd caught her on the stairs. She had no man. She was free. Free to tangle with a bounty hunter.

Right.

"She'll get one," he said, swallowing half the pie in one bite. It wouldn't be him, but she'd get one. Hell, she had Tucker in her pocket now. How many men could a woman use?

"That's the plan," Sarah said simply, pushing her empty plate away from her.

Jack forced coffee over the wedge of pie in his throat

and leaned back in his chair, tipping the front legs off the floor.

"Where do I fit into this plan?" he asked, cutting the fat off the conversation.

Sarah smiled and sipped her coffee, thinking carefully how best to say it. Jack Scullard wasn't stupid and he didn't have the look of a brawler; by the cut of his cloth, he made a good dollar hunting bounty. He showed pride; that could make a man rile easy and she had no wish to rile Jack Skull. But that pride of his could be turned to her plan, if she put it to him right.

A man's pride was a powerful thing when married to his lust and she was a mother ten times over if Jack Skull didn't have it bad for Anne. A man would need to be dead not to stir when Anne walked across his trail.

Jack Skull wasn't dead.

"I won't lie to you," she began and Jack was instantly cautious. People didn't begin that way unless they had considered lying and decided either to tell the truth or skim along the edge of it. "Anne has a beau, of sorts." Bill Tucker, who'd come to fetch her from the depot. "But he's not . . . they're not . . ."

"He's slow to the spur," Jack said, understanding in that moment what this woman wanted from him.

"That's one way of saying it."

"You want to think of some more, I'll stick around and finish my pie."

The anger in his voice was so suppressed that she barely heard it. But she felt it.

"More pie?" Sarah said, trying to coddle him into a sweeter mood.

"This is about all I can swallow," he answered, saying it all.

He was going to bolt; the fact was in every angry movement, in the shadows behind his eyes, in the set of his hat; but he couldn't run, not until she'd set things up properly for Anne. What could she say that would get a bounty hunter to stay? Put that way, the answer was obvious.

"There's things you don't know, being new to Abilene," she said, leaning across the table, whispering. "Anne's only known Bill for a few weeks and he's been a proper enough beau, when he's here. But he's not often in Abilene. Travels all over the country, doing God knows what, and not a braggart when it comes to talking about his business. Lord knows how unusual that is; I never knew a man who made an honest dollar who didn't want to tell you every detail of the conquest. But not Bill. Off and doing only the Lord knows. And poor Anne, hoping he might want to marry her and her not certain of what to think. Of what sort of man she might be tangling with."

She was striking blind and she hit dead center. She could see it in his face, in his blue eyes, but she didn't know what she'd said that had turned him around. It didn't matter. It was clear by just looking at him that the way had suddenly opened for him to pursue Anne.

"You like Anne," she stated, certain of it. "You'll court her?"

Sarah couldn't know that he was seeing a dead girl in his mind, the breath pressed out of her. A beautiful girl lying on the prairie, dark hair splayed out like a shawl, alone in the dark. A girl who got hooked up with a man she should have steered clear of. A girl maybe too much like Anne Ross.

"Ma'am, if you'll excuse me, I'd better get to work."

He laid money on the table for the food without flourish; Sarah hardly noticed, so keenly was she watching his face. He had to get to work? She didn't know what he meant. Until he winked.

Chapter Ten

The dog had his body wedged so tightly between Bill and the door frame that anyone would have thought Dammit was Bill's dog. Anyone not from Abilene. Everyone in Abilene knew that Sarah's husband, Roy, had picked the dog up somewhere on his way home from the war, named him, and given him to Sarah. At least the dog was still around. Though if Bill had even whistled, Dammit would have run after him to Powell's. Personally, Anne thought it was insulting that even a dog wouldn't have loyalty to his mistress. But Dammit was a male and that seemed to explain it all.

"*Stay*, Dammit," she said, squeezing out of the door with Bill, forcing the dog to stay inside.

"I wish that dog had a different name. It doesn't seem right for you ladies to be cussing all day long because of a dog," Bill said once they were outside.

"Uncle Roy named him and Aunt Sarah won't change it. Miss Daphne doesn't like it much either."

"I wouldn't think so," Bill said.

Dammit whined on the other side of the door and

scratched at the wood. They moved across the porch to stand on the steps. Another scratch. Anne just smiled and shrugged, hoping Bill wouldn't pursue it; there was nothing she could do about the name of Sarah's dog and she didn't want to be asked to try.

"How did the trip go?" she asked, changing the subject. Dammit whined and sniffed the crack between the door and the jamb. "Will you be able to stay in Abilene for a while?"

"It went well," he said. "They're going to run a line connecting Junction City and Council Grove, Emporia, Burlington, all the way to Denison on the Red River. Land prices might as much as double. Good opportunities there."

"So you'll be leaving again?"

"I'll be around for a while." He smiled charmingly. Everything he did was charming. It didn't seem as attractive as it once had, say, a week ago, before that outlaw had tumbled at her feet. "I make a good living, Anne."

"I'm sure you do," she said. She could feel her mother's eyes on her back through the lace curtain fabric. She smiled. Bill smiled in return. Surely her mama could see his smile from where she stood.

"But I want you to know," he said, pressing her hand. His hands were nice, long fingered, the nails pared, his skin cool. A bit sweaty. "We'll talk more about my prospects tonight, when I come for you. Seven, remember?"

"Yes, I remember."

"We'll eat at the Demorest, a big dinner. Eat light today so you'll enjoy it."

"I think we're having cold chicken for lunch," she said.

"That sounds perfect." He kissed the back of her hand, a gallant gesture, and backed down the steps, holding on to her hand until their arms were extended fully. He reluctantly let go of her hand. It was very romantic, almost conspicuously so. "And, Anne?"

95

"Yes?"

"Wear the blue dress. I can't take my eyes off you when you wear blue."

She was wearing ivory.

"Of course. The blue dress."

As soon as he left, her mama joined her on the porch. Dammit had been closed off in the kitchen.

"From his look, I'd say he'll ask you to marry him tonight."

"I really haven't known him for very long, have I?"

"I'd say long enough for him to know what he wants," Nell said, looking sideways at her daughter. Anne wrapped an arm around the porch post and leaned into it. "It's what you wanted."

"I know," Anne said softly, lying to her mama, hating it and doing it anyway. It was better than the fight that would come if she admitted that she didn't want to marry Bill or anyone else.

"He's a fine-looking man with good prospects," Nell said. "He'll give you children." A child was the best a man could give. It was what they did best. It just wasn't enough; not for her. Her life was going to be bigger than that.

"Was that how you felt about Papa? A fine-looking man with good prospects who would give you a child?"

"It doesn't matter how I felt, but I got my child. I got you, Anne." Nell said it softly, gently, her eyes full of sudden tears. "What would my life be without you?"

Anne gave her mother a quick hug, heavy with guilt, and then wrapped herself around the porch post once more. "It's just that I . . . I hardly know him." Better to ease her ma away from the certainty of a wedding this week; she didn't want to break her heart.

"You don't know anyone until after you're married anyway," her mother said, rubbing quick hands across her eyes.

It was a frightening thought, to marry a stranger, no

matter how long you had known him, and find out years later if you had joined yourself to a friend or a foe. But she knew how it would turn out if she married. That's why she wasn't ever going to marry. But she couldn't tell her mama that, not when it was all Nell lived for.

"If you say no, you'll lose him. He's got too much pride to ask twice," Nell said.

And then she would be alone again, living in a house of women, all related by blood. The days empty and the nights eternal. No bumpy rides.

Anne blushed and tucked her face into her arms. He was the problem, the bounty hunter. Thinking about a man like that, feeling what he made her feel just by looking at her, was what got a gal in trouble every time. She wasn't going to get in trouble. She wasn't going to let a man worm his way into her life, rotting it from the inside out. She was going to be smart. She was going to use a man before he could use her, and she was going to stay free. Even if her nights were long and smooth and endless.

"Anne?"

Anne lifted her head and looked into her mother's careworn blue eyes. They all had blue eyes, with the exception of Miss Daphne, who had the blackest brown.

"It's all right, Mama," she said. No need saying all she was thinking; it wouldn't do any good and would just cause a lot of trouble. "I need to press the blue if I'm going to wear it tonight."

Nell smiled and kissed her daughter on the temple. "I'll do it. You sit and enjoy the day. The Topeka train is due soon. I'll see you at lunch."

Anne watched her mother go in and then looked back out onto the quiet street, still clinging to the porch post. She hung on to it as if it were the only solid thing for a hundred miles, which was exactly how she felt. Bill hadn't been all that much to manage; he was gone more than he was here, but suddenly he wanted to talk weddings. Why now?

She knew the answer and wanted to kick herself for her stupidity; Jack Skull, in town for just shy of a week, hadn't shown her anything but the most modest interest, and that just this morning on the platform. Up until then, he'd been almost rude; he'd certainly been eager enough to avoid her at every opportunity. She'd given him lots of opportunity. The way he'd all but run from her at the hotel had been humiliating, especially after she'd tumbled against him. Of course, today he'd been different, standing so close to her and being downright impolite. That's what had set the spur to Bill. He was defending his claim against another man. It was what a man would do. She'd wanted Jack to run Bill off and she'd accomplished the opposite. How to fix it? How to make a man leave his claim?

That was easy. Bring in more guns. Jack Skull was bristling with guns. All she had to do was get Jack to dig in and court her and Bill, if he was sensible, would run. Bill was very sensible.

It shouldn't be a problem. Jack had at least noticed her today, talked with her, stood next to her. It was a good start. She wouldn't be much of a woman if she couldn't get more out of him than that. It wouldn't be too hard.

She liked the look of him, the sound of his voice, the way his chest had felt pressed against her own for that brief instant on the stair, hard and flat and hot. She'd wanted to press herself against him, wrapping her arms around his waist, nestling her head under his chin, safe. It was fool thoughts of that sort that got a woman in trouble. Safe, indeed.

Jack was on the steps before she saw him coming, probably because her head was buried in her arms, burrowed in thought. He was beautiful; he was everything a man should be, hard and lean and rough. She wanted to wrap herself around him like a rope; she tightened her grip on the post, hanging on against the impossible urge.

"Ma'am." He tipped his hat brim.

"Hello." She smiled and then bit her lip.

"I've come to apologize for being so forward on the platform today. We haven't been introduced, not formally."

It was a good thing she was hanging on or she would have fallen over like a leaf in the wind. Never on earth would she have imagined that Jack Skull would apologize to anyone for anything he did. And certainly not for ignoring social niceties.

"It's all right. I mean, I didn't mind." Now she sounded forward and completely shameless. "I know who you are." That was better, give him an explanation as to why she hadn't minded that he started talking to her without an introduction. It wasn't a completely honest explanation, but it left her reputation a little cleaner.

"Is that a good thing?"

She wasn't sure how he meant that until she saw the glint in his eye. He was teasing her. Jack Skull was teasing her. Surely that was a good sign. Hadn't Sarah always told her that boys tease girls when they like them? But that was years ago; did men tease women?

"I don't think you need to worry."

"If you say I don't, then I won't."

He seemed to want her to continue, to say something light and fun and teasing in response, but she couldn't think of anything. She'd never had a conversation with a man that had felt anything like this. Bill never teased her. She never even teased the dog.

They stood awkwardly for a few minutes. Somehow, she'd trampled the conversation he had started and neither one of them knew how to pick it up again. Out of the corner of her eye, Anne could see the curtains twitch;

it was either Mama or Miss Daphne and neither one made her feel one bit more comfortable.

"Well, that's all I came to say," Jack said, backing down the step into the dirt.

The train whistle sounded and Jack looked into her eyes with sudden eagerness, putting words in her mouth she would never have had the courage to say on her own.

"Would you like to accompany me to the train? It's coming from Topeka and should be—"

"Sure, Miss Ross, I'll escort you."

He offered his arm subtly. She ignored the offer. The curtains twitched again as they turned away from the house. Jack tipped his hat . . . at the curtains. So, he had known they were being watched; she only hoped he understood that had been the reason she wouldn't take his arm. It must have been Mama who had been watching; Miss Daphne wouldn't have let her leave the porch with a bounty hunter.

They walked slowly, his steps shortened to match hers, dust rising with every step they took. It had been a dry, cool spring. Miss Daphne's flowers weren't going to do well unless they got more heat and more rain. Anything that put her grandmother in a foul mood was to be avoided, even contrary weather. Thinking of the weather and her grandmother were fine topics if she wanted to forget that Jack Skull was walking at her side. Fine topics, except that they weren't working. Every breath was forced; her ribs seemed to press down against her lungs, her heart to beat sideways. He did things to her that didn't need doing.

"Why do you watch the trains?" he asked as they walked.

She looked askance at him. He wasn't looking at her, his eyes were skimming the boardwalk, the storefronts, the flat distance of the prairie, never still, searching. He wasn't even looking at her, but her heart thumped sloppily. She was just shameful. They were intruded upon by

Jim Conner, which was a delight; that kept her from having to answer Jack's question about why she met the trains.

"Good day, Anne," Jim Conner said.

"Good day, Jim."

"Meeting the train from Topeka? Well, you'd better get on, it's been in for a full two minutes now and it's not a long stop."

It was awful, the way Jim ignored Jack. Though Jack didn't seem to mind; he ignored Jim just as completely.

"We'll make it," she said cheerfully, including Jack.

Jim didn't say another word.

"That was Jim Conner, from the stockyard," she explained softly to Jack.

"Seems everyone knows of your interest in trains," he said. "Or is it that you're expecting somebody?"

For a stranger, he was striking too close to the mark. No one around here had ever stopped to think about why she met the trains. It was a common enough pastime. She'd used to come with Sue Ann until her friend married and moved out of town. That she kept up the practice on her own wasn't cause for comment. She wasn't going to flatly refuse to answer; she was going to divert him with a question of her own, staying just on the edge of polite protocol.

"We were all surprised when you decided to stay in Abilene; bounty hunters don't usually stay long."

"You know a lot of bounty hunters?" This time he looked at her. Those blue, blue eyes were trained right on her. She stumbled on a rock in the road. He made a move to steady her and then stopped, letting his hand drop.

"Of course not."

"Of course not," he repeated softly.

Had she insulted him? Did he want her to admit to knowing a passel of bounty hunters? Which, naturally, she didn't. She'd never wanted to get anywhere near a bounty hunter until she'd seen Jack come off that train like a bull out of the pen, hard with muscle and with the spark of a fight in his eye. She'd never seen a man like him. He was absolutely nothing like Bill.

Which was the problem. She could take a full breath with Bill.

"I was so sorry about the girl—Mary I think her name was? What happened?"

They were at the station and Jack took her elbow and helped her up the few steps to the platform. She didn't need the help, she could have skipped those steps in the dark. His mouth tightened and he looked at John Campbell, the stationmaster, who looked right back. John had a special, disapproving look for Anne; she blushed and smiled weakly. There was no doubt now that Miss Daphne would know about her special escort to the station. Her stomach muscles clenched in anticipation as she kept her smile in place for John and Jack and all the world to see, but she felt sick inside at the scolding she knew waited for her back home.

Jack led her down to the far end of the platform and stood between her and John Campbell, shielding her from the stationmaster's eyes, breaking eye contact between them. She looked up at Jack and saw that he was staring down at her. Their eyes held for just a few moments and she saw that he knew, knew the state of her fear and saw the dread that was hanging on to her skirts. He knew and he was trying to protect her from it in any way he could, without actually killing someone. And just when she would have hung her head in shame at being so sick with fear, he winked and looked away, his eyes searching the featureless prairie.

He winked. The moment was gone. Her tension thrust away from her by his simple, discerning act. How had he known it was just what she needed? It didn't bear thinking on. She needed him to manage Bill for her, that was all. Winking wasn't going to have any place in that. She'd make sure of that.

"Where did you find her?" she asked.

His eyes narrowed and he took a shallow breath that she could hear, even on the windy platform.

"I haven't been to Abilene in a few years. Don't remember your friend Bill being here then. How long has he been here?" he asked, ignoring her question.

"A few months."

"What's he do?"

"He's a land developer."

"You mean a speculator."

Jack obviously did not want to talk about the murdered girl. She did not want to talk about Bill. She had no idea how to get Jack to stop talking about Bill. Talking about Bill made her feel underhanded. Standing here with Jack, she wanted to forget all about Bill. Seven o'clock was hours away.

"You been seeing him long?"

Anne just stared at his second button. It was made of horn and the thread was black. Maybe if she looked away, Jack would stop asking her these questions.

She turned to face the station. Facing John Campbell was better than talking about Bill with Jack.

"He must travel some with his work. You get to see him often?"

"I see him enough," she said softly.

"It must be hard on a man, having to be gone so much from the girl he's courting. He is courting you, isn't he?"

She didn't know what to say to that. If she answered truthfully, Jack might walk right off this platform since she would be declaring herself another man's girl; her invitation for him to accompany her didn't cast her in too soft a light, either. But she couldn't lie; he could ask anyone and hear the truth. In fact, he wouldn't have to ask; there were plenty of folks who'd shout it out to him as he passed.

"Why don't you just tell me to mind my own business?" he said, his voice soft and gentle. Amused.

She turned to face him, her fingers clutched together. Again, he seemed to know what she was feeling. No one had ever tried to see into her thoughts the way he did. She felt naked in front of him, exposed and vulnerable. That wasn't good.

"That would be very rude," she said.

"So what?" He grinned. He had the most engaging smile. Those laugh lines hadn't lied.

"I just couldn't do that," she said, trying not to fuss with the strings of her reticule.

"Why not?" He took a step nearer. She snapped one of her strings.

"I've been taught—"

"I've talked to your aunt; it ain't that," he said on a chuckle.

He'd talked to Sarah? About what? Knowing Sarah, remembering the focus of their most recent conversations, she blushed to think.

He was laughing at her and she didn't know why. She had no idea what to do about it. Bill never laughed at her. Bill rarely laughed with her. Bill didn't laugh much at all. It was just possible that she didn't either. There hadn't been much to laugh about in her life. She had absolutely no idea what to say to him, especially since he was standing so close. Because he was standing so close. He'd shaved recently; there was a small slice of a cut near his left ear. Why was it even that looked wonderful on him?

"Miss Ross, you need to speak up for yourself or any fool man will take up with you."

She didn't have anything to say to that. It wasn't true. No one wanted her to speak up for herself. No man had ever tried to take up with her. Until now. And she didn't mind it a bit.

What was wrong with her? She knew what lay at the end of this trail and she wasn't going there. She lived in a houseful of women who'd followed that trail and she'd learned better. There was nothing there, nothing but the emptiness of a man's name.

"I'm sorry," she said. "But you don't need to worry about me. No man has ever tried . . . I mean, there has never been anyone who . . . it's just that I . . ."

"You're scaring the life right out of me, one day at a time," he growled. "You don't know what I'm talking about, do you?" He took a step closer, his boots brushing the hem of her skirt. She stayed right where she was. Seven o'clock was such a long way off; why, it wasn't even lunchtime yet. "You can't just go off with any man, letting him touch you and get close to you. There's dangerous men in this world, Miss Ross. . . ."

She didn't pay much attention to his words after that. He was leaning down to her and she rose up on her toes, lifting her mouth to his, ignoring everything she knew of men, just for this minute. Just for a minute, she wanted to get close to him, to taste him, to feel the pulse of him on her lips. Just once, she wanted to surrender.

He hesitated just for a second, just before their mouths met; she closed her eyes and tilted her head back, showing him that she was surrendering, that she wanted this kiss at this moment more than she remembered wanting anything. He seemed to growl a bit and then he kissed her.

It was the kind of kiss that could drive a girl into some real deep trouble.

It was hunger wrapped in gentleness, roughness cloaked in restraint. It was deep and thorough and wet and it was over much too fast.

He lifted his head, pulling away from her. She leaned

against him, her mouth seeking his still, until he held her by the arms and pushed her away from him.

"Do you kiss Bill that way?" he said in a soft growl.

She opened her eyes slowly and blinked away the haze. "No."

The Topeka train whistle sounded sharply just a few feet from where they were standing. Anne jerked as if whipped and turned away from Jack, shamed beyond words, only to face John Campbell. He looked as though he'd like to whip her, right then and there. But he'd most likely let Miss Daphne do the job.

Anne rushed off the platform, her skirts swinging against her legs, not giving him a backward glance, which Jack thought was smart. The first smart thing she'd done since he showed up on her porch like a stray dog. Jack watched the stationmaster until the man stopped looking at Anne and turned to face him. It didn't take long for the man to duck his head and turn back to the station depot. Jack was left alone on the platform as the train pulled out of Abilene. What stuck with him was how naive that gal was with men, and the memory of that kiss. And the memory of her telling him that she kissed Bill.

What got into him when he was with her? This was the second time he'd made a fool of himself with her on this platform, acting like a bull with a cow when she had her tail up. Anne Ross wasn't a cow twitching her tail; she was a proper lady and he was acting more bullish each time he saw her. Trouble was, she didn't know the first thing about heading off a man who was charging after her. She shoulda stopped that kiss. He'd thought she was going to and couldn't stop himself when she didn't. She shouldn't have looked at him as though she wanted to melt into his bones, as though she would have gone on kissing him until the sun set if he hadn't held her off. He didn't have much practice at holding women off of him and he sure didn't want to learn with her. Damn, but she was a fool woman to lean into a man that way.

There was a killer out there who'd just love to find a woman like Anne Ross under his hands.

Jack slapped his hat against his leg and jumped off the platform to the dust below.

"Why didn't she tell me to mind my own damn business?"

Chapter Eleven

"John, don't often see you in here this time of day. Beer?"

Shaughn stopped sweeping to step behind the bar and pour out a beer before John Campbell had a chance to answer.

"Rye," John gritted out. "And you'd better save that beer for yourself when I tell you what I just witnessed over at the depot."

"Not another killing," Shaughn said slowly, setting down the half-full glass of beer and pouring out a jigger of rye.

"Of a sort. The killing of a fine girl's reputation," John said, taking a swallow from his glass. He in no way came close to finishing it off in one swallow; he wasn't much of a serious drinker.

"A girl's reputation was killed at the depot? At ten-thirty in the morning? How?"

"You wouldn't need to ask how if you knew the man who did the killing. Specializes in killing." He took another swallow.

There was only one man in town who specialized in

killing. And there was one girl, one fine girl who was at the depot several times a day, who had caught that man's eye, caught his eye right here at this bar. Shaughn reached for the beer.

"What happened?" he asked after he had downed the beer and set the glass carefully on the polished bar. He had to know. He felt somehow responsible since Jack Scullard had spotted Anne standing right here in his saloon. But maybe it wasn't all that much; people liked to talk, especially about someone universally hated, and Jack Skull was that. Might not have been much at all. After all, what could happen on a railway platform before supper?

"First of all, he escorts her to the depot like she was his personal property, and that when she comes fine enough on her own seven days a week without any help from him."

Shaughn relaxed. "Now that doesn't sound so bad—"

"That ain't all." John took another swallow, a bigger one than the first, and it went down easier. That was the nice thing about drinking; it got easier. "He's standing there, talking to her like he's got the right. Just about nose-to-nose he was."

"Talking ain't no crime, John."

"And then he kissed her." John Campbell took his final swallow and finished off his rye. His glass hit the bar like a club coming down. Shaughn flinched and, on reflex, poured another. He poured two, one for each of them.

"You mean like a kiss on the cheek?"

"Hell, no, I don't mean a kiss on the cheek! It wasn't no grandma kiss he gave her, Shaughn. It was a kiss!"

"Oh." Shaughn swallowed his rye. It went down hard, but he needed something hard to straighten out his thinking. "What'd she do?"

"Stood there and took it." John looked sideways at Shaughn and took another swallow. His glass was almost empty again.

"She didn't hit him or raise a fuss?"

"Anne?" John snorted. "Would Anne raise a fuss if a hornet crawled into her corset?" John grumbled, slamming his glass down again. It was empty. "Course she didn't raise a fuss. She didn't even raise a hand to slap his face."

"Oh." Shaughn finished his drink, thinking. Thinking was getting harder; he didn't usually drink hard liquor and never before supper. "What'd you do?"

John blanched and made a face as if the rye were going to come back on him. "What could I do?" he blustered. "He has two guns strapped down and I've got nothin'. I'm no fool to tangle with a man like that. A killer."

"Oh. Yeah." Shaughn nodded, clearing away the glasses. It made sense. He wouldn't want to tangle with Jack Skull either, even with guns of his own. It would have been different for Anne, being a woman. She could have slapped his face and come away unbloodied.

"Good morning, John," Martha said, coming into the room from the back. "Not often we get to see you this time of day. I was just bringing Shaughn something to eat. Would you like some pork stew? Lot of fat on that pig, cooked up nice and rich."

John looked the worse for that description and walked to the door, carefully. "No, thank you, Martha, I need to get back."

Martha watched him out and then turned to her son. "What were the two of you doing, sitting in here drinking when you should be about your business? I've never known John to drink before dinner and I've rarely seen you drink with the customers. He *did* pay?"

Actually, he hadn't, but Shaughn was certain he would. When he felt more himself.

"He had some hard news to pass along and wanted a drink or two to get it out."

"Not Miss Daphne?" Daphne Todd was the oldest female in the community and, though she was fit, no one could last forever. "My, but I thought she looked flushed at the last meeting of our sewing circle."

"It's not Miss Daphne."

Martha handed him the bowl of stew she'd brought from their kitchen, right out back of the saloon. Shaughn looked at it, noting the swirls of cooling grease that marbleized the brown surface of the stew, and toyed with his spoon. Maybe if he stirred it up . . .

"Then what? Are they moving the lines? Will we lose the railroad?" Abilene was failing, but it would be death to lose the railroad. The trains were the life of the town, especially since the cow trails had moved west.

"No. He saw something at the depot this morning that ruffled him up."

That said it all, really. Only one person in town made a life out of hanging around the train station and it wasn't John Campbell, he only worked there.

"Did Anne finally board one of those trains and get out of here?" Shaughn only shook his head and continued to stir his stew. "Shaughn O'Shaughnessy, it *was* Anne! If you don't tell me what happened this minute, I'll dump that stew on the floor!"

Not such a bad idea, the way his stomach felt with that rye rolling around. Shaughn looked up at his ma and said, "She got good and kissed." When she smiled and started to shake her head, he knew why. Everyone knew that Bill Tucker was back in town. "By Jack Skull." She stopped smiling.

"And John Campbell watched?"

"I won't say he watched, but he saw it."

"Don't pick at words with me, Shaughn. If John saw it, he could have done something about it."

"Against Jack Skull?" Shaughn gave up on the stew. "Ma, what was he supposed to do? Die to save her from

111

a kiss? Besides, the way he tells it, Anne didn't exactly fight him off."

"You don't expect a grown man like John Campbell to fight Jack Skull but you expect little Anne Ross to?"

"Well, now, she's a woman."

"And?"

"And women can take care of themselves in situations like that."

"Against a killer?" she huffed, hands on her hips in frustrated fury. "When there's a dead girl lying in the doc's office right now?"

Shaughn's face blanched like John's had done just moments before. He hadn't thought of that. The rye bubbled and burned in his gut and he fought to keep it down. It just didn't pay to have hard liquor before dinner.

"Eat your supper, Shaughn," Martha said, beyond all patience with her son and with men in general. "I'm going to see to the dishes and then I'm going to pay a visit to Nell and see if she knows what's run afoul of her daughter."

"Now don't go stirring things up worse than they are."

"I don't much see how things could get worse, but I'll be discreet. I don't want to cause poor Anne any more trouble than she's already in. As to Jack Skull, I don't hold anything against the man for his chosen line; we need bounty men, after all, but he should know that it's not his place to dog after a nice girl like Anne."

"I agree," Shaughn said. And he did. Bounty men kept their distance and kept their place with no one needing to explain why.

Martha had just closed the door behind her when Powell ambled in, pipe between his teeth. "Good day, O'Shaughnessy."

"Good afternoon, Powell. Slow day at the livery?"

"Slower than Campbell's seeing at the depot," he said through a blue haze of pipe smoke.

A Kiss to Die For

Shaughn nodded and got out a clean glass. He should have known; Powell came by every day but not until dusk. It was hours till nightfall, about seven o'clock this time of year.

"You thirsty for rye or beer?"

"Beer," Powell said easily. "I've lived long enough to see worse than this."

"I guess there's some good in that."

"Don't know how," Powell muttered. "Anne's not lived so long; this is bad enough for her. If she was here, I'd spot her the rye myself and tell her she owed me nothing. Can't get much worse than a girl of her standing being mauled by a renegade like Jack Skull. Why, I wouldn't put my worst nag in the way of him and his kind."

"I heard," Shaughn said, passing the beer across the well-worn bar.

"And was I right?" Powell poked his pipe stem into the air surrounding Shaughn. "Man doesn't get a reputation like Jack Skull has hanging on his spurs by spitting up-wind. That gal was playing it smart by not setting her spurs into him; you never know what a man like that will do when he's riled, except that you won't like it. Let him steal his kiss and then move along, out of his territory, and keep your distance from then on. Smart girl, that Anne. She knew when to fight and she knew when to hold her cards."

"You ever seen Anne fight?" Shaughn asked, drying the glass John Campbell had used on a snowy white bar towel. His ma was particular about such things.

"Can't say I have, but that don't mean she ain't got it in her. Never met a woman who couldn't give as good as she got, and maybe some better. Anne's likely the sort of gal who picks her fights careful and she did a good job in not picking a fight with Skull. I've never seen a man who would put up with less fuss than that man. Meanest

113

eyes I've ever seen. 'Bout froze my tongue to my teeth first time I saw him."

"I heard you did plenty of talking," Shaughn said, putting the glass away and wiping down the surface of the bar.

"Just holding my own, that's all. Man was a splinter away from walking off with my stock, cool as you please, and with no regrets, let me tell you. He's a hard man, that Skull is, with a pile of bodies to mark his passing."

"He's been in here a time or two. I never had no trouble," Shaughn said, feeling contrary.

"That's 'cuz you were willing to give him what he wanted. Plain as that. Try telling him no and see how you fare. You don't think Anne stood a chance against him? That little thing, why if she'd even of turned her face to keep him from laying ahold of her, he'd have shot her dead then and there. He's that mean."

"That's the talk," Shaughn admitted. He hadn't paid much attention to it; Jack Skull had been tolerable enough in his saloon and he didn't ask for more than that. But this thing with Anne, that changed the game some. It wouldn't do to have Jack Skull sniffing after Anne. No, that was no good.

Powell upended his glass and drank his beer in long, full swallows. He set the glass down gently, which Shaughn appreciated, and wiped his full, upswept mustache carefully.

"That's the talk because that's the man. I just hope he's not around long enough to prove it. We haven't had a killing here since the trail moved west and I don't care to see any more killing soon. That Anne, she's a sweet one."

"You think he'd kill Anne?" Shaughn asked, studying Powell.

Powell put his pipe back in his mouth and shuffled to the door. "I can tell you firsthand that the man don't take no for an answer. Gets real ornery when what he wants can't be had."

"You think he wants Anne."

"He kissed her, didn't he?"

Powell turned his face to the cold spring air and walked outside. He didn't hear if O'Shaughnessy had anything to say to that. Probably not. What was there to say? Jack Skull was a killer and he had his eye on Anne. Poor little gal.

There wasn't much action on the boardwalk as he made his way back to the livery. Wind was kicking up, blowing dust as high as a rail fence, but it wasn't cold and it wasn't wet so he paid it no mind. The cold days were gone and the blistering heat of summer still weeks off; these were the golden days, days of moderate temperature, moderate wind, moderate thunderstorms, and the occasional tornado. One of Abilene's finest seasons.

Mrs. Walton was charging her way down the boardwalk, dragging one of her kids with her. A boy, it was, with red cheeks and glassy eyes and the normal share of bruises. She wasn't going to stop, he could see that, but he was feeling talkative today.

"Good day to you, Mrs. Walton. Where you headed?"

"Good afternoon, Mr. Powell," she said, hardly slowing.

"Trouble following you today, Mrs Walton?" He gestured to her son, who was at that moment wiping his nose with the palm of his hand. She slapped his hand away from his face.

"Joel's feeling poorly, Mr. Powell, and I'm taking him to see the doc. I'd like to catch it now before it snares any of the others. Nothing wears me out quicker than a houseful of sick children."

"Likely one of them spring fevers; had a few myself in my day."

Joel Walton looked up at Powell, gray and grizzled, brown teeth clamped on his pipe stem, with wonder. No one alive remembered Powell as anything but old.

"Most likely. Thank you for asking," Emma Walton said. "Do you happen to know if the doc is in his office?"

"Haven't seen him," Powell answered, pulling out his pipe. "Just left O'Shaughnessy's."

There was something in the way he said it that made her pause and look at him again. She handed Joel her handkerchief. "Oh?"

"Talking about what happened just a bit ago over at the depot."

Emma moved closer, patting Joel absently on the back and taking her own few swipes against his nose with her handkerchief. Emma calculated quickly; the train from Topeka had come in about an hour ago. Anne would have met that train as she met them all, with the exception of those that stopped in the dead of night. Miss Daphne drew the line at allowing her granddaughter to traipse through Abilene in her night rail and slippers. Bill Tucker was back in town. Jack Skull was still loitering about, looking for trouble, no doubt. It seemed safe to guess that the news was about Anne and concerned either Bill or Jack or both, though why Jack Skull would have any reason to go anywhere near Anne Ross was a puzzle.

"Is Anne all right?" she said, fairly confident that she was close to the mark. Aiming true with limited information was her God-given profession; she was a mother.

Powell grumbled against his pipe stem, having just lost a fair-sized portion of his thunder.

"Right enough," he said and waited. When Emma was relaxing into a smile, he added, "If you call being man-handled by Jack Skull 'all right.' "

She'd had the players picked correctly, but she would never have imagined that scenario. That fact showed on her face. Powell smiled and bit down on his stem, taking a puff of self-satisfaction.

"Was she hurt?" Emma gripped Joel's hand as if she

expected him to be shot out from under her protection. If Jack Skull could attack a woman like Anne, he was capable of anything.

"Not bloodied, if that's what you mean. That gal has too much thinking to rile a killer like Skull; nah, she just let him steal his kiss and then skittered off home to her mama."

"You mean he actually kissed her? At the depot?"

"Full on the mouth and held her arms down to do it," Powell relayed with immense satisfaction. One would think he had done the kissing himself. "Not a thing she could do about it, what with him forcing himself and being a killer and all."

"Did he . . . did he threaten her?"

"Well, I don't think he asked her pardon, do you? He took his time about it, crowding her, touching her, then kissing her like he'd be about it till Sunday service rolled around. Poor gal couldn't do a thing to stop him. She saw that murdered gal, same as the rest of us. She saw what happens to women what say no to a man determined."

That was true. And Jack Skull had shown up just about the time as that murdered girl, who was also pretty and dark of hair. Just like Anne. Just like her Lillian.

Dr. Carr walked onto the boardwalk from the boot maker's just ahead and Emma remembered that she had been on an errand to see him and that she was holding Joel by the hand. It was just horrible the way the thought of Jack Skull intruded, threatening the normal course of life. She should never have sold him that horse, no matter how much she needed the money.

"Excuse me, Mr. Powell, but there's Doc Carr now and I must have him take a look at Joel."

"Shore," he said, tipping his hat and continuing on down to the livery. He didn't have much more to say anyhow.

Emma hurried down the boardwalk, the rising wind pushing at her skirts and threatening the security of her hat, but she persisted until she caught up to Doc Carr at the door to his office. In no time, Joel was sitting in a chair that faced the light coming from the window and opening his mouth for the doctor and all the world to see. Only the doc looked.

"A little red, he's congested, nothing serious. Keep him quiet, give him apple cider vinegar and honey in warm water every two hours while he's awake." Joel suddenly felt very sleepy; he could hardly keep his eyes open. He hoped his ma was watching. "He should be fine in a few days." Joel's hand moved of its own accord up to his nose. "And get him a handkerchief." Joel's hand crept back down as his mother flushed her embarrassment. He sniffed, loudly.

"That's a relief," Emma Walton said, opening her reticule to pull out her pennies. Others might pay in poultry, but she had been taught better by her folks. Besides, she had the money Jack Skull had paid for Joe. "I have so much troubling me right now that I'm afraid I couldn't stand another burden."

"Oh?" A lot of weight rested on that one word. They both stopped to let it settle in the air between them. Joel sniffed.

"You've heard about what happened at the depot this morning." It was not a question.

He had heard something at the boot maker's, but it had been garbled and rushed, besides being unbelievable. He had the time now to listen to a fuller tale and Mrs. Walton was the sort of woman to have her facts about her.

"No, I've had a rather busy day so far. What happened?"

Joel slouched in his chair in preparation for a long wait. Since only apple cider vinegar and warm water waited at home, he was content to sit where he was.

"You know that Jack Skull, the bounty hunter, is in town."

"I do," he said in clipped tones.

"Oh, that's right, you went out with him to find the dead girl's folks. How did that go?"

"Just fine," he said. He wasn't going to give information when he was supposed to be getting it.

Sensing she was losing a sympathetic ear, Emma continued. "Well, this morning, when Anne Ross went to meet the Topeka train, Jack Skull attacked her. Right on the platform."

Doc Carr picked up his bag and stood up hurriedly. "Attacked her how? Did she lose consciousness? Why didn't anyone come for me? I should have been there. She'll need me," he said in a rushed mumble.

"No, not that way," she said quickly. "He held her arms so that she couldn't fight him off and then he kissed her full on the mouth."

Malcolm Carr sank slowly into his chair and let his bag rest on the floor near his feet.

"He kissed her," he repeated. "Was John Campbell there?"

"Isn't he always?"

"And he did nothing?"

Emma shrugged. "Against Jack Skull?"

"Where's Anne now?" He was rising to his feet again, the color coming back to his face.

"At home, I would think. The next train's not due in till four."

"Thank you, Mrs. Walton," he said, all business again. "As I said, Joel will be fine in a few days. Don't forget the apple cider vinegar."

"Of course not," she said, rising to her feet. The doctor rose with her and held the door as they passed through. Joel sniffed.

Malcolm Carr put a sign on his door saying he'd be

back in thirty minutes and then left the office. He went straight to the sheriff's.

The door was open. Wind was blowing dust into the room so that the air was golden with it. Nobody paid it much mind.

"Have you heard about what happened—"

"Heard it five times already, Doc. Don't need to hear it a sixth."

Sheriff Lane got up from his chair and grabbed the broom from the corner. The floor was developing little piles of sand. He used the broom to prop open the door, which was starting to swing in the wind.

"Have you arrested him?"

"Arrested him?" Lane looked at the doctor as he sat back down in his chair and tilted the front legs off the floor. "For kissing a girl?"

"But Anne is—"

"Don't matter who the girl is. Kissing's not a crime."

"But Anne—"

"Didn't put up a fight. In my book, that means she was willing."

Carr placed his hands on the desk and leaned toward the sheriff, his expression grim and determined.

"Did it occur to you that she might have been too afraid to resist him? There is a dead girl lying in my back room being readied for burial. Anne saw that woman, hell, the whole town did, when that bounty hunter brought her in. Don't you suppose that Anne might have been thinking that she'd get more of the same if she put up a fight?"

"You think he would have killed her, right there at the depot with the Topeka train sitting there and John Campbell watching like a bird dog, if she had turned from his kiss? Is that what you think?"

"I don't know what the man is capable of, but I do know that he kissed Anne Ross in broad daylight!" Malcolm roared.

A Kiss to Die For

"And by all accounts, she kissed him back," Lane said quietly. "Look, Malcolm, I don't like this any more than you do. Not this man and this girl, but I can't arrest a man for kissing. Not even when it's Anne."

Malcolm ran a hand through his hair and took a deep breath. "I don't like it."

"You and everybody else in town." Lane smiled lightly, easing the tension. The doc was plenty agitated. "I will have a talk with him, if that helps. Pass that around, if you would."

"Fine."

"Thank you, Doc."

Carr didn't answer as he walked out the door; he had spent all his energy in anger and outrage. Sarah brushed past him, coming in just as he was leaving. Malcolm tipped his hat and kept moving, content, for the moment, to let Lane handle the situation.

Sarah walked in, adjusting her gloves as she came, a victorious light in her eyes.

"Good afternoon to you, Charles," she said, smiling. "I thought you might be wanting to talk with someone from the family about now."

"You know," he said.

"Me and everyone else," she said, sitting down with her back to the open door. The wind blew the ribbons that trailed from her bonnet; she ignored them and kept her eyes on Sheriff Lane.

"Then you know what's being said, that Jack forced himself on her and that she was afraid to resist him . . . that he kissed her . . . publicly."

"No one disputes that he kissed her . . . publicly," she said calmly, the trace of a smile on the edges of her mouth. "I don't believe she was either forced or fearful."

Lane leaned forward in his chair, banging the front legs down onto the floor and raising a small dust cloud. "You sure about that, Sarah? Did Anne tell you that?"

121

"Anne didn't have to tell me, Charles. I have eyes."

"What does that mean? Are you saying that he's been hanging around her?"

"I'm saying that he's a fine-looking man. I'm saying that Anne's of marrying age," Sarah stopped and smiled fully. "I'm saying that Jack Skull is a man who knows how to commence a courting."

"A courting," Lane repeated. "What did you two talk about over your apple pie, Sarah?"

Sarah smiled and shrugged.

"Did you say something to set Jack on Anne's trail?"

Sarah smiled and removed one glove, a finger at a time.

"Are you saying that you encouraged Jack to court Anne, that he had your approval?"

"We talked. He's a nice enough man, no matter his profession."

"You set a bounty hunter on to your niece?" Lane's voice was rising noticeably with each question.

"I don't appreciate your tone, Charles, and I don't see what business it is of yours or of the rest of this town. Who Anne sees, and marries, is her own affair."

Stunned, Charles looked at Sarah for a few moments, studying her composure, which was complete, and her face, which was relaxed. She slowly removed the other glove and set the pair of them in her lap.

"Does Miss Daphne know?"

Sarah jerked and the gloves fell to the dusty floor.

"I didn't think so," he said with a smile. "What's she going to think when she hears about this kiss? And she surely will the way folks are talking. She going to open up her hand so that Anne can fall into Jack's lap?"

"Anne deserves a proper courting and more than one beau to buzz around her," Sarah said stiffly, picking up her gloves.

"So this is about Bill Tucker, too."

"This is about Anne, Charles," Sarah said, her spine stiff

against the wooden back of the chair. "I only want good things for Anne."

Charles scraped his chair legs against the floor as he leaned forward. "And Jack Skull is a good thing?"

Sarah didn't answer. Charles was being horribly bossy.

"The man's killed."

"And so have you."

"It's not the same," he said, running a hand through his hair.

"It is to the men who're dead and I don't believe he killed without provocation."

"Fine. But what's provocation to you and him might be a sight different, Sarah. To have killed as many as he can lay claim to would indicate a real touchy man."

"He's dealing with dangerous men—"

"And always comes out alive."

Sarah fidgeted with her ribbons, suddenly intensely annoyed that the wind was blowing them all about.

"You said he wasn't as dangerous as people made out."

"Sarah," Charles said softly, "that doesn't mean he's right for a girl like Anne."

"Well, someone's got to be and he deserves his chance same as any other," she snapped.

"Did he say he wanted a chance with Anne?"

This time she smiled. "He kissed her, didn't he?"

Charles smiled back, though his smile was weary. "That he did, by all accounts."

Sarah stood and smiled up at the sheriff for a moment before she turned toward the door. The wind blew against her skirts so that the outline of her legs was clear against the weight of the fabric. Charles didn't seem to notice. Sarah sighed. No one ever seemed to notice.

"You warn her to step easy with Jack, Sarah. Anne's not used to his sort with their rough ways. That's obvious." He was thinking of that very public kiss.

"I won't do anything of the kind, Charles. Anne is entirely too cautious as it is."

She left before he could tell her what else she should be doing regarding her own niece. Blasted men, thought they knew everything.

She wasn't halfway home when she saw Bill coming out of the barbershop, as clean shaven as a babe. Just the person she most wanted to see.

"Hello, Bill," she said, coming up beside him. He did what she expected; took her hand and bowed over it. Sometimes his manners rubbed her wrong and now was one of those times. Why couldn't he be the kind of man to kiss a girl in broad daylight? Anne deserved that kind of excitement before life ran her down.

"Hello, Sarah," he said as he lifted his head. Then he said nothing, just stared down at her with his mouth as straight as string. Not like him at all. Something must have given him a face as bleak as a blizzard in March, something that was bothering him badly.

Sarah smiled.

"Have you seen Anne since this morning? No, I guess you haven't, being so busy and all."

She gestured with her eyes toward the barbershop. Busy man, to leave his gal to find her own amusements while he primped. Poor Bill hadn't expected Anne to be any place but where he put her; and why should he worry? There wasn't a man in twenty-five square miles who was fit to court Anne, or there hadn't been, until Jack Skull rode in. It would serve him right to lose his gal for being so slow and so shy with his attentions. She'd talked with Jack, shown him the gate was open, and he'd been off like a shot; kissing Anne full on the mouth with half of Abilene looking on and Anne not minding one bit. There was nothing slow or shy about Jack Skull.

Before Bill could answer that, she spoke again, deciding to ride him a bit. "I suppose you've heard what happened at the depot today," she said gently. He looked so mad and so pitiful that she almost could find it in herself to feel sorry for him. Almost. "Bill, you've got to know that Anne's a smart-looking woman, ready to build her own nest, and when a man comes along and shows her that he appreciates her, that he's serious . . . Well"—she shrugged—"she's going to listen. And you can't blame her for that." Bill opened his mouth to speak, his blue eyes hot with angry intensity, but Sarah cut him off. "It's too bad you spend so much time away from Abilene, not giving Anne the attention she deserves, but I expect you know what you're about, being such a smart businessman and all. Good day, Bill," and she sailed off down the boardwalk with brisk steps, the wind pushing her along from behind.

Bill stared after her, the words he had been about to speak tangled around his tongue like a cord. He didn't see Jack enter the sheriff's office behind him. It was probably for the best.

Jack didn't say anything. He stood in the doorway, his shoulder braced against it, and looked at Lane. Lane didn't invite him in, didn't invite him to sit, didn't offer him a drink. He needed one.

"Had yourself a morning, didn't you?"

Jack shrugged one shoulder and ambled into the room, taking the fact that Lane was speaking to him as an invitation to come in and not get shot.

"Didn't figure you for a ladies' man," Lane said, opening his drawer and pulling out the rye.

"I ain't."

"You'll do," Lane said, pouring out two drinks. It was early, but it had been quite a day so far.

Jack took his drink and sipped it; he wasn't sure how mad Lane really was and he wasn't going to play it wild.

"What made you do it? Anne 'n' all," Lane asked.

"You have to ask?" Jack smiled crookedly before taking

another swallow. She was the prettiest woman he'd seen in years, maybe the prettiest north of the Red River, and that was conservative. He'd never seen a woman like her. He'd never known a woman who made him feel the way she did, like he wanted to lay his brand all over her and protect her from every kind of predator the world could cough up, while he devoured her himself.

He wanted to know why she spent half her time jumping in her own skin and the other half trying to be better than a preacher's wife. He wanted to know why she let a man like him lay hands on her. And he wanted her to let him close enough to do it again. Hell, if she didn't want him up close to her, he'd just have to convince her. He was enough of a hand with the ladies to do that.

"Yeah, I have to ask. I've heard things about you, Jack, but courting women wasn't one of them. What's different now?"

Jack put down his drink on the edge of the desk, thinking. He had no secrets to keep, not about Anne, so he might as well tell what had started him on her trail.

"Her aunt's mighty persuasive."

"I figured it for something like that. She have to persuade you much?" Lane smiled over the rim of his glass.

"Some," he said. He'd never have gone near her, no matter what his blood did inside him when he looked at her, if her kin hadn't opened the chute on her and waved him in. He wanted her, wanted her any way he could have her, even as a pretend beau to spur another man on. If that's what opened the door to her, he'd take it. But now that he was in, he had his own game to play and it wasn't as the spark to light another man's fire. He wasn't that much of a fool.

"Anne's got a beau—she tell you that?"

"She told me that right off, that's why she was talking at all to a man like me. Seems he doesn't pay her enough mind, leaving her to herself more than he should. I'm supposed to make him sit up."

"You're off to a start, what with this morning."

"Yeah," Jack mumbled, picking up his drink again.

But that wasn't why he'd kissed her. He'd kissed her because he couldn't stop himself, and he was a man who always stopped himself, especially with a woman like her. He didn't have any call to be rubbing up against so fine a woman. She ought to know that. Hell, the whole damn town knew that.

"What's with that gal? She doesn't have the gumption to save herself from drowning," he said to Lane.

"You saying that you didn't expect to get away with that kiss?"

"I'm saying that she ought to know how to handle herself with a man by now."

Charles Lane set his glass down and carefully corked his rye. The drawer slid open with a long squeak and slid back shut with a muffled bang, the bottle rolling against the sides. It was a time before he lifted his eyes to Jack's.

"You know that man we were talking about? The one who'd die for a stray dog?"

Jack finished his drink and set the glass down. "Yeah."

"Name's Bill Tucker and he's been courting Anne all spring."

Chapter Twelve

Martha O'Shaughnessy hadn't wasted any time in getting to Nell. Nell turned as white as flour when she heard, but didn't say a word, either in acceptance or denial. Miss Daphne was in the garden picking greens for supper and heard the tail end of the story as she came through the back door. Martha obliged her by repeating it. Miss Daphne didn't turn white, she turned pink, but she managed to hold her tongue in front of Martha; they were all members of the same sewing circle and it wouldn't do to be the center of such a fuss with her words being bandied about by women who didn't have to suffer her trials of life. Martha left, settled in her own mind that she hadn't done anything but her Christian duty and was not spreading gossip. After all, it was the *truth*. Miss Daphne and Nell waited in the parlor for Anne to come home.

When Anne came home, it started.

"Anne, did—"

"I'll talk to her, Nell," Daphne interrupted. "You just sit and keep still awhile."

Nell closed her mouth and sat back in her chair.

A Kiss to Die For

Anne closed the door softly behind her, wishing she had the grit to run down the street and jump on a train going anywhere. With the gentle click of the door, she closed herself in to face the nearest thing to the wrath of God she'd face this side of heaven.

"Anne," her grandmother began softly, "you've disappointed me and brought shame and disgrace to our family by your wanton and unseemly behavior today." It would have been bad enough if she'd stopped there, but she didn't stop. Miss Daphne never stopped.

"You've been brought up in a fine home, having had the grace to be born into a family of untarnished reputation and you have seen fit, by your unrestrained and ill-considered actions today, to take those gifts, given from God Himself, and throw them down into the dirt."

Anne pressed back against the door, the feel of the handle a wedge of pain on her spine. She didn't move. She wasn't sure if she even blinked.

"The Lord has not seen fit to give me an easy life, left alone to support two daughters on my own and you, my only grandchild, but I have not complained. I have not asked God to make my load any lighter, I have taken what God gives and I have not shirked my duty." Daphne's voice rose in volume with every sentence; she spoke with all the divine authority of Moses on the mountain.

"That you have turned from all that you have been taught and thrown it under the scuffed boots of that killer is self-seeking disobedience of the worst kind. You commit your foul acts and then run home to the family who has loved you and cared for you since your birth like a mockery of the prodigal son. He, at least, was truly repentant. He had known true degradation and isolation. If you are going to wallow with the pigs, Anne, you should at least have the dignity to be truly repentant of your acts. Perhaps it is that you have not known true degradation and isolation. You have a home where you have been shown respect and love and you do not know enough of the world to be truly thankful for these gifts that God, in His mercy, has given you."

There was silence for a moment. Her mother was pressed against the cushion of the love seat, her hands in her lap, her fingers twined. Her grandmother stood before the hearth, pulled to her full height, chin up; God's anointed one surrounded by the unrepentant and unredeemed. Anne kept her back against the door and her eyes on her grandmother's feet; her left leg was going numb. She didn't dare move away from the door and shift her weight for fear it would be interpreted as a lack of proper contrition to seek her own comfort.

"What do you think Bill will do when he finds out about your very public display of impropriety?" Daphne continued. "Do you think him the sort of man to turn a blind eye to such an affront? Do you think he will willingly saddle himself with a wife of so little propriety, so little modesty, so little self-control? And do you think that Bill Tucker will be able to ignore the damage to your reputation that your display at the depot has caused? What man will want a wife of such loose morals?"

The answer seemed obvious. No man would want a wife who displayed the character traits of impropriety, immodesty, licentiousness, and self-indulgence. That had been the idea. Except she hadn't had a thought in her head when Jack had brushed up against her skirts and looked into her eyes. When his mouth had touched her, she had forgotten her own name.

Bill's kisses were private, cool, and self-controlled. Jack's kiss had been the opposite in every regard. Out of control, hot, pushing her plan to escape Abilene down to the dust beneath her feet. And she had liked it, wanted more of it.

Not good.

"Anne? I asked you a question and you will do me the

courtesy of answering me in my own home."

"I'm sorry, ma'am," she said softly.

Miss Daphne looked her over carefully, her eyes slits of concentration. "I hope you are, Anne, because you have certainly made God cry rivers of tears over your rebelliousness. How will you ever enter His kingdom acting this way? Did Jesus not say, 'Be ye therefore perfect even as your Father which is in heaven is perfect'? What you did today is not in line with His perfection and His standards."

"I don't think one little kiss will get Anne thrown out of heaven, Mama," Sarah said, coming into the room from the back.

"Don't contradict me, Sarah," Daphne said briskly, not taking her eyes off Anne. "And why didn't you come in the front? My family does not enter the house from the back, like hired help."

"I tried, but the door wouldn't budge," Sarah said with a little smile for Anne.

Anne made herself take a step into the room, away from the solid security of the door.

"Anne, are you truly repentant?"

"Yes, ma'am, I'm sorry. I didn't mean to cause a fuss and I didn't mean for him to kiss me and I didn't mean to bring shame on you."

Daphne pursed her lips and tightened her apron strings before saying, "Very well. We'll let it lie. For now."

"Yes, ma'am."

"Come, Nell, help me pick some more greens while Sarah and Anne roll out the crust for dessert."

Having been given their assignments, each woman went to her task. The weight of Daphne's pronouncements pressed upon the women for a while before time and task eased it off. Anne worked the dough while Sarah mixed up the soft filling that would make up the type of pie Miss Daphne liked best.

"Well, are you going to tell me how it was?"

Anne looked up, saw the sparkle in Sarah's eye, and ducked her head as a blush crept up her throat.

"Does everyone really know about it?"

"Yes, everyone really knows." Sarah smiled, stirring, the bowl balanced on her left hip.

"Even Bill?"

"Especially Bill."

Anne didn't say anything, thinking that through. If Bill knew, her chances with him had narrowed to wafer thin. Bill Tucker was black-haired, blue-eyed, and handsome. He was successful, personable, and affable. He was good husband material. Jack was lean as jerky, tough as string, and dusty. He was hated, feared, and avoided. He was a bounty hunter and no girl in her right mind tied up with a man who hunted bounty. Would Bill believe he was being thrown over for a bounty hunter? Would anyone believe it? She had to have a reason, if asked, and she had one. Even better, it was a reason rooted in truth.

She liked Jack better.

He made her feel things, things that would probably get her scratched out of the Book of Life, things that a God-fearing woman would never allow herself to feel. Things that a smart woman wouldn't let herself feel.

She still liked Jack better. And she didn't want to stop feeling what he made her feel, even if it didn't last very long. She wasn't going to let herself get tangled up with any man, even if he could kiss the breath out of her. She had more grit than that.

But did that mean her soul was in peril? Could a kiss be what separated her from heaven?

"Anne, if you mash that dough any more, it'll be as delicate as hardtack."

She eased up on her rolling. Maybe she'd better talk with Reverend Holt; he'd know if her soul was secure. He'd know if a kiss could be eternally fatal.

"Well? I'm waiting to hear about you and Jack."

Anne looked up at her aunt and said, "I'm going to let him court me. Jack, I mean."

Sarah grinned widely and picked up the pace with her stirring; Miss Daphne hated lumps.

"That good, huh?"

Anne matched her smile and, for once, didn't drop her eyes.

"That good."

Chapter Thirteen

She'd kissed Jack Skull.

He ran a hand through his hair and looked over to her house. It sat on the edge of town, big and wind-worn, isolated and intimidating. He'd thought of her that way, he realized. A woman he couldn't reach and wouldn't touch. But if a bounty hunter could lay hands on her, then that opened a door for him into her life. She hadn't kicked up a fuss over that kiss. That told him a lot and all of it was sweet.

It was better if they didn't fight, at least not until the end.

She was well surrounded by family. That had always played against his natural desires to have her. That, and she was so close. Maybe too close. He lived in Abilene. It wasn't smart to take a woman, make her your own, in your own town. Too many eyes to see. Too many mouths to talk. That kiss with Skull had proved that, if it needed proving.

She was too close.

But he wanted her. He'd always wanted her. There'd

been family and the townsfolk. That had held him back. Now there was the bounty hunter. More than one man courting her made it easy. The door swung wider and he eased himself in, feeling the fit.

She was looking to marry, the whole town knew that. The door swung wide open. He wanted to hear her say the words. To hear her say she'd marry him. To let him touch her, to turn into his kiss, to smile her willingness. That's all he wanted.

All he had to do was get Anne to look at him. He could do that, easy. She liked him. She always had.

It was more than smoke that billowed out from the roof vents late that afternoon; it was pure flame, orange and alive.

Neil McShay, who owned the dry goods shop across the street, saw it first and stood in dumb horror for a moment before his lungs took over and he shouted, "Fire! Fire at the Cattlemen's! Everybody out! *Out!*"

Isaiah Hill ran out of his boot shop without stopping to look at the fire, shook his head in a daze, and then ran back into his store. He ran back out carrying leather buckets for the water line that had to form quickly, before the winds whipped the fire out of all control.

The door to the hardware and tinware shop banged open and John Wells ran out carrying metal pails, his long legs flying with urgency. The sun was low in the sky and the wind had been picking up all day. One good stiff wind and all of Abilene would be gone by midnight. Even the railroad wouldn't matter anymore; no trains would stop at a ghost town of charred timbers that smelled of smoke. There would be no chance to relocate with a healthy bankroll or a nice stockpile of goods to sell. All would be gone, house and livelihood at once.

The fire had to be stopped.

There were short and breathless bursts of conversation as the town converged.

"Was it lightning?"

"Didn't hear no thunder."

"Don't always hear it."

The sky was clear; the wind had pushed any clouds to the far reaches of the horizon and was holding them there, having itself a time fanning the flames in Abilene.

Moses Webster was standing on the boardwalk, watching his hotel being devoured by fire. He didn't say anything. He watched, his mouth soft with shock.

"Did everybody get out, Mose?"

Moses turned to look at the speaker, his eyes wide and unfocused. "Nobody in there but me."

"You sure, Moses? You sure there's no one in there?" Sheriff Lane asked, unbuckling his holster, ready to run in if there was the need.

"Yeah. I'm sure," he said, looking Charles Lane in the eyes, showing him that he knew what he was saying.

"Thank God for that," Lane said, his voice low with feeling.

The lines formed quickly, the men of the volunteer fire brigade falling back on their training and leading the others. There wasn't a man, woman, or child who lived in Abilene who wasn't there in the bucket line, helping bring water to a thirsty fire. Even Joel Walton was there, his nose running unheeded, forgetting even to sniff.

The wind swirled through the town, down the street, seeming to seek the fire it fed. The people kept their heads bent to their task, not bothering to waste breath on cursing what had fallen upon them so suddenly. Moses Webster had been led across the street and he alone of them all watched and did nothing. It was not expected that he do anything more than what he was—grieving, making a slow and stunned mental catalogue of everything he possessed being eaten by the fire that ran across the peak of the roof and burst forth from the window frames. The fire was a prisoner, destroying all in its escape from the wooden confines of the hotel.

Jack stood next to Powell, who stood next to Shaughn, who stood next to Charles, who stood next to Neil and on it went, a line unbroken of men and women who ignored the heat and the wind and the blackened air to fight the fire with all they had. It was powerful little, but it was a fight none would turn from. Prairie towns lived in constant fear of prairie fires and the wind that drove them. There was no time now for weakness or tears, anger or fear. There was time only to pass the bucket and pray that God would stop the wind.

"Lord Almighty, take what you will from us," Reverend Holt said loudly, praying for them all as he stood in the line. He was a powerfully built man, thick with muscle and barrel-chested; he did not shirk in helping his brothers under God. "We give it all to you, we give you Abilene, the hotel, the saloon, the church, and the stores. We know that you test those who love you. We know from the book of Job that Satan prods you to test your servants so that he may gloat when they fail. But, Lord, we will not fail!"

Amens were whispered up and down the lines. God would do what God would do and they would fight the fire until every ember was cold and black.

"Take what you will from us, we will not turn from you. We will not doubt and we will not despair, for we know that no one and nothing can snatch those who love you out of your hand. Not fire. Not wind."

A gust of dusty wind pressed hard against their legs, pressing against their resolve and, weakening, lost.

"Take this wind from us and give us the strength to fight!"

"Amen, Reverend!" came a wobbly chorus from throats tight with soot and dust and heat.

Arms blurred in motion, heads bent in labor, and lips murmuring prayers for safety and strength were there for God to see, if He chose to intercede. The wind ran off out onto the prairie, a weak and listless foe, beaten and humbled. A prayer answered.

The fire raged.

But they were beating it. It burned and flared, hot and molten yellow, within the confines of the outer walls of the hotel. It was not spreading.

By dusk, it was over, though the embers were still alive and red, waiting for a chance wind to give them roaring life. Buckets of dirt, plentiful in Kansas, penned them in, smothering them. But the dirt was quickly hot and they knew the fire only awaited a better time to burst into flickering life again. If they could beat the fire's heat back until tomorrow, then it would be truly over. Second fires burn hotter than the first and were nigh impossible to put out. If the charred remains of the Cattlemen's burned again, it would take the town with it. Powell, Chris Dodd, and Neil McShay would stand watch during the night and no one feared they would sleep away their vigil; it was that important to them all.

"Does anyone know how it started?" asked Tom Monahan, the owner of the mercantile.

"Didn't hear no thunder, but I was with the stock," Jim Conner said.

"It was a hot fire. Never seen a fire burn so hot and so fast," Isaiah Hill from the boot shop said, wiping a sooty hand across a blackened face. One of the Walton kids brought him a cupful of water from a pail he was carrying round; Isaiah drank it down and nodded his thanks.

"Same here and I saw a scorcher up in Deadwood once. Took out three buildings before it was stopped and it didn't burn near as hot as this one. Them flames was high and strong, not wispy and struggling," said Everett Winslow, owner of the Demorest Restaurant.

"Did anyone hear any thunder or see lightning strike?" Powell asked, rubbing the bowl of his pipe, too dry in the mouth to want to light it.

"Nope and I was looking out the window when it happened. I didn't see anything but the flames. No lightning," said Neil McShay.

Nobody said anything for a bit, chewing that one down. Fires didn't start without some effort.

"Moses? You sure you were alone in there?" At his distracted nod, McShay asked, "For how long?"

Moses was starting to pick through the smoking rubble; the love seat that had graced his lobby was in one piece but blackened beyond saving. The stairs to the second floor reached up to open sky. There was nothing above the ground floor.

"Mose?"

"Huh?" He turned to face McShay.

"Who was the last one in the hotel, besides you?"

Moses Webster thought for a moment, a moment that stretched out. Thinking was an effort.

"Jack Skull."

"Figures," Isaiah grumbled.

"What figures?" Lane said, coming up to get a drink from the Walton kid and his bucket.

"That the last person in the Cattlemen's was Jack Skull," said Powell, shoving his pipe into his shirt pocket with angry energy.

"Now what's to that?" Lane said before he upended his drink. Water never tasted so good to him.

"You doubt that he's mean enough to burn a man's business to the ground for the sheer perverse pleasure of it? You didn't see him at my livery. He's probably going to hit me next."

"Now that's talk that can get a man killed, Powell," Charles said sternly, dropping the cup back in the bucket.

"You put a bridle on that tongue of yours before you talk yourself right into a cell."

"You think he'd come to get me himself? You think I'm in danger?"

"Nah, I think you'd talk that man into a noose without raising a hair. It's him I'm trying to protect, not you."

"But that fire started somehow, Sheriff, and there warn't no lightning," Isaiah said.

"This isn't the first fire to take down a building. It won't be the last. You can't lay them all on the bounty hunter just 'cause you've taken a dislike to him."

"He was the last one in the building, 'cept Mose," McShay said, who saw himself as an eyewitness and if he kept talking, would convince himself that he'd seen Jack throw the match.

"And he was staying there," Lane reminded him. "What man burns down the place where he's stored his gear? Did you bother to think that he lost about all he owned in that blaze, same as Webster? His gear was stashed in his room and he didn't come out with it, did he?"

"I saw his gear. It wasn't all that much," Powell said in a surly rumble.

"But all he has," Lane repeated, driving the point.

A small crowd had gathered around the Walton boy and his bucket; that was the excuse they would give if anyone bothered to ask, but the real draw was the talk about Jack Skull, the fire, and how the two were hitched. The way they all felt about Jack, the two had to be hitched with an iron halter and they'd keep talking if they had to forge the iron themselves with the heat of their own rage and suspicion.

Anne could feel the way the mind of the crowd was headed as she and Sarah stood on the edge of the growing throng. Jack, who'd done as much as anyone standing here to fight the fire, was going to be blamed for starting it. No town welcomed a bounty hunter, that was certain, but he had kissed her under the open sky and with half of Abilene looking on. That hadn't won him any friends. But Sheriff Lane was handling it; he wouldn't let the town run after Jack with a rope. She didn't have to feel guilty about that kiss and what it had done to a man's already shaky reputation. She didn't have to get into the middle of this fight.

"And now he and the others who were staying at the Cattlemen's will need some help," Lane said. "Can anyone donate clothes and such to the folks who were staying there? McShay?"

"I have some dress goods that I could part with," he said. "Some shirts and underclothes, combs and brushes and hats."

"Thank you, Neil," Charles said sincerely, glad for both his generosity and the turn in the conversation.

"I'll organize the donations, Sheriff," Sarah volunteered, "if you can get people to bring it all to your office."

"I'll do that, Sarah," Neil McShay said, "and you can use my store to organize; I doubt the sheriff wants his jail piled high with shoes and shirts."

"Thank you, Mr. McShay," Sarah answered. "If you can get the other shop owners to contribute what's needed, I'll find out who was staying in the Cattlemen's, what they need, and arrange to get it to them."

"Don't forget Mr. Webster," Anne said softly. Moses was still walking through the wet and filthy wreckage of his material possessions, burned beyond all recognition to anyone but him.

"Best find him a place to stay tonight and for a while beyond that," Charles Lane said. "He looks as lost as a lone wolf pup."

"I'd be happy to make the arrangements for anyone who needs a bed, Sheriff," Anne offered. "Could you just get them corralled together? It would make it easier."

"Of course, Anne. There were five guests of the hotel; I'll round 'em up and have them ready for you at the saloon."

"You get them lined up with a bed and I'll bring over the goods they'll need to survive and start again," Sarah said.

"I'll help," Neil said. Sarah gave him a quick look, but said nothing. Folks were generous in a calamity.

"When you have them settled, bring them over to the Demorest for a meal, on the house," Everett Winslow said, his wife nodding her agreement.

It was clear to Anne they had all forgotten that Jack was one of the people who had just been offered free lodging, free food, and free clothes. But she hadn't forgotten.

"I'll see you at the saloon in a few minutes, Sheriff. I'm certain it won't take long for me to find beds for these poor people."

The crowd slowly drifted apart, some hanging back, eager and ready to offer a bed to some poor passing stranger in the name of charity. Giving to those who suffered surely made a man feel noble.

"We have a bed, Anne," Mrs. Walton said. "I can double up the twins and Joel since they all have the same sickness, shift Bob and Tim in with Zeke and Luke, move Ellen and Lillian, and that frees up my bed. I'll have it made up with fresh bedding in no time." Anne didn't see how Mrs. Walton was going to get a spare bed out of all that shifting and moving, but then, she didn't know what the normal sleeping arrangements were for the Waltons anyway.

"Thank you, Mrs. Walton," she said. "I don't know if there were any women staying at the Cattlemen's—"

"Anne, in times like these, a woman can't be particular. It's my Christian duty to open my home to a stranger in need. Why, I might be entertaining an angel unaware!" At that, Emma turned to Joel and said, "Go pick me some early blooms to put on the table, Joel. We want to show our best." For the angel, Anne almost said.

Joel sniffed, ran his hand with businesslike authority across his nose, and trotted off down the street.

"I have room in my bed," Neil McShay said. He said it in such a way, with such an odd tone to his voice, that Sarah and Anne turned in unison to look at him.

"Thank you, Mr. McShay, but you've already done so much—"

"Not at all, Anne, happy to do my part. Won't hear a word from you that says I can't have the privilege of helping a neighbor in need."

"Well, thank you again."

"Don't require thanks," he said. "Now, Sarah, let's gather some of those articles you were talking about." He escorted her into his store by the elbow. Sarah's bustle twitched gracefully as she walked by his side. He held the door for her and she proceeded him in. Anne watched, oddly fascinated; Mr. McShay was behaving strangely. It was most peculiar.

Anne looked across the street to where Moses Webster was walking through the debris that was his home and his business; his pants and shoes were covered in black soot, his hands matched as he turned over piles of rubble, looking for anything that might have survived the fire. Alongside him were his neighbors, her mother and her grandmother among them, ignoring the fact that they were all slowly and methodically being covered in soot as they helped him sort through what remained of his life.

The crowd around her had thinned to none. Those who weren't helping Mr. Webster at his hotel were gathering what they could to give to the victims of the fire. She had arranged for two of the guests to have beds, but there would be one guest no one would want, one guest who would not be welcomed into a home with a bed drawn down and flowers on the table.

Claudia Dain

It was a good way to get closer to him, which would force Bill to keep off. That was all she wanted, for Bill to back off a bit. That was what should happen, with Jack right under her roof. It wasn't that she wanted to be near Jack; no, it was that she needed him as a wedge against Bill. It was a good plan. It should work.

Anne smiled. All that was left was to make the offer. He had to accept; where else could he go? And her grandmother would have to allow him into her home; it was her Christian duty and who knew what that comprised better than Miss Daphne? The glory of it was, it was the right thing to do; how could anyone fault her for Christian charity?

How would he be able to resist courting her if she was so close to hand? How much easier would it be to keep Bill at arm's length when Jack was under the same roof? Anne smiled again and walked down the street to the saloon.

Jack was tipping up his glass to wash the smell and the feel of smoke and grime from his throat. A bath would have been good, but the bathhouse was under repair and the hotel was a memory. As was all his gear. He had no clothes but those he wore and they had looked better. What he did have was his guns. His revolvers were on his body, as always. His rifle was close at hand, either in the scabbard on Joe or, as now, in the buckskin sheath that hung down his back. He was always armed. Mostly empty ammunition bandoleers covered his body like strings of boils, heavy with purpose, declaring blatantly that he hunted men. He had lost all that he had carried with him into Abilene, but, with his guns, he could still earn money. And he could stay alive. Staying alive was good.

The saloon was as close to full as he had yet seen it. Everyone in town had been at that fire and everyone had helped put it out. O'Shaughnessy had spotted everyone the first round of drinks and his arm had been liberally pouring ever since. Jack downed his third beer, but it was going to take more than drink to wash away the memory of that fire. Hard, watching a man lose his home and his way to earn all at once.

"Guess you lost it all."

Jack turned his head slightly. It was the old man, the one who was always propping up the corner of the saloon with his chin on his chest. He was bearded, rumpled, dusty, and, strangely, friendly. Maybe a common calamity did that to people; maybe it was the comfort of safety that kept them hostile.

"Yeah," Jack answered, "just about."

"See your guns made it through all right."

"Only because I never take them off."

"Guess you're glad of that now."

Jack smiled and signaled that he was ready for another drink. "I've been glad of that more times than I want to remember."

The old man leaned into the bar, resting his elbows on it, watching as O'Shaughnessy filled Jack's glass. Jack twitched a finger and O'Shaughnessy filled another for the old man.

"I recognize the Colt, but that other one's a mystery," the old man said before taking a polite sip of his beer. "Who makes the one on your right hip?"

"Le Mat."

"Ain't never heard of Le Mat."

"You say that's a Le Mat?" a man asked from down the bar.

"Yeah," Jack answered quietly.

The man made his way down the bar to stand next to Jack. Jack felt suddenly crowded in and he backed off, leaving his beer on the counter.

"Don't mean no harm," the man said, doing some backing off of his own when he saw Jack's reaction. "My name's Wells. I own the hardware and tinware shop in town and I've always wanted to set my hands on a Le Mat. Heard some stories about them in the war and wished even then I'd had one to hand."

"Rebs had 'em," Jack said, slowly approaching his beer. He didn't want to offend Wells, seeing as he sold ammunition in his shop. All his extra rounds had gone up in that blaze. He was down to maybe a hundred rounds and carrying all of it.

"Yeah." Wells laughed. "That's when I wanted one the most. Is it true, it being double action?"

"Double action? Whad'ya mean?" O'Shaughnessy said.

Jack didn't have to answer, Wells took it up for him. "All you do is squeeze and there you have it, no cocking of the hammer for each round. Fires off like pouring cream, so they say. Fast."

O'Shaughnessy looked at Jack, his gaze dropping to the gun closest to the man's right hand. No cocking? How fast could a man fire when all he had to do was touch the trigger?

"And ten shots in the cylinder," Wells continued, sounding more and more like a salesman for Le Mat.

"Ten? Didn't think they made such a contraption," Isaiah said, coming down the bar to join in.

"I heard of 'em," the old man said, "heard ole J.E.B. Stuart himself had one. Served him well, they say."

"He did and it did," Jack said softly, taking another swallow of beer.

"That ain't all," Wells said, ignoring the pause Jack's comment had caused. "It's more than a pistol. It's got a sixty-caliber smoothbore alongside that fires buckshot. It's a hand cannon; formidable and reliable," he said proudly, sounding like the man who had invented it. "Hell, nothing ever goes wrong with a Le Mat."

The talk at their end of the bar stilled at that. A gun

that fired ten forty-two-caliber shots without cocking while buckshot came spouting out the middle?

"Damn," Isaiah said.

That about said it.

"Still, ain't never heard of it before now," Isaiah said after a time of respectful silence.

"Most folks call it a grapeshot revolver," Jack supplied. "It's a nice little piece."

"Sure sounds sweet," the old man said.

"I don't suppose you'd let me have a look at it?" Wells said.

"When I come by to get some boxes of ammunition, I'll pull it out. Not here," Jack said.

The saloon was crowded with people he didn't recognize, all pressing against the long dark length of the bar. He wasn't going to pull his gun here unless he was going to use it.

"It'll take metallic cartridges? That's all I carry now," Wells worried.

"Yeah, this is a late model. Metallic is what I want."

"Course, I've got plenty for the Colt—'bout all anybody wants anymore—but what about your rifle? I don't recognize it."

"I do," said the old man.

Jack turned to look into the man's eyes, whiskey brown and surrounded by a crisscross of heavy lines. His brows met over his nose and spiked up, pointing to four strong lines across his forehead. His beard was brown and gray and hiding thin lips. Jack didn't recognize him.

"I saw my first one in Fort Kearney, time that Nelson Story came through with his cows," the old man said, leaving his beer on the bar, enjoying being the center of attention for that small moment in time.

"That's right," Wells said, "he drove three thousand head from Texas to Montana with Sioux, Cheyenne, and

147

Arapahos dogging every step. With how many cowboys to see the job done?"

"Thirty," said Jack as he finished off his beer.

"Had thirty to start," the old man said. "By the time they got to Kearney they had one down and two wounded. Twenty-seven men for three thousand cows and five hundred of Crazy Horse's best."

"And the Remingtons," Wells put in, "those rifles counted for something."

"They counted for plenty, the way I heard it. The cattle Story let fend for themselves while he and the boys circled the wagons. Crazy Horse, he knew what he'd do, he'd just let them fire off a round and then he'd come at 'em while they hurried to reload. Only this here rifle don't need no reload, just slip in yer round and fire it off, and so tough that there's no way to blow out the breech. Nice, accurate weapon in a fight."

"So how many of Story's men made it out?" Shaughn asked.

"All of 'em. But Crazy Horse lost more than a few; counted it as bad medicine and after a couple more passes at 'em on the trail to Montana, he finally threw it in and let 'em ride on."

"Never seen one before," Wells said, gently letting his eyes rest on the stock of the rifle Jack had slung on his back, the buckskin sheath soft and darkened with age.

"Ain't many out there, only the thirty that went with Story," the old man said.

The men in the saloon were quiet, looking at Jack. He could feel their eyes on him, feel the questions in the air all around him, questions they didn't dare ask and that he'd never answer anyway. They wanted to know what it was like to drive a herd with five hundred Sioux between you and the next water. They wanted to know what it was like to load and fire until all you smelled was powder and smoke. They wanted to know if he had really ridden with

Nelson Story all those long, hot miles from Texas to Montana.

Jack said nothing. He knew, and that was enough.

Anne walked in, with Lane right behind her. The mood was broken; the noise level rose steadily and men looked into their beers, letting the memory of that drive wash away under a cap of foam. Jack was just as happy to let it go.

Women didn't come much into saloons; there was no law against their coming in, but it was a place for men, with rules men understood and talk men could understand. Having a woman in the place changed the air almost. They could feel it. Anne could feel it. The men kept their faces down in their cups. Anne hurried to do what she had come to do. Everyone wanted her to hurry up and go.

Damn if she didn't come right up him.

"Mr. Scullard?"

The place quieted like a burial ground.

"Ma'am?" He turned to face her.

It was the first time he'd seen her, really seen her, since that kiss at the depot. He'd seen her at the fire, working like the rest of Abilene, but that had been different. This was face-to-face and quiet. Real quiet. Everyone in that saloon was holding his breath to hear what Anne Ross had to say to Jack Scullard. Everyone in that room knew about that kiss.

Anne got a little red on the thin skin of her throat and coughed a bit to cover her nervousness.

"Mr. Scullard," she repeated, "Sheriff Lane and I met on the boardwalk and we have arranged for a bed for each guest of the Cattlemen's. Each guest except for you."

"That's fine, ma'am, I can make my bed up out on the prairie or even in the jail, if there's room—"

"No, I . . . I—" She stammered and the redness on her

throat crept up to her cheeks. "There's a bed for you in my house."

O'Shaughnessy dropped a glass on the floor behind the bar. No one turned to look at the sound of it shattering.

"Now, Anne," the sheriff said, his eyes shifting uncomfortably around the room, "there's no need—"

"That's right," Jack said, taking her by the arm and steering her toward the door. She didn't have enough sense to get out of the way of a moving train, offering up an invitation like that with half, the worst half, of Abilene straining to hear every syllable of it. "I can look after myself and—"

"I'm not going to let you go without a bed, Mr. Scullard, not when everyone else has been provided for! Why, I wouldn't be doing my Christian duty, isn't that right, Sheriff?" She was letting him walk her out the door, but she wouldn't keep her mouth shut. Still, it was the first time he'd seen her show her teeth with even the hint of a growl. He couldn't honestly say he didn't like it.

"Now, Anne, I can't say I think it's proper for you to take in a man—" Charles said.

"You didn't say a word when Emma Walton took in that medicinal salesman, Sheriff," Anne argued, her cheeks flushed.

"That's different," he said, helping Jack to lead her out onto the boardwalk, away from all those listening ears. It didn't work; Jack could hear the scuffle of boots on wood as the mob of them shuffled to the door to keep up with the conversation.

"I don't see how," she said, standing between the two men.

"Now—"

"You're not going to say, 'Now, Anne,' again, are you, Sheriff?" she asked, her foot beginning to tap lightly on the boardwalk. "I can't do less than everyone else, can I?

I can't ask folks to take in strangers and then not do the same myself, can I?"

She sure was cute, standing there, her face flushed and with a trace of soot on her lashes and swiped on her chin. Showing the first signs of fight he'd seen in her yet.

He wondered if she'd shown that much spark with dog-lovin' Bill and just exactly what those kisses were like that she shared with him when he was in town. Like he was right now.

That was the last thought he had before he opened his mouth.

"Thank you, ma'am, I'd be obliged to stay with you." Could hardly be a better way to keep his eye on Bill Tucker.

It was damn bad when a man started up lying to him-self.

Miss Daphne stood wedged between the edge of the door and the jamb, refusing entrance to her home in every way available to her. Dammit stood pressed against her leg, growling.

"Anne, I don't know what you were thinking to issue an invitation without any preparation or forethought," Miss Daphne said through thin lips.

"Ma'am," Jack said softly, "she was just seeing that every-one who lost a bed because of that fire found a place to stay, and she spent the best part of the afternoon seeing to it. If you don't have the room . . ." He let it slide; Anne lived in the biggest house in Abilene and everyone knew it.

Daphne's pride in her home was pricked. "Of course we have the room, but I don't open my home to just anyone who happens to be passing."

Anne sucked in her breath and seemed to shrink down an inch or two. Jack shifted his weight, the spurs on his heels jingling like bells. He smiled slightly and said, "I'm not passin' by, Miss Daphne. I'm an invited guest. Invited by your own granddaughter in a time of tragedy for the whole town. I think it shows her raising that she was so free with her hospitality."

And if Daphne declined to let him stay, she'd be shaming both Anne and herself with her lack of charity.

"Besides," he added, "I don't plan to be a burden. I'll pay the same rates that I did at the hotel." They needed the money. The chipped paint and sagging porch told that tale.

"I don't run a boardinghouse," Miss Daphne snapped irritably.

"Of course not, ma'am," Jack said easily. "I'm just a guest of your hospitality who's helping to pay for the extra bother. I'll be gone as soon as I'm able and get out from under."

There wasn't a woman in that house who had any trouble in believing that a man would git when he was able.

Brown eyes bored into blue. Jack held his ground easily, meeting her stare and returning it without effort. Anne wanted to crawl back down the steps and burrow under the porch; she just hated this sort of thing. It was the combined presence of Jack and Miss Daphne that kept her rooted. Abruptly, the door flew open, the battle over. Dammit crept onto the porch, hackles raised, still growling and showing his teeth.

"Dammit, get in the house!" Daphne said sharply.

Jack smiled suddenly and said, "Thank you, ma'am, for the kind encouragement. You sure make a man feel welcome."

Daphne blanched white as a sheet, her mouth softening in shock.

"She was talking to our dog," Anne whispered as Jack walked into the foyer.

"You sure about that?" he asked, taking his hat off and holding it in his hands.

"Of course, I'm sure."

"Your grandma always cuss like that?" he whispered with a smile.

"She wasn't cussing," Anne whispered back. "His name is Dammit."

Jack smiled and ducked his head down, trying to hide it. Maybe Anne wasn't as far out of his reach as he'd thought at first look. Any girl with a dog named Dammit . . .

Miss Daphne stood with her hands clasped before her in the parlor, her expression as stern as her posture was rigid.

"You may show our guest to the maid's room, Anne. And I don't want any of your weapons accidentally discharged in the house!"

"No need to worry, ma'am, they don't discharge unless I want 'em to."

Daphne couldn't seem to find the words to answer that.

Anne hurried down the hall that skirted the parlor and edged along the kitchen wall. The maid's room was at the back of the house, next to the kitchen. It wasn't really a maid's room anymore; they hadn't been able to afford a maid in years. The room now functioned as a canning room and looked like it.

Anne started moving glass jars out of the room, her arms full and awkward with the effort. Jack stood in the hallway and watched her, an amused expression on his face. He didn't help her. He just watched her. The jars rattled and clanked together as she tried to hurry, tried to avoid his eyes, tried to forget that he was so close and would be staying in the same house with her. And with her mother, aunt, and grandmother. That calmed her down some.

He seemed to fill up every space he occupied. It wasn't just the hall, he had done the same on the platform, under the wide sky with no walls in sight. She felt her breath get tight in her chest just looking at him. He was lean, but his shoulders almost filled the doorway. Blue eyes watched her. He didn't look at the room she was trying to clear of kitchen paraphernalia, he was looking at her. Only at her.

She dropped a jar. It didn't break only because it landed on the bed. He'd be sleeping in that narrow bed come tonight.

She dropped another jar. She made a quick lunge for it; it bounced off her hands and landed dully on the floor to roll clumsily at his feet.

He bent to pick up the jar and held it easily in one hand, fighting a smile. She ducked her head and took it from him, leaving the room with her arms full of glass jars. They'd all go in the kitchen for now, stacked in a wooden box and stored under the worktable.

When she got back to the room, he was standing in it. Next to the bed. He'd thrown his hat on it and was running a hand through his hair. He had longish hair, soft brown in color and waved on the ends. Pretty hair.

She couldn't think in anything but short bursts when he was around. Just impressions, quick as June bugs, that would flit and fly from pillar to post.

Would he kiss her any time soon?

"You didn't have to ask me to stay."

Her eyes found his and then lowered in embarrassment. "I thought I should."

"And you're a gal who always does what she should."

He sounded amused and maybe irritated. She couldn't figure out why that would be so. She had invited him because it was her Christian duty to find lodging for those without a bed. She had invited him because she wanted him near so that he would court her, keeping Bill off her tail. It was that thought that kept her head bent. It surely wasn't Christian to so boldly arrange for one man to go against another.

154

A Kiss to Die For

"Why'd you kiss me?" he said, moving away from the bed and walking toward her across the small room.

Her head jerked up. "You kissed me!"

"Then why didn't you push me off?"

He was standing so close, she could see the soot lying on the surface of his eyebrows, so close she could see that one of his shirt buttons was broken in half, so close she could see the shadow of his beard on the chiseled angle of his jaw.

"Is that what I should have done?" she said, her voice just above a whisper.

"I'm sure your ma's told you already."

Oh yes, she'd been told by just about everybody that she shouldn't have allowed that kiss. A kiss she'd been so eager for she would have followed him to the Great Divide to get it. But a nice girl, a smart girl, didn't admit a thing like that, even if she was bad enough to think it.

She was going to be smart. She wasn't going to get tangled with any man.

"Why did you kiss me?" she asked.

"Wanted to," he said simply, his blue eyes suddenly hot with color. "I'm not a man who does what he should. I do what I want." He breathed the last.

She watched his mouth as he said it. He wanted to kiss her, or had. Did he want to again? She wanted him to want her, to want her enough to keep trailing after her until she escaped Abilene, leaving him behind with the rest of them. That he trailed after men for money, hunted them down no matter where they went, she chose to ignore. No man chased a woman for long; there wasn't any profit in it.

"What do you want now?" she asked, forcing herself to act bold, hoping she was flirting.

What did he want? He wanted to tumble her back on that bed and kiss her till she couldn't take a breath that wasn't his. And then he wanted to shake her senseless for letting him. He knew she'd let him. The trouble with Anne was she'd let anybody push her around any old time they took the notion, and leave her apologizing for the trouble that spilled out after.

Jack looked at her, at her bright eyes and her hope that he'd take up with her. Hell, she didn't have enough sense to know he wasn't the sort of man who should be on the same side of the street as her, let alone in a tiny little room with a door and a bed.

Did she think he was something he wasn't? Didn't she understand what it meant that he hunted bounty; that he was no man for the likes of her?

But Bill Tucker wasn't the man for her either. That's what he was doing here, keeping Bill off her. But Sarah had hooked him as bait to draw another man in. Well, hell, he'd have some fun of his own before she shoved him out of her life. If she was smart, she'd shove him. But Anne didn't seem to have much shove in her. That was the trouble. She was walking straight to her own killing and picking flowers on the way.

"If you want me to kiss you," he said roughly, "ask straight out. I'm no Saturday night beau."

He looked angry. She wasn't afraid. He was Jack Skull and she wasn't afraid. He was right, he wasn't her beau. Bill was. But Bill didn't make her feel like this, thank God, or she might have wanted to be his wife, to chain herself to a man when all a man did was run as far and fast as he could. She didn't have to worry about that with Jack. He wouldn't want to marry. He'd know she could never marry a bounty hunter. Wouldn't he? He'd never push for that, the way Bill and her family did. He didn't want her to do the one thing she'd made up her mind never to do.

"I shouldn't," she said, looking at his broken button, at his suntanned throat, at his curling hair, but not at his eyes.

"Probably not," he said, the anger in his voice gone.

He was not going to force it or her. He was giving her the choice and she knew that no matter what she decided, he wouldn't be angry. Bill would have been angry.

Or maybe he knew how she would answer. Maybe he knew how his kisses made her feel.

"Kiss me," she whispered, her eyes downcast, wanting it. Dear God, she wasn't supposed to want it.

"Yes, ma'am," he said.

A finger tipped her chin up. She closed her eyes. She didn't want to see laughter in his look.

His mouth hovered over hers, close enough to feel but not close enough to touch. His nearness made her tremble. His arms wrapped around her, holding her, gentling her. His mouth lowered to touch hers and she felt the breath go out of her as she leaned into him. His arms tightened and her nipples brushed against his shirt. She could only lean toward him, wanting the contact, the feel of him on any part of her. It was like hunger, like emptiness.

His mouth was soft and persuasive and she pressed herself against him, wanting more, sensing there was more.

His mouth opened over hers and he pulled her into him, his tongue demanding, enticing. Bill had never kissed her like this. She didn't know a kiss could be like this.

Her arms wrapped themselves around him, around those narrow hips and flaring back, past all the belts of ammunition, to find the shape of the man. He was hard as wood, broad and lean at once, and ridged with muscle. Bill was softer and wider. This was better.

His arms pulled her in and his thumb trailed down to sculpt the shape of her breast. Her nipple throbbed in response. His tongue demanded urgent attention, pressing deep and fast in her mouth. She tasted him and

157

breathed in his smell and didn't even think to compare him to Bill.

Her thoughts had been jumbled before; now they were lost. She could only feel and want. Only respond to what he was doing to her. Unafraid. Stupidly unafraid.

"All settled in?"

Sarah's voice made her jump in her skin and she pulled guiltily away from Jack's heat. Jack slowly let her go. He did not look guilty; he looked as if he'd been tumbling with a cougar. Without a word, she left the room, her eyes on the floorboards, her color high.

"I'd ask what you were doing with my niece, but I'm afraid I know the answer."

Jack picked up his hat and put it back on with casual ease. It took all his effort to look casual when he was as tied up as a fresh-roped stallion.

"I'm courting your niece the only way I know how." With a soft smile, he added, "It seems to be workin'."

Chapter Fourteen

The sheriff knocked on the door just as supper was being prepared. Nell answered, her arms dripping water from washing the greens. She was not inclined to invite Charles to stay and eat.

"Good evening, Nell," he said, taking off his hat when he saw who it was.

"Evening," she said tightly.

"You recovered from fighting that fire? I saw you there and was plenty impressed by the amount of work you did to try and save the Cattlemen's."

Nell pursed her lips and tilted her head at a sharp angle, holding Lane's eyes with her own. "I wasn't there to impress you, Mr. Lane. I was there to help a neighbor, which is my Christian duty and one which I don't shirk. And I don't need to 'recover,' I'm a healthy woman in the prime of life, not a bedridden matron."

Charles clutched his hat, crushing the back brim. "Of course not, Nell, I never meant any such thing as that. Why, you're a handsome woman. I've always said so and never heard no argument otherwise."

Nell's head tilted violently in the opposite direction. "Are you saying that you bandy my name about, comparing me to other women? Just who do you think you are, to discuss me as if I were a prize cow?"

"Now, Nell," Charles said, twirling his hat in his hands and crushing the brim all around, "I didn't mean it like that. You know that I wouldn't do anything to—"

"And I never gave you leave to call me by my given name, Mr. Lane. Please remember that when you're discussing me over drinks in the saloon!"

She turned and marched off, sideswiping Jack as she stomped back to the kitchen. Jack didn't mind; listening to another man get tied up by a woman put him in a real pleasant mood. He looked at the mangled hat in Lane's hands and smiled. Lane jerked his hat behind his back and swore softly.

"You finish your business here or did you want to talk to me, too?"

"Where'd they put you?"

"In the back, next to the kitchen."

"Well, let's go on," Charles grumbled. "I've got some things to tell you."

"You could have told me at the jail. I would have been by directly."

"I needed the air, thought I'd walk down here."

"And how was the air, down here?" Jack said over his grin.

"Cold as January," Charles mumbled, closing the door to Jack's room behind them.

Jack leaned his back against the closed door. Charles walked to the far wall, looked out the window, and then looked back at Jack.

"Poked through the fire," Lane said. "Looks like it was accidental, though I'm not a top hand with fires."

"What were you thinking?"

"I was thinking that you're not real popular."

"I'll take your word for it."

"Maybe somebody'd want to get you out of Abilene?"

"How many people heard about me kissing Anne? I'd guess about that many would want me on the next train out," Jack said evenly, his eyes not dropping.

He was talking about Anne, but he was thinking about the killings. He was roped close to Abilene because of those killings. Maybe the killer knew that. The sheriff sure did. Might be better if folks thought he was staying because of Anne. Might even protect her better than she could protect herself. Hell, she couldn't protect herself from a tick.

"That'd be one reason," Lane acknowledged. "Any others I should know about?"

"No. But if anybody asks where I was when that fire started, I was in the saloon. With three witnesses."

"If anybody asks, I'll tell 'em," Lane said pleasantly.

"How about telling me about Tucker?" Jack said, easing off the door and coming more fully into the room that was now his. "When'd he hit Abilene the first time?"

"Maybe four months ago, maybe a bit more. He came scouting through before he settled."

"How much has he settled? I heard he traveled around some."

"Yeah, he's on the loose a bit," Lane acknowledged. "He's always off, checking on land and finding buyers. Comes back to Abilene to register the deeds and the sales. Always seems to have a pocketful of money. Always a smile on his face."

"A pocketful of money will do that for some people, give them something to smile about. You ever get the idea he was smiling about something else?"

"Like women?"

"Like women," Jack said with no trace of a smile.

"The only woman he's buzzed around here has been Anne. I don't know where he was before he came here.

He didn't offer and I didn't have no call to press."

"And Anne didn't have no call to complain."

"No," Lane said with the beginnings of a smile. A man didn't like to be alone in his female troubles. "She's seemed happy enough with him."

But she had kissed Jack in full light and bright public and then again in this very room. Tucker didn't have her held all that tight. Still, there was a hungry look about that woman that didn't have everything to do with kissing; she was looking for something to fill up a hole somewhere in her. He knew the signs of that well enough.

"But he's not made his move."

Lane shrugged. "Not yet, but the talk is that it'll be soon."

Neither one of them mentioned that Jack's kiss might have something to do with the timetable.

"What's the talk on the ladies in this house?" Jack asked. "I've never come across so many women in one family who ain't got a man."

"They've all been married, all's except Anne, and that'll come." Lane chuckled. "Daphne came into Abilene with a husband and two girls. She's still got the girls. Her husband, Malcolm Todd, was something big with the railroad and they came when Abilene was just a river and a patch of grass with only the hope of cows. The rail line moved west and so did he. Climbed on that train he'd help build and took off."

"The line moved a few years ago," Jack said. "Them girls must have been old enough to marry by then."

"Sure they was," Lane agreed, "but Miss Daphne, she keeps a close line on family and, married or not, those girls weren't going to stray. Sarah's man went off to war, came back when it was over, and lit out the day after his homecoming. That was seven years ago."

"What about Nell's man?"

Charles swallowed a grunt of disgust. "He was a lawman

in Missouri. Local hero. Went bad and went west."

"Left his wife and daughter?"

"Yeah, left Miss Daphne, too."

There was something to that. A man wanted to make his own home with his own woman; he didn't want to marry a daughter and get a mother-in-law, especially one who wouldn't disappear.

"Makes your case kinda hard," Jack said.

"What case?" Lane scowled.

"Anne's mama." Jack smiled slightly.

"There ain't nothing like that there," Lane grumbled.

"You said that right." Jack grinned. At least the joke wasn't on him anymore.

There was a quick knock and the door opened before Jack could say a word. He didn't pull his gun; anyone who would knock first didn't have to be afraid of what he'd find on the other side of Jack's door.

Nell poked her head in, then flattened her lips when she saw the sheriff. Jack felt his grin get bigger.

"I just wanted to know if you expect meals with what you're paying for the room. We don't have a lot, Lord knows, and—"

"I leave it to you, ma'am; you decide what's right and I'll abide," Jack said softly.

"Well, I don't think it was right for Anne to offer to house a stranger, no matter what. She should have come and talked it over with her elders before proceeding. As to the food, the hotel doesn't provide—"

"Now, Nell," Charles interrupted, "that doesn't seem very neighborly, considering the circumstances. Why, this man has lost all he had."

"He's got guns enough," she muttered at Lane, "but I'll give him meals since it's my Christian duty. You can have Anne's portion since she won't be eating with us tonight, Mr. Skull," she said, turning to Jack. "She's got an arrangement with her beau and won't be in the house this evening."

"The name's Scullard, ma'am," Jack said, "and I thank you for the meal."

Nell's eyes softened in response to his soft tone of voice. "You're welcome, Mr. Scullard. I hope you enjoy it. I'm sorry about mangling your name. It won't happen again." She shut the door softly behind her as she left the room.

"The women in this family sure don't have much bite," Jack said when she'd gone.

"I thought Nell was sharp enough," Lane grumbled.

Jack couldn't stop the chuckle that filled his throat and only laughed harder at Lane's scowl.

"Think about it, Sheriff," he finally said, "Anne's mama had her back up but she spit nothing at all and settled down quick. Anne apologizes to anyone who'll stand still long enough to listen. Sarah, now that Sarah, she's got some spine, but she let her mama scare her man off. No bite."

Lane nodded and worked at straightening his hat brim. "You're right, but Miss Daphne, she's got teeth for the whole lot of them. Sarah has more powder than Nell, and Anne the least of all. But that Anne, she's a sweet gal. Swim a river to fetch you a sack of flour."

"Yeah, even if her legs were broke," Jack said. It wasn't a compliment and Lane knew it. "Now Nell, if you was to do the asking, would break your legs and tell you to get your own damn flour."

Lane put his hat on; it looked respectable enough to go out in daylight. "You don't want to hear what Miss Daphne would tell you to do with your flour," he said as he walked out the door.

Chapter Fifteen

He could see them from the porch steps, set out like petrified wood, stiff and proper, waiting in the parlor for Anne's beau to come fetch her. Truth to tell, they were all fine-looking women; even Miss Daphne had her points. The glow of lamplight lit them softly, making dark hair shine and the lines of age fade like tracks in a sandstorm. Fine women and not a man among them.

Except for Bill Tucker.

Jack bent his head, turning his eyes away from the domestic contentment of the scene in the parlor. He had his Colt to clean and he'd best get it done while the light was still with him. He knew without asking that Miss Daphne wouldn't abide his cleaning his guns in her house; it was a dirty, greasy business and he supposed there wasn't a woman alive who'd wish the job done in a bedroom.

He didn't care where he did it and had spent the better part of his life living out of doors anyway. He cleaned his guns every time he used them, and every few days whether he had used them or not. Most of the time, they got hard use.

He was a good, steady shot. It had taken him some time to get good and he'd lose the skill quick enough if he didn't keep it up. Problem was, he'd been in Abilene a good bit and hadn't fired off his guns as often as he'd have liked. One advantage of living out under the sky, he could fire off a few dozen rounds without bothering anybody. Couldn't do that living under Miss Daphne's roof. Just thinking of her reaction forced a smile out of him.

"What are you doing here?"

Jack looked up slowly. The polished leather shoes, the creased pants, the brocade vest, the silk tie, the proud and flustered expression: Tucker.

"I live here," Jack said, enjoying the confusion on Tucker's face. "Hotel burned down today. Remember?"

"Of course I remember."

"Well, the offer was made for me to bunk here. I accepted."

"Here? Wasn't there any place else you could have gone?" Bill looked as if he were going to pop a blood vessel.

"Don't know," Jack said and then smiled. "I like it here."

He clicked the Colt back together and holstered it smoothly, almost in a single motion. Bill looked at that action, swallowed, and stopped talking.

"I notice you don't carry," Jack said. "Why's that?"

"Never saw the need," Tucker said, the arrogance thick in his throat.

"Trust others to take care of you, is that it?" Jack asked, his voice relentlessly casual.

Tucker flushed from the throat and said, "I can take care of myself, been taking care of myself for more years than I want to count. Not everyone needs a gun."

"True, but most everyone needs somethin'. I once knew a man down on the Rio Grande, he used a whip. Could kill flies with that thing."

"Jiggs Maron," Tucker said, his eyes alight with recognition.

"You knew him," Jack said.

"He taught me, when I was starting out."

"You ran cattle, then?"

The memory of Jiggs had relaxed him, made him remember; he was talking now and not thinking much. That was good. *Keep talking, Tucker. Spit it out.*

"Up the Chisholm, three times," Bill said.

"Dusty work," Jack said, pushing the memory, wanting him to savor it. "A good life, though, for those who can stand it."

"Hard work, but my whip sang by the end of the first drive; I could make that line go anywhere I wanted."

"Been up the Chisholm Trail myself. Never saw you. Did hear of a man who liked his whip, though; used to do some loco things with it."

Bill looked down and recollected whom he was talking to. He closed his mouth.

"You meet Anne back then, when you were riding herd?"

"No."

"All the trails led to Abilene for a while there; surprised you didn't see her."

"It was a different town then."

"That's the truth," Jack said. "All farmers and merchants now. Not the town it was."

"It's a better town, respectable."

"Sure, and you're helping to make it so, right? You sell land, I hear, and do fine at it. Takes a bit of traveling, don't it?"

"No more than you, with what you do."

"As to traveling, I'm sure I do more. You been to the saloon in Topeka? The one with the purple walls?"

"No, I don't get that far east," Bill said.

Jack could feel his discomfort and confusion; Tucker

didn't want to talk. Jack was being friendly; they were two men who had some things in common, talking it out. For Bill not to talk would make him look like he was holding out, hiding something. The fact that he was talking when he so clearly didn't want to told Jack a lot. Why would a man who had nothing to hide care if it looked like he had something to hide? An innocent man would say, "I'm not talking with you and I don't give a damn what you think." Bill seemed to care, talking against his inclination.

"How about Junction City? You ever see Fat Alice? She's something to see, you ever get that way. Good land around Junction City, even down toward Council Grove."

"There's good land everywhere," Tucker said.

"Guess that's why you're doing so well."

"That and I work hard." Bill said bristling.

Jack looked at his thickened waistline and soft hands. "Yeah."

If Bill had had that whip he seemed so fond of, he might have gone for it then. But he didn't have it.

"Come on in, Bill. Anne's waiting," Nell said from the doorway. The light flooded out onto the porch, though not as far as where Jack sat on the step; he remained in deepening shadow. Twilight was sliding into full dark at a nice clip. Bill went in without another word for Jack. Jack stayed outside. No one invited him in.

For a man who'd lived most of his life outside, he didn't know why he had the sudden urge to be invited in.

Yeah, he did, and she stood right in that parlor, accepting a kiss on the back of the hand like it was nothin', letting a man touch her who had no business touching her, with her whole family looking on and smilin' their pleasure. Lord, even the dog was smiling, his tongue hanging out, his tail going like a windmill. Even the dog . . .

Jack eased off the porch and into the night, leaving the

warm glow of the houselights firmly behind him. He wasn't leaving Anne alone on the dark streets of Abilene with a man who was that friendly with a dog.

They didn't see him as they walked to the restaurant, though he followed close enough to hear the pride in Tucker's voice and the hesitation in Anne's. They didn't see him when they entered, but he watched the warm reception they got when they walked to their table. People smiled and greeted them, Tucker grinned and clapped a fellow on the back, Anne smiled without showing her teeth and sat down when Tucker pulled the chair for her.

She didn't show her teeth much, not in talking or smiling, or even in eating, for that matter. Bill did most of the talking. Bill did the ordering. Bill did the gesturing. Bill did the smiling and the laughing. Anne did the listening.

It appeared to be a one-sided courtship with the weight on Tucker's side.

Jack stood in the darkness that blanketed the main street of Abilene, hidden from all eyes, in no one's thoughts. That was just the way he liked it. He didn't want anyone sniffing along his trail. He didn't need anyone at all.

He watched Anne in the golden light of the Demorest, her dark hair shining in a wavy mass atop her head, her skin smooth and glowing, her blue eyes brilliant in the gentle lamplight. Her expression guarded. Why would a gal be wary when out with her regular beau? Bill leaned across the table, smiling, talking excitedly. Anne smiled politely and rested more firmly against the back of her chair. A fool would have no trouble reading that picture; Bill's aggressive pursuit, Anne's passive withdrawal. And he was no fool. Except maybe where she was concerned.

She had leaned into him, seeking his kiss. She had come to his hotel, seeking him out. She had pressed herself against him not three hours ago, demanding a kiss from him that he'd been too ready to give. She hadn't been wary, or cautious, or reserved. Not then. She was being all those things now with Tucker. Damn, but the woman had it tumbled; she was supposed to encourage her town beau, not the dusty-heeled bounty hunter.

She didn't have the first idea of how to look after herself.

That's why he was following her. She couldn't be trusted on her own with a man—he knew that well enough from personal experience, and her mama ought to know it, too. But Bill Tucker was an approved beau for Anne and looked on the verge of asking her to be his woman, that was the difference. A mama would make allowances if the man was ready to submit to the halter.

But Bill Tucker had ridden the trail, traveled a lot, and was good with a whip. And dogs tied themselves in knots for him.

That's why he was following them. Anne needed someone to watch out for her, and Bill just plain needed watching.

Anne turned at that moment to smile at a woman at a nearby table, her first genuine smile of the night. Tiny dimples appeared in each cheek and her cheeks flushed pink. The woman said something and Anne chuckled, ducking her head for a moment and then raising it, her face alight with pleasure, her light blue eyes crescents of momentary delight. Then Tucker said something and Anne calmed down, pressing her lips against her smile and readjusting the napkin in her lap. Tucker nodded to the woman and she nodded back, her smile still in place. Tucker'd only managed to knock the smile out of one of them and it was coming to be a sure bet that it'd always be Anne.

What kind of beau would knock the smile out of a woman?

What kind of gal would let him?

The kind of gal that needed watching.

Without knowing how it happened, he realized that he'd hired on for the job of doing just that.

Jack stayed in the shadows, watching the couple in the warm light of the restaurant, chewing on a piece of hardtack that had been stuffed into the bottom of his pocket. Miss Daphne hadn't had to spring for his supper after all. She must be as pleased as punch about that.

He was still standing in the dark, his back holding up the storefront across the street from the Demorest, when they came out. Tucker took Anne by the arm and led her down the street toward home while Anne was fussing with fastening her cape. The spring night air wasn't cold enough to show breath, but it wasn't much warmer. She'd need to have that wrap firmly tied down. Couldn't Tucker have waited while she got herself pulled together before he dragged her off down the street?

Jack eased off the wall and followed them, leaving the boardwalk to walk in the quiet of the dirt street. He needn't have bothered being so careful; Tucker was so busy listening to himself talk that he wouldn't have raised his head for a stampede.

"Here, let me help you," Bill said, positioning himself in front of Anne so that he could grab hold of the ribbons that would hold her wrap shut.

"No, I can manage it," she said softly, her voice muffled as she tried to look down to a spot just under her chin.

"It would have been easier in the light," he said, his large fingers mixing in with hers and getting everything jumbled up even more.

"Yes, it would have," she said, except he hadn't given her a chance to get her cape on before he had charged out of the restaurant with her by the arm. It was hard to tie a ribbon with only one hand available. Bill didn't seem to realize that.

She finally got herself together and breathed a sigh of accomplishment. Bill was looking down at her with a smile on his face. She smiled back. He lifted her chin up with one finger and smiled even bigger. He always did that before he kissed her.

Anne's smile faltered and she jerked her head away from his touch. It was just a little jerk, but he noticed.

"What's wrong, Anne?" His voice wasn't raised, but he kept that one finger firmly planted under her chin, forcing her face up to his. It was uncomfortable. "You'll kiss Jack Skull in broad daylight? A man like that? A man you hardly know? But you won't kiss me now, when we're alone?"

She flushed and wanted to walk around him, just leave him there in the dark of the street for embarrassing her like that. But she didn't move. She did jerk her head away from his extended finger and backed up a step to put some distance between them.

"I'm sorry about that," she said. "I . . . I don't know how that happened." That was the sad and honest truth. "I'm sorry you had to hear about it." A flat-out lie.

"Anne, the whole town's heard about it, those that didn't actually see it," Bill said, the anger in his voice as bright as a lamp. "Didn't you think that people'd be worried about you? You mixing with that bounty hunter and them all knowing about you and me. Are you sorry it happened or sorry I found out about your infidelity?"

Anne's head came up at that, her blue eyes suddenly as sharp as a blade. "Acts of infidelity are reserved for the married. I'm not married." And never would be, if she had her way. Which she would.

"Let's talk about that," Bill said, easing off on his own anger to assuage hers. He moved in close to her, pulling her under the shelter of his arm as he continued on down the street.

There weren't any lights up ahead. The Demorest, with

its golden light pooling on the dirt street, was long behind them. Up ahead was only darkness and in the far
distance, the lights of home. All the stores in between
were closed and dark. The moon was out and the sky was
clear, but it was only a crescent moon and its cold, spring
light was feeble. Bill guided her carefully along the boardwalk, their steps loud and hollow in the night, his arm
snug along her shoulder. Her right arm was pressed so
close to his side that she couldn't move it.

"You know how I feel about you, Anne," he said, his
eyes circles of sincere blue under the dark sweep of his
thick brows. He didn't wait for her to answer. "I think
you're the prettiest girl between here and Texas, and the
sweetest."

He turned his face and kissed the side of her face, just
near the ear. She shivered. He tightened his grip and
stopped walking. Anne, by necessity, stopped too.

Jack didn't stop.

"I've wanted to ask you something all night, Anne." Bill
turned Anne in his arms and raised her face for a kiss.
His mouth came down on hers softly, confidently. It was
a gentle kiss, designed to inspire a gentle response. Bill
seemed pleased.

Jack wasn't.

"Kissing in public," he said from the darkness. "That
just might be illegal."

This time it was Bill who jerked away, whirling to face
the voice of the man he couldn't see. Anne closed her
arms over her chest and ducked her head down, ashamed
to the core. Kissing two men in one day; she'd get a reputation for being just plain common.

"Then you'd be the first to be arrested," Bill said, making her want to groan in shame. "Besides, she's spoken
for."

Anne's head jerked up and she looked at Bill for the
slimmest moment before looking at the spot where Jack's

173

voice had come from. Jack stepped into her range of vision, coming out of the darkness like a wraith and looking as dangerous as one.

He still looked good.

"You asked and she answered?" he asked Bill.

"Well, no, but we—"

"Then I'll escort the lady home, with your permission, ma'am."

Jack's eyes raked over her and she felt herself flush to her feet. Bill was forgotten in that instant. Unfortunately, Bill seemed to realize it.

"I don't leave a woman in the middle of the evening," Bill said. "I'll escort Anne home."

"Ma'am?" Jack asked, waiting for her to say what she wanted him to do.

"Come on, Anne," Bill said, taking her arm firmly.

Jack stepped up and stood in front of Anne, blocking her. If Bill forced it, she'd have to run right into Jack Skull, chest to chest. Bill wasn't going to force it under those conditions.

"Answer him, Anne," Bill said in exasperation.

She knew what she wanted. It wasn't going to make Bill happy. What was worse, she knew that Jack knew what she wanted.

"Thank you," she said softly. "Please join us."

"Yes, ma'am," Jack said, taking her other arm and walking off down the street. For a second or two there, he thought Bill might be left behind. He caught up quick enough, hanging on hard to Anne's arm. The woman would probably have bruises tomorrow.

Why didn't she say something and shake him off?

Same reason she didn't shake him off; she was too polite to make a fuss over her own murder. Jack shook his head at her dangerous vulnerability.

"You don't want to be here, you can go anytime," Tucker said, misreading Jack's action.

"I want to be here," Jack said. "I'm the sort that does what he wants, not what he should."

Anne coughed a bit and lowered her eyes to look at the dirt under her toes.

"I didn't figure you for anything else," Tucker said scathingly.

Jack figured he was counting on Anne's presence to protect him; he didn't see Tucker as the sort who'd say something like that without a witness around to make sure he didn't get hurt. Trouble was, he was right, at least around Anne. Jack didn't want to do anything to make her any more skittish than she was. Tucker didn't seem to give a damn.

"You take a good look, Tucker," he said, "and you'll see right clear what kind of man it is you're talking to."

"I know the kind of man. I don't need to look again."

Jack laughed and looked up at the starry sky. "What you gonna do when Anne steps out from between you 'n' me, Tucker? You gonna stand and face me, telling me you don't like the sound of my spurs?"

Tucker didn't say anything. That about said it all.

"He doesn't mean anything," Anne said quietly. It wasn't a sure bet whom she was speaking to; could have been to both of them.

No one said anything for a spell after that. The sound of their footsteps on the dirt was soft and indistinct. He let the sound of it soothe him, urging the anger out of his blood.

Here she was, kissing two men in one day, one of them a stranger and the other a shade too slick. And when they growled over her as if she were a scrap of bone, she didn't get mad like she ought, she got sorry and apologized. For someone else. Damn, but she should be hissing at Tucker for bullying her and snapping at him for horning in where he had no call. But she wasn't doing anything like that; when anyone else would get mad, Anne Ross got sorry.

And found herself with two escorts shadowing her home.

Well, he wasn't leaving.

The body of that poor gal, lying dead on the prairie, thinking she was being courted by some smooth-talking man, lay like a heavy blanket on his mind.

He damn sure wasn't leaving.

Anne was stuck in the middle, without an arm to call her own. Her head came to about his shoulder, even with her hair piled up like it was. Her arm was soft under his hand, soft and round. She smelled as clean as prairie grass.

Even sharing her with Tucker, he liked walking beside her.

The lights from her house seemed to grow larger and brighter and then they were on her porch. All three of them.

He still wasn't leaving.

"You can leave anytime," Tucker said, eyeing him furiously.

"Thanks. I'll stay." Jack nodded.

"I have something I want to say to Anne. Privately."

"I won't repeat a word of it," Jack said, sitting down on the step and looking up at the two of them.

Anne didn't say anything. She just looked up at Bill like she was real sorry that things weren't going his way. And sorry that she couldn't do anything about it.

"Anne," Tucker said, "don't you have anything to say? Can't you encourage this . . . guest of yours to—"

"Still shoving Anne in between, are ya?" Jack said. "No use roping her into doing what you ought to do. I ain't leavin'. I want to be right where I am. You want me to move, you just keep takin' it up with me and see where you land."

He said it pleasant enough, but his smile was miles gone. There was nothing the least bit amusing about a man who'd shame a girl into doing his fighting and then make her feel shamed that she couldn't see it done.

Tucker looked ready to kill.

Anne laid a hand softly on his arm and smiled up into his blood-suffused face. "I had a wonderful time tonight. Thank you for taking me to dinner."

"You're welcome, Anne," he said stiffly, pointedly ignoring Jack, who was staring at the two of them with all the subtlety of a rattlesnake. "I'll be by tomorrow and we'll talk. Alone."

"Of course, Bill." She smiled sweetly. "Good night."

"Night."

Jack sat on the step watching Tucker fade into the darkness. He sat until the sound of Tucker's boots whispered out into nothing. Then he turned to look at Anne. She was staring off into the dark, after Tucker, looking flustered and uncomfortable and sorry. What was she going to apologize for now?

"Not even a good night kiss," he said with a hard and angry edge to his voice, "or is that my job?"

He could kiss her, he just couldn't be seen with her. Those were apparently the rules, unspoken but understood. He understood just where he stood in her polite little life; he knew what he was and what he would never be. And it made him mad. All of a sudden, just like that. And he knew she'd apologize and take it on herself and that just made him madder.

She turned abruptly to stare into his eyes and then dropped hers in embarrassment, obviously studying the condition of the porch boards; they were wearing through in a couple of spots. Did she always have to be so blamed sorry about things that had little or nothing to do with her? Couldn't she ever get mad?

"Well, doesn't he usually kiss you a time or two before

177

the evening's over? He's kissed you once tonight already, right out on the street. I saw that one."

Anne twisted her hands together and then crossed her arms to keep herself still. She wouldn't look at him.

"Go ahead and tell me," Jack said.

"Why are you mad?" she said softly.

"Mad? I'm not mad, not even a little bit," he said, his voice hoarse and throaty even to his own ears. "You want to kiss two men in one day, that's your business. You want to have two men bellowing over you like you're a prize cow, you go right on and enjoy yourself."

"I'm not enjoying myself," she said. She looked like she was about to bust out and cry. And then apologize.

He was furious with her. Why wasn't she telling him to get off her damn porch and mind his own business instead of horning in on her evening with her proper beau? Why wasn't she marching into the house, into the safety of female numbers? Why was she standing on a half-dark porch, looking up at him with sad and sorry blue eyes?

Damn, but he didn't want to feel this way about her, like he had to take care of her, like she needed something real bad and only he could give it. Tenderness, that's what it was, and he wasn't going to give it. There was no space for tenderness in him. That had been burned out of him long ago and it was well gone.

"You're not enjoying yourself?" he asked brusquely, standing up. "Well, I know how to fix that. I know what you like, don't I, Anne? You like what I got, don't ya?"

He was talking to her as if she were no better than a sporting gal, wanting her anger, wanting her to fend for herself. She did neither. What was wrong with her that she couldn't fight back?

Anne blushed ten shades of red and lifted her face to his, unafraid. It didn't matter what he said; she knew he was mad. She'd be mad too if he'd kissed her and another woman in the same day, and she'd had to watch. Sarah might think it was great fun for her to have two beaus, but she wasn't managing it well. She was just terrible at courting. Good thing she didn't need to be good at it. All she had to do was keep everybody happy, her mama and Sarah and Miss Daphne and Bill and Jack, until she could run off to some town where she didn't know anybody and could worry about pleasing only herself. She just had to get ready, to be ready. Pretty soon now. Pretty soon and she'd be gone, away from them all, Jack, too. He was mad, but she wasn't afraid. What was it about him that made her unafraid?

She was a fool not to be afraid. With what he was feeling, she was a fool.

"Why don't you ask me for it?" he prodded, stalking her, hemming her in as she stood with her back to the rail. "Go ahead and ask. I'll give you what you want."

If she had a lick of grit, she'd run in the house and slam the door on his fingers. She didn't run.

Lifting her face, her eyes on his, she whispered, "Kiss me."

She didn't know why she did it. It wasn't as if she wanted a man. It wasn't as if she cared about him. It wasn't as if he would be any part of her future. No, she didn't want him. Not for anything. But she'd take his kisses. Just for now, she wanted his kiss. That one small touch of him on her, on her life, on her body. Nothing else, not one thing more. Just his kiss.

With a moan of desire mingled with self-disgust, he bent and kissed her, giving her whatever part of him she could take.

At the first touch, she seemed to melt against him, her arms going round his neck and pulling him down close. Her body pressed against his, from top to bottom, her breath coming on quick and hard, like a horse fighting his rider. But she wasn't fighting. No, she was yielding, giving, urging him to give her more of whatever he had that she wanted. She seemed to want it all. His arms wrapped around her, pulling her tight, and he opened her mouth with his tongue. She opened to him quick as lightning, groaning when his tongue touched hers. Sweet breath, soft heat, warm welcome; she offered all.

He could taste no fear in her response, not even when he slid a hand up to coast over her ribs and rest on the underside of her breast. She just kept kissing him back, holding nothing back, unafraid.

He was afraid for her.

She didn't have the weakest instinct for survival. And she needed to. There was a trail of bodies leading north to Abilene.

And here she was, ready and willing to give her kisses to a man who was a stranger and rough as a cob, to boot. She'd kiss herself right into a grave. But he couldn't stop kissing her, even knowing all that. He couldn't turn away from what she was giving so sweetly. He couldn't stop giving her that little bit of himself. If she was going to drown in his kisses, he'd go right down with her.

The porch door slamming put an end to it, bringing them both up for air.

"You coming in, Anne?" Sarah asked.

"Yes," she said, running quick hands over her hair and down her skirts. Her skirts were safe; he hadn't lifted them. Yet.

"Good night, Mr. Scullard," she said, not looking at him.

"Miss Ross." He tipped his hat.

The door slammed behind her. Sarah just stood leaning against the door frame, grinning.

"You seem to be doing all right. Bill still alive?"

"Yeah," Jack said, walking across the porch to where she stood.

"Where you going?"

"To bed."

"After that kiss? You'll sleep in the jail. Across town."

Jack studied the wry amusement in her blue eyes and saw that she was dead serious. No way she was letting him anywhere near her niece.

Smart woman.

"Yes, ma'am," he said, adjusting his hat as he walked down the porch steps into the night.

Lane was just throwing out the dregs from the coffee-pot when he showed up.

"You got a spare bed in there?" Jack asked, cocking his head toward the cells.

"What you need a bed for? Ain't you got a good soft one over at Miss Daphne's?"

When Jack shrugged and kept his mouth shut, Lane smiled as he rammed the lid down hard on the tin pot. It made a noise that echoed three miles out.

"She threw you out, didn't she? Didn't figure she'd go for you dirtying up her sheets. You didn't last long, but no one does."

"Wasn't Miss Daphne," Jack said as he followed Lane into the jailhouse. "Was Miss Sarah and it's only for the night. I'll be back over there tomorrow."

"Sarah? She wouldn't throw a man out into the street no matter what his stripe." Lane sat down and leaned back in his chair, his legs up on the desk, ready for a long story. "What'd ya do?"

Jack didn't tell long stories. "Kissed Anne."

"What? Again? What are you doing, following her around?"

That was too much true so Jack didn't say anything.

"Well, at least it was dark this time."

It wasn't too dark on the porch of Anne's house, but Jack didn't say anything.

"You can't keep your hands off that gal and you won't be over there tomorrow, I can promise you that," Charles said. "They don't have much use for men over there and

181

that's a known fact in these parts. You better walk careful in dealing with them women."

"They've had their share of man trouble," Jack said, sitting down. Charles got out the bottle and poured. Appeared that if Lane wasn't going to get to hear a long story, he was prepared to tell one.

"You ain't heard the worst," Lane began. "Sarah? Her man, Roy's his name, he marries her, runs off to war a month or two later, comes home a year after the war's done, spends his night of marital rights, and then lights out again. Now, none of this happened round here, but word gets out. That woman came to Abilene thinking she was lower than dirt. Time's taken care of some of that, but a woman don't forget that her man run off."

Jack didn't say anything. He took a drink and leaned back in his chair.

"Now, Miss Daphne, I told you about. Her man left on the train he helped build, but what I didn't tell was that he had a pretty young gal keeping him company just down the line. Word of that sort of thing gets out pretty quick since the train is always going back and forth, you see. Well, Miss Daphne, she's held her head up and kept her spine straight and not said a word about it. She's a hard woman, but she's respected."

"And Nell?" Jack took another swallow. He'd been drinking more since coming to Abilene than he ever had in his life.

Lane finished his drink in a long swallow and banged his cup down on the desk.

"He was a marshal and respected. A prime match, everybody smiling about the fine couple they made. Well, he was on the go most of the time, riding out, chasing outlaws. Time got to be where he was gone more than he was home and became more outlaw than lawman. One time, he just didn't come back." Lane shrugged, "It happens."

"You sound like you were there," Jack said quietly.

Lane poured himself another and drank off half of it before he answered.

"I was. I was his deputy."

Jack and Charles sat silently for a while, letting things settle down. The light flickered, sending tortured shadows against the wall and up into the air. It was quiet out on the street. A dog barked, twice, down near the stockyard and then was still.

"You've been dogging her a long time," Jack eventually said.

Lane smiled in wry humor and nodded. "I have. I knew right off she was the one. She didn't. She still doesn't."

"You must remind her of her husband; every time she looks at you, she remembers."

"Yeah," Lane said, taking another healthy swallow.

"Anne must hate men by now," Jack mumbled, studying the contents of his cup.

Lane chuckled sadly. "Nell does. Hates them all, especially lawmen."

"Yeah"—Jack tipped up his drink and downed it in a swallow—"I guess she would."

The two men set their empty cups on the table. Lane put the bottle back in the drawer.

"You can always quit," Jack said, throwing his hat down on a cot in the corner.

Charles smiled at the joke. It was a joke. He was a lawman, it was all he wanted to do and he was good at it. More, he believed in it. He'd seen Tim Ross turn bad and it had turned his stomach. He was going to be the man Ross should have been. God willing, he'd get to be the husband Nell should have had.

"Yeah," Lane said and blew out the lamp.

He was playing in the dirt, hidden from the only home he had ever known by the brush along the Brazos River. He knew the name of the river because his mama had taught him. He knew how to lay out a house because his daddy had taught him that; his daddy had built his house. His home.

He worked now, just like his daddy, at planning his own house by the river. It was a small house, but then, he was a small boy.

With a stick, he carved the shape of his house into the dry dirt of the land, his tongue sticking out between lips compressed with effort. His bedroom, the fireplace, the door, a fancy kitchen for his own bride: all scratched into the hard dirt of Texas. He stood up and looked it over, the brush coming to his shoulder. In the distance, he could see the roof of his daddy's house. He could hear the chickens and the stamp of the horses; he could hear his mama when she called. But he couldn't see her and she couldn't see him when he was crouched down in the rough square he had decided would be his bedroom. He was far enough away for privacy and close enough for safety.

He was happy.

The sun was hot on his head, just a sliver away from being too hot. It was hot enough to warm him down to the center without burning. Sometimes a breeze would come sliding down the river and he would feel the trace of moisture on the skin of his face before the heat took over again.

He scratched again at the dirt between his knees, deciding to add on another bedroom for his children. He would have a son.

His mama called out again, calling him. She'd made something for him, a treat of apples and crust and cream. He wanted the treat, but he knew that his mama would send him to bed for a rest after he had finished eating. It was that time of day. He crunched lower into the brush, delighting in the knowledge that she couldn't see him, and worked on the last line in the dust that would finish his house.

The shot rang out against the heat and the quiet.

Jack jolted upright, heart pounding, sweat thick on his neck and his chest. The dark was thick around him and he took a few breaths to stop the shaking that rattled his chest like an old man's. Running his hands through his hair, he forced himself to calm down, to ease himself back into sleep. It would work. He'd get control. He'd done it night after night.

Chapter Sixteen

He came in time for breakfast and was served royally. Grits, hotcakes, steak, eggs, and biscuits all steaming merrily from the center of the table, his plate pristine and white, awaiting service. He got it. Mounds of good, hot food with a fragrant cup of coffee served in a porcelain teacup and saucer all but surrounded him at the table. The women stood like servants, awaiting his smile or a word of appreciation. He was free with both. Dammit sat at his feet, tail pounding on the floorboards with flagrant joy, muzzle resting on his thigh: a picture of devoted contentment.

Bill had come for breakfast.

Bill was working up the wind to ask her to marry him and everyone in the room expected her to say yes. What would happen when she said no?

"Anne, freshen up Bill's coffee," Miss Daphne said from her place at the stove, where she was frying up some potatoes to go with Bill's steak.

"Yes, ma'am," she said, reaching for the pot and pulling herself out of her daydreams at the same time. Her plan for using Jack to scare off Bill hadn't worked. No, it was Sarah's plan to use Jack to light a fire under Bill that had worked. Mercy. She wasn't ready for this fight; she didn't want to have it at all. She just wanted to be plumb gone one day, free from expectations. She might even change her name.

Where was Jack? Why wasn't he here to pull the reins? Gone, just like a man. Probably because he had the impression that she was loose. Hard for him not to think that when she was always asking him to kiss her.

"I'll be back before you know it, Anne," Bill said, smiling.

Was he leaving again? Well, that was good. Maybe he'd leave town without asking for her hand.

"I'm so glad," she said, smiling back while she topped off his cup.

"We'll have our private talk when I get back in a day or two," he said softly.

She smiled even more fully and said, "Good."

"There must be some prime land in Junction City that keeps pulling you back there, Bill," Nell said. "Weren't you out there just last week?"

"Yes, ma'am, and I've got the lady who owns it about ready to sell. Her man's gone and she never wanted to come West much in the first place, so I'm just nudging her along, you might say."

"Well, I'm certain you'll make out just fine," Miss Daphne said.

"So am I," Sarah said, pulling out fresh biscuits.

It seemed there was nothing much to add to that without sounding foolish, so Anne just kept her mouth shut and put the pot back on the stove.

Jack didn't show up in time for breakfast.

After a strong look from Miss Daphne and an exasperated one from her mother, Anne offered to walk Bill to the train that would take him the forty miles east to Junction City. Bill accepted gladly.

Jack wasn't on the front porch.

Anne allowed Bill to take her arm and walk her to the station. She forced herself not to look for Jack's gun-draped body as they walked through town.

Jack wasn't on the boardwalk that banded the main street of Abilene.

She still held her head up and her chest out, looking with smiling eyes at Bill, just in case Jack could see her from inside one of the buildings. Bill appreciated the effort, anyway. He squeezed her hand and leaned down to whisper, "I'll be back as soon as I finish up in Junction City. I'd ask you now, but I want it all to be just right."

"I can wait," she said. And she could.

She couldn't allow herself to put off any longer meeting with Reverend Holt; her spiritual condition was dangerously weak, fed by the lie she was living more fully every day. Her family would be laid flat if they knew what she was planning. She needed to talk things out, get the reverend's view on her plans, maybe even get his approval. But no matter what he said, she was leaving. She just didn't want to feel so guilty about it.

Jack was on the platform, watching her.

A tingle that had nothing to do with Bill standing next to her shot down her spine. She smiled her first heartfelt smile of the morning and aimed it right at Jack. Bill didn't seem to notice.

Jack didn't smile back.

Bill wasn't smiling anymore either.

"You watching or riding?" Jack asked, talking to both of them or either of them. He didn't act like he cared which.

"Bill's taking the train to Junction City," she said.

Anne and Bill climbed the platform steps and Jack looked at Bill, ignoring her altogether, it seemed to her.

A Kiss to Die For

"Business or pleasure?"

"I don't owe you an explanation," Bill snapped.

"Business," Anne chirped.

"Long trip?" Jack said, his hands relaxed and next to his guns. No matter where he rested his hands, they were near his guns.

Obviously, he planned it that way. Maybe he was so used to his guns that he didn't think about them anymore, maybe they were so much a part of him that he didn't realize how he looked to everyone. Watching him, the wary look of him, the way he kept his eyes on Bill and his hands easy, she knew the sudden truth. He knew exactly how he looked and he never for a moment forgot that he was a dangerous-looking man carrying potent firepower. He was the most aware man she had ever seen.

"Nothing you need to know," Bill said, clasping her arm. Anne suddenly remembered Jack's gibe of last night. Was Bill hanging on to her because that gave him the freedom to talk tough? Would he be as bold without her by his side? Jack didn't think so.

Anne tried to move away from Bill. He held her tight by him. To protect her or to protect himself?

"Just a day or two," she said to Jack, answering his question while gently trying to disengage herself from Bill's hand on her elbow. "He's trying to buy some land from a widow woman over there."

Jack's eyes hadn't left Bill's face as she answered, which was flatly irritating. Maybe she was the only one who had relived that kiss until after midnight. Maybe he kissed every woman he had a passing acquaintance with the way he kissed her; after all, she was hardly more than an acquaintance by most standards. But his kisses changed every standard she'd ever heard of, which was the pity of it. She wasn't going to be snared by the power of a kiss. Especially when he couldn't be bothered to remember it.

"A widow?" Jack asked, his eyes cold in the morning

189

light that slanted like a drift of snow across the wooden platform. "You known her long?"

"Long enough."

Jack smiled and that was cold, too. "I'll just bet."

Bill grabbed her tighter. His grip pinched and her fingers were going numb. He didn't seem about to let go.

"Bill, you'd better get on. You know how you hate to be in the back of the car."

She turned and gave him a kiss, full on the mouth. He was so startled that he hardly did more than breathe and let go of her arm. She never kissed him, unless it was at night and he started it, never good-bye at the train. She was really kissing him for Jack's benefit, hoping to provoke Jack. Hoping that Jack would just once this morning look at her.

He looked.

He'd been trying his damnedest to keep his eyes off of her, hard to do since she'd been pressed up against Bill like siding on a barn. Now, he looked his fill for the eternity the kiss she planted on Bill seemed to last. Oh yeah, she'd started it. The gal seemed to like to kiss, no matter who the man was.

A less than civil thought since Tucker was her proper beau. He was the one who'd been stealing kisses and getting away with it. With her full approval and participation.

The whistle blew, Anne pulled herself off Tucker, and turned to face him. He met her look. She looked both wistful and expectant; what did she want him to do? Flatten Tucker for kissing the woman he was obviously working up steam to marry or kiss her himself with Tucker looking on? He knew what she wanted him to do; he knew the look of her well enough by now, but he couldn't do it. There was no bridge taking him to where she wanted him to go and he wasn't going to build one now, not with Tucker about to climb on a train out of Abilene, off to meet a woman who was holding something he wanted.

Jack knew that Anne would be safe if he kept near her. Or if he kept near Tucker. The way he was feeling, after watching her kiss Bill as if he were the last man in Abilene, Tucker was the safer bet. If he stayed with Anne in Abilene, he'd do more than just kiss her. For all that she liked kissing, she didn't seem to have any notion of where kisses like that took a man. She had just enough feminine know-how to make her dangerous and more than enough to make her foolish, at least in her ability to watch out for herself. She had no ability there; she just threw herself at a man and trusted he'd do the right thing. Trust thrown free like that was a ticket to trouble. He didn't want any trouble with her and he didn't want her getting into any on her own. With both him and Bill gone, she'd be safe enough. He'd be safe enough, too. She was digging in too deep and he didn't have what she was looking for. He needed a spot of breathing room and he was going after it before he drowned in her blue eyes. Jack turned away from the questioning look on her face and went and bought a ticket for Junction City.

Breathing room.

Tucker looked like a gored bull, but there was nothing he could do to stop Jack. Anybody could ride the trains, any time they had the price of a ticket. He had the price and he paid it.

When he climbed on, the train had already started moving off down the track. He stood at the rear door and looked back at Anne. She stood like a little porcelain doll, all alone on that big wooden platform, as desolate as a child at getting left behind. He was leaving her behind, but she was safe. He knew she was safe while he had Tucker in his sights. And with Tucker on his way east, the woman in Junction City needed him.

*   *   *

The train pulled out, taking the only two eligible men in Abilene with it. She'd kissed them both and they'd both left her without a second thought. That in itself told its own tale. Everything she'd suspected about men and women was true, not that she'd ever doubted it. Men left. She knew it. She'd seen it for herself. Men left. They might marry, but they didn't stay. It was good to be reminded of that again. Jack made everything, all she knew, a bit fuzzy. It was good to get clear again.

She needed to get clear and stay clear. It was time to talk to Reverend Holt.

She found the reverend alone in the parlor of the parsonage, for which she was thankful. He was reading his Bible, but he put it down fast enough when he saw he had company.

"Anne! What a surprise! Come in, come in, I'm glad to see you," he said, a bit loudly. Anne turned to look out the nearest window to see if anyone was listening. No one seemed to be, but then you could never be sure in Abilene.

"You're looking lovely," he said, rising to his feet as he closed his Bible. It was a quite ordinary-looking Bible with a worn leather cover and well-thumbed pages; the dye had worn away on the spine where he held it, leaving the indistinct imprint of a pale hand. "Up early to see the seven twenty-five off? Anyone interesting on the train today?"

"Good morning, Reverend," she said. "Yes, Bill Tucker and Jack Scullard both got on the train this morning."

"Is that right? Traveling together?" An odder couple couldn't be imagined.

"Oh, no," she quickly assured him. "Bill had business in Junction City and Jack just . . . left."

"He's staying with you, isn't he?" Anne nodded and sat when he indicated a seat. The room was spare but comforting, clean and well tended with a masculine feel to it.

There wasn't a room in her house that had that feeling. "That was kind of you, especially considering how folks in this town feel about him."

Anne just nodded, guilt pouring through her veins like a spring river, hard and fast. She hadn't invited Jack out of kindness, she'd invited him in to get him closer and take advantage of what he offered.

"How'd Miss Daphne take it, when he showed up with his gear and looking for a bed?"

"She wasn't happy about it," Anne said, "but Jack just sort of made his way in. My grandmother didn't have much to say against it once he was standing in her foyer."

He wished he'd been there. Miss Daphne outtalked was something he'd yet to see.

"Umm, Reverend Holt," Anne said, trying to ease into what she had come to say. She sat for a few moments in strangled silence. There didn't seem to be a way to ease into this kind of conversation.

"Is there a problem, Anne?" he said, saying the words for her.

"Not what you'd call a problem, more of a question."

"I'm here to serve, Anne, fire away," Holt answered, leaning back in his chair.

Anne leaned forward in hers and folded her arms across her chest. "Just how bad is it, in God's eyes, to . . . to . . ." She couldn't say it. How could she admit to using one man to keep her family happy and another man to keep everything upset? She was using people for her own ends. There was nothing very Christian about that. "To . . . disobey your elders." She'd done that, too. And meant to do it some more, when she left Abilene.

"How old are you, Anne?" he asked.

"Eighteen."

"Getting close to marriage, I'd guess," he said, smiling.

Anne dropped her gaze to rest on the spine of his Bible. "I suppose so."

"Well, any girl who's old enough to marry probably doesn't need to worry overmuch about obeying her elders, not when she's as sweet and agreeable a girl as you are."

He clearly hadn't heard about her daylight kiss with Jack.

"My grandmother—"

"I know all about your grandmother and I know all about you," he said with a warm smile. "You're as obedient a daughter as I've ever seen."

"But . . . Jack . . ." Anne dropped her eyes to her lap and sat fidgeting with her fingers.

"Jack?" he repeated, his expression showing his confusion.

"I kissed him," she whispered, the words so soft they barely moved the air.

"You kissed him?"

She nodded.

"What did he do?"

Anne looked up. "He kissed me back."

"And your family knows about this kiss," he said, slowly putting it together.

"Everybody knows," Anne said.

"So Jack Scullard is courting you?"

Would she let a man kiss her who wasn't courting her? She knew the answer to that, but she wasn't prepared to admit the bald truth to Reverend Holt. Some things were better left unsaid. Most things, actually, were better left unsaid. It made for a more peaceable life.

"Yes, he is," she said. And he might be. She didn't know for certain. She was no expert at courting styles. Maybe they did things like courting different down in Texas. They did everything different down in Texas.

"You like Jack?" he asked.

"Yes, I do," Anne answered softly.

"What about Bill?"

"I like him, too." She knew that made her sound flighty and shallow and even a little fast, but it was better than sounding manipulative and calculating.

"I've been hearing that Bill's starting to talk marriage. Have you been hearing that, too?"

"He hasn't said anything outright," Anne said.

"Does Bill know about that kiss with Jack?"

"Everybody knows," she said again.

"And he's still coming around?"

"Yes," she said.

"That says a lot about his intentions, doesn't it?"

"I suppose."

"Does Jack know about Bill?"

"Yes."

"What does that say about him?"

Anne's color came up, two spots of warmth on her cheeks, and she looked the reverend in the eyes. "I'm not married, Reverend Holt. Jack's free to court me. In fact, it was Sarah who told him I was . . . available."

"Sarah?" He seemed surprised. Well, she had been surprised, too.

"What I came to ask you, what I need to know," Anne said, "is that, can you, is it possible for a person to . . . be damned for kissing?"

Miss Daphne had implied it, the whole town was talking about it, and it was all she was going to admit to. She just couldn't ask the reverend if she was going to be damned for selfishly using two men to deceive her only blood kin. She knew the answer to that. He wasn't going to be able to tell her anything that would give her any comfort.

"Are you asking about Jack's kiss?"

"Yes, I am," she said.

"It is absolutely not possible for a person to be damned for a kiss," he said firmly. "Give it no more thought, no matter what anyone else tells you. You just enjoy your courting season, Anne. You'll be married soon enough.

But be careful how many kisses you pass out in the meantime," he said with a grin.

In the long cold light of a spring dusk, they stood. They faced west, watching the lavender sunset of a cool sky; she delicately fingering the gift he had just given her, he with an arm about her waist. He turned her in his arms as the sun cast its last golden light and she went willingly, eager for the kiss he would give her. She had only been kissed once before and that the awkward kiss of an overeager boy.

These kisses were of a man.

He had trained her to his kiss, teaching her the feel of him, the size of him, the taste. She knew him and delighted in it. He was all she'd ever dreamed a man could be.

They were to be married in the morning.

She hadn't asked her ma yet, her ma had hardly seen him, just at a distance. He'd said he needed to keep his presence in the area a secret. He traveled in his work so she hadn't seen him more than two days in all the weeks she'd known him. But he was the man for her. Her ma would say yes, had to say yes when she understood that she'd have no other.

This was the man she'd spend her life with. This was the man she'd face death with. And all the days in between.

She threw herself into his kiss, wrapping her arms around his neck and sighing her delight into his mouth. She was dizzy with the taste of him, breathless with yearning, suffocating.

Chapter Seventeen

"Yeah, heard about it when I was in Junction City. She was from there, ya know. The place was hopping when I caught the train this morning; the sheriff over there, Gates, was sending a wire off to the U.S. Marshal and trying to keep folks away from her body, both at once. No deputy over there, too small. Doc was away on a birthing so the body was just laid out in the saloon. Naturally, they closed the place down because of it. Some folks were riled at that; folks got a right to drink even when there's been a murder. Maybe more."

"But was it the same as the gal here, that Mary that was found?" John Wells, the owner of the hardware and tinware shop, asked.

"The same kind of murder, you mean?" Bill asked. "Yeah, same as same. Something pulled tight around her throat, her face bloated and discolored. Nice-looking gal, from what you could tell of what was left. Blond and busty with a little snub nose."

"She have kin?" Neil McShay asked.

"Her ma was crying full out, but silent." Bill shook his head in grief. "Terrible to see it."

But he didn't have any trouble talking about it. Had been talking about it since getting off the morning train. And folks had been listening. As well they should.

"You know, Jack Skull was over there, in Junction City," he said as a carefully planned afterthought.

"Thought I saw him leave town. With you," Isaiah Hill said, spitting out a stream of brown tobacco juice to pattern the dirt street.

"Yes," Bill said easily, "I had business there with Widow Blake. Been meeting with her for a few weeks. But what business did Jack Skull have in Junction City?"

A small crowd had grown around Bill and a crowd did not work to his purpose; he had hoped to spread his tales of suspicion quietly, one man to one man, and then have the story of murder take root in the dirt around Jack Skull's feet. But Abilene was too small a town and the people too willing to believe the worst of a man they already instinctively disliked to let the story spread slowly. Where there was a crowd, Sheriff Lane would appear. He didn't need that.

"Jack's business is his own," Lane said from the edge of the crowd.

"But he didn't tell you, did he, Sheriff, why he was leaving?" Isaiah pressed.

"A man's business is his own, Hill, until he breaks the law. Then it's my business. Jack didn't break no laws by leaving Abilene."

"You two are getting thick, it seems," Douglas Currie, the banker, noted, puffing on his slim cigar.

"As thick as it takes to find the one who's murdering these girls."

"You heard about that gal in Junction City?" McShay asked.

"Got a wire from Sheriff Gates."

"What's he know about this?" Currie said.

"About as little as anybody," Lane said slowly, the

weight of his words and the authority of his presence shifting the crowd until he stood at its center and Tucker at its rim. Tucker was just as glad; he didn't want to be noted as the source of this tale, he just wanted people to know that a girl had been killed in a town where Skull had been. He'd accomplished that. "Her name was Elsa, new to this country with her ma. Pa died somewhere east of the Mississippi. She was working as a baker, made the lightest pies for miles, Gates said. Spoke the language fine, though her ma is slower to it. She's having a tough time of it now, doesn't understand half of what's said, can't answer questions, doesn't seem to know anything."

"Convenient for the killer," Tom Monahan said, his wife at his shoulder.

"Yeah," Lane said, "he's not stupid, that's for sure. Leaving a pretty thin trail."

"How about Skull? He on the trail?" McShay said.

"Jack and I are working on this together and I think you should know that he's been working on finding this man for months."

"All he need do is look in a mirror," Hill said, spitting for emphasis.

"Now, that's enough, Isaiah," the sheriff said forcefully, fingering his gun belt gently. Of all the things he did, his gunplay was the only thing gentle and easy about him. Treated his guns like polished eggs, drew them out with whispered movement, fondled the hammer like a lover, and fingered the trigger like a silken thread. And hit what he was aiming at with delicate precision; first time, every time. "The man has a hard reputation, but he's earned it being tough on outlaws. He ain't no lawbreaker himself."

"You ever know him? Before he came here?" Monahan asked.

"No," Lane answered truthfully, "but you get to know about a man, word gets around."

"No word seems to have gotten around about that

killer," Nell said from the edge of the crowd.

Charles turned to face her and said plainly, "It will."

The air was so thick between Charles and Nell that the crowd thinned out to give them room to tangle. Most went back to their business, some stayed out of range but within earshot. They weren't disappointed.

"I never thought to see the day when Charles Lane would defend a known killer, especially knowing that he's living in my house—"

"Nell"—he cut her off sharply, his black eyes hard as basalt—"you playing with a man's life, a worthy man at that, just because he up and kissed Anne, is a shameful thing."

"There's nothing shameful about protecting my own child from a well-known killer!"

"That man has never once killed anyone who didn't need killin' and a man don't deserve to hang because he's courting your girl. I thought better of you, Nell. Personal dislike ain't no excuse for injustice. Ma'am." He tipped his hat and marched off down the boardwalk, boots scuffing against the wood.

Never, in all the years she'd known him, had Charles Lane shown her such disrespect and disregard. It shocked her into leaving her mouth hanging open for just a moment as she watched him walk away from her; she shut it with a snap of teeth and marched herself on home, her own booted feet raising a muffled clatter from beneath her swinging skirts.

The train whistle sounded just then and Anne was there to meet the train. She'd met Bill's train earlier that morning, heard his story about the murdered girl, heard also his carefully spoken belief that Jack had done the killing. She didn't believe a word of it. She didn't believe it and she knew she was a fool. There were two dead girls now, and the killer was as free as he had been yesterday, but she trusted a bounty hunter with a reputation as hard as gunmetal. She didn't know anything about him except that he made her legs feel like melted butter whenever he looked at her and that he had a name for killing. Both of those facts meant trouble, yet here she was, hoping he'd get off the next train.

She was in real bad trouble.

How long since she'd met him?

Nine days. Nine days exactly. She'd counted. Nine days and three kisses. It sure didn't amount to much, yet she was in deep, thick trouble anyway. He had got ahold of her somehow and she couldn't shake him loose.

Somehow? Oh, she knew how. She just hadn't understood that a kiss could be such a deadly thing coming from the right man. Or the wrong one.

She was remembering each and every moment of those three kisses when he stepped off the train. He looked tired. His hair was tangled, his face stubbled, and his eyes reddened. He looked wonderful.

He looked glad to see her, his head lifting at the sight of her on the platform, a smile coming into his eyes. And then he looked plain mad. He still looked wonderful.

"You here to meet Bill's train?" he said, pulling his hat down tight and low.

"I meet all the trains; Bill happened to be on the eight-fifteen."

"And I happen to be on the eleven O-five," he said, walking past her.

She fell into step beside him. He must have known that she would. It was probably pathetic, the way she dogged him. She couldn't seem to help it. He didn't look like he was going to kiss her.

He was mad that she'd met Bill's train. But it wasn't the same, it wasn't anything the same, what she felt for him and what she felt for Bill. And she had no idea how to tell him that. He probably didn't want to hear it. It was better for her not to say anything anyway. She didn't need the kind of trouble that followed him like a dog. She didn't need Jack Skull, no matter how he made her feel. She just needed to keep things peaceful.

Having Jack around sure didn't make things peaceful. How come she wanted him around anyway?

Jack didn't want to hear one word out of her mouth. He'd seen her standing there, looking like the sweetest homecoming a man could reach for, and she'd given the same gift to Tucker. Lord, she gave the same to any danged stranger who fell off the train in Abilene. Any killer who happened to find his way to her door would get the same open-armed welcome and hopeful smile and she'd end up as dead as Mary and Elsa and all the rest of them. Dead with a throat black and purple, choked by misplaced trust and dreams of romance.

But she wasn't looking for any dream of love in his arms, no, it was his kisses she liked, pure and simple. And he wouldn't have any cause to complain as to that, except that someone was out there, trading kisses for death. A girl who was prey to kisses was walking a rope over a windy canyon; sure to fall. Sure to die.

And here she was, trailing after him, waiting for the kiss she knew he'd brought her. Knowing he wanted to kiss her and hold her safe from all the darkness in the world, knowing he'd give in to her eventually. Knowing that he couldn't turn away from the kiss of welcome and warmth that was already written in her eyes.

"Welcome back," she said, reading his wants too clear for his comfort.

"Thanks. Abilene pay you to meet the trains and welcome folks? Good business on their part, but I got business of my own with the sheriff. You go along, now."

"You know I don't get paid to meet the trains. You know I . . . I was hoping you'd come back."

"Like you was hoping Bill'd come back?" He didn't

look at her. She was rushing to keep step. He didn't let himself slow down.

"I knew he'd come back," she said, flustered. "I don't want to talk about Bill. I'm just so glad you're back."

"Yeah."

"Yeah," she repeated, meaning it. He could hear that she meant it and it kicked at something inside him, something tied up and tied down. Nobody'd ever cared if he came or went. He didn't have time for this; he had to find a killer. He had to make sure Anne didn't find him first.

Good way to make sure she stayed alive was to keep her with him, keep her safe.

Yeah. That was a lie he could live with.

"But if I'm bothering you, which it seems I am, I'll just take myself off."

For her, it was a mouthful. They were as close to fighting words as he'd heard yet out of her. And then she said words that hit him like a fist to the belly.

"I'll find Bill and invite him to supper."

Like hell she would.

Jack reached out and took her by the arm. "It's too early for supper. You come on with me to the sheriff's."

"Bill likes to eat early," she said stiffly. Oh yeah, she was digging the spurs in. But he knew what she wanted, what she wanted more than she wanted Bill sitting at her table.

Jack pulled her around to face him and then backed her slowly against the wall of the stable. Her face paled and her eyes went wide, but she went. She didn't fight him. That's what would get her killed, she didn't fight, didn't see danger when it had its hands around her waist and was pressing against the long fall of her skirts.

He was danger. He shouldn't be anywhere near her, couldn't she see that? Hell, the whole town saw it, but not she. She just kept looking up at him, her eyes blue and soft and trusting. She'd get herself killed without any trouble at all, just the way she'd get herself kissed, just by looking at him. Just by relaxing into his hands when she should have been tensing in outrage. Just by raising her face, her lips parted, her breath sweet when she should have been cussing him out. She probably didn't know how to cuss. Trouble was, she knew how to kiss.

Trouble was, he couldn't stop himself from kissing her, out on a public street, again.

He wrapped his left arm around her and kissed her, gently. It was a welcome-home kiss, full of happiness and satisfaction and joy. When she wrapped her arms around his waist, it turned into a bedroom kiss, and the open street was no place for that; he was having trouble keeping his right arm free and near his gun and his eyes open and scanning the street. Her kisses made him forget to stay watchful and wary, made him forget that there was a world full of people who wouldn't mind seeing him dead. And with him dead, who would protect her?

Jack eased himself out of the kiss as slowly as a man leaving home for the last time.

"Come on, Anne," he said softly, his thumb brushing against her jaw. "I need to talk to Lane and I want you with me."

Her eyes glowed bright at his words and she linked her arm in his and walked peaceably by his side down the street to the sheriff's. Hell, she'd follow a bear into his cave on his promise to share the honey.

Lane was glad to see him.

"Gates sent me a wire."

"Then you know what happened," Jack said.

"Jack, the whole town knows. Bill Tucker got in before you, remember?"

"Yeah, I remember," he muttered, offering Anne the seat he usually took. There wasn't another. Lane remained standing as well.

"Anne, you might not want to hear the rest of this," Lane said.

"She's staying with me," Jack said softly, resolutely. There was no arguing it. Charles studied Jack and then shrugged.

"Tucker's pretty fired up about this murder and getting anyone he can to listen to what he has to say. He doesn't have any trouble getting people to listen, not the way things run around here."

"No law against talk," Jack said.

"No, but when it builds folks up to a lynching, then it gets troublesome."

"I can take care of myself," Jack said quietly.

"What is it that Bill is saying?" Anne asked.

"Now, Anne, I told you, you might not want or need to hear this," Lane said, looking at Jack as he spoke.

"She's already heard the worst of it," Jack said. "Somebody's already told her about Elsa."

They all knew who had told her and told her not one bit reluctantly.

"I can't believe that Bill would do something like that," she said, believing it anyway. "And why would anyone believe Jack killed that girl?" She'd set Jack against Bill and Bill was taking his revenge. The load of guilt she toted for playing one man off against another just got heavier.

"Elsa," Jack said. "Her name was Elsa."

"Elsa," Anne repeated absently. Why was Jack always adamant that these girls be referred to by name? Maybe because he had known them? The thought stirred and twisted, like a flea in the straw, scratching and hopping in her mind. Unwelcome.

"You're going to have to start believing a lot of things you'd be more comfortable not knowing," Jack said.

Anne had nothing to say to that.

"What'd you find in Junction City?" Lane asked.

Jack leaned against the wall and hooked his thumbs in

his waistband. "The same as before. Nothing different."

"Gates told me as much."

"Seems like a good man."

"He is. How was he taking it?"

Jack shrugged. "The best he could. Keeping a good, tight lid on things there, from what I could see. Elsa's ma, she's taking it hard. That girl was all she had left in this world. It's going to be hard for her to get along now."

"Gates let slip in his wire that you'd given the ma a roll of bills and were trying to get her on the next train east."

Jack shrugged again. "Just trying to help. There's nothing for her here now and she'd be more comfortable with people who can at least speak her language."

"Bill didn't tell me that," Anne said.

"Bill didn't stick around long enough," Jack said tersely.

"Any sign of who did it?" Lane asked.

"Just the same as before. No one knew she was seeing anyone; can't get much out of the mother, so we don't know what she might have been told."

"Well, I guess we'll hear more from Gates as soon as he knows anything. He's sending wires all over, trying to hitch up with the marshal."

"Good," Jack said, leaning away from the wall and coming to stand behind Anne. "I'll take Anne home now. I'll be back."

He wasn't going to tell Lane all the reasons he thought that Tucker had done it, not with Anne sitting there. And there might be some questions Lane would have for him, like how come he happened to be in Junction City just when there was another murder? Lane wouldn't want to have that talk in front of Anne, not the way he protected her. Hell, they all protected her. She inspired that sort of thing. Not that it would do her any good. She needed to learn how to protect herself.

He and Anne hadn't gone far down the boardwalk when Isaiah Hill clumped up to him.

"You ain't finished your business in Abilene yet?"

"No, I ain't," Jack said and kept walking, keeping Anne at his side.

"Anne Ross," Hill rasped, "you were brought up better than to keep company with a man like this. Is this how Miss Daphne taught you?"

"No, sir," she said softly, keeping her eyes on the ground and her feet moving.

"I'm a guest in this lady's home," Jack said coldly, "and I'm escorting her home."

Isaiah Hill spat and walked on.

"You get your hands off that girl," Powell said, coming out of the dark interior of his stable to face them. "And you do your manhandling somewhere besides the back of my building!"

"Kissin's not a crime," Jack said softly.

"It is when you do it on my property and with a girl who should have better sense than to be seen with the likes of you!" Powell was so angry that his pipe fell from his mouth; he caught it with one hand and stuffed it in his pocket.

"Anne's a woman grown, Powell, and she can walk out with anyone she fancies. I ain't forcin' her," Jack said.

"I ain't convinced o' that an' even if it was true, then someone should warn her about them other gals who was walking out with the wrong sort."

"Then warn her," Jack said, pushing past him. "I ain't stoppin' you. I'm trying to warn her myself."

That left Powell speechless long enough for them to leave him behind.

Anne was more flustered and embarrassed than she had ever been in her sheltered life. And Jack knew why.

He waited until they were about fifty yards from her fence before he asked her, "Do you think I did it?"

"No" was her first response and then she frowned down into the dirt. "I mean, I don't think so." She looked sideways at him to see if he was offended. He didn't look it.

"Go ahead, say what you're thinking."

She hardly ever heard that. In fact, she never did. No one ever encouraged her to say what was on her mind, because if they did, there just might be a tussle. No one went looking for a fight, except maybe a bounty hunter.

"It's just that, well, people seem to think you might be the one . . . though there's no proof of it. Is there?"

He shook his head. "No, there's no proof it was me."

"But then, there doesn't seem to be any proof that it isn't you."

"That's right," he said easily, looking down at her, the wide brim of his hat leaving his face in full shadow. "It could be me. I could've killed them gals. They got mixed up with the wrong sort of a man and got killed for it. You think about that now," he said.

"If you'd done it, you wouldn't be talking like this."

"How do you know? You know how a killer talks? How he puts you off his trail? How he builds your trust, strand by strand, until he's got a rope thick enough to strangle you with?"

She backed up, suddenly edgy. His face was shadowed and his voice had gone dark.

"You think you can save your life by backing off a step? Why, I can lay hold of you any time I want, Anne. All I need do is reach out."

He pulled her to him by the back of her neck, his palm rough and warm against the soft skin of her nape. She tripped toward him, reluctant, yet coming on. Unable to stop. Maybe even unwilling.

"How you gonna save yourself now, Anne?" he said softly.

She could see his eyes now. They were cold blue, but the pulse in his throat beat hot. He was cold and hot and she didn't know whether to run or stay.

Was this how those girls had felt just before the air had

been shut off, the need to breathe rising up so strong that only the hand of their killer had been stronger? She felt the rise and fall of her breathing, forced and heavy with Jack standing so close. And still she didn't move away.

"You come toward me and you're coming toward death," he said. "Can't you see that?"

She couldn't see anything, anything but him. Her breathing came fast and hard, as if she were trying to save up for when she couldn't breathe anymore. For when he kissed her.

She stared up at him and she didn't see death in him. Not a bit. She watched his mouth, studying the slant and shading of his lips, the clean white of his teeth, the dark shadow on his upper lip where his beard would be the thickest. But she didn't see death.

"Lord, you're a bigger fool than I am," he breathed. "Back off, Anne. You got a pinch of sense, you'll back off."

She did have sense. She'd made up her mind long ago to have sense. She wasn't going to be the kind of woman who needed a man. She wasn't ever going to be that big a fool.

But she didn't back off.

Jack let loose of her neck and took hold of her hand.

"That's it," he said. "I'm going to teach you how to drive a man off. And you're going to do it, too. No back talk."

Back talk? She followed him obediently to the livery, where he picked up Joe and rented a mare for her. She didn't even say a word when he rode with her out into the wide silence of the prairie.

Maybe she was as big a fool as he'd named her.

They were only a few miles out of town, but they could have been fifty miles from anywhere. The sun was high and the wind cool, but it was sunny and there was no sign of rain, so there was nothing to complain about. April in Kansas could be troublesome. The prairie stretched out all around them, a golden green sea of emptiness, the only sound the stirring of the wind in the long grass.

They were alone. He was armed. He was mad. And she still wasn't afraid.

She was ripe for killing. He was going to make sure, here and now, that she stayed alive.

"Take my six-gun. It's heavy and there's no way to carry it polite-like, but it does the job," he said, handing it to her, empty of cartridges. He wasn't a fool to hand a woman a loaded pistol.

"Why?" she asked, holding her hand out and taking the gun.

"Because you're going to learn to shoot, that's why."

"I am?"

"Yeah, and we're starting today," he said. "I'd give you a rifle, but I know you'd never carry it." Plus, the killer would be up close and a rifle was no good for the shooting she was going to have to do.

"I don't need to learn to shoot."

"The hell you don't," he muttered. "You take this gun and you do what I tell you. You do what I tell you and you just might come through this alive."

"You don't need to cuss at me," she said.

"Glory, is that Anne taking me to task? You just might survive if you learn to fight back a bit," he said, his smile hard.

She smiled slowly and then looked down at the gun in her hands. It looked mighty big in her grasp. That was good. A nice, big bullet would come firing out of that barrel.

"It's heavy," she said.

"Yeah, but you'll get used to it since you'll be carrying it all the time from now on."

"I couldn't possibly carry this all the time."

"Yeah, you could and you will. I do. I don't have a problem with it."

"Well, it's your job."

"And now it's your job to keep yourself alive. Don't make me name you a slacker. This is one job you'll do well."

"I'm not a slacker."

"Good, then this will be easy for you."

She looked up from the gun and stared into his eyes. He could read her confusion and it pulled at his gut. He looked down, ignoring his guts and everything else.

"You know what those girls all had in common, Anne? They were pretty, they were looking for a man, and they were unarmed. I can't help your being pretty, but I can take care of arming you."

"I'm not looking for a man," she said softly.

He jerked his head up to look at her. "No? You do a good job of acting the part."

She just looked at him, her blue eyes soft with shame.

"What?" he asked.

"Nothing," she said, lowering her gaze.

He wasn't going to hunt that rabbit now. It might have been that she wasn't looking for a man, that they just came after her without her doing anything to herd them in. She was pretty enough to get that from a man. Hell, he'd been ready to follow her after that one look on the platform when he'd rolled into town. But that wasn't the problem now. He had to teach her to kill the man who came after her before she got killed herself. That's all he was about. He wasn't going to spend time with her doing anything, thinking anything, else.

Yeah, and when did he get to be such a good liar?

"You know what a gun is for, Anne?"

"Of course. It's for shooting." She held the gun down at her side, the metal buried in the folds of her skirts.

"Hell, no," he said. "It's for killing. A gun was made to kill. You remember that. You pull this gun, you shoot to kill. Don't you ever pull it out and not pull the trigger. Don't you ever leave it unloaded. An unloaded gun won't help you. Might as well carry a hammer. Understood?" He said it harsh and he meant to be harsh with her. She had to toughen up. She was so soft, she was going to die of it.

"Yeah," she said, sticking her nose up in the air. That was good. He wanted to get her back up some. Looked like he was doing a good job of it.

"Good. Now, we'll try some dry-firing, to get you used to the idea. Then we'll put in some rounds."

"Fine," she said.

She was looking at him hard, like she was trying to work herself up into a burst of anger. All to the good. Now, if he could only get her not to apologize for it later.

"Lift it up," he said. "No, don't hold it straight-armed; you don't have the strength for it. Bend your elbow, turn your body sideways, makes you a smaller target."

She did it, but she looked stiff, the gun an awkward thing she held away from herself. Had he ever looked like that? He couldn't remember. He'd been carrying a gun for as many years back as he could count. He felt as natural holding a gun as breathing; in fact, it was because he was so good with a gun that he was still breathing. It was a hard world and a man had to be hard to get along in it. He knew that. How was it that Anne was still so soft in a world so relentlessly hard? He couldn't figure it, but he was going to fix it. He wasn't going to have her death on his soul or carry the image of her broken body in his mind for the rest of his days. No, sir. He was going to save her by teaching her to save herself. That was the best way. It was the only way. He wouldn't be around forever and she'd have need of the skills he could teach her.

"Go ahead and pull the trigger. Try not to move the gun," he said.

She pulled the trigger and the gun wiggled in her hand like a snake she'd caught up.

"You're moving the gun," he said.

"It's heavy!" she said, lowering it.

"You won't notice it after a while, that's a promise," he said, standing beside her and taking the gun from her hand.

"I don't need a gun," she said, looking up at him. Her eyes were the blue of the sky after a long winter. She had oatmeal-colored freckles on her nose and along her hair-line. She looked like a girl headed for trouble and he was a man who had a habit of chasing trouble. But he wasn't going to chase her.

He wasn't going to kiss her.

Yeah, he was turning into a first-rate liar.

"What do you need, Anne?" he asked, his mouth inches from hers. " 'Cause I ain't got nothing to give you, Lord knows."

"I don't need anything," she breathed. "Not a gun. Not you. Not anything."

"No? Not anything?" he said, inching down toward her mouth. Her lips were pink as penny candy, soft and warm. "Not even a kiss?"

"No," she whispered.

"You sure about that?"

He touched his mouth to her temple, trailing his breath down the soft ridge of bone that made her cheek, toward the gentle mound that was her mouth. Her lips opened and she sighed, the air brushing against his ear.

His hands came up, skimming her torso, sliding up over the swell of her breasts. She rose into his hands and sucked in a hard breath.

"You sure, Anne?" he breathed against her mouth, his hands on her breasts, feeling the weight of her, the heat

213

that came through her clothes to burn his hands.

He wanted her. He'd wanted her from the moment he saw her, her sky-blue eyes staring at him as he laid hard hands on an outlaw. He wasn't for her. He was too rough, too close to being an outlaw himself, for him to get anywhere near her soft innocence. Yet here he was, with his hands on her and his mouth on her and all his thoughts circling like dirty crows in the clean blue sky of her. He wanted to blame her for letting him get too close, but it was he. He was to blame. He couldn't make himself walk away from her. She would have to be the one to do the walking and he'd have to make her see that that's just what she should do.

His hands slid up to her throat and her eyes closed as she tilted her head back for the kiss she thought was coming. He almost did kiss her. He almost gave in to the sweet vulnerability of her exposed throat and softened mouth. But he didn't. He didn't kiss her. He gave her something else. Something he prayed she wouldn't ever forget.

He pressed his hands to her throat and tightened his grip, the feel of her pulse hot and strong under his fingertips. He could feel the life in her slowing as her eyes flew open, wide blue in the shock white of her face.

"What you gonna do, Anne?" he whispered, his voice coming harsh from the back of his throat. Her breath was flattened by the strength in his hands; he could feel her dying and he watched her as she tried to pull away.

"Not enough," he said, staring down into her eyes. "Not near enough. I got you good. How you gonna get loose of me? How you gonna save your life?"

"Stop," she said on a squeak.

"Make me," he said, feeling the heat of her, the pounding of her heart, the flutter of panic just beneath her skin.

She pushed against him. He didn't move. It was nothing, two little hands without any weight behind the push; she couldn't shove him off.

"I'm too strong for you," he said. "Or you're too weak. Either way, you're mine."

Her eyes were going red and she was tearing up. He wouldn't let it stop him. She had to understand just what it was she was facing. He was death. Anyone under heaven could see he was death and danger and aching solitude. There was nothing else to him. There was nothing else in him.

"Fight me, Anne. Take your life out of my hands. Fight back," he urged, giving her enough air to breathe, giving her the will to fight.

She kicked him. He grunted. It was a good solid kick, but his boots took the worst of it.

"Kick me in the knee. Kick hard. Try to make it pop," he said.

She did and she missed.

Her hands came up and pried at his thumbs, trying to pull him off. His hands were stronger than hers by a long mile; she wouldn't get him off that way.

"Use your thumbs," he said on a growl. "Try to take my eyes out."

She did, she did try, but he turned her in his arms so that he held her from the back, her arms trapped beneath his. She couldn't reach his eyes. He had her good and there was nothing she could do about it.

"What do you want?" he whispered against her ear.

"Let me go!" she whispered.

"Hell, no!" he breathed, taking in the warm, sweet scent of her. "What do you want?"

She was crying, but she was still fighting him, kicking and twisting, her hair tumbling down, covering where he had his hands on her. But he still held on. He still had her.

"The gun!" she said on a choked sob. "Give me the gun!"

"Damn straight," he said, letting her go.

She backed away from him, her hands to her throat. First smart move she'd made since he'd met her. Why it bothered him, he wasn't going to consider.

"You got a man on you and you want to get him off? You need a gun," he said. "You don't wait, you don't think, you don't wonder. You just flat-out pull that gun and shoot him. He comes in close, you press that barrel to his middle and you fire."

Her tears hung like rain on her cheeks, wild and soft, but she was nodding. Accepting. Believing.

"I don't care how heavy that gun gets. I don't care if you know him or not. I don't care if he comes on you from behind and you never even see his face. You pull that gun and you fire. You fire until you got nothing left but air in those chambers. You empty that gun into him. You got that, Anne? Understood?"

He could feel the weight of something rising up in him and he swallowed it down, blinking it off and away from him. He had nothing to give her but this. He'd protect her if he could. If he couldn't, he'd give her the means to protect herself. That's all. That's all he had.

"You all right?" he asked, taking a step near her. She backed up a step and he let it stand.

"Yeah," she said. Her voice sounded soft and high, like she was fixing to cry.

"I didn't want to hurt you, just scare you," he said, taking off his hat and hitting it against his leg. "How'd I do?"

"You did good," she said and he could hear the smile in her voice, though her face was still wary. That was good. Being wary was always good.

"Yeah, I scare lots of folks. It's about time you joined the herd," he said, smiling back at her.

"You want to scare people?" she said, walking toward her mount, not taking her eyes off him, keeping her distance. Smart.

"Yeah, certain people," he said, walking parallel to her,

keeping the gap between them open and wide. "Makes it easier. They don't fight so much."

"I thought you liked to fight," she said.

"I don't like it. It's just that I don't mind it. Fighting has its uses."

"Like what?"

He shrugged and put his hat back on. "Like keeping the outlaws away from the innocent. I'll fight for that. It's worth a bruise or two."

"I guess," she said, looking down at the prairie grass at her feet.

"Anne?" he said, stopping. She stopped and looked at him. "Some things are worth fighting for. You need to figure out what those things are."

She blinked and let out a soft breath and then she smiled. "Well, until I do, how about showing me how to fire that gun?"

She got the hang of it pretty quick, once she got over the noise of the explosion when the hammer hit the rim. Turned out, she was a pretty good shot, when he could get her to keep her eyes open.

"Don't worry so much about aiming, just point and shoot." Anything she'd be shooting at would be right close to her, but he didn't want to hammer that point in too hard. "And empty it, don't leave bullets for him to fire at you. You fire one shot, he gets the gun out of your hand; then he's got five to pump into you. Don't do him the favor. Let him use his own weapon, don't make it easy for him to use yours."

"All right. I get anybody in my sights, I'll keep firing until there's nothing more," she said. "I'm going to be real ruthless, I keep spending time with you," she said, grinning, holding the gun like it was a thing she was afraid to touch. Yeah, she looked real ruthless, all right.

"Yeah, you can form your own gang of outlaws; then I'll come hunting for you."

Her smile wavered and then fell. "I think I'd like that."

"What? You going to turn outlaw?"

"No," she said, shaking her head slowly. "You hunting for me, coming after me."

Damn.

"No, you wouldn't like that," he said, trying to figure a way to make her believe it. "Nobody wants a bounty hunter on their trail."

"Not a bounty hunter," she said, her voice a mere whisper. "You."

This wasn't good. Not what she was saying. Not how she was looking. And not how he was reacting to it. He wanted her. He wanted her and he could see the day when he'd track her south of hell just to touch her again. Just to look into her eyes. Just to feel her breathe into his mouth.

"Not smart, Anne," he said softly, looking down at her.

"I know. Not smart. And I was going to be so smart," she said, her voice a small whisper of sound lost on the wide tumble of the prairie.

He wanted to . . . hell, he wanted to hold her against all the trouble in the world and keep all of it from touching her. He wanted to hold her, to touch her, to be the wall that stood between her and pain. And he couldn't do any of those things. He couldn't. He knew he couldn't. Trouble was, he still wanted to. Even knowing that all he could do was fail, he still wanted to.

A woman did strange things to a man; made him want to be bigger than he was, made him want to rise up and be better. Just for her. Because of her.

He was a damn fool.

He took a step toward her and she matched him, closing the gap between them, her eyes soft and wet with emotion.

"Ain't you afraid?" he asked.

"Not of you," she answered. "Never of you."

He took her in his arms and groaned. She laughed, a hiccup of sound that she buried in his shirtfront.

"You laughing at me?" he asked, pressing her against him, his chin resting on her hair.

"No, I'm laughing at me. How smart is this? How smart am I?"

"You can still be smart," he said, knowing he was giving her good advice, holding his breath against the chance that she'd take it. Maybe he wanted her to be as big a fool as he was. Yeah, maybe that was it. He didn't want to be in this alone.

"It's too late for that," she said, and she pulled his mouth down to hers and kissed him.

It was too late for that. She was past smart. She was walking the same road her mother and her aunt and even her grandmother had walked. She was tossing away everything she had—her freedom, her good name, her plans—for a man. Because she wanted a man who was plainly not the right man. No, it was more than want. It was need. She needed him. She needed Jack Scullard.

No, it wasn't smart.

She was repeating the pattern she'd sworn for ten years that she'd break. And for the first time, she understood just what it was that made a woman give it all up for a man. Suddenly, she had a whole lot of sympathy and understanding for the women in her family. It was hard to stand against the depth of this sort of need. No, it was impossible.

But shouldn't she at least try?

Jack's kiss deepened and her thoughts sank to the pit of her stomach and rolled there, useless and empty. The wind brushed her skin with a tenderness that was odd for wind; her skirts brushed against her legs enticingly, caressing her, and she swayed to the sensation; the feel of his lips on hers was exquisite torture, so soft, so demanding, so drugging. She could hardly see. She could only feel, her senses sharp, her hunger great. Her resistance gone.

It was Jack who ended the kiss. It was Jack who always ended the kiss. With a lopsided grin, he brushed her tumbled hair back over her shoulder and then walked her to her horse. Without a word, he helped her mount. Without a second look at her, he headed them back toward town, his hat pulled low against the dropping sun.

They didn't say a word as they rode across the prairie and into Abilene. Nothing was said as they handed off their mounts to the boy at the stable. They kept their silence as they walked to her house and then they were at the door.

"You keep that gun with you and you keep it loaded. Wear a belt around your waist and tuck in it that. I don't have a holster that would fit you. No arguments," he said.

"No arguments," she said, looking up at him. His eyes were so intense, his expression so severe, and he was so beautiful.

They walked into the house together and Jack went back to his little room, the thud of his boots marking his passage. Anne went into the kitchen where the women were gathered.

"We heard him come in with you," Nell said. "You'd think he'd have the decency to take off his spurs before walking over these wood floors."

"I wouldn't expect anything approaching decency from that man," Daphne said, pouring herself a cup of coffee.

Anne waited for Sarah to say something in Jack's defense. Sarah said nothing. In fact, Sarah looked almost as worried and disapproving as the others.

"You met him at the train, I suppose," Daphne said.

"Yes, I did."

"Well, I don't suppose that could be helped, but you need to keep your distance from him. In fact, I'm going to talk to Charles Lane this afternoon and see if he'll put up Mr. Skull in his jailhouse. I would think those accommodations would be more than sufficient for a man of his ilk. Bill must be extremely distressed to know that a bounty hunter is staying in the same house with you. I should have put my foot down about it when he first showed up at our doorstep, but Christian charity forbade it. But now that there's been talk as to his guilt in all these murders, and while I wouldn't think of judging a man without benefit of all the evidence, I think it would be prudent to keep our distance. After all, we are judged by the company we keep."

Anne knew what she was supposed to say. She knew what she was expected to say. She just didn't want to say it. It was wrong. It was all wrong and she didn't want to keep quiet about it, though that was the path that would keep the peace. Maybe, just maybe, some things were worth fighting for.

"Jesus consorted with sinners, tax collectors, and adulterers," she said softly, trying to keep the trembling out of her voice. "I don't think a person should be judged by anything other than his own behavior, and Mr. Scullard's behavior in Abilene has been fine, just . . . fine."

"Anne!" Nell said in disapproval.

"Sheriff Lane doesn't think Jack is guilty of anything and he's the law," Anne continued, her resolve growing with each syllable.

"Charles Lane has been very contrary lately," Nell sniffed.

"Well . . ." she groped. "The sheriff in Junction City didn't think Jack was guilty either or he wouldn't have let him leave town!"

"Even if he's not guilty of these horrible murders," Daphne said, her voice as brittle as an icicle, "he's stepped past the bounds of propriety. I didn't want to mention this again because I didn't want to shame you, but we've already discussed the flagrant impropriety of his kissing you. The fact that this immoral act took place in full daylight and in public only makes it worse. But, Anne, what is worse is that you've changed since that man came to town. You're not the sweet-tempered woman you were reared to be. You're becoming ill tempered and disobedient. I don't have to think twice as to the cause. Bad company breeds bad ways."

Anne looked at Sarah, searching for another voice to defend Jack. Sarah did speak, but she said the wrong thing.

"He is a bit wild, Anne."

She'd lost Sarah as an ally. Anne drew herself up, her hands clasped in front of her more in nervousness than resolve, and said shrilly, "I kissed *him!*"

"Nonsense, Anne," Daphne dismissed.

"Excuse me, ladies," Jack said, sticking his head in the door. "I'm sorry to interrupt, but I was wondering who to thank for washing out my things while I was gone last night."

Nell blushed red. "I did it." It sounded like the most abject confession. Under the circumstances, it was.

"Thank you, Miss Nell, that was kind of you. Of course I'll pay you for the service, if you don't mind. I like to pay as I go." He pulled out a stack of silver dollars and set them on the table.

It must have been twenty dollars, too much money for room, board, and laundry. It was more cash money than they'd seen in six months and all their eyes were focused on it, shining delicately on the table, as if they thought it would disappear if they blinked.

They needed that money. Jack knew it. They knew it. Galling as it was, they needed the money more than their moral pride.

"Thank you," Miss Daphne said formally, reaching out to pocket the money safely in her own apron. She breathed a sigh when she felt the weight of it and heard the muffled clink of coins bumping together.

The three older women eased away from facing Jack, embarrassed and maybe a little ashamed. Jack just smiled and jerked his head for Anne to follow him to the front of the house. She followed him on shaky legs; the confrontation in the kitchen had been both worse and better than she had ever believed possible. Worse because she still felt sick to her stomach for disagreeing with her grandmother and mother and aunt. Better because she was still breathing and hadn't been thrown into the street. Yet.

She was still catching her breath when Jack leaned her against the front door and gave her a quick, hard kiss on the mouth. His arms bracketed her, trapping her against the door, sheltering her from everything that existed outside of his arms. Sheltering her from the whole world. She knew it was a lie, that a man couldn't and wouldn't protect you from anything, but she wanted the lie. She threw herself into it, trying to forget she knew the truth about men. She wrapped her arms around his waist and snuggled against him, starting the kiss again when he would have ended it. Keeping the lie alive with her very breath.

Softly, fully, his mouth met hers. He closed the distance between them until his leg was pressing against the wedge of her thighs. Some instinct told her to keep her legs tight together. Just as softly, the kiss ended.

"That was real hard for you, I know," he whispered.

Dazed and groggy, she shook her head. "No, I like it."

"I mean back there, in the kitchen." He grinned, brushing his index finger down the planes of her face, from temple to cheekbone to jawline. "I thought you did good, nobody was getting the better of you."

"You did?" She grinned back.

"I did." he smiled. "But don't do it for me, Anne. Do it for yourself."

Do what for herself? Get in scrapes that only made the people around her mad? What good did that do? It seemed likely advice from a bounty hunter; he made his wages getting into scrapes. She wasn't going to listen to him. He was a means to an end, that's all, and she wasn't going to forget the end. And if she liked his kisses in the meantime?

Thinking that, she stood on tiptoe and kissed him quickly on the mouth. He not so quickly kissed her back, wrapping his arms around her and pulling her tight against him. She'd never felt so safe in her life, but that wasn't a thought she could let sit. Men only promised safety, but the promise was a lie. A lie. A lie, but this kiss was so real. Something this real couldn't be a lie. And if it was?

If it was, she'd take from him what he could give. She wouldn't let it go any further than kisses. She'd hold the line there. She would. She still needed him to hold Bill off and now she needed him to teach her to shoot. So she needed him for a few things. That didn't mean she couldn't live without him.

Nibbling on her lower lip, he gradually ended the kiss. Almost. He came back once more for a firm kiss of finality, which she met with blatant eagerness. In the end, it was Dammit scratching at the door that ended all kisses.

Jack readjusted his hat as Anne opened the door. Late afternoon sunlight poured through the opening with the dog, who only snarled briefly in passing through the house on his way to the kitchen and his snack.

"I'll be back," Jack said, walking out. "And, Anne? You shouldn't keep letting me kiss you."

He was right. She shouldn't.

Chapter Eighteen

"He's never talked to me like that before. I wish you could have been there to hear it."

Sarah smiled as she swept the floor. "I wish I had."

"In all the years I've known him, he's always been polite, attentive, considerate," Nell said, wiping down the bread board.

"Ignored," Sarah summed up.

"I am a married woman," Nell snapped.

"You sure about that? Tim Ross could be dead five years now, hell, how long's he been gone? Ten? Fifteen? He could have died the day he rode out for the last time. I'd say you're single."

"Sarah! Watch your mouth!" Nell looked guiltily out the kitchen window to where Miss Daphne was watering her morning glories by the back fence. Too far for her to hear what went on in the kitchen. "How long you been cussing?"

"Since I figured out that I'm a single woman, too. My man's been gone about seven years and I'm just starting to think that makes me about as unmarried as a woman can get."

"I think it's because you've been talking to Jack Skull."

"That, too." Sarah grinned.

"Everything's different around here since he came to town," Nell said, hanging up the dish towel next to the stove.

"I'd have to agree," Sarah said. "Bill's paid more court to Anne in the last week than he has in the previous month. And then there's the way Charles has been acting, if what you say is true. . . ."

"Oh, it's the truth, believe me! I haven't been talked down to like that by a man since, well, since . . ."

"Since Tim was around?"

"I'd rather not discuss it," Nell said a little stiffly.

"I don't blame you," Sarah said, slipping an arm around her sister's waist and giving her a quick hug. "Let those memories stay dead, as dead as I hope he is."

"That's not a very nice thing to say."

"Maybe not, but it's the truth and I felt like saying it. For once."

"What's the matter with everyone lately?" Nell sighed, frowning. "First Anne and then Charles and now you."

"We could blame Jack." Sarah grinned, putting away her broom and taking off her apron. "Or we could thank him."

"Thank him? What for? I know it's because of him that Anne's got her back up and Charles near bit my head off."

"And for the first time in years, you're looking at him twice. Now, I do think Jack's too wild for Anne. I meant that, but if he's the one who put a touch of bite in Charles, then maybe it's a good thing he came to town."

"I am not the least bit interested in Charles Lane," Nell said, her posture stiff and forbidding.

"Well, then, in the spirit of all this free-talking that's been happening around here, you might just want to tell him that."

Nell faced her sister, her arms crossed and her chin up. "I just might."

Anne walked into the middle of it, when her mother was as fit to fuss as she'd ever seen her. Anne had about had the fight kissed out of her and was not eager to renew the battle concerning her interest in Jack Scullard. Anne's lack of eagerness didn't matter a thumbnail to Nell.

"I suppose he kissed you again," she began, more angry at the moment at Charles and his presumptions than with her daughter and a stolen kiss or two.

Anne fought the blush that heated her breasts and throat. "I kissed him," she said as forcefully as she could manage. She was using Jack; she wasn't going to let him take the blame for it. At least not without a bit of kick.

"Don't be ridiculous, Anne. You know I'll never believe that about you, though I am willing to believe that he didn't force you. You are attracted to him, that's obvious enough, though I can't see why."

"Have you really looked at him, Nell? Beyond the stubble and the guns he carries?" Sarah asked.

"Of course I've looked at him and what I see is a hard man with a dangerous reputation."

"Nell," Sarah said with a crooked smile, "you've been without a man for too long."

"Nonsense. In fact, in some ways, he reminds me of Tim."

"Jack is like my father? How?" Anne hardly remembered her father; he had left for good before she was five.

"You know I don't like to discuss your father, but, yes, some things they share."

"Like?" Anne pressed.

"Like"—Nell stalled—"they both hunt men and seem to get a good deal of pleasure out of it."

"And?"

"They both have that quality, that toughness caught up with shy charm, that women find so attractive."

"It sounds like a bad thing."

It did. She didn't want to tangle with a man who was like her father. That meant she really was following the same trail her ma had. How many nights had she lain in bed, crying for the home and the pa she'd lost, vowing that she'd never let it happen to her again? Enough nights to make her attraction to Jack impossible. But she didn't need him, not that badly. It was only attraction. She wasn't going to let it go any further than it already had. But she wasn't going to be put off just because her mama didn't like him.

"It is," Nell said softly, turning away from her daughter. "I want you to stay away from Jack; he's not right for you."

"I think he is," Anne said quietly, but there was a firmness to her reply that made both older women sigh in frustration. "And I *did* kiss him."

When Nell turned around to argue further, Sarah spoke.

"You go on, Nell, and have your talk with Charles. I'll talk with Anne. I feel responsible for this, with my meddling."

"Fine." Nell sighed, smoothing down her hair, preparing for her next battle. Lord, life had been so much more peaceful before Jack Skull had come to Abilene. "Thank you," she said as she left.

Anne faced Nell with all the openness of a penned mule.

"I *did* kiss him," she repeated.

"I believe you," Sarah said. "And I'll bet my shoes he kissed you back."

Anne failed completely to contain her blush. "He did."

"Man would be a fool not to and Jack Skull is no fool, but, Anne, he's a man grown, hard and dangerous, just like your ma said." Sarah held out her hand and kept talking before Anne could interrupt her with arguments. "Don't fool yourself, Anne. Just 'cause a man knows how to talk sweet, it doesn't mean he'll be sweet. How do you think he got the reputation he has? Being nice? No, he's killed time upon time and learned to trust no one. If a pretty girl shows him that she likes him, well, he'll take her up on it and who can blame him? I don't and I'm the one who put him on your trail. But, Anne, I wanted you to have a proper courting, with more than one fella knocking on your door. You've had that. But your real beau is Bill and Jack might be scaring him off. You don't want that 'cause Bill's the one who'll marry you. Jack's not the type."

"How do you know?" she asked.

She didn't want to marry anyone, but how did a woman know when one man was the marrying kind and another wasn't? If her aunt could see that in a man, why couldn't she see it in her? She wasn't the marrying kind and all they talked about was when she was getting married.

"Experience. I've seen too many like him. Your pa for one. Roy for another. Even my own pa; he could charm prairie dust into lying quiet in a tornado."

"That sounds more like Bill than Jack; he'd more like shoot the dust out of his path."

"Maybe so," Sarah said, "but he's the man who's got himself tangled up in your blood and that's the difference. You want a man you can manage and that's not Jack."

That wasn't any man. A man just couldn't be managed, not reliably and not well. She knew that, even if Sarah didn't. That's how she was smarter. She had to be smarter. She wasn't going to end up like all the women of her family, losing her heart to a man, giving herself to him in marriage, and then getting left. No one was going to leave her. Not again. Not ever again.

She was going to be the one to do the leaving and she just wasn't ready to leave Jack yet. Not just yet. And he wasn't tangled up in her blood either; no such thing.

She'd cut him loose when the time was right. She still needed him now to push Bill off, that's all. Her blood had nothing to do with it. She was smarter than that.

"He was there, but I never did see him with Elsa, just Widow Blake, who was healthy when I left her," Jack said.

Charles leaned back in his chair until he was propped against the wall. "Yeah, it looks bad, him being there and there being another killing. Course, you were there, too."

"I wondered when you'd get to that," Jack said easily, leaning back in his own chair in the sheriff's office.

"Couldn't ignore it, not and do my job."

"Yeah, I guess not."

The silence filled the space between them, each man thinking of what had to be asked and what would be answered.

"You do it?" Lane asked.

"Nope," Jack said.

"Didn't figure it that way, not when you been doing so much talk about finding the killer. Doesn't figure, to pull down so much attention on yourself. And this killer, he don't make his courting known. You haven't exactly made a secret of what's going on between you 'n' Anne."

"And what do you figure is going on?"

"A mighty fine courting, if you're an honorable man."

"And if I'm not?"

Lane shrugged and banged his chair legs down on the floor. "A man could get hanged for doing what you're doing to a girl like Anne."

"What am I doing?"

"Getting her thinking of marriage, for one."

"For one?"

"For two, getting her ready for what comes after."

Jack grinned and lit a slim cigar. "You must think my kisses are real convincing."

Lane snorted. "Don't matter what I think. It's Anne

you're firing up. You've got that gal strung from here to Kansas City, obvious as moonlight on snow."

Jack got up and walked to the door; it was time for supper and he was hungry. And he was tired of talking about Anne, a gal that was using him for her own ends without a thought to him. Yeah, she was a nice girl, but nice girls had their own weapons. Trouble was, she didn't have the first idea what she'd stirred up in him and he wasn't thankful for it. Not a bit. Wonder what she'd do if he acted on all the urges she'd sparked in him. Might be fun to find out.

"Do I need to get a rope ready?"

"Only if you want to pull her off me. I didn't start this."

"Meaning?"

"Meaning I'm on the job till her aunt pulls me off. Marriage was never part of the deal," he said and walked out the door.

Jack missed Nell by five minutes, which was just as well. She'd come for Charles.

She'd combed her hair, gotten herself a fresh handkerchief, which was lightly sprayed with precious cologne, and brushed the worst of the dust off her boots. Charles noticed every bit of it and tucked his shirt in a little tighter. Then he finger-combed his hair. Then he pushed in his desk chair and they faced off, like the two adversaries they suddenly were. She started it.

"I came to see if you want to apologize."

"Apologize? For what, Nell?"

She sniffed her reluctance and turned away from him slightly, giving him her profile. "For being unnecessarily unkind to me before."

"You mean when I wouldn't let you join that necktie party forming up on the street for Jack? Excuse me, Nell, but I don't let the kind of wild talk that was going on out there build any wind. It's a wind that kills and has nothing to do with the law."

"You're doing it again."

"So are you."

They didn't say anything for a while after that. Nell was regrouping and Charles was waiting for the next assault. It came.

"You never used to talk to me like this before, before *he* came. You used to be so polite and kind; I always felt I could count on you, Charles. I always thought we were friends. Old friends."

He couldn't help thinking just then about how well Jack was doing with Anne after less than two weeks. He'd known Nell for the better part of twenty years and wasn't half so far. Could be that Sarah was right; Jack knew how to commence a courtin'.

"You did? Old friends, huh? Why, I can remember times when you wouldn't say hello to me if you bumped into me on the street. Is that what old friends do?"

"You know I never did any such thing," she said.

"I know damn well you did."

"Stop cussing. Is that how you talk in front of a lady?"

"What is it you want to be, Nell, lady or friend?"

He'd moved closer to her, the long length of him towering over her. She'd never quite realized how tall he was or how muscular. His body was still hard, his stomach flat, even after all these years. She pulled her own stomach in and lifted her chin.

"I would hope that I could be both," she said.

"Or you could be something more," he said gruffly, crowding her until she found herself backing up. Her breath lifted up into her chest, and stayed there.

"Nell! What on earth are you doing in here with the sheriff? I'm certain he has important business to see to," Daphne snapped from the open doorway.

"And I'm seeing to it right now," Lane said, still looking at Nell. She felt her nipples rise up against the fabric of her cotton dress.

232

"Charles Lane!" Daphne barked. "My daughter has better manners than to loiter in a jailhouse with no proper escort. This is hardly appropriate—"

"Miss Daphne," Charles interrupted, "I've got things to say to your daughter and I'd like to say them in private. If you'll excuse us?"

"I most certainly will not! If you have anything to say to my daughter, you will do so in the proper way at the proper time and—"

"Miss Daphne? I ain't waitin'. Nell will be home later."

He ended the conversation by slamming the door in the old woman's face. Nell was speechless, her breath rising to get caught in her throat; she'd never seen Charles like this before, why, he was almost . . . wild.

Daphne was far from speechless.

"Charles Lane," she said from behind the closed door, "your manners have gone straight to the devil since that bounty hunter came to town."

Charles slid home the bolt without once taking his eyes off Nell. Leaning back against the door, he crossed his arms and smiled.

"Yes, ma'am, Miss Daphne. Yes, ma'am."

"Heard you were back," Shaughn O'Shaughnessy said, putting the beer down in front of Jack.

"I'll bet you did," Jack said, reaching for his drink. "You serve food here? I'll pay you double not to have to go to the Demorest." He wasn't feeling up to staring that woman down just to get a plate of grub. It was shaping up to be a long day.

"Yeah, my ma'll serve up something sometimes, something simple; not like what you'd get at the Demorest."

"I'll take it," Jack said. "Whatever you've got."

"I'll tell her."

O'Shaughnessy was back after a few minutes with a plate of food.

"You got lucky; this just came out of the skillet."

The plate was piled high with beefsteak and fried potatoes seared golden brown.

"Thank your ma for me. It's a nice spread."

Jack took the plate and sat at one of the gaming tables in the corner of the room. The old man who usually slept there was gone. O'Shaughnessy swept the floor behind the bar. The saloon was empty but for the two of them. Jack couldn't have been happier.

"I ever tell you that my ma, she thinks your name is kinda familiar?"

"No." Jack shoveled a mess of potatoes into his mouth. He was real hungry.

"Yeah," Shaughn said, leaning on the broom handle and looking out at the street. "She's got a head for names and yours struck her like a ringing bell."

"Yeah, well," Jack said over the steak in his mouth, "she's not the first to know my name."

"Nah"—Shaughn grinned, looking over at Jack—"not your handle, your real name, Scullard. She's sure she's heard it afore."

"Well, tell her to pass it around," Jack said and took a swallow of beer. He was damn tired of being known as Jack Skull; never did much like it and it was growing real thin about now.

O'Shaughnessy went back to his sweeping. "She'll worry over it till it comes to her, and it will. She's got a head for names."

"I heard," Jack said over a thin smile.

"Heard about that gal over in Junction City."

"Elsa."

"Yeah. Terrible. Heard it was just like the other one. What'd she look like, anyway? Pretty?"

"She looked dead," Jack said, pushing away his empty plate. He wasn't going to talk about that woman as if she were nothing but news.

"Junction City, that's right close to Abilene. It's a mercy no one in Abilene's been killed yet. You think that murderer is going to try for one of the girls here? You think Abilene might have a murder?"

All he could see was Anne, her dark hair limp in the dirt, her blue eyes closed forever because of a purple slash across her throat. Anne, who was too trusting to push a man away when he got too close.

Jack stood up abruptly, making his chair squeak back along the floor. "No. There's not going to be a killing in Abilene." *Not while I'm breathing.*

He paid O'Shaughnessy two dollars for the food and the beer and walked out, right into Anne.

"There must be a train due in," he said, catching her arm.

"There is, the Union Pacific from Salina," she said. "Care to come?" She'd seen Bill over at the dry goods store. Was it her fault that she'd have to walk by there to get to the train? It certainly wasn't her fault that Jack had offered to walk with her. Some days, you just got lucky.

"Yeah, I've always wanted to see a train out of Salina," he said wryly, holding her by the arm and escorting her down the boardwalk. "Must be somethin' to see."

"It is!" she said, grinning. "This one has a red cowcatcher and blue wheels and the brakeman wears a red-striped hat." She was laughing, teasing, a thing he'd yet to see her do. What was that about? He looked around for Tucker; she sure was putting on a show for someone and she didn't need to smile and tease for him to trail after her.

He was as good as roped and tied and she was holding the iron that'd mark him.

"I just gotta see a man who wears a red-striped hat," he said, pulling his hat down low so that his eyes were in deep shadow beneath the brim.

She laughed, looking up at him, her smile wide and

unguarded. She was leaning into him, her shoulder brushing his chest. He leaned away and kept rigid, getting a tighter grip on her arm to hold her off. She was too easy with herself, too loose and free with her laughter and her closeness. It was too easy to want a woman who acted that way. Too easy to think you could have her, to believe she wanted you the way she was teasing you to want her. She didn't want him. She wanted Tucker. She smiled at Tucker, too.

Had Elsa smiled up at the man who had killed her?

Had Mary?

Who'd watch out for Anne when he left town? Who'd keep her safe? Not Miss Daphne, she kept her like a dog chained in the yard, confined but not protected. She needed to use that gun he'd taught her to shoot and not be sparing with the rounds. Hell, maybe she couldn't afford to buy another box and would be too cautious in her firing. There was no protection in a gun if a body wouldn't squeeze off a few rounds.

Hell, he'd buy her another couple of boxes, just so she'd have enough. Maybe even take her out to the prairie again, for target practice. Maybe just hang close to Abilene until he was sure she was safe. Safe. There wasn't a safe place in this world, especially not in Kansas, especially not for a woman. Especially not now.

Maybe he could settle here, keep an eye on her for a while.

Jack shook himself mentally. It wasn't going to play out that way.

That wasn't the game he'd signed up to play. Sarah had made it pretty clear that his job was to get Tucker to sit up and take notice. Well, he was sitting straight enough now. That meant he was about out of a job, at least the job Sarah had in mind for him. But he wasn't leaving Anne to face the killer on her own.

"Where's that gun I gave you?" he asked.

"I didn't have a belt strong enough to hold it. I'll get one. I'll wear it. Tomorrow."

"You do that," he said. If he had to buy her a belt to hang a six-gun on, he'd do that, too.

He wasn't handing Anne over to Bill, with a gun or without it. There was something about that one that set his fingers itching. He wasn't leaving Abilene until he had Tucker pegged down and dried out.

"How long you been keeping company with Tucker?"

The smile got wiped right off her face. She stopped looking at him to look down toward the station.

"Not long. I really don't know him well at all."

"Funny. The other night you seemed to know him well enough."

"Well, when he's in town, we . . . we see each other some."

"Yeah? How often's he in town?"

"Oh, I don't know."

"Don't tell me you don't know when your regular beau's in town."

He was getting mad. He couldn't help it. She'd kissed Tucker; told him so to his face. Rubbed his nose in it; not a real friendly thing to do.

"He's not my . . . regular beau. He's just courting me."

She was starting to fuss with her hat. She wasn't leaning into him anymore. That was good. It went better for him when she kept her distance.

"So, how often is he around to court you? How often is he gone?"

"About as much as you," she said, a little sharply for her.

He had to tuck his head to hide a smile. Anne fighting back always made him feel good, like maybe she'd come out of this whole thing alive.

"So, he's like me? How else is he like me?"

They had almost reached the station. The stationmaster

was keeping an eye on them, but there wouldn't be anything to see, not this time. Anne was mad enough to keep her distance.

"I didn't say he was like you," she said, looking down at the ground as she walked, her pace no longer strolling and playful, but brisk.

"No? He don't hang around you, like me? He don't kiss you, like me? He don't get invited in to set in your parlor, well, hell, that's not like me, is it?"

"I told you," she gritted out, climbing the steps to the platform, "he's courting me."

"And what am I doing, Anne? Am I courting you?"

"I don't know what you're doing," she said in a near whisper.

The hell of it was, he didn't know what he was doing either.

He wanted her, but he knew that she was playing a game with him as the pawn to get her proper beau to propose. He wanted to keep her safe from a killer on the prowl, a killer who went after girls close enough to touch a wedding day and no sense to protect themselves. He wanted her to want him just as badly as he wanted her, but she didn't and the whole town was pushing her away from him and Anne was just the sort of person to let herself get pushed. The only thing Anne wanted out of him was his kisses; she seemed to have a real firm attachment to his kisses.

And the trains. She had a true passion for meeting each and every train that rolled through Abilene. Why?

"Who are you waiting for, Anne? Who's going to get off this train one day?"

She kept her posture and her face composed, but she didn't turn to face him. No, she kept looking at that train.

"I'm not waiting for anyone."

"Then why come?"

"I just do. I've been coming here since . . . since, well, since we got here."

"What do you think about when you watch these folks get on and off the trains? You think about leaving?"

She took a deep breath and turned to face him, her eyes bright and glistening. "Yes, I think about leaving. I want to get out of Abilene someday and it'll take a train to do it."

"Is that what I'm for? To get you out of Abilene?" he whispered harshly. It sounded true and fit what he knew. He was being used, by Sarah for her purposes, and by Anne for her own. It didn't matter what he wanted. Nobody cared what he wanted.

Damn, but she looked guilty.

"No," she said quickly, then, "I don't know. I've never told anyone before. They all think . . . I don't know what they think. But I want to get out. I want to leave," she said, her voice hard.

"Where do I fit into that? You want me to buy you the ticket? You want an armed escort? Hell, I'll ride with you as far as . . ." *Forever.* "Dodge. You want to see Dodge? Rough town. A girl like you needs a man like me to keep the scum off, right? Is that what I'm for? Is that what you got in mind for me?"

"I'm sorry," she said, her eyes soft.

"I just knew there'd be an apology in there somewhere," he bit out. "You been doing a lot of thinking, sounds like," he just about snarled. "Ever think about what I wanted? What I'd like?"

"Well, of course, I just thought," she stammered, getting a pretty little blush going, "I mean, I thought that we . . . well, you have kissed me."

"Why shouldn't I? You keep letting me!"

Her eyes flared at that and good, hard anger took the place of embarrassment. "I'm not letting you. You're just doing it!"

"Doing it all by myself, am I?"

"I . . . I . . . I thought . . . there've been times when you . . . just last night, you, by the door."

"Hell, I thought you were asking me, the way you were actin'."

She blushed red and clasped her gloved hands together like she wanted to strangle something. Probably him.

"I didn't know that's how it looked. I'm sorry."

"Damn it, Anne, if you're mad, be mad. Don't apologize for every damn thing."

"Don't you cuss at me! And you don't have to kiss me, either!" she snapped.

She turned around and stomped off like a stallion who's had his face kicked one time too many. He watched her walk off, her bustle bumping with each and every step, that little white bow bouncing.

"At least she didn't apologize for that," he said to the air.

They rode into town from the other end, so Jack missed their arrival, not that he'd known they were coming. He'd come north on his own, used to working alone, needing no one. At least that's what he thought. These two thought Jack Skull just might need a bit of help, even if he never did ask for it.

Emma Walton saw them first, living on the edge of town like she did, and recognized them for what they were straight off. She hustled her kids out of the yard and into the house and shut the door before anyone could ask her anything. Once she had her back against the door, she could admit that she wasn't surprised; bad company followed after its own.

Powell came out of his livery and watched them ride silently and sedately into town. He wasn't fooled for a minute. They had the same look as Jack Skull, hard and well armed and used to trouble. At least they had their own mounts.

Sheriff Lane was talking to the doc about nothing in particular when he saw them. He may have been the only person in town who was glad to see them, with the possible exception of Doc Carr, who thought they might just be the men to gun down Jack Skull for that string of murders.

Not likely, since they were his closest friends.

"Howdy," Lane said from the boardwalk.

"Howdy," the dark one answered. The fair-haired man didn't say anything. Lane wasn't alarmed; some folks just weren't talkative.

"Looking for somebody?" Lane asked.

"Yeah, trailed him up this way," the black-haired man said, remaining seated, his hands resting easily on his saddle horn. He could afford to rest easy, his partner was keeping watch while he kept his mouth shut. "Looking for Jack Skull."

"He's here," Doc Carr offered quickly. "Staying just down the road."

The black-haired man smiled and said, "Thanks. Looks like you're eager to get rid of him."

"I'm not," Lane said, taking control of the conversation. "Come on in. We'll talk. Doc? I'll see you."

"Thanks again," the man said, dismounting. Only when he was on the ground did his partner dismount. They watched out for each other carefully; an old habit and one they had no wish to lose.

"Name's Lane," he said, motioning them into the jailhouse.

"Callahan," said the talkative one. "And this is Gabriel."

"You've traveled a bit, looks like," Lane said.

"Not without reason," Callahan said.

"What's the reason?"

"I think you know. If you don't, I'll talk to Jack first,"

Callahan said without any attempt to be polite. Lane didn't mind.

Callahan was taller than most and lean as a whip with shoulders like a young bull's. Black hair hung straight down to his collar. His eyes were matching black and his features lean and hard. For all that, he didn't have the look of a man with Indian blood, not that it would have mattered. With the way he carried himself, Lane couldn't think of a man who'd challenge him.

Gabriel was slightly shorter and built like a man who'd laid track for most of his life. He was thick with muscle and hard as brick with sandy hair and dark blue eyes. It didn't look like he was much of a talker.

"I know," Lane said, offering the two men a drink. It was a lucky thing that he had four cups and had just washed two of them. They took the proffered cups silently, showing their appreciation by how fast they drank it down. "We've had three up here, all recent."

"All since Jack's been here?" Callahan asked.

"Yeah, or thereabouts. None in Abilene."

"Not yet," Gabriel said. His first words. Not pleasant ones.

"Not ever, if I have my way," Lane said, taking a drink for himself.

"I hope you get your way, at least on this," Callahan said.

"Jack expecting you?" Lane asked.

"He would if he had a lick of sense, which he don't," Callahan said with what passed for a smile.

Lane smiled back, a half smile to show he understood. "I take it you're friends?"

"Yes," Gabriel said. It was almost a challenge.

Lane just chuckled. "He needs 'em 'round here; there's a whole herd of folks who'd throw him on the next train, if they thought they could get away with it."

"They couldn't," Callahan said.

"And they know it," Lane said. "That's why he's still here."

"That and the murders," Gabriel said.

"Yeah," Lane said without any trace of a smile.

"Any clues?" asked Callahan.

"Nothing to speak of," answered Lane. "According to Jack, they're all about the same; pretty girls, strangled, no one knew who they were seeing on the sly. The marshal is working the outlying areas while all us sheriffs are holding the towns. The last one was in Junction City. Gates is taking it pretty hard."

"No one takes it easy," Callahan said.

"Especially Jack," Gabriel said.

"Yeah, he takes it right hard, every time. You know why that is?" Lane asked.

"His story, not mine," Callahan said. For the talkative one, he could hold his tongue when he had a mind.

Lane nodded his acceptance of that answer, understanding the depth of friendship that would provoke it. These men wouldn't betray a confidence, real or perceived, and that spoke well of them and of Jack.

"How'd you hook up with Jack?" Lane said, pouring more drinks for them all.

"We were in the Rangers together before the war," Callahan said. "Drifted together afterward from time to time."

"And now's one of those times?"

"Yeah," Callahan said, tipping up his cup.

"What about you, Gabriel? You meet Jack in the Rangers?"

"I knew him some before that," he said.

Lane nodded and drank. Gabriel wasn't going to offer more, that was clear.

"So, where's Jack?" Callahan asked. "Looks like the last hotel in town is burned out."

"You know the Cattlemen's?" Lane asked.

"I've been in Abilene before." Callahan shrugged.

"Punching cows?" Lane asked.

Callahan smiled slightly and shrugged in answer, not really answering at all. Lane let it drop.

"Jack's staying with a family of ladies at the edge of town; they offered him a bed."

"A family of ladies?" Callahan said, smiling. "How old are these ladies?"

"One old, two middling, and one young," Lane said.

"The young one offered him that bed, right?" Callahan laughed.

"Yeah," said Lane. "Why's that funny?"

"It just is," he answered. "Sounds just like Jack."

"She's a nice girl," Lane said, all traces of humor rubbed out of him.

"I'm sure she is," Callahan said, "and she'll stay that way. He knows what he's doin'."

"Yeah, it sure looks like it." Lane scowled.

His conversation with Nell hadn't worked out like he'd hoped. She'd been silent and sullen, refusing to talk to him. She'd looked about ready to slap his face when he came right out and told her he was nothing like Tim Ross, that he wasn't the sort to run out on a woman, that he was a better man than the first man she'd chosen. Not even a bolted door had held her in then; she'd shot off out the door and down the street before he could figure out what he'd said wrong. Wouldn't a woman be glad to know that the man who wanted to court her wasn't the kind to run off when the pasture looked better on the other side of the river? Whatever it was that Jack said to Anne, he sure didn't get that kind of response; no, Anne hung on Jack like a halter. Whatever Jack was doing, he knew how to do it.

"Thanks for the drinks," Callahan said as he and Gabriel set down their cups.

"It's nothing," Lane said. "That house is—"

"We'll find it," Gabriel said.

Lane watched them leave, long legged and heavy with guns. He didn't doubt but that they would.

Chapter Nineteen

She'd been an absolute fool and she wasn't going to be one anymore. She was going to be smart and the smart thing to do was stay away from Jack Scullard. He was pure trouble. Unmanageable. Unpredictable. Dangerous. Hadn't he almost strangled her? He surely had and she'd smiled it off, making pleasantries with him, being polite when she should have been aiming that gun of his right at his middle. That's what a smart woman would do. That's what she would do if he ever came closer to her than a quarter of a mile. For all she knew, he could be the killer and all his talk of teaching her to protect herself mere playing on his part.

A killer would do something like that, toy with his victim before strangling her. Sure he would. Killers were capable of anything. Jack was capable of anything. Anything except being manageable. All she'd wanted was a man to force Bill off; that's all he'd had to do, and he'd messed it up by kissing her too often and too well. Well, she'd manage on her own. She'd get rid of Bill and she'd do it without any help from Jack; Jack was causing more trouble than he was saving. Just like a man.

She'd get Bill to back off and she'd do it her way, nice and gentle and permanent. She wasn't getting anywhere she wanted to be by having two men buzzing around her like horseflies. That had been ill conceived.

Jack would be easy to avoid. Wasn't he always telling her that she ought to keep her distance? Wasn't he always taunting her about wanting his kisses? Well, she'd take his advice. He ought to be real happy. She sure would be.

Getting rid of Bill was going to be a bit more of a mouthful, but she'd do it. She had to. She wasn't going to let him slither his way into her life and into her bed. She'd leave town first and, knowing Bill, he wouldn't follow. He wouldn't be able to find her if he did. Now Jack, if Jack made up his mind to track her to Chicago, he'd find her. She knew that.

It was a good thing he wasn't going to want to find her.

It was a good thing she was going to keep her distance from him. He was pure, undiluted danger. Any fool could see that. And she wasn't a fool.

Except with him.

She'd wanted him from the moment she first laid eyes on him. Just like that. She'd wanted to walk right up to him and curl up in his arms, sure she'd be safe forever. He'd had the look of a dangerous man, there was no lying about that, but she hadn't felt the smallest prick of fear, even though she could see that he was a man who should be feared and was. For her, he'd been safety, rest, home.

That's why she had to keep her distance. He was danger. He made her want things she'd decided long ago never to want. She was going to keep to herself, living life on her own terms and with her own company.

All she had to do was find Bill and make that clear to him.

* * *

She found Sheriff Lane instead, or he found her. He had the look of a man who'd been searching her out.

"Anne, there you are," he said, taking her arm and walking with her into his office.

The light was murky inside, dust floating in the air and sparkling like fairy powder. What Abilene needed was a good rain to settle the dust. Sometimes mud was better than breathing in dust.

"Hello, Sheriff Lane," she said. "Were you looking for me?"

"Well, not hard, but I did want to talk to you," he said, holding the chair for her.

She sat down, aware of the solid weight of him at her back. How long had she known Sheriff Lane? For as far back as she could remember, seemed like. But for all that, they weren't real close.

Why was that?

"Yes?" she said, turning her head slightly, wanting him to move into her line of vision.

He moved slowly to his chair and sat down.

"I wanted to talk to you about Jack."

"Oh?"

He shifted his weight, reached over to open his desk drawer, and then slammed it shut without taking anything out.

"Yeah," he said. "Now, Anne, Jack is . . . well, he's mighty rough."

"Not any rougher than any other bounty hunter, I guess," she said.

"Well, no, maybe not, but his reputation—"

"He's good at what he does and folks know it. Is that what you mean?" she said. She was fighting him, softly, politely, but she was doing it.

It felt pretty good.

"Now, Anne, you just let me say what I got to say," he said.

"I thought I was helping," she said with a smile.

"I don't need no help to say this," he said, rocking forward in his chair and leaning across the desk. "You ought to keep your distance from him. He's not the sort for a girl like you."

"A girl like me?" she said, leaning forward, closing the distance between them. "What kind of girl is that? You think I'm not smart enough to handle myself with a man—"

"Now, I didn't say any such thing," he said, rubbing the wood with his hands. "He's just not your sort. You got to know that yourself."

"I don't know that I think I have a 'sort,' Sheriff."

"Why, of course you do. A girl like you, with your face and, and your pretty ways, could get any man," he said. "There ain't no doubt to that."

The room seemed darker all of a sudden, as if a cloud had passed through the endless dust to hide the shimmering sun.

"Thank you, Sheriff," she said. "You don't need to worry about me, though. I'm not interested in Jack Scullard, not the way you mean it."

He leaned back in his chair, his expression easy and relaxed. "I knew you had good sense, Anne. I just felt it was my duty to talk it out with you. I'd hate to see you hurt."

"I don't want to be hurt, that's a fact," she said, rising to her feet. Sheriff Lane rose with her. "The thing is, I think I do all right at keeping myself out of trouble. Don't you?"

"Well, sure you do, Anne, sure you do. It's just that Jack—"

"Thanks for the advice, Sheriff. I'll keep it in mind," she said. She walked to the open doorway, glad for the wind and the sunlight of the open street. "I guess you're going to talk to Jack, too, warning him off me? I guess you should. I could do that man a serious hurt, don't you think? A woman with my pretty ways can cause a man some problems, if she puts her mind to it. Good afternoon, Sheriff."

Yeah, it felt real good.

"Anne? How are you?" Doc Carr said.

He had come out of his office, buttoning his vest as he did. He looked fine, standing in the cold spring light, his hair dark and shining with oil. He was a man who took pride in his grooming, that was sure; his boots were always polished and his shirts pressed. He never let his beard build on up him, like some men she could name. He was a good doc, too. Abilene had sure needed him.

"I'm fine, Doc. Just fine," she said, nodding her greeting.

"That's good to hear. I've been worried about you, what with that bounty hunter in town and all those murders piling up. You have a care, won't you?"

"Sure I will. I'm not going to get in any trouble," she said. And she sure wasn't. She was throwing that bounty hunter out of her life and Bill along with him. She'd be just fine once she got clear of men and their troublesome ways.

"No woman means to get in trouble, Anne," he said, taking her arm as he stood with her on the walk. "But it happens. I'd hate to see anything happen to you. You light up this town, you know that?"

"No, I didn't know that," she said, easing his hand off her arm. "But it's nice of you to say."

"Nothing nice about it. I'm a doctor; I can see what's under my eyes."

He smiled as he said it, and he had a real nice smile, warm and welcoming; she just didn't feel too warm in return. Every time she had someplace to go, someone just had to slow her down.

A Kiss to Die For

"You sure can talk sweet, Doc. No wonder your patients don't complain," she said, moving away from him.

"You keep clear of Jack Skull and you won't have cause to complain. You keep him away from you and you'll be all right," he said, his eyes serious.

"I think I'm all right now, Doc. I surely do. But thanks for the advice."

"Howdy, Anne," Shaughn said as he swept off the walk in front of the saloon.

She just never was going to find Bill at this rate.

"How're you, Shaughn? You seen Bill anywhere?"

"Nope, not today. Though it's early. Listen," he said, leaning on his handle, smashing the bristles of the broom into the wood. "You doing all right?"

"Just fine," she said. She must look like something hung on a cow's tail, with all this talk coming at her. "Why?"

He shrugged, his shoulders heaving the fabric. He was a well-muscled man; it would be easy to go to seed standing behind a bar most of the day, but he hadn't let it happen. Still, he was fairly young. He might thicken up like two-day stew in a year or so.

"Jack Skull's been trailing along after you pretty good. That's got to put a girl on the sharp end of a quill. Then with all them murders . . ."

"It's a sin and a crime, that's for certain. But you don't need to worry about me. I can take care of myself."

She really was going to need to start wearing that gun. It was the hard truth that a murderer was hunting unmarried girls. And she was going to stay an unmarried girl. That about put her at the top of whatever list he might be working on. Of course, he might not be anywhere near Abilene.

Then again, he might be in Abilene.

Anne shivered and crossed her arms over herself.

"A spring wind sure can blow cold, can't it?" Shaughn

251

said, stepping closer to her. Anne took a step back and when the flush of guilt swept over her at such an overt act of rudeness, she ignored it.

"It sure can. I'd better get on, Shaughn. Miss Daphne is going to be put out with me for dawdling when she expected me home half an hour ago. Give my best to your ma."

"I surely will, Anne," he said to her back as she walked away. "You give that Jack Skull a wide range, now. He ain't no man to be messing with you. You take care of yourself."

Oh, she would. She was going to start by standing up for herself more. It hadn't been so bad and there was even a certain amount of fun in it. She was going to finish by getting that gun and strapping it to her side. She just might pistol-whip the next person who tried to tell her whom she could talk to and whom she had to keep clear of. She got plenty of that at home from Miss Daphne; she didn't need it from every man in town, too.

No, things were going to change some. She'd found something worth fighting for: her own independence. It wasn't going to be a revolution, but just a quiet and dignified little revolt. She was going to take care of herself good. And she was going to start with Bill, if she could only find him.

Bill got found, but not by Anne.

Miss Daphne cornered him as he was leaving the bank, grabbing him by the arm as if he were her escort. He wasn't escorting her; he was listening to her while she clutched of his arm.

"I'm going to do you the courtesy of speaking honestly with you, Bill. I think we know each other well enough for that."

"Why, yes, ma'am," he said, "and it pleases me—"

"Just shut your mouth until I have my say, Bill. I'm

going to assume that your intentions to my granddaughter are honorable because I believe you to be an honorable man."

When Bill looked like he was going to open his mouth to say something, a sharp look from Daphne made him close it.

"I think you and Anne have a fair understanding of each other, having spent the better part of a month keeping company, so I'm going to tell you straight out that if you intend to ask her to marry you, you'd better stop playing around about it or that bounty hunter is going to cut in on you and steal your girl. If you want to marry my granddaughter, you'd better see it done and done quick. Do I make myself clear?"

Bill could only stare down at her, his eyes wide and his mouth slack.

"Close your mouth," she snapped.

"Yes, ma'am," he said instinctively.

"Well?" Hard brown eyes looked up into his, waiting.

"Yes, Miss Daphne. I want to marry Anne," he said firmly, once he'd swallowed down his shock.

"Then get to it. That bounty hunter is like flies on honey with her. You either snap her up or he will." And with a flurry of skirts, she marched on down the street toward home, leaving Bill, in every sense of the word, in the dust.

Which was where Anne found him, standing in the dust of the street, watching her grandmother sail toward home.

"Bill?"

He whirled as if she'd whipped him.

"Anne! I've been looking for you." He smiled.

"Here I am." She smiled back. "I've been looking for you, too."

"Shall we walk? I have something I've wanted to say to you for days now." Bill took her arm and led her down

253

the street, away from her home in the distance. "I kept hoping for the right moment, wanting everything to be just the way I had it in my mind."

"What do you mean?"

Here she'd gathered up her courage to face him on her own and tell him he could commence courting someone else and he looked to be digging in even deeper. Of course, she could be reading him wrong.

"Oh, moonlight and flowers; the way a woman likes things. But I don't want to wait any more to get it right; I just want to get it done. Would coffee in the middle of the day be all right with you?"

No, she hadn't read him wrong.

They were ten steps away from the Demorest when he made the offer, so she nodded and let him lead her in. She could end things just as well in the Demorest, she didn't have to do it out on the street. He drew out her chair with a gracious smile and patted her hand when she sat down.

Jack never patted her hand. Of course, Jack never pulled her chair out for her, either. Jack's big skill was in kissing her. Unfortunately for her, it was a skill he'd perfected.

Didn't matter; she was going to give him a wide range now, too. She was done with men. They made a mess of a woman's life.

Everett Winslow brought two cups to their corner table and poured out the coffee. Bill was declining sugar when Everett set the bowl in front of Anne; she liked three teaspoons with her coffee. Bill never seemed to be able to remember that.

"Anne," he said, pulling her hand across the table to rest in his. His hands were soft; nothing like Jack's, which were tanned and calloused. "You must know how I feel about you." His blue eyes twinkled. Jack's eyes, of a much clearer blue, never twinkled; they glittered like broken glass in the sun. "I've spent enough time with you to know what a lovely girl you are and what a respectable family you come from. If it wasn't for your aunt's dog . . ." He smiled, chuckled, really. He meant it as a joke. It was a joke that fell flat on the table between them and lay as dead as a bee in January.

If Jack ever had call to ask her to marry him, would he want her to be lovely and respectable and without a dog named Dammit? Would Jack call her a girl when he always treated her like a woman?

It didn't matter what Jack would or wouldn't do, or what Bill was doing either. She was done with both of them.

Anne's answering smile faltered and she wanted to pull her hand back and put it safely in her own lap. Common courtesy required that she do no such thing. She bolstered up her smile and tried to relax.

"Pie?" Everett Winslow interrupted. "We've got apple and sweet potato; too early for any of the berries yet. And I think Emmie's got a custard in the spring house."

"No, thank you, Everett," Bill said. "We'll let you know when we need anything else."

Anne would have liked some apple pie; she never got any at home. But if Bill didn't want pie, she wasn't going to get any pie. She had a feeling Jack would have let her order her own pie.

She really wanted to pull her hand back.

"You must know that you're the most beautiful girl in Abilene," he said softly. That might have been true, but what was surely true was that she was the only unmarried woman in Abilene under the age of thirty. "And you must also know that I have never wanted to marry before. Before now," he amended.

He'd said it. He was going to ask her to marry him, even if it seemed as if he had to puff himself up with a whole lot of words to get the thing done.

For a man this hesitant, he ought to take her "no" real easy.

"Bill," she said, looking at the tabletop. Her fork had something crusted on the handle. "Bill, I'm real flattered that you'd ask, real flattered."

"You don't need to feel flattered, Anne, I'm just speaking the plain truth. A man would have to travel far to find a girl like you. I want you to be the mother to my kids, Anne. I want to hook my life up to yours, give you my name and my life. You want that, too, I know you do."

"Well, Bill, that's real sweet of you, but I don't think—"

Against everything he knew of decency, Bill leaned across the table and kissed her very lightly on the lips. "Say yes," he whispered. "I just know you want to say yes. You're mine, Anne, made for me. I know you want what I'm offering. I can give you everything."

He kissed her again before she found the wit to pull away from him. He kissed her hard and hot, his breath a weight that pressed against her mouth. She held her breath unconsciously and tightened her neck, resisting him, rejecting his taste and his scent. He eased off and kissed her softly, tenderly, a caress to convince and confuse.

It was nothing to get swept away over and it didn't carry her anywhere, not the least little bit.

Bill didn't seem to notice.

He was just walking into the parsonage when she found him. She had expected to find him at the saloon or with Charles. Finding him on the steps of Edward Holt's house had stunned her for a moment, but was not so great a shock as to render her speechless.

"I'm not as sure of you as I once was," Sarah said, stopping him cold. "You're a bit more than Anne can comfortably handle. Might be better all around for you to back off."

"I'll back off when that killer's caught," he said. "Anne, and you, are just gonna have to get used to me until then."

"What's one to do with the other?"

"Dead gals lying all around the country and you have to ask that?" Jack said, adjusting his hat. "I'm staying. Anne don't seem to mind me."

"With those kisses you're handing out?" Sarah said on a snort.

"Just doing my job," he said.

"Well, you're off that job."

"Then I'm on another. I'm sticking like a burr to Anne until that killer is as dead as those girls, and if I have my way, I'll take him out the same way he did them. That'd be justice," he said softly.

"I won't argue that," Sarah said, "but I'll fight you myself if you hurt that girl. She's not the sort to take to a rough-and-tumble man, not for long."

That was the truth. There wasn't any sort of quality woman who'd take to him; he was all wire and no cotton. But that was just what she needed to keep her out of harm's way. When that killer was caught, killed, and buried, then Anne'd be free of him. Not until then. It didn't take any time at all to kill a man, it was just taking too damn long to find this one. Tucker looked good for it and he'd be real happy to lay it on him, but something there didn't feel right. Tucker was too obvious. A man who killed on the sly was tough to pick out of a crowd. Tucker just about shouted to be noticed.

"Fine. When the killer is caught, then I'm out. But not until then," he said to Sarah. "Now, if I'm going to do my job, tell me where Anne is."

Sarah hesitated and then said, "She's at the Demorest."

He walked in just as Anne was getting herself kissed. She seemed to be enjoying it well enough.

Too damn bad.

From now on, the only one who'd be kissing her was he, whether she liked it or not. He had a feeling she'd like it well enough.

"Back off, Tucker. Anne needs kissing, I'll see to it."

Jack ignored Tucker after that and moved behind Anne's chair. He pulled it out enough for her to get up, 'cept she didn't move.

"Get up, Anne. I'm takin' you home," he said.

It was Tucker who stood, his face as red as sunburn and his eyes shooting fire.

"No, you're not," Tucker said loudly. Sure he was loud, there was a roomful of witnesses. "I'm having a private conversation with Anne—"

"Didn't look too private and it didn't look like talking either," Jack interrupted. "Anne don't need to have more conversations with you like that one."

"What Anne and I do is none of your concern!" Tucker was really yelling now, building steam for a big blow. Too bad he wasn't carrying; now'd be a good time to end the problem of Bill once and for all.

"It is now. I'm planning to marry her." Where that came from, he didn't want to know, but it would do the job of getting Tucker away from Anne for good and of getting Anne out of the killer's sights. Unmarried, unspoken-for women were what he aimed at. Anne wasn't going to walk around unclaimed anymore. And she wasn't ever going to be with Tucker again. He'd see to that.

Anne looked like she was going to fall off her chair. Jack grabbed her by an arm and urged her to her feet; if things were going to get rough, he didn't want her sitting like a stone in the middle of it.

"I'm proposing to Anne," Bill bit out, reaching out for Anne.

Jack pushed her gently behind him. He wasn't going to let Bill Tucker anywhere near her and now, he'd given himself the right to control her. Protect her. Just until he was certain she was safe. There wouldn't be a wedding. He'd have found the man he was hunting before there'd need to be a wedding.

"Sure takes you a stretch to build up steam, Tucker. Don't take much effort to open your mouth and let the words tumble out, unless you're not too sharp on the notion to begin with. Or unless you keep waiting for a private moment, say, out on the prairie? That what you been waitin' for?"

"I've been courting Anne—"

"On and off," Jack finished.

Tucker looked worn out with fussing and turned his attention to Anne. Jack kept her by his side. She stayed where he put her. Smart girl.

"Anne," Tucker said, "you know how I feel about you, the plans I'd made, the future I'd hoped for. I want to—"

"Tucker, you're all show and no go," Jack said. He put his arm around Anne's waist and pulled her to his side. She was warm and small and trim and he was suddenly more happy than he'd been in years. "I want you for my woman, Anne," he said gruffly. He hadn't planned on saying that, but it fit the moment. He had to convince Tucker and everyone else in the Demorest that Anne was his to protect. That was why he'd said it: instinct. Yeah, and he trusted his instincts.

In the place of Anne's response, he heard only silence. He turned enough to study her profile. She was looking at Tucker, but was leaning into him. And she wasn't saying a word.

It was on the edge of town that Sarah ran into Nell. Nell was on her way home. After realizing what she'd started, Sarah was on her way anywhere but home.

"You look like you just wrestled a bull to the ground. Or had another talk with Charles," Sarah said.

"It amounts to about the same thing," Nell answered.

"He's stuck his spurs into you again, has he?"

"Everything's gone wrong lately," Nell said with a frown. "Have you noticed that? Everything used to be so pleasant."

"You mean predictable," Sarah said. "And I don't think everything's going wrong." At least she hoped not. She really should have known better than to tangle with a bounty hunter.

"No?" Nell shot back. "Have you talked to Miss Daphne lately?"

"No, and that's why I'm not heading home any time soon."

"Well, I have, and got an earful about my conduct with Charles."

"What happened? And how did Mama get in on it?"

"Get in on it? She was shoved out of it. Charles slammed the jailhouse door in her face. And locked it."

"Oh," Sarah said, her eyes wide and her smile wiped clean. "I guess what I just did will be pouring kerosine on an already hot fire."

"What did you do?" Nell asked, her face going white in anticipation.

"I ran Jack down and gave him a push in the wrong direction; he's asking Anne to marry him right now, if I know men. And I do."

"Good Lord, Sarah," Nell breathed, her face going from white to ash gray.

"Yes," Sarah said back, her face losing some of its color in companionable empathy. "It's going to be pretty bad when she finds out."

"Maybe she won't find out."

"She will when Anne says yes."

"You seem sure she will."

Sarah smiled again, ruefully. "Oh, I'm sure."

"Mama will blame me."

"Why you? You didn't invite him to stay in the house or invite him to propose to your daughter."

"No, but after Mama heard me talking with Charles, 'loitering in the jailhouse' as she put it, she blamed me for setting a bad example for Anne by keeping bad company in 'inappropriate settings.' I'm sure to get blamed for it if Anne actually marries Jack."

There was nothing to say to that. A mood of gloom and desperation hung over them both. The wind kicked up, sending dust swirling in a large, thick cloud down the street. Nell hurried off so that she would be safely and innocently at home when the storm of Anne's proposal hit. Sarah hurried into the dry goods shop so that she would be far away when the trouble started, for it was sure to start at home and spread outward, like the retort of a rifle shot. The farther away she was, the less likely she was to get hit.

"Blowing up out there some," Neil McShay said as Sarah hurried in and closed the door behind her. "We may get rain yet this month."

"That'd make Miss Daphne happy; her spring flowers are struggling and you know what store she sets on a fine display around the house."

"I sure do." Everybody did. "Saw Anne walking by with Bill a bit ago," McShay supplied. "Looked like they were headed for the Demorest."

Sarah stopped brushing the dust off her skirts and said, "You didn't happen to see Jack trailing along after, did you?"

"That bounty hunter? What d' you care about him for? He's nothing for you to be thinking of."

"Now, Neil McShay, I'm not going to hear a word against that man." Especially since he was probably proposing right about now. Couldn't insult family. "He's holding down a job and he's interested in Anne and that's enough for any man to be."

"Oh," he said slowly. "Well, I guess that's Anne's business."

"You can say it is," Sarah said stoutly. She was going to get it bad enough from Miss Daphne, she wasn't going to take it from Neil.

"All right, I say it." He smiled in conciliation. "Now, all it takes for a man to be a man in your eyes is that he be working and interested? Why, Sarah, I'm a right nice-looking fella, when my hair's combed, own my own business, and . . . I'm interested."

Sarah blushed to the roots of her hair. She hadn't blushed since she was fifteen.

"You're blushing." He smiled. He had quite a winsome smile and a nice thick moustache. The blush picked up a little heat and stayed put.

"Why, Neil, your wife's been gone just three months now; this doesn't seem quite proper."

"It's been nearer to five and there's nothing improper about it," he said, coming around in front of the counter. Sarah backed into a barrel and kept on moving.

"Neil, you've got to have ten years on me. Don't you think you're a bit old to be chasing women around your store?"

"Sarah, I'm not *that* old. What do ya think killed Ida anyway?"

Sarah backed up against the bolts of fabric he had on the wall and edged to her right. Neil just grinned and kept coming on. She wasn't scared; actually, it was kind of fun.

"I'd heard she died in bed."

Neil wiggled his eyebrows and then winked. "That's right."

Sarah laughed outright and backed herself into a corner. If Mama ever heard about this, she'd think Nell's tussle with Charles mere shadow play.

A Kiss to Die For

"Neil, I don't have time for such nonsense. I've got to get Anne married."

Neil came as close as the circle of her skirts, reached up behind her, and pulled down a stick of hard candy. He held it in front of her as an offering, his twinkling eyes and his wide smile showing how little he was offended.

"Get it done, Sarah. I'll be here."

Sarah took the candy, wearing a grin as big as a painted doll, and slowly walked out of the store. She hadn't been so flattered in ten years. And she wasn't going to forget to come back to McShay's real soon. She was in trouble with Daphne anyway and her pa always said, "In for a penny, in for a pound."

Chapter Twenty

Anne could only stare at Bill, shock riding her hard and deep. She'd wanted the two men to drive each other off and all that had happened was that she was the bone they were fighting over. She should have known. Now she was staring at the worst possible outcome—direct conflict. This was exactly what she'd been trying to avoid. The tension and aggression between Bill and Jack was suffocating, oppressive, and she couldn't see a way to end it happily for all. Someone was going to be real mad at whatever she had to say. If she could think of something to say. Maybe, if she stayed real quiet and still, they'd work something out between them and she wouldn't have to say a thing. That was something worth wishing for.

She could feel Jack looking at her, but she didn't dare meet his eyes. She wasn't sure what she'd see, but looking into Bill's eyes was bad enough. He looked ready to burst with angry expectation and frustration. Poor Bill, he'd had a time of it since Jack had arrived.

There just didn't seem to be anything she could say that would make it all work out so that everyone was happy with her. Why hadn't she ever thought of this when she'd been playing Jack against Bill?

Maybe because when she was with Jack, she didn't think of Bill at all. But she couldn't ignore him now, not with him standing not three feet off, looking like he'd carry her from the place if she delayed one second more. He sure hadn't thought his proposal would end up this way or that he'd have to wait for her answer. Bill sure did like to get his way.

"Anne, you can't be actually thinking of refusing me? You have to know that I'm the better man, after all the time we've spent together . . . and he's just a . . . just a bounty hunter!"

"That's right, Anne," Everett Winslow chimed in. "Bill's a respectable man, make a proper husband for you."

"Anne," Bill said softly, "listen to him. I'm the man for you and you're the woman for me. You know that."

They were all talking at her, trying to convince her, telling her what to do. Only Jack was silent. There was something bone-deep pleasant about a man who didn't prod and push.

She looked at Jack then. He was still looking down at her, his face composed and easy, his eyes even a bit amused.

"I guess you haven't got anything to say," she said.

"Nah," he said slowly, "I figure you know what you want."

She sure did. She wanted to get out of here, out of this fight, out of Abilene. Jack was the only one who ever even gave a thought to what she wanted. He was the only one who ever gave her a minute to listen to her heart, to try to find out what *she* thought, what *she* wanted, and how to get it. He gave her room to breathe, to think, to move, without ever leaving her side. She didn't know how he did it, but there was a comfort to it that should have set her running.

She stayed put.

"Think, Anne, think about what I'm offering you and what he's got," Bill said. "Think about them murders and how they started when he came to town. Think about how he gave that gal's mama in Junction City money to get out of town, so there'd be no witness, no one to point the finger."

Even then Jack said nothing, though his hand tightened on her arm in silent anger. The fact that he didn't open his mouth to defend himself against such a wild claim made him seem all the more innocent. And made Bill look like a donkey that had his mouth open to the wind. Bill talked too much. It surely was starting to wear thin.

It was then that two men came in, men who looked like Jack in that they were strung with rounds of ammunition and heavy with guns. Jack nodded, but that was all. He didn't leave her side and he didn't let go of her. And he didn't pressure her for a decision, telling her what to think and what to say, just so he'd get what he wanted. A feeling of safety settled on her, comforting her.

But wasn't that always the danger of Jack?

"Problem?" the dark one asked the room in general.

"We're waiting for the lady to tell us just who she's going to marry," Jack said calmly.

"Who's in the runnin'?" the dark-haired man asked.

"Me 'n' him," Jack said.

"You?" the blond asked, his eyes wide.

"Me."

"Not much contest in that," the dark one mumbled, except that they all could hear him, including Bill.

"This man is Jack Skull," Bill snapped, "a bounty hunter and probably a murderer of young women."

"Hell, Jack don't hurt women, unless kissin's a crime."

Anne turned to him at that, her eyes wide and suspicious. That tore at the comfort she'd been feeling with

Jack. It sounded just like a man to run around the country, kissing anything in skirts. It was hard news, but she needed to hear it. It wouldn't hurt to have a long conversation with this stranger, getting all the details, just so she could remember not to trust Jack any more than she would any other man. That's what she'd do if she was smart.

"Shut up, Callahan," Jack said smoothly.

Callahan just smiled.

"You sure you asked her to marry you?" the blond asked. "That don't sound like you."

"Shut up, Gabe," Jack said with a tight smile, "the lady's got a decision to make."

"She's made it," Bill announced, coming to take Anne's other arm, uncomfortable at being so suddenly outnumbered.

Jack moved her behind him as quick as a June bug and faced Bill down. "I didn't hear her say nothin'."

"She will, if you get out of here," Bill said.

"I'm not leavin'."

There was really nothing for her to think about, not if she ignored what everybody else wanted and followed her own instincts. Bill was getting too wild to manage, too set on marrying. Jack Skull wasn't the kind to marry, but he was the kind to look for a fight just for the pure pleasure of fighting. It was all talk for him. Bill was serious. And there was no way out of this until she made up her mind between the two of them. She knew what she had to do and she'd just have a long talk, quiet and reasonable, with Jack about it later.

"Yes," she said quietly from behind Jack's broad shoulders.

Jack turned to face her, his back to Bill. "You sure?"

He looked down at her, his eyes blue and soft. He knew she'd been talking to him and he'd waited for her to decide, without pushing at her. That was a nice quality in a person, even if it all was just a pissing contest with Bill.

"Yeah," she said, surprised to find herself smiling.

He smiled back, as big as the sky, and her smile faltered. Mercy, but he was a dangerous man. It was hard to be smart around such a man.

"Lord, Anne, what will Miss Daphne say?" Everett groaned, throwing his apron down on a table in disgust.

"Who the hell cares?" Jack grinned.

Yeah, he was some dangerous man.

"Now that's settled, I could use some food," Callahan said, lifting his leg over a chair and easing himself down into it.

"And coffee," Gabe said.

"Anne! Think about what you're doing—" Bill whispered hoarsely.

"The lady's decided," Jack said, looking over at Bill, his hands on Anne's waist. "Don't make it worse on yourself."

Anne couldn't look at Bill; she felt too guilty at how she'd manuevered everything. She used Jack's body to hide herself as much as possible and she held her tongue, wishing Bill away. Jack seemed to read her wish.

"We're going to sit down for some pie; you want to join our party, you can stay. Otherwise, you can go."

He said it easily enough, but there was a note of command underneath and Bill heard it. They all heard it.

Bill grabbed his hat and shoved it on his head; even trying to avoid looking at him, she could see that his face was black with fury.

"You've just made the biggest mistake of your life, Anne. I only hope you live long enough to regret it."

"You leave now," Jack growled, "and I'll let you go unbloodied. You ever threaten my woman again and I'll kill you."

Anne shivered. He meant it. He meant every word. She'd never heard words thrown with such pure intent and straight meaning. Jack sounded like he wanted to kill

Bill and couldn't wait for the chance. But Bill walked out without looking back. And Jack let him go.

"Gettin' married has softened you already," Callahan said from his spot at the table. "I remember a time when it took less for you to kill a deserving man."

"I'm getting older, wiser," Jack said, escorting Anne to the table. "I don't want to kill a man when I'm about to have a piece of pie with my intended. Too messy."

"You are getting old." Callahan laughed, stretching his legs out. "When are you going to introduce us?"

"Anne," Jack said lightly, "this is Tim Callahan. And this is Chase Gabriel. Both from Texas. What they're doing here, I don't know," he finished in a tone just shy of condemning.

"Hello," Anne said softly, still coming to grips with the notion that she'd just said she'd marry Jack. He sure was talking like he'd meant it; Bill was gone. He could rest easy and let it all out as a joke, especially in front of his friends. That he was acting so serious about it left her speechless.

"Ma'am." They both nodded, Tim Callahan lifting his hat to her. Chase Gabriel just looked her over. She straightened her shoulders and lifted her chin, returning the look.

"Mr. Winslow," Jack called out, his arm on the back of Anne's chair, his nearness proprietary, "we'll have four coffees, four pieces of apple pie, and extra sugar."

Everett grumbled but he didn't hesitate, not when faced with the three men plunked down in his establishment. They were fighting men and looked every inch of it. Totally unexpectedly, Jack Skull had reinforcements.

The pie and coffee appeared without delay. Jack shoved the sugar bowl toward Anne. He didn't need to be reminded that she liked sugar in her coffee. Anne settled back in her chair, feeling slightly befuddled about her agreeing to marry Jack. She needed to talk to him quick, before news of it spread all over Abilene and landed at Miss Daphne's feet.

Callahan and Gabriel dug right into their slices of pie; Mr. Winslow wasn't slight on his portions, no matter how he felt about his customers. Jack just sat back with his arm around the back of her chair, a real satisfied expression on his face. He took his time and ate his pie one bite at a time; his friends ate theirs in two or three gulps, their cheeks bulging and their throats working. They were on their second cup of coffee before Anne had swallowed once. It was good pie; flaky, light, and sweet. Still, she was having trouble swallowing. The idea of marriage was caught in her throat.

"I haven't had a nice slice of pie since, . . . when was it?" Callahan asked the air above his head. "That time in Miles City or maybe that fancy place in St. Louis?"

"What about that place in Brownsville, just before the Chisholm drive?" Gabriel asked.

"Yeah, that was good pie. Blackberry," Callahan said with a dreamy expression.

"You come up here to talk pie?" Jack asked.

"Nah," Callahan said, "but I don't mind. I like remembering. Course, it's rude to cut you out, ma'am." He nodded in apology.

"That's all right. I don't mind," she said. It kept them from talking marriage and that was good.

"You know why we came," Gabriel said.

"I know why you think you came," Jack said, tipping back in his chair. "And you can go on home."

"Well, we're not going," Callahan said with a smile, "so we're here for a while. Extra hands never hurt no job, Jack."

Jack said nothing for a while, just looked down at his pie, taking a bite every now and then. Finally, he said softly, "Guess not."

Their mood relaxed at that.

"Well, I guess we'd better find us a place to stay. This town's short a hotel and it'll take some doing to find ourselves a bed," Callahan said.

"I could help you—" Anne said.

"Nah," Jack interrupted, "they can take care of themselves. The prairie's not too bad, this time of year."

"Hell, Jack, it's a cold wind blowing out there," Callahan grumbled.

"You'll get along," Jack said easily.

"I guess you got a place," Gabriel said.

"I do and there's no room for more," Jack said.

"I can guess where," Callahan said. The eyes of the two strangers turned to Anne and flicked over her lightly. Anne flushed instantly.

"Good," Jack said, "then you know you'll have to fend for yourselves. The jailhouse isn't bad."

"You speaking personal?" Callahan grinned.

Jack shrugged and Callahan laughed softly. "Hell, I guess we can bunk there as well as anywhere."

"You watch your mouth, Callahan," Jack said. "You're cussing in front of a lady and I have it personal she don't take to it."

"Ma'am," Callahan apologized. "Won't happen again."

Callahan and Gabriel scraped back their chairs on the wooden floor and stood to go.

"We'll see you later, Jack, and it was a real pleasure to meet you, ma'am. You're a real lady to take on a man like Jack Skull."

"Shut up, Callahan," Jack said calmly.

"Ma'am," Gabriel said softly, "I wish you well on your marriage. Jack's a lucky man."

"Thank you," Anne said to both of them.

"You better be getting on, too, right, Jack?" Callahan smirked. "Ain't you got to go meet with the preacher and get things arranged?"

Jack had just finished his pie. Anne had just picked at

271

hers, her stomach so tight with emotion that she could hardly breathe. What she'd managed to swallow lay like a stone in her middle. She didn't want any more.

"You ready to go, Anne?" Jack asked, his eyes still soft and blue and warm with some emotion she couldn't name but wanted to bathe in, it warmed her so. Stupid. She needed to get away from him as fast as she could run.

"Yes, I am," she said.

When they were out of the Demorest, the streets of Abilene quiet and dark, she said, "I didn't see you as the marrying kind."

"No man sees himself that way, but it happens," he said.

"But not to you," she said. *Not to me.* "I know what you did back there, that was for Bill, that was just men talking, trying to best each other."

"What?" He stopped her and turned her to face him. She couldn't quite look into his eyes, so she stared off over his left shoulder.

"You weren't serious, I know you weren't. I won't hold you to anything. You probably just wanted to drive off Bill. Well, you have. That's all there is to it."

"You don't understand men at all, do you, Anne?" His voice was low and hard, filled with an anger that she could feel throbbing out from him. "Well, hell, that's fine, because I understand women real good. I understand you."

"Excuse me?" she said, looking up into his eyes.

"Yeah, you ought to ask to be excused, but you won't. Hell, I played my part, didn't I? I got you free of Tucker. Your aunt, now she thinks that you need to find a man to be happy and she'll use me to get you one. What she don't know is that you don't want a man, but you'll use me to get rid of one for you. Hell and damnation, I'm real popular when the women of your house need something done. But what about what I want? You give any thought at all to what I might want?"

He understood things too well, that was the trouble. He didn't want a wife—what man did?—but he didn't want to be played for a fool either. A man sure didn't want it to get out that he'd been played.

"You don't need to do anything you don't want to do," she said, turning from him, walking on. "I'm certain you don't want a wife."

He grabbed her arm and spun her around, pulling her in close. She could feel his breathing against her chest and her own breathing faltered.

"You don't know me, Anne. You don't know the first thing about what I want."

"I know—"

"You keep still," he said, tracing a hand down her face to her throat. "You listen to me. I'll tell you what I want. I want you to marry me. I want you to want to. Understood? You've got three days to get there and then, by damn, you're going to be my wife."

"You won't force me to marry you. Not you."

But she couldn't quite see his eyes in the shadows of the night. His hat was pulled low, hiding his features from her. Where was the man who didn't push and prod? Where was the man who let her find her own way?

"You don't know me," he said, his voice a husky throb that touched her face like a rough caress. "You want to escape marrying me? You got to leave Abilene to do that." He laughed, soft and quick. "Can you do that, Anne? Can you leave Abilene? 'Cause that's your only way out."

"Do *you* want to get married?" she asked.

"Let's just say I want you to want to."

Pride. It was all about pride. His, of course, not hers. Well, she wasn't going to give in to male pride.

"Not an answer," she said, turning sharply and walking away from him. He let her go and kept step with her.

"It's good to see you got some fight in you, Anne. It gives me real pleasure to see it. This town sells you short."

"What does that mean?"

Jack looked at her sideways, his eyes showing light against the dark slant of his brows. He was a handsome man. He was going to be her husband. Or so he said. She would have to leave Abilene to keep it from happening. But he couldn't make her say the words, could he? Even if she stayed? No one could force her to do that.

"I meant that you're a grown woman," he said, "and more than half this town treats you like an adorable half-wit."

She didn't stop walking toward home, she had at least that much self-control, but the surge of anger that burst up with that casual remark was as hot and high as heat waves in August. A half-wit? He thought that the respect and concern and pure affection that her friends and neighbors in Abilene showered on her was the pitiful condescension they'd give to a half-wit?

"Bill doesn't call me a half-wit," she said through clenched teeth, her feet speeding up without any plan on her part. Jack kept pace with her and, for once, she wished he wouldn't.

"Maybe not," Jack said, "but he treats you like one."

"I don't know what you're talking about," she said, huffing in her hurry to get on, to get away from him. "Everybody likes me."

"Sure they do," he said, "and why not? You work damn hard at being agreeable."

"There's nothing wrong with being agreeable."

"No?" he said, pulling her up short just before they reached the light that flooded from her home to light the dust of Abilene. "Even when you go against what you want to do?"

"I do exactly what I want and right now I want to go home," she said.

"You do exactly what you want? Every time?" he prodded.

A Kiss to Die For

"A person should do what's right, should want to do what's right," she said.

"Then how come you keep kissing me?" he said and she could see his grin shine white in the dark.

"I just *knew* you'd say that," she flared and jerked her arm out of his and marched up the steps. "If you were so offended, you should have just . . . shot me. In fact, since the fact that we've kissed a few times seems to rile you so, you won't want me for your wife and that's fine with me. More than fine. Perfect."

He grabbed her around the waist and turned her to face him. "Nice try, Anne, but no go. I'm the man who does what he wants." He pulled her into his embrace, his arms wrapping around her. She didn't fight much. Did she ever? "I asked you to be my woman. For always. Nobody made you say yes, but I'm the man who's going to hold you to it."

His words made her stomach drop to her feet and flutter there like a June bug in September. Could anything be for always? She wanted something in her life to be for always.

"Why should I marry a man who thinks I act like a half-wit?" she mumbled, her face almost pressed against his chest. He smelled like soap and clean cotton.

"Now you're fighting like a woman," he said with a smile. "Makes me feel like we're married already. I never said you act like a half-wit; I said you were treated like one."

"But I wouldn't be treated like one if I didn't act like one," she said, pulling back. Her ma was watching from the window, and one of the Walton kids, the one who worked for Powell, was standing in the street and making kissing noises on the back of his hand. She was making a spectacle of herself and Jack was helping.

She didn't like it. She should put a stop to it. Lots of things she should do. Had she ever done any of them?

"You just need to stand up for yourself more," he said calmly. "Take care of yourself better." How did he have the nerve to instruct her on proper behavior? He seemed almost amused.

"So you're saying that I *do* act like a half-wit?"

"Of course not, it's just that, well, you *shouldn't* go around letting men kiss you," he said in an angry rush. At least she wasn't the only one mad now.

"I don't let men kiss me!"

"You let me kiss you! Again and again!" he said, taking off his hat and slamming it against his leg. Dust flew.

"Well. I'm so sorry," she bit out, turning her back on him and walking up the stairs with stiff little steps. "You won't ever have to *suffer* through it again since I'm not about to marry you!"

"Not marry me?" he said slowly, his voice deep and severe. She'd never heard him like that; it made the hair on her arms stand straight up. "Oh, you'll marry me. I asked. You answered. That's that. Understood?"

She didn't look at him. Didn't dare, really. He sounded mad enough to kill and, though she was learning to talk to him like she couldn't with anyone else, she still didn't enjoy all this fuss. If she'd eaten any more of that pie, she'd have thrown it up, right now. She wondered what the Walton kid would have done with that.

"Fine," she said, showing him her back.

"Good," he said.

"You can leave anytime," she said stiffly. "I'm perfectly capable of making it inside, half-wit that I am, without any help from you."

"I'm getting damned sick of people telling me I can leave. I'm staying."

"Stop cussing," she said, her chin up and quivering.

"Stop meeting the train," he said. "Whoever you're waiting for won't get off. And you're not getting on."

She turned and fired, verbally, for he'd hit hard and

in her most vulnerable spot, but she wasn't going to admit the worst of it. "I'm sure you're right," she said, her voice quaking with suppressed emotion. "I'm sure I'll never get out of Abilene, just like I'm sure you'll never stay. One day it'll be you who climbs on and leaves and never comes back." *No one ever comes back.* Hidden tears scrambled up her throat to lodge in her mouth.

Jack's scowl was wiped clean off. He moved toward her, his arms open, and enfolded her within his strength. She let him. She didn't have the strength to fight him. Let him call her a half-wit. She didn't have the heart to fight him.

"I'm not leaving, Anne," he whispered against her hair. "I'm not ever leaving."

"Everyone leaves," she mumbled against his shirt, swallowing her tears. She never cried about this, not anymore. All her tears had been used up. She had promised herself never to cry about it again.

"Not me," he said forcibly. "You've had a rough time, but you won't be getting a rough time from me."

Not a rough time? He was all rough time; impossible to manage, difficult to ignore, and determined to stay. Were they all just as determined to stay before they finally left? Had they believed their own lies of constancy? Did Jack?

She didn't want him to stay. She didn't need him now that Bill was gone. She didn't need these vows from him. He could go. She wanted him to go, just like she wanted to go, leaving Abilene and all the trouble of family behind.

"So you say," she said.

"I mean it," he said.

"You called me a half-wit," she mumbled, turning her head to rest it against his chest. Let the Walton kid do what he liked; she was going to press herself against Jack because he was a wall she could lean on. Just for now.

"I'm not going down that trail again," he said. She could hear the smile in his voice.

"Coward," she whispered, wrapping her arms around him. He was lean and hard and warm. Safe. Even though it was a lie, it felt good. Maybe this was why women kept believing the lie; it felt so much better than facing the truth.

"You'll never be alone again," he promised. "I'll never leave you." He kept saying it. Why did he think she needed to hear him say it again and again? Why did she let him keep repeating the words?

"That's if I marry you," she said.

He turned her face up with his hands and kissed her. Hard. He obviously didn't give a damn whether her ma or the Walton kid saw them or not. After a while, she didn't care either.

His arms wrapped around her, pulling her in tight, his hands pressing her hips to his. She could feel the hardness of him, the unrelenting masculinity of him, and wanted more. Her nipples were tight and they rubbed against his shirt, that warm, blue, cotton shirt he was wearing that had a broken button. She wanted to pull that shirt off him and run her hands over his hard body, feeling the muscle and the skin of the man who promised he wouldn't ever leave her.

She didn't give a damn what her ma saw or what Miss Daphne found out.

He was that dangerous.

When he finally let her go, she almost stumbled and had to lean her head against his chest to get her balance. Her breath was ragged and short, her vision blurred.

Jack smiled and ran his thumb over her cheek.

"And give that up? Yeah, you'll marry me."

She pushed him away and he dropped a step down. "You're not winning me over talking like that."

"I already won, Anne. Can't you see that?" He

shrugged, hooking his thumbs in his pants. "But you want me to stop? I'll stop. But you gotta tell me."

He was everything she didn't like about men: arrogant, selfish, hard with pride. Except that she liked him anyway. That was what was wrong with women; they had all the facts, facts as hard as any man, and they still made the wrong choices. But not her. Not her. She wasn't going to be like her ma; she wasn't going to raise a child on her own, living in the haze of a past she remembered wrong, like a dream turned inside out. She was going to leave here and she was going to do it alone.

"Go away," she said, planting herself firmly on the porch, the light from the windows at her back. She could see him clearly in the light, his blue eyes hard with amusement, his lips lifted in good humor. All at her expense.

"Nope, I won't go away," he said, stepping up to the porch. "You don't have the words to make me go. You only have the words to make me stop. To make me stop touching you. And kissing you. And wanting . . . you."

Her heart hammered underneath her suddenly aching breasts. She told her heart to shut up and keep still.

"You better find those words right quick, 'cause here I am. I'm going to kiss you, Anne. I'm going to kiss you and take us both outta here with the sweetness of it. This kiss is going to take you clear out of Abilene."

She stood, her feet planted on the boards of the porch as if someone had nailed her to it. His eyes were intense, buried beneath the long slant of his brows; he licked his lips and touched her, his hands on her waist, his eyes on her and nothing else. Like she was the only thing on God's green earth he wanted to be looking at. Like she mattered.

His touch, the look of him, sent her pulse running and her breath hopping. She couldn't breathe, not with him so close. He smelled like sunlight and apple pie, like leather and gunmetal, like promises and vows.

No man could smell like that. No man could be all that. She was losing her mind like she was losing her breath.

His hands swept around her back to enfold her, pulling her to him, pressing her against his length. He was hard all over, up and down, front and back. She could feel the movement of his muscles underneath his shirt and she sighed at the sensation. His mouth brushed over the rim of her ear, moving down, licking the lobe, skimming the skin of her throat, her pulse against his lips.

All while she stood on Miss Daphne's front porch.

"You shouldn't do this," she said. It was a whisper, breathy and high.

"Why not?" he said, his voice a tickle against her skin.

Why not? There must be a reason, some reason why he shouldn't be touching her like this, holding her like she was precious and beautiful, kissing her like . . . like . . . like she wanted him to. Like he always did. Like he wanted to drown in her, learning to swim in her blood, sharing his breath with her, breathing in harmony with her. Sharing her life. Sharing her dream.

Merciful God, he was in her blood. He was tangled in her blood and in her very breath. How was she going to get free of this?

"You gotta stop," she said, his lips hovering over hers so close that she tingled with the nearness.

"Tell me to stop," he said and then he kissed her, his tongue surging into her mouth with such powerful strokes that she had to remind herself to breathe.

Her hands wound around his neck and she stood to meet him, her mouth open under his, her heart laid bare. She throbbed for him, a low, demanding pulse that tore at her heart. She clung to him all the more fiercely, stupidly.

He lifted his mouth from hers and trailed kisses across her face. "One of these days, I'm gonna kiss every freckle on you. That'll take some doing," he said, his breath a caress.

"Stop," she said, her head buried against his chest, hiding her weakness from herself. "Please. Stop."

He ran his hands over her hair, stroking her, and pulled her in closer. Then he backed her up against the porch post and pressed into her. Her legs opened of their own will and he nestled into her. The throbbing between her thighs pounded in her ears.

"Make me stop," he said.

Make him? She couldn't make him. She couldn't make herself do what she wanted; how was she supposed to get him to do anything, anything at all?

She drew in a sharp breath and then sighed it out. "I can't," she said, lifting her face to his. "I can't make you. I can't even make me."

"You can," he said. "You got more grit than you think." He pressed against her and she could feel the hard length of his manhood against the soft cushion of her petticoats.

She moaned and pressed back, kissing her way up his throat, hungry for the taste of him, the pure male heat of him. Grit? She was mash, nothing but mash.

"I don't," she said. "I can't. You—"

"No," he said, cupping her breast with his hand. "You can. You only gotta say you don't want me. Then I'll stop."

She was throbbing from unseen wounds. She couldn't stand. She couldn't see straight. She was lost in him and because of him and she hardly even remembered that she didn't know her way out. Not want him? She didn't want him. He was a man and she didn't want any man. Wasn't that what she had decided? Wasn't that what she'd worked out in the quiet of her thoughts? That was the trouble. She couldn't think. How could she be smart if she couldn't think?

"Tell me to stop. Make me stop," he said, his voice a throaty command. "Damn it, Anne, you gotta fight me."

Claudia Dain

"Why?"

She lifted blind eyes to his, her mouth open and seeking. Why did she need to fight him? There was a reason, she had decided that long ago. She knew she had to push him out of her life. No, no, that was wrong. He was never supposed to have gotten into her life in the first place. How had he come close enough to touch her life?

"Please," she said, her voice barely audible.

"What?" he said, his voice raw like an open wound.

"Don't stop," she said.

He kissed her, his mouth on hers hard and hot, his tongue invasive, his touch possessive. All the things she had vowed to reject. All the things she had told herself to hate. All the things she craved.

With a moan, she melted against him, welcoming him into the heat between her thighs.

With a grunt, he escaped her, holding her off and keeping her back.

"No," he said, holding her back by the shoulders when she would have crumpled against him. "No, it's not gonna be that way. Three days. We got three days."

Three days. Could she last three days?

Chapter Twenty-one

"You don't want me to stop, do you?" he asked.

She hesitated, dropping her head, but not moving off.

"I think you should. This ain't proper," she said. But she didn't say it real convincingly.

"Well, if you think I should, then I will. I won't do anything to dishonor the woman I want to marry," he said.

Her head lifted, her dark eyes full of surprise and pleasure. Yes, this was what they all wanted, what they all held out for. Dangling the promise of marriage was to hold a woman's heart, a woman's very life, in your hands.

"Marry?"

He smiled and held out his arms to her, welcoming her in. Unlike the others, this one hesitated.

"But . . . we hardly know each other."

"I knew you were the one from the first moment I saw you. A man doesn't like to admit to being felled by a woman, and so quick, but there it stands. I love you. I want you for my wife."

Yes, words of love and devotion always sat well on a

woman's heart. There was not much she could do to fight against that. Only one woman had ever said no to him and she'd paid hard for that mistake.

She smiled, her vanity caressed, and took a step nearer.

"We should go talk to my pa," she said, toying with a strand of her dark hair.

"And we will," he said. "Just one more kiss. Please?"

"Come on, Anne, if you're going to shoot it, you got to clean it," Jack said.

"Well, I don't have to shoot it."

"We're not going over that again," he said.

The prairie stretched out around them, comforting them by its very expansiveness. Kansas was all sky and cloud held down by the thinnest line of earth. A man could breathe in the space of Kansas.

"I think the one who is making me shoot should be the one who has to clean."

"Yeah, you would think that," he said, grinning.

They'd been spending time together every day. Jack had eased off on his kissing. Anne didn't need any more of that, not now. What they needed was time to get to know each other so that Anne could walk into marriage clear-eyed. She was confused, any fool could see that, and he didn't want her that way. Hell, he wanted her any way he could have her, but he was going to take the high road, no matter how much Callahan laughed.

He was spending too much time with her, valuable time, when he should be out hunting a killer. In three days' time, a girl could get killed. But he wanted to give Anne that three days to get to know him. She didn't want to get married, he knew that; it was his job to get her to change her mind. Once she was his, he'd go off and find his man and finish the job. No more dead girls. Not one more dead girl. Anne married meant she was safe. He'd be free to go, knowing she was safe. It was those other gals who weren't safe.

This sitting around was about killing him, but he'd do it. He'd give Anne that. He just wished he could settle down some in his thinking about that killer. What was he doing now? What gal was he planning to kill?

"I think I'm getting better," Anne said.

Jack shook off his thoughts and watched her. She was holding her gun a bit more comfortably now, not so heavy-handed. Her shots weren't too far off either. She still flinched with the first round and it took her some time to get up the grit to fire it off, but once she had heard the first retort, she got used to it and then fired off all the rounds real quick. She hit with about two of them. Still, a loaded gun was a powerful deterrent; it might be enough to keep her safe. Trouble was, she still had trouble firing off that first shot. A gun wasn't much use if you wouldn't pull the trigger for fear of the noise.

"Yeah, you look pretty good," he said.

She looked at him over her shoulder as she loaded in more shells. "How do you mean that?"

Damn, but she was a flirt. He sure did like that about her.

"I mean it just the way you want it," he said, picking up the empty shell casings. You just never knew when you might have to load your own shot.

"Good," she said, grinning.

She sure wasn't the skittish thing he'd found when he first came to Abilene. She was a bit more able to speak up for herself—all to the good as far as he was concerned. He knew it wouldn't go down smooth with her family, but they were wrong. A woman needed to speak up, same as a man. The world wasn't an easy ride; he wasn't going to have Anne tromped to death and have her say nothing against it.

She was going to be his wife.

It felt strange. He hadn't planned to take a wife. Did any man? Didn't seem likely. Still, he wasn't going to kick against it. He wanted her, that was sure, and he wanted to keep her safe. That about summed up the idea of marriage, as he far as he knew.

"You finish shooting those off and then you're going to break down that gun and you're going to clean it," he said.

"Yes, sir," she said, taking a breath and then slowly squeezing off a round into the target he'd set up about ten yards off. What she'd have to shoot wouldn't be any farther away than that.

"You think by being agreeable that you're going to get out of it, you're wrong," he said.

"You sure about that?" she said before turning back to the target.

"Yes, ma'am, I'm sure," he said.

She chuckled and fired off the last five rounds real fast, which was her style. The first shot was slow and then the others followed in quick succession. Not a bad habit. He'd let her keep it. If only she could fire off that first round faster. Well, with any luck, she'd never have to fire at anybody.

He laid out an old scrap of blanket on the ground and the rag he used to wipe his gun. He was kneeling and waiting for her by the time the last shot echoed off into the wide Kansas sky.

"You're ready?" she asked. "You don't need a minute . . . ?"

"You get yourself down on this blanket. We got work to do," he said, his voice serious, his eyes not.

She laughed and shook her head at him. "You trying to scare me?"

"How'm I doing?"

"Not bad," she said. "I sure don't want to get on that blanket with you . . . and clean that gun."

A Kiss to Die For

"Well, that's too bad 'cause that's all that's happening on this blanket, Miss Ross."

"I heard you were dangerous," she said.

Yeah, she was feeling prime, sure of him, sure of herself. That was good. He'd given her that.

"I am, when crossed. You don't want to cross me, Anne. It's not pleasant."

"I think everything about you is pleasant. And dangerous."

She wasn't teasing him now and his heart jumped up to crush his voice. Damn, but she did things to him that he hadn't thought could be done. She was a helluva woman. It was worth marrying to keep Anne Ross alive.

"Much obliged, Anne. That was real nice," he said when his voice came back.

She just looked down at him, her blue eyes a match for the sky that wrapped itself around her.

"Why are you sad?" she said.

"I'm not sad."

She knelt across from him and put the gun down between them on the blanket.

"You are. There's a sadness in you, deep down."

"That's not sadness, Anne, that's aloneness."

And that was the sorry truth. He was alone. He'd been alone for his whole life.

"Funny, I've wished for a little aloneness for most of my life," she said.

"It's not funny. Not when you've got it."

"You don't know my family," she said, trying for a smile and almost making it.

"I know them, well enough anyway. They're not so bad. They just care about you, that's all."

"I can care for myself," she said.

"What about me? When you marry me, I'll care for you."

"Am I marrying you? When did I decide that?" she said,

287

changing the tone and direction of their talk.

"Now, Anne, don't be making yourself out to be a liar,"
he said, sitting down on his heels. "You know right well
that you'll marry me. Tomorrow. Three. The church. Any
questions?"

"Yeah," she said, sitting down on the blanket. "How do
I take this gun apart?"

"Smart girl," he said, showing her how to release the
cylinder from the barrel.

"My hands are getting greasy."

"Too bad."

It didn't take long to show her how to clean the grease
and dust off of the revolver. What took a while was getting
her to remember how to put it back together again. It
took her six tries.

"How long did it take you to learn to do this?" she
asked.

He thought about it, thought hard, and couldn't come
up with an answer.

"I don't know. Seems I've always been able to break
down a gun."

"You mean you were doing this as a child?"

"I guess so," he said.

They were quiet awhile at that. He made her take it
apart and put it back again. She did it with only three
mistakes and she fixed them without his having to say a
word.

"What else did you do as a child?" she said, keeping
her eyes on the gun, polishing it with the rag.

"Not much. Same as most kids, I guess."

"Well, I scrubbed the floors and then got to play with
a rag doll out by the kitchen coop when I was a child.
You do that, too?" she said, her blue eyes twinkling.

"Nah, I missed that," he said. "I guess I learned to ride.
And rope. And shoot."

"Those are man skills," she said. "What did you do as a boy?"

"A boy becomes a man. I learned what I'd need."

She pondered that, looking out at the prairie, brushing a strand of hair out of her eyes with the back of her hand.

"Who taught you?"

"Folks."

"Your folks?"

He swallowed and watched a misshapen band of crows fly across the clouds.

"Just folks."

She didn't say much after that. Hell, he knew how it sounded, but he wasn't going to lie about his upbringing. Course, that didn't mean he had to spell it all out for her either. He wasn't going to do that. There was no point in dragging yourself back over stony ground when it was well behind you.

The gun was put together and she handed it to him. Her eyes looked into his, real serious, all the twinkle smashed out of her.

"We'll be getting married tomorrow. Three. The church," she said.

"I don't want you marrying me for pity," he said, standing, sticking the gun in his belt and then shoving it back at her. She had to carry it for it to do any good. He had enough guns for himself.

He wasn't going to have her like this. He wasn't doing her a good turn out of pity. He wanted her, wanted her alive and safe and breathing for as long as God decided to keep her aboveground. He wasn't going to be taken because she pitied what she couldn't understand. He was a man. That was all he had to be and he'd made it. He didn't deserve pity and he didn't want it.

She stayed at his feet, small and crouched down against the dirt of Kansas, and looked up at him. She met his eyes, smiled, and then looked away. Off and away to the far distance.

"I don't pity you, Jack."

That was the honest truth. The only one she felt sorry for was herself. She was going to marry him. Not for his kisses, she was smarter than that, and not for his looks and not even because it would make Miss Daphne howl in anger. No, she was going to marry Jack Scullard because he needed her. Jack Skull, feared and respected, was alone. In the whole wide world, he was resolutely alone. Who would have thought that Jack would need her? But he did. He purely did.

She guessed that, somehow, the need in him more than outweighed her own need to be free.

So, they were married, married in the church by a very subdued Reverend Holt, and were now enjoying a small reception in Miss Daphne's immaculate parlor. Miss Daphne hadn't wanted it, of course, but she wasn't going to air their troubles in front of the whole town for small-minded people to titter over; no, she'd give the reception and put her brand on the wedding so that no one could say she'd failed in her familial duty. That had been her parting shot. She hadn't said a word to Anne since.

That was the first advantage to being Mrs. Scullard.

The reception was subdued. Jack was out on the porch with Sheriff Lane and Mr. Callahan and Mr. Gabriel, their voices lowered in talk, their heads together. He wasn't in the parlor with her, while she tried to keep her smile in place and placate the nasty looks from her friends and neighbors. He was out there, where it was safe.

"Congratulations, Anne, on your marriage," Constance Holt said.

"Thank you," she murmured, accepting the light hug the reverend's wife pressed upon her.

"I know there's been some nervousness about this

union," she said softly, her blue eyes kind, "but I wish you and Jack a happy marriage. It's one of the Lord's greatest blessings."

"I suppose it is," Anne said politely.

"It sure has been for me," Sue Ann Weaver cut in, edging into the conversation and raising the volume. "Being married to Rob was the best thing I ever did; why, before, I hardly could afford a new dress once a year."

"It's wonderful Rob's doing so well," Constance said.

"Oh, he's doing fine, but it's that his daddy has some money and helps us out every once in a while. That's where the new dresses come from."

Anne blushed. For Rob.

"Who's Jack's family, Anne?" Sue Ann asked. "I ain't never heard of no Skulls around here."

"The name is Scullard," Anne said, "and my husband isn't from around here; he's from Texas."

"Speaking of folks not being around," Jane Rivers joined in, "where's Bill Tucker been hiding himself? I haven't seen him in days and he was always one to come in every day or so to buy a little of this or that."

"I haven't seen him either, so I can't help you," Sue Ann added happily. "Seems he made himself scarce when Anne up and picked Jack Skull for her man. Must have broke his heart."

"Yes, I would think it did," Jane said with casual condemnation. "That man sure was taken with you, Anne. I'm sure he thought—"

"We all thought," Sue Ann pushed in.

"—that you two would—"

"But they didn't," Constance Holt said. "Anne's made her choice. I'm sure she's content with it. Congratulations again, Anne. All my very best to you and your husband," she said just before she went across the room to talk with Nell.

Leaving Anne alone with two very disapproving people.

"I heard from Everett Winslow that Bill was real upset over your picking Jack over him," Jane said.

"I guess he was," Anne said.

"And I heard that Jack threatened to kill him," Sue Ann said somewhat gleefully. "Maybe that's why Bill's not been around; maybe he's running for his life."

"And who could blame him?" Jane said. "He's no gun-slinger."

It was said scathingly. Anne flinched. Jack had worn his guns, minus the ammunition belts, to their wedding. He wore them now. He was most definitely dressed as a gun-slinger.

"What happened, Anne?" Sue Ann asked, edging closer, making Anne slosh her tea over the rim of her cup. "Did Jack really say he wanted to kill Bill?"

"No, not really."

Maybe if she wore guns, people like Sue Ann would walk a little more softly around her.

"But sort of?" Sue Ann asked, her eyes alight with morbid interest.

"No, it really wasn't anything like that."

"Well, what was it like? Did he say he would kill him or not?"

"Well, he said he would if—"

"I knew it! I knew that man had killing in him!"

She definitely needed to get a gun.

"But it was only if—"

"Oh, there's always some reason for that kind of man. But they'll kill; it's what they do, isn't it?"

Something small but deadly looking, with a real fat barrel.

"He is a bounty hunter," Jane said stiffly.

"And I've never made a secret of it," Jack said from the edge of the room.

Anne breathed a sigh of escape. Jack would take over now; he'd manage all this confrontation and accusation better than she could. He *was* wearing all the guns in the family at the moment.

"Why should you?" Callahan said, coming in from the porch with Gabriel on his heels. "It's honest work."

"And lawful," Gabriel said.

Jane Rivers just sniffed and nodded to Anne before putting down her cup and saucer; she made her good-byes to the ladies of the house and left. Yes, wearing a gun sure made a difference in how a person was treated. Sue Ann stood openmouthed in fascination. The three men who stood before her looked nothing like her husband Rob. There wasn't an ounce of farmer in the three of them together. Before she could say anything, Rob came up and took her elbow and walked her clean out of that house.

"I don't mean to break up your wedding party, Mrs. Scullard," Callahan said with a smile, "but me and Gabe's got to get on."

"Oh, I'm so sorry you have to leave so soon." She smiled. "When will you be coming back?"

"Well, that depends," Callahan said, looking down at his boots. "We're hunting a man and won't be back till he's found."

That statement put a heavy lid on her party. Folks just started disappearing out the door until only the reverend and his wife, the sheriff, and the doc were left. And her family, they stayed in the room and stared right at her. Would carrying a gun have any effect on her family? Probably not, as they knew she'd never shoot one of them. Which was too bad.

"Oh?" the doc asked. "Who?"

"Bill Tucker," Callahan answered. "Can't help wondering where he is."

"And what he's doing," Gabriel added.

"I'm certain that he's engaged in nothing more than his own business," Miss Daphne said stiffly.

293

"Then he won't mind us looking in on him," Callahan said smoothly.

"I'm sure that a man of Mr. Tucker's character only wants a chance to be alone just now. What with all that's happened in the last few days," she replied, looking right at Anne.

Anne wanted to crawl under the stairs and curl into a ball. Or buy a gun. Or leave Abilene. Maybe all three.

"Nothing's happened in the last few days that a decent man would have a problem with," Jack said, standing next to Anne and pulling Daphne's gaze to him, drawing her fire. He was awfully good at that and she sure was awfully grateful, though her stomach was still in knots.

"I'm sure that I won't argue with you about what a decent man does or does not," she said.

"I sure appreciate a woman who refuses to argue, ma'am," Jack said. "Appreciate it a lot now that it's my wedding day and the day's about through. How about Anne goes on up and gets settled? I'll be up directly."

Anne blushed pink and dropped her head. This was not going *at all* as she'd planned. Reverend Holt and Constance left quickly, Sheriff Lane said a brief and somewhat stiff good-bye to her mother, and Doc Carr said a very formal good-bye to her grandmother. Neither one of them said good-bye to Jack. Callahan and Gabriel didn't say good-bye to anyone but Jack and her. In five minutes, she was alone in the parlor with her grandmother, her aunt, her mother, and . . . her husband. The only one who looked happy at all was her husband. It might have been that happy look on his face that propelled Miss Daphne from the room. She didn't say good night to anyone, but she looked with cold self-satisfaction at Anne as she walked by her on the way to the kitchen.

"Nell," she said ringingly, "you go on up with Anne. Sarah, you'll help me with the cleaning up. There's a pile of dishes to wash tonight."

A Kiss to Die For

"But I thought I'd like to help Anne—" Sarah said.

"That's a mother's duty and, unfortunately, you are not a mother."

"Humph," Sarah grumbled softly. When Miss Daphne was out of the room, Sarah whispered to Anne and Nell, "I'll be up later."

"So will I," Jack said, looking only at Anne. Winking at her, he went out on the porch and lit a cigar.

Anne watched him go, frozen. Until her mother pushed her toward the stairs. She went up them, one heavy leg at a time. She'd done it, done what she'd sworn she'd never do. She'd become a wife and now she had to face the devil and give him his due.

No, now Jack wasn't a devil. He was merely a husband. Well, and weren't the two just too close for her comfort?

"Nervous?" her mother asked as they entered her room and closed the door.

Anne went to the window and looked out onto the street in front of the house; she could see the smoke of Jack's cigar rising sporadically in the twilight air.

"I guess so," she answered, turning to face Nell. "I didn't think I'd end up married. To a bounty hunter," she added.

If there hadn't been any point in telling her ma her plans before, there was even less so now. She needed a new plan, one that would accomodate being the wife of a bounty hunter. She didn't know if she could make a plan that big. How had she ended up here? Married, and to the one man everyone took pleasure in hating. It wasn't going to be a pretty life, not if it went on like this.

But it wouldn't go on. He'd leave, or she would. There were lots of places to get lost in between California and Kansas. She might even go east, to Chicago. A girl could get herself good and lost in Chicago; so lost that nobody would be able to find her. If anybody came looking.

She'd been wrong about Jack needing her, must have

been. There was no one better at looking after himself. Why, the way he'd handled himself at the reception proved that. He surely didn't need her. If she lit out, he'd scarcely notice. Probably.

"When I married Tim, he was the town hero. He'd just shot a man, killed him, a real bad man who was on the run. The townsfolk would have voted him in as president, they were that taken with him. Everyone was just as pleased as they could be that I'd married him."

"Even Miss Daphne?"

Nell chuckled and spun her daughter around to continue disrobing her. "Especially Miss Daphne. You know how she likes everything done just right? Well, Tim was the right man at the right time."

"And look how that turned out," Anne said.

Her mother looked at her hard. "Why, Anne Ross Scullard! I was happy with your pa. He made me feel things, wish for things . . . I was just flying with the clouds whenever he even looked at me."

Yes, she'd heard this before, all her life in fact. Men did that. They turned you around so that you couldn't find ground and then left you flat, all memories of flying lying in the dust with you.

"And then?"

"And then he turned bad, a little bit at a time," Nell said softly, her fingers fumbling with the buttons. "And when that happened, folks started avoiding me, like I'd turned bad with him."

"Everyone?"

"Everyone, everyone except Charles," Nell said slowly. "Charles never did change."

"But you hadn't changed. You were the same person," Anne said. She'd been so little, she hardly remembered any of it. She remembered that her father had black hair and large hands, that his boots had been loud on the wooden floors of their home, and that when he hadn't come home for a long time, they'd moved. Moved back home with Miss Daphne.

"I was the same," Nell said, "but folks don't see that. They see you as being the same as the man you marry."

"That's not fair," Anne grumbled.

"Life's fair?" Nell said, smiling. "Maybe I'm not saying it right. It's not that they see you the same, but that they respond to you the same. You and your man, you're one. You share more than a name, you share your life."

Share her life? With Jack? Jack was just for now. Jack was kisses that made her drunk. Jack was safety and passion and laughter. Until he left her. Or she left him.

"Until he leaves," Anne said aloud as her dress fell to the floor in a delicate heap.

"Until he leaves?" Nell asked. "What are you talking about?"

"Men. Husbands. They never stay. They leave," Anne said, looking down at the floor and the flattened heap of her dress.

"Anne, that's not true," Nell said heavily.

"Yes, it is." Anne looked at her mother, her arms crossed over her breasts. "It's always true."

"No, it isn't. Look at the Holts."

"Miss Daphne says it takes thirty years to see if a marriage will stick." Her granddaddy had left after twenty-seven.

"But that's—"

"That's the way it is. That's the way it's going to be. One way or the other." And it would be her way. She'd leave him before he could leave her. She'd pick the time and the place. She'd move on, make a new life, start over. She'd be the one to leave.

Nell stood and held Anne in her arms, rocking her gently to and fro. Her ma hadn't done that since she'd had been a child, right after her father had left. That pain was behind them. She'd made sure of that. That pain wasn't ever going to touch her again.

"You don't marry a man thinking he's going to leave you, Anne. Only God knows what's coming. Maybe I made a poor choice in a man. God willing, you made a better one." Nell kissed Anne's cheek. "Enjoy every day you've got, not because you're afraid he'll leave, but because every day's a gift." Nell rocked her daughter and kissed her temple, smoothing the hair away from her face. "I don't have the best judgment in men, but I don't think Jack'll leave."

Sarah opened the door and hurried in; she'd escaped from Miss Daphne, for the moment.

"He won't leave until he's taken advantage of his marital privileges," Sarah said, misinterpreting what she'd heard. Nell and Anne didn't correct her; their conversation had been too private to share, even with Sarah. Nell patted down Anne's hair and bent to pick up Anne's dress.

"What exactly does that mean?" Anne said, crossing her arms over her suddenly sensitive breasts.

"You're her mama, you want to tell her?" Sarah asked Nell.

"You want to tell her so bad, you go ahead," Nell said, hanging up the dress in the wardrobe.

"You know those kisses he's been handing out?"

Anne was sick of blushing, but she did it anyway. "Yeah?"

"Like that, only everywhere. If you're lucky," Sarah said. "With Jack, I think you're going to get lucky."

Chapter Twenty-two

"I never figured you to marry," Callahan said.

The porch was shadowed in twilight, a wind kicking around the corners, pulling at the flaking paint. The rest of the wedding guests had gone on home a while back. They were alone, except for the women in the house.

"I never figured it either, but here I am," Jack said.

Why tell them that he'd never thought a woman would have him who didn't have to be paid for it first? That was nobody's business but his own. That he'd come by a woman like Anne, well, that just proved that God looked kindly on fools and sinners.

"What you gonna do with her now?" Gabriel asked.

It was a question. He couldn't take her with him when he hunted bounty; that was no life. He'd have to leave her. At least he'd be leaving her safe. No married women had been killed; he was going to have to count on that.

"I'm going to do my job and leave her to do hers," Jack said. "She's safe now. I can finish this thing. It needs doing and I got to get to it."

"Whoever he is, he's been pretty slick," Callahan said, leaning against the post.

Claudia Dain

"Yeah, well, I can handle it. Once I get hold of him, he's not going anywhere."

"The trick is to get hold of him," Callahan said.

"Yeah," said Gabriel.

"Yeah," said Jack. "You thinking I'm not up to it?"

"Nah, just that you might need some help."

He didn't like the idea of help. Help could leave you flat and worse off than if you'd done it alone. Except now he had Anne and her family to think about. He didn't like the idea of leaving a houseful of women to fend off whatever came in from the prairie.

"Sure," Jack said, accepting the offer.

The two men shifted their weight and exchanged a glance.

"What?" Jack asked, watching them.

"That gal sure has softened you," Callahan said. "You never was so easy as this before."

Jack just grunted, sure Callahan meant it as a joke. Well, pretty sure.

It was near dark when he went upstairs. He'd finished his cigar; that was more than enough time for her to get herself ready for her wedding night. He was more than ready.

When he got to the top of the stairs, he realized that he didn't know which room was hers; all the door were closed against him. He knew that Daphne and Nell and Sarah were downstairs, because he could hear the sounds of women softly talking over the equally soft clink of china submerged in water. It was a nice sound, real homey. But even though they were downstairs, he didn't want to open up the door to any room that wasn't Anne's. The way Miss Daphne had looked at him all day, she'd most likely accuse him of stealing and he didn't want a thing in this house. Except Anne.

"Anne?" he called softly.

"Yes?" he heard after a bit of hesitation.

A Kiss to Die For

The sound came from the right, but there were two doors on the right and he couldn't tell which one had her voice behind it.

"You going to invite me in?" he said.

After a longer hesitation, the door nearest the stairs opened, just a crack, but a crack was all he needed. He pushed the door open with his fingertips and eased in. She was wearing a gown of thin cotton that had buttons all the way down the front; all those buttons . . . he got hard, then and there. She must have sensed it because she backed up real quick and banged her hip against the base of the bedstead. It must have hurt, but she was too scared to say anything. She stood there, staring at him as if he were going to kill her, rubbing her hip with her hand.

For a cigar's worth of waiting, Anne didn't seem too ready.

"You're beautiful, Anne," he said, his voice gentle and even. He used the same kind of tone when he was getting the feel of an unfamiliar horse; seemed like the same kind of situation. But Anne didn't need to know that. "That's a real pretty gown."

"It's nothing special, nothing new, I mean."

"Doesn't need to be new to look good on you. You'd look good in a saddle blanket. At least to me."

"Thank you. I think."

Her eyes were wide and open, the whites showing clearly in the dim light from the single lamp. She looked ready to bolt.

He moved toward her, hand outstretched and palm up, offering her his hand, offering her his touch. She backed up and put her hand to her throat.

"Come here, Anne. I only want to kiss you."

She pressed her lips together and kept her distance.

"Don't you want a kiss?" He smiled, taking off his rifle. She watched him carefully, completely, silently. "You're my woman. I want to kiss you, to feel you in my arms, pressed up against me, with your mouth hot on mine. Don't you want the same?"

He took off his holsters, one at a time and laid them on the floor next to the bed. His rifle he laid atop the dresser. He took off his belt and watched her turn white as flour.

"Didn't they tell you nothin'?" he asked softly.

"They told me some things," she whispered back, her eyes on his boots, where she could watch him without meeting his eyes.

"What things?" He unbuttoned his shirt, slowly, just the way he was going to unbutton all those little white buttons that ran from her neck to her feet. One small button at a time.

"They said ... they said 'it' was just like kissing, only ..."

"Only what?"

"Only better."

He opened up his shirt and without any fuss, pulled out his shirttails. He was tanned brown from living outside for so many years; some women liked a man like that, some didn't. He hoped Anne liked what she saw. He threw his shirt on the floor in the corner. Her eyes flickered up to his waist and then hurried back down to his boots. And then flickered up again to his chest. And then dropped back down to his knees. Progress.

"That's no lie," he said, sitting in the room's only chair, a rocker, to kick off his boots. The first one was the hardest; it fell with a thud to the floor and he kicked it out of the way. The second one slid off more easily and he dropped it on top of the first. "But they didn't tell you near enough, did they?"

"No, at least, I don't think so."

She was still holding on to her throat, as if she wanted to squeeze the air right out of herself, but her breath was coming on strong anyway. And real fast. Yeah, she liked what she saw.

"Well, I wish they would have, but I'll fill you in. If you want."

His socks he tossed on top of his boots. They were clean, so he didn't worry about the smell. He'd washed up good and proper before this wedding, wearing the best clothes he had, getting a shave and a haircut. Anne had run her hands through his hair a time or two when he'd kissed her, so he'd kept it at the collar, figuring she liked it long. For himself, he didn't care.

He stood up and eased open the top button on his pants. Her eyes jerked up to focus on his waist as if he were the only thing in the room. That was good. That was just where he wanted to go.

"You know, men and women, they're put together different," he said pleasantly.

"I know that much," she said with a scowl. He stood with his hands on his hips and that's where she was looking. That was fine with him. More than fine.

"Well, that's good, Anne." He grinned. "I never did take you for a half-wit."

"Now I'm the one who's not going down that trail again," she said with a little smile. He smiled back. This was going better and better.

He undid another button. Anne stopped smiling. She also stopped strangling herself; instead, she crossed her arms over her breasts and swallowed something that sounded like a moan. He hoped that meant she liked what she saw.

She did. He was corded with muscle, lean muscle riding his belly and sitting on his shoulders, rippling with the smallest movement. It was mesmerizing. She couldn't stop looking at him. His chest was near hairless, but a line of brown hair traced its way down his belly to land somewhere below his partially opened pants. He was a hard man, looked rock hard every square inch of him, but it was the kind of hard that compelled. She wanted to press up against him like she had before, but against that skin . . . she just knew he'd be hot. Hot and smooth and hard. It wouldn't be like before at all. Everything was different now.

"You don't notice it much, the difference, in kissin', but it gets real noticeable . . . later. Can't hide it then," he said.

He wasn't going to be able to hide it much longer now, the way he was talking. He didn't know how he was going to get his pants off without Anne running from the room, or else dropping in a dead faint. The thing to do was distract her and he knew just the way she liked best.

"Like what?" she asked, her voice curious even if her posture was guarded.

"Like . . ." He shrugged. "Like we don't have the same parts and your parts and my parts, they just sort of . . . blend. It's like when we kiss; your mouth and mine, touching, blending, opening . . ." Lord Almighty, he was a fool to talk like this when Anne wasn't near ready to help him out of the hole he was digging for himself.

"I like the kissing," she said softly. She wanted him closer, wanted to touch the muscles on his arms and chest. She could do that if they kissed. And kissing was safe; she knew about kissing. She could manage the kissing, but the rest of it? She didn't want any man to get that close. Or she hadn't. Until Jack. Until now.

"Don't I know," he said, shifting around in his pants. "How about you come over here and let me kiss you?"

"Dressed like this?"

"You wanna take it off?" He smiled.

"No!"

"Then come as you are," he said, hooking his thumbs in at the top of his pants. Anything to keep from grabbing her and pushing her to tears. He wasn't going to start his marriage like that.

He gave her credit for guts; she came on. Or maybe it was just that she liked his kisses too much to turn one down. It didn't much matter, as long as he coaxed her within range.

The lamp was on the table behind her as she walked slowly across that bare wood floor; he could see the outline of her through the white cotton. Lord, she was shapely, even without a corset. And she was scared, her body was trembling and she was chewing her lip. It was going to be a long night.

"Come on, Anne, you've got nothing to worry about. You know what this is like."

"But what about what comes after?" she said, looking up at him with both fear and trust.

"It'll come when it'll come; let it take care of itself."

"But—"

"You know I won't hurt you, don't you?" he whispered, running his hands over the dark length of her hair. "I'll never hurt you."

"It's just that, Sue Ann told me—"

"Never mind what anybody else says, just listen to me," he said, stroking her back and turning her face up to accept his kiss. He kissed her on the corner of her mouth and she trembled at the tingle it caused. "I'm your husband. My job is to take care of you and I'm going to do it, every day of my life I'm going to do it." He kissed the very top of her cheek and felt her eyelashes brush down as her head tilted back. "You can trust me, can't you?"

"I want to," she breathed, her eyes closed.

"Then do what you want. Do what you want with me, here, now. Go on, Anne. Don't hold back. Not now. Not with me."

He kissed her then, his hand going up her back until he cupped the back of her skull. She was so delicate; the slightest pressure would break her neck. She relaxed into the kiss, her breath coming out as a sigh and her trembling easing off as her fear lessened. With his other hand, he undid the very first button, the one that lay just on top of the pulse point in her throat.

His hands skimmed, as light as goose down, over her breasts. She pulled herself away from him. He pulled her back and kept kissing her. He plunged into her mouth with the most gentle of persuasions, twining tongue with tongue, sharing breath.

He unbuttoned the second button.

She didn't seem to notice. Or maybe it was that she didn't care. Or maybe, just maybe, she was trying to trust him.

His hands came up again to brush against the peaks of her breasts. When she moved her body away from him this time, he wrapped his arms around her and held her tight, pressing her breasts up against his bare chest as he kissed her. She didn't fight him off. Progress.

He trailed his mouth down the side of her throat while his hands traced her hips. That second button hadn't opened up much more of her than neck and throat, so he kissed her at the opening and then nibbled his way up, where he sucked and bit the soft, supple skin of her throat. It'd leave a mark, sure, but he didn't care. She was his woman. And she liked it. He'd make sure she liked it.

With one hand, he lifted a breast, enjoying the soft weight of it in his hand, and when she would have protested, bent down and flicked her nipple with his tongue through the thinness of the cotton.

She moaned and leaned into him, gripping his hair with her hands. He was sure glad he'd left it long.

"Anne? Are you all right?" Miss Daphne demanded from the hall side of the door.

Anne jerked like a calf when the slack's played out of

a lasso and her eyes flew open to stare at the door.

"She's fine," Jack said, running a hand through his hair in frustration. The mood sure was broken now.

"Anne! Answer me!" Daphne barked.

"Yes," Anne said. "Yes, I'm fine."

"Well," Daphne said crossly, "I thought I heard something and just wanted to be sure. Is there anything I can get you before I go to bed?"

"No, no," Anne said, blushing and running her hands up and down her thighs in nervous agitation. "Good night."

"Good night, Anne."

They could hear her door close and then there was quiet. But she was right next door and they both knew it. Damned if he was going to wait; Anne needed some good, hard kissing to make her forget that her family was perched all around her like a flock of vultures. It was his wedding night and he was going to have one, no matter who came knocking on the door.

The time for talk was over.

Before she could say a word, he pulled her to him and kissed her, his tongue invading her mouth before she could think to protest. He rubbed his hands against her breasts and when she acted like she was going to pull away, he pulled her right back and caressed her breasts like they were meant to be touched; gently, relentlessly, and, God willing, eternally. It didn't take more than a few seconds for her to stop fighting him. She sure wasn't much of a fighter.

That was when he backed her up so that she'd fall down on the bed. She looked like she was going to say something, so he kissed her, quick, and undid that next button. It opened the fabric that covered her breasts. Pushing it aside, he licked her, kissing her there the way she liked to be kissed on her mouth. She thrashed beneath him, but she didn't fight him. That was good.

"It's good, isn't it? You want this."

He moved his other hand up and thumbed her nipple while his tongue played hard on the other. She moaned and put her hand over her mouth. So, she wanted to keep quiet; he had Daphne to thank for that.

He undid another button.

Now he had enough play in the gown so that he could ease it off her shoulders and down her arms. Lord, she was a beauty. Smooth skin, soft as brushed flannel, and white as bleached linen. Breasts full and round and topped with nipples of baby pink. And all that dark hair spread beneath her, deepest black in the light of that one lamp. She was like something you hear about in stories, something you'd never expect to find and actually be able to hold. And she was his. His woman. His wife.

She couldn't fight him much now, not with her arms pinned to her sides by the gown; not that she looked like she wanted to. No, she looked like a woman far gone in passion, tossing her head and looking up at him with eyes dilated by desire.

He undid the next button and pushed aside the gown.

He looked at the mound of her belly and the jut of her hipbones and the beginnings of the black hair that marked her womanhood. He ran his hand over her, touching only what he could see. Anne lifted her hips slightly off the bed and whispered, "Kiss me."

He did, palming her breasts and playing with her nipples as he took her mouth with his own.

A drawer slammed next door. Anne jerked her mouth from his, froze, and then tried to cover her nakedness with her hands.

"Hell."

He ripped through the rest of the buttons, sending them flying to the floor, where they hit and rolled. Anne jerked to a sitting position and tried to crawl under the blanket she was lying on. It didn't work. He made sure of that.

"Trust me," he whispered, touching the coil of curls that shielded her, pressing her down against the bed, kissing her savagely. She pressed against his shoulders a bit, trying to lift him off. He wasn't going anywhere and it was his job to make sure that she didn't want him to. He kept kissing her, his tongue like a knife that stabbed and twirled without leaving any blood. No blood, but lots of heat. He bit her neck again while he flicked her nipples and was rewarded when she lifted into his hands and her arms, still trapped in the sleeves, clutched at his back.

He slipped a knee between her legs. She was tense at first and then she relaxed. He kissed his way down her, first one breast and then the other; she was soft and sweet, like peaches or thick cream. He couldn't get enough.

He slid a hand down to cup her and felt the hot wetness of her passion. Anne bucked, trying to get his hand off her. Like hell. He stroked her gently, learning her, teaching her what passion felt like. He could feel her bud rise up, stiff and small against his finger, and he started to flick it gently, so very gently, with his fingertip.

Her moan of pleasure about set the curtains swinging.

There was the bang of a door and then pounding on the door to Anne's room. Jack didn't need to guess who it was. He was clear out of patience.

"Anne! What's going on in there?"

Jack leaped out of bed, threw his discarded shirt over Anne to hide her nakedness, and opened the door.

Daphne looked real surprised to see him.

"What's going on?" he repeated coldly. "I'm pleasuring my wife. Now, if we can't get any privacy here, we'll go out on the prairie. It's not my first choice; a woman's first time should be in a bed in a room with a locked door, but one way or the other, I'm going to pleasure her."

309

Daphne, it appeared, had nothing to say. She looked a little gray around the edges, in fact.

"Understood?" Jack said, all his banked fury in that one word. "You stay in your room and keep your nose in your business and we'll stay in ours. And that goes for anyone else in this house who wants to knock on my door tonight."

Two doors clicked closed at that.

"Good night, Miz Todd," he said, his eyes relentless. He wasn't going to give her the grace to walk back to her room without his watching her every step of the way. She made it; she walked back to her room without another word spoken, and it was the first time he'd seen her that her spine wasn't as stiff as a broom handle.

Jack closed his own door and turned to face his wife. She looked pitiful; she was trying to organize the twist of fabric her gown had become and get it back on her. It was not going to happen, not if he had his way, which he would.

"I don't think we should do this," she said, not looking at him, trying to line up her buttonholes with her buttons.

"Anne, if you think that, you really are a half-wit," he said.

When she looked up at him in instant irritation, he stripped off his underwear. She didn't have a word to say after that.

"This is what a man looks like, Anne. This is what he looks like when he wants a woman and, Lord Almighty, I want you. And I'm going to have you and you're going to like it. Understood? You speak up if you have any questions about what's going to happen to you tonight, 'cuz, Lord knows, I don't want you scared. But I do want you. And, darlin', you want me."

Jack pulled her to the edge of the bed and stripped the gown off her arms and threw it on the floor; she wasn't going to crawl back into that thing when he wasn't looking. While she was sitting there, naked as the day she was born, he kissed her. Kissed her hard and fast and deep while he spread her legs and kneeled between them. With his hands, he enjoyed the weight of her breasts and he toyed with her nipples until she moaned into his mouth and wrapped her arms around his neck, holding his head to her. It didn't look like she was in the mood to fight him off. Was she ever?

He wrapped his arms around her good and tight and pulled her up against him, forcing her legs wide. Still kissing her, he trailed one hand down her and fondled her womanhood till his fingers were wet with her. She started to shake, her whole body quivering as if she had the chills of fever. He knew what fever shook her.

He eased her torso down on the bed, her legs still hanging over the side, where she thrashed and moaned, turning her head from side to side as if she were looking for something. He knew exactly what she was looking for and he knew where to find it.

He knew how to get her where she wanted to go.

Still fondling, still caressing, teasing, he sucked hard on her nipple. Her fingers clutched at the bed and she had the sheets fisted in her hands. One of her hands found a pillow and she grabbed for it, throwing it over her face. As soon as it was there, she groaned, loud. That pillow did a fine job of muffling the sound.

He eased himself into her, gradually stretching her to fit him, letting her adjust to the feel of him. Her legs jerked and she grabbed for his shoulders, pulling him in to her, down to her. He slid his hands down her thighs and pulled her legs up, knees bent. She opened up, was opening up, to him; he could feel the easing, the tight space, hot and wet, that she made for him inside her. He was halfway in and knew that the rest would not be easy. Better quick than slow, he decided.

Thumbing the tiny nub that pressed against his hand,

he brought her quickly to her release. As the contractions gripped her, he pushed in, hard and quick.

She screamed. He didn't know if it was from pain or pleasure. He couldn't see her face. The pillow covered where her head was supposed to be.

While she clung to him, he rode her, with her legs and arms wrapped around him, grunting with each thrust. It didn't take long before he felt the contractions of his own release and when they passed, he laid his body on hers with a sigh of contentment. She held him to her as her legs relaxed and her feet came to rest on the floor.

He leaned up on his elbows to study this woman whom he had made his. All he saw was the pure white of a pillowcase.

"First time I've made love to a pillow," he muttered as his head dropped back down next to hers.

Later, when they were snuggled in bed together and modestly tucked under the blankets, he held her in his arms. The house was quiet; of course, it had been quiet since his pronouncement. But this was the quiet of peace, of sleep, of rest. A dog barked somewhere out in the night, distant and mournful. The house creaked as Dammit walked down the hall, nails clicking on the wooden floor. Far off, a train whistle blew, signaling its location and its purpose.

Anne shifted her arm and tucked the blankets more firmly around her, shutting Jack out. She was naked, they both were; Jack had said he wasn't going to allow that nightgown back in this bed the whole night long. If he had meant to sound anything but sweet, he had failed. He had taken a cloth and wiped the blood from her legs, apologizing for hurting her when he was being as tender with her as a mother with her babe. He had held her, tucked her in bed, and climbed in and enfolded her in his arms. If he thought she needed comforting, he was wrong. Not about that. It was as good as she'd feared, stronger and more binding than she'd ever let herself imagine.

The train whistle blew again, farther off now, the sound just a cry in the night that drifted off and was gone.

Gone.

She had thought and planned all her life to avoid this moment, but it was one thing to plan around a faceless and nameless man, it was much harder to do it when the man had a face and the face was Jack's. Besides, it was too late for all that now. She'd made her choice; she'd gotten herself married. How long it would last was the only question now.

Maybe it would depend on how badly he needed her. She'd believed that yesterday, hearing the lonesome pain in his voice when he had spoken of his life before becoming a man. He needed a wife, a woman to hold his place in the world, a woman to give him a home. Maybe he wanted her for that. Maybe it really was something as strong as need, what he felt for her.

If he needed her, she'd stay.

If he needed her.

But if he left, if he lit out like her pa and her uncle and her grandpa had done . . . Well, he wouldn't leave, not first. She'd do it first. She'd leave him. She wasn't going to sit around and wait for a man to come back anymore. There'd been enough of that. She wouldn't be the kind of woman who sat and waited for her man to come back. She wouldn't be the kind of woman she'd been all her life.

But if Jack left today, tomorrow, in a month or a year, would she wait? Would she? No lies, not to herself; the weight of lies a man told when he was promising a woman the sun for a bonnet was a heavy enough weight of lies. She wasn't going to add to it by lying to herself.

Would she wait for Jack? For a day? A week? A month?

She would.

She would and that was her misery.

Loving him would only make it worse. She couldn't love him. If she did, the leaving that was sure to come would kill her.

"Did I hurt you?"

Anne closed her eyes and whispered, "No."

"You're quiet," he said, reaching out his hand for hers and interlocking their fingers.

"It's the middle of the night. I don't usually talk much in the middle of the night."

"You could start," he said softly. "I'm here. I'm listening."

"For how long?" she said and then wanted to bite her tongue in half. It was too vulnerable a question to throw at a man; it left her feeling more naked than she already was.

"What do you mean, 'how long?' For as long as it takes."

"And how long is that?"

Jack leaned up on one elbow and stared down at her, his face pale and chiseled in the moonlight. "What are you talking about?"

"Nothing," she said.

"Now I know I'm married," he said under his breath. He turned her to face him with gentle hands. For a killer, he was the most gentle man she'd ever known. "Look at me, Anne."

She looked at him and pulled the blanket up to her chin, hiding underneath the covers.

"Talk to me," he said. "I don't want to hear what's 'right' or what's 'polite,' just be honest, with me and with yourself. Trust me, Anne," he breathed.

She wanted to, that was the worst of it. She wanted to bury her head against his chest and sob her worry away, but that wouldn't work because she'd only sob him away with it. Hadn't she cried and cried every time her daddy had left and hadn't he just stopped coming back? There was nothing to cry about now anyway. Nothing had changed. Still, her throat closed against the pain of tears trying to find a way out. There was no way out.

"If you can't trust me now, when can you trust me?" he urged.

Never. She could never trust him.

But maybe she could talk to him. She could talk to Jack like she could talk to no one else; he let her talk, without judgment, and listened. When he got mad, it was honest anger that didn't belittle her, not fury over who she was or how she behaved or how she made him look. Talking with Jack left her feeling clean, sometimes confused, but never ashamed. Maybe she could tell him what she was thinking. Maybe she could trust him with her thoughts. Just a few.

"Anne? What is it?" he said, brushing his lips over her brow and holding her close.

"Someday," she said against his chest, "someday you'll leave."

"What do you mean?" His breathing slowed and he held himself still.

"There's no other way to say it," she said in a choked voice, pressing down the sting of unshed tears.

His arms stiffened around her and he opened a space between them. "You think I'd do that? You think I'm the kind of man who chucks his wife when he decides he's got somethin' better to do somewhere else?"

He was mad.

"If you think that little of me, why'd you marry me?" he asked hoarsely, backing up from her to lean against the headboard. He wouldn't touch her, not even under the covers. "Oh, I know. Those kisses. I got you so hot and bothered that you couldn't see straight."

"That's not true!" she said, clutching the sheet to her breast and sitting up to face him.

315

"Right," he said sarcastically.

That made her mad; here she was trying to tell him her thoughts, her *fears,* and he was getting his back up because she liked his kisses? Would he be happier if she *didn't* like his kisses?

"You think I'd marry a man just for his kisses? What kind of woman do you think *I* am?"

"A woman who likes to kiss and lets too many men kiss her."

"You don't know a thing about me!"

"I know enough," he snarled, getting out of bed. Leaving her.

"And I know a few things, too," she said on a rising sob. "I told you you'd leave me. Men leave. It's all they do."

Jack stopped putting on his pants and turned to look down at her. She was sitting in the dark, holding the sheets around her as if they were her last protection against the monsters of the night. Looking at him as if he were one of those monsters.

"Anne, I'm not leaving," he said, sitting down on the edge of the bed and reaching for her hand.

"Yes, you are," she choked out.

"I *won't* leave."

"You're already half out the door."

Jack kicked off his pants. "I can't leave like this," he said with a soft smile. "See? I'm not leaving."

"Men can always leave; they don't need pants to do it."

"Well, I do," he said, stroking her hand with his thumb. "I've got a bad enough name in this town without stomping around in my boots and my hat and nothing in between."

Anne smiled past her tears and hung her head, her hair spilling down to hide her face. "I'm sorry. I never should have said anything."

"If there's one thing I'm going to do in all the years that I'm not leaving you, it's to get you to stop apologizing for everything. You get mad. I get mad. It don't mean anything. Nothing's broken here, Anne. I'm not going anywhere."

"How do you know?" she whispered, her hair hiding her face and her tears. Nothing could hide the pain in her voice.

"I just know," he whispered back.

Anne shook her head and swallowed hard against the pain in her chest.

"I know," he said, "because I know who I am. I'm not a man who leaves his woman."

"You don't know," she said. "I've seen it before. I've seen it my whole life."

He pulled her against his chest, letting her bury her head against his warmth, stroking her hair, absorbing her hurt, and offering her unrelenting comfort. It was wonderful, in a painful way, to be able to hurt and cry and have no one tell her to stop. No one tell her that she had to put a good face on it and keep her dignity at all costs. She didn't want dignity, not now; she wanted someone to love her and protect her. Someone who would stay. She wanted the impossible.

She wanted it anyway.

"I know what you've seen," he said softly, rubbing her back with long, firm strokes. "I know about all of it."

"No one knows all of it."

"I expect that's true, but I know enough to understand. Lane told me."

"When?"

"Back a few days, maybe last week; long enough ago for me to think on it. Long enough for me to figure out why you're always running to that train."

Anne froze in his arms, afraid of what he was going to say. She didn't want to hear him say it. She didn't want to be that exposed, like a side of beef quartered and skinned and left to hang.

317

"Don't say it," she said on a whisper.

"The pain's not in sayin' it. The pain's in livin' it, Anne," he said gently. "You go to the trains, not because you want to leave, but because you're hoping, wishing, that one of the men of your family will come home again. You want 'em to come back."

That was true enough. She could have gone anytime. There was nothing holding her here, except the hard ties of family and the wish that maybe her pa would find her here. It wasn't so hard to find a person if you were looking. All he had to do was look and she would have been here, waiting. But he hadn't come because he hadn't looked.

"They never will," she said softly. "They go. They don't come back."

She'd known it was true even as she waited, but saying it made it real. Her pa wasn't coming back. Her uncle and her grandpa weren't coming back. No amount of waiting was going to change that.

"That may be true of them, but it's not true of me." He lifted her off his chest and looked into her stinging eyes. "Those men were bastards, one hundred proof, to run off and leave their women and their kids. I'm not like that."

Looking into his eyes, she could almost believe him. Resting in his arms, she was halfway there. She'd never heard a man so mournful and solemn about family. In Jack's voice, she heard the echo of her own longings and her own dreams. Even, just a little, some of her own pain.

She wanted to trust him.

She was so very close to trusting him.

"Kiss me, Jack," she said, leaning toward him, wanting the comfort of his arms and wanting to give him comfort in return.

His kiss was gentle and full of heartbreak. She put her arms around his back, feeling the hard pull of muscle and

318

the slick smoothness of skin. And heat. He was so very hot.

He held her softly, the hard possession of their first mating gone to be replaced by tender caresses and slow meanderings over bared skin and loose limbs. With his hands, he told her that he would never hurt her. With his mouth, he promised to want her forever. With his body, he claimed her. So gentle, so thorough, so leisurely in his taking of her. Laying her down, smoothing his hands over her breasts and stomach and hips, sliding fingertips over the tops of her thighs and across her ribs, kissing her eyes and her cheeks and her throat. And her mouth. Giving himself to her. Taking her for himself as a precious thing, yearned for, sought after, and found. Kept. Treasured. Cherished.

Loved.

She wanted it to be so. She wanted to believe his hands and his kiss, to sink into the softness of unhurried love, knowing that same love would be there tomorrow and tomorrow. To rest in love. To love without fear. To be loved.

She wanted to be loved.

He spread her legs slowly and she reached up for him, urging him down to her by the soft fall of his hair. The cords of muscle in his arms and chest stood out in the pearl-gray light of night; if she did not know him for who he was, she would have been afraid. He was a hard man, hard in body and hard in deeds, but his spirit was not hard.

He said he wouldn't leave her and he was a man who said only what he meant to say. And who wanted the same of her. It was a great gift, this shared talk of no boundaries and no barriers, if she could accept it. If she could believe it.

He came into her in one hard push. She wrapped herself around him and took him into her, feeling the fullness he brought to her, the heat and the completeness that were so much a part of what he was teaching her about the marriage bed. His strokes were slow, measured, full, and she matched him, kissing his throat and his shoulder, holding on to the ridged planes of his back. Wanting him, wanting everything about him, and eased down to her soul to know that he wanted her. Even for this. Even if only for this.

The tension building inside her pushed aside all thoughts and feelings until she was lost in sensation, remembering only that Jack was with her and Jack would take care of her. That he had promised never to hurt her. She trusted that. And with the freedom of trust, Anne fell down into pure sensation, pure ecstacy, trusting Jack to protect her as she fell. Throbbing hard against his thrusts, pushed to a place of no boundaries, she could feel only Jack. He was in her, a part of her, in a place where they were one. Whole. Together. Pulsing. He held her, his breath loud and sharp in her ear, falling with her, holding her as they fell together.

He was sweating, his back shining in the dim light, the curtains moving in the narrow breeze of the partially opened window. He held her, kissed her temple, kissed her breast, and left her body. But he didn't leave her.

Their breathing settled down to normal. The wind blew suddenly cold and she moved to set the bed to rights, wanting the comfort of a blanket, wanting the haze of sleep to take her while she lay in Jack's arms.

"Where's my pillow?" she said, patting the bed, looking for it.

"I threw it on the floor," Jack said, reaching down to get it. "Just a precaution."

The sound of their shared laughter followed them as they fell into sleep.

* * *

A Kiss to Die For

His mama called out again, calling him. She'd made something for him, a treat of apples and crust and cream. He wanted the treat, but he knew his mama would send him to bed for a rest after he had finished eating. It was that time of day. He crunched lower into the brush, delighting in the knowledge that she couldn't see him, and worked on the last line in the dust that would finish his house.

The shot rang out against the heat and the quiet.

His mama stopped calling.

Lifting his head, he could just see where she lay, the red of her blood running over the hard-packed dirt so fast there wasn't a chance for it to sink in. His daddy fired twice from the corral and was answered with the crack of a dozen shots, rifle shots. He knew the sound of a rifle. Men rode in, trampling his daddy into the dirt, and collected the herd of horses that was his daddy's living. They rode off on horses covered in sweat and dust; they rode off as quietly as they had ridden in. Except this time, there were no rifle shots.

The sun was still hot, only now it wasn't hot enough to warm him.

He shivered until the sun set, seated firmly in his own scratched-out little bedroom next to the Brazos. He stayed there, in the last place he had felt safe, all the night through.

Sometime the next day, a woman who had shared flour and salt with his mama came by with her man. He could hear her crying clearly all the way to his little house in the dirt. But he did not raise his head.

Calling, calling . . . He could not answer her. She found him, in time, and held him to her bosom. She did not smell like his mama and her bosom felt different. He let her hold him anyway. She bundled him up in her shawl, still shivering, and walked him to her buggy.

His house got ruined when she had clutched him to her, the lines blurring and rubbing away until it resembled nothing but random scratches in the dust with some of the walls of his house lost altogether. He couldn't help looking back at his house as she

321

led him away. She wouldn't let him look at all at the house that
his daddy built. Her man was doing something with his daddy
and mama, he couldn't see what. He didn't try very hard to find
out.

The flour and salt woman knew that his family had relatives
in New Orleans; she paid for the train ticket herself and bought
him a new pair of pants and a pair of shoes that were too big.
He wore them anyway. He'd been to town before with his daddy
and knew the shopkeeper by sight. He knew the man at the livery
and the man at the train depot. He knew the sight of the town;
it was familiar.

She settled him on the train, putting his basket of food between
his thigh and the window and asking if he didn't have to use
the privy just one more time. He was too embarrassed to answer,
even though he did want to use the privy just one more time. She
told the conductor to watch out for him and make certain he got
off when he should. She told him that he was going to family,
that he was going to be just fine. She had that tightness in her
voice that his mama got just before she cried. He didn't know
why this woman would want to cry. She must be different in that
way, too, not just in her smell and the feel of her bosom.

The train made all the sounds of a train getting ready to go
and so the flour and salt woman got off after telling him again
to sit still and not eat all his food at once. Even through the
smoke, he could see that she waited on the platform, waving and
holding the end of her shawl to her mouth, as the train pulled
away from all he had ever known.

In an act of desperate disobedience, he lunged to his feet and
pressed his face to the window. His food basket tumbled to the
wooden floor; he ignored it. The town was behind him and the
train was surging forward with noisy speed toward the east. His
daddy had taught him his directions. His face he kept turned
toward the west and the life he was leaving behind him with
every turn of the wheels. He could not sit and he could only look
back. Behind him was all that was familiar.

Behind him was the last home he would ever know.

A Kiss to Die For

He awoke with a start, covered in sweat, and reached for his gun. It was in his hand before he'd taken his first full breath. It steadied him, the feel of his gun in his hand, cold and smooth and heavy.

Anne sat up and reached out to him, her hand on his leg.

"What's wrong?" she asked.

"Nothin'. Thought I heard something." He made himself lower his gun, made himself set it on the floor next to the bed.

It was almost dawn, the sky still black, but the black of a night that knows its time is short. The stars were gone, overpowered by a sun they couldn't yet see, and the air was dead still. Trouble was, she could see pretty well in that light.

"You're sweating. Did you have a nightmare?"

"Just hot. Not used to sleeping two to a bed," he said, winking at her in the dim light. His breath was still ragged. He brushed the hair out of his eyes and smiled at his wife. "Can't wait to get used to it, though."

Anne didn't smile back. She pushed his hair back from his face and then ran a hand up and down his back. It was real comforting. He was afraid that was the reason she was doing it.

"What's wrong, Jack?"

"Nothin'."

"Now I know *I'm* married," she said wryly. "Tell me."

Jack slid down in bed and pulled her on top of him, cupping her bottom with his hands and grinning up at her. "You've been a married lady for a whole night. What do you think of it?"

She pushed herself away from him, bracing her hands on either side of his head, and said, "I think you have one set of rules for me and another for yourself. That's a one-sided game by any account."

"I told you, men and women are different."

"And I told you, I'm not a half-wit. We aren't that different. Talk to me."

"Nothing to talk about."

"One-sided," she said, rolling off him and sitting next to him on the bed. "I don't recall you asking me whether I wanted to share any of my secrets with you."

"You didn't share them, I found them out."

"Bull. The fact is, you know them and it wasn't easy for me. You told me that I could trust you. Are you going to trust me?"

It was an important question; the weight of their future rested on it. He didn't want to tell her what he kept tied down tight inside him. She couldn't do anything about it and it didn't help to talk about it. Trouble was, he understood women. She'd never open up to him again if she felt he was shutting her out. A woman liked a free rein to walk all over a man's life; the best thing a man could do was pick a woman who walked carefully. Come to that, Anne was the most careful woman he'd ever seen.

"Yeah, I'll trust you," he said and pulled her back against him, her back against his chest while he leaned against the headboard. He'd tell her, but he didn't want her looking at him while he did it. A man had some rights to privacy, even with his wife.

"It's a dream I have, that's all."

"The same dream?"

He made an agreeing sort of noise.

"How often?"

"More often than I like."

"Tell me about it. Is it a real dream or a pretend dream?"

"What?"

"You know, a dream that has real people in it and real things happening or—"

"It's a real dream. Too damn real."

"What happens?"

Her hair was soft and thick against his chest, her bottom warm as she nestled between his outstretched legs. The last thing he wanted to do at the moment was talk. But he didn't want to break the trust he was building with her, so he talked.

The things a man did to please his woman.

"I'm a little kid and I'm playing in the dirt next to the river, the Brazos, down in Texas. I can hear my folks a way off, but I'm hiding in the tall grass, digging lines in the dirt with a stick."

Making the home he'd always wanted, but could never have. Until now. Until Anne.

He hadn't wanted to talk about it, but now that he'd started, it seemed to flow up out of him. The images rolled through his mind like they had a thousand times, only this time his eyes were open and it wasn't so bad. It wasn't like he was living it over and over.

"And then I hear a shot and my ma's lying in the dirt, blood running out of her, and my pa's shot a few times and then our horses are run off. And I'm left in the grass by the river."

She didn't say anything, but she shifted sideways and wrapped her arms around his waist, pressing her face to his belly. He could feel her breath on his skin, unexpectedly comforting.

It wasn't so bad, telling her. His gun was just a few inches from his hand, lying on the floor, ready to be grabbed up. He could get to it. Nobody could get him; he was ready. He was always ready now.

"I'm there awhile, through the night anyway, and someone, a woman, comes and takes me off. She buys me some clothes and sets me on a train heading east, off to kin. Folks I ain't never seen before. She gave me some food and I knocked it all over the floor of the car. I felt real bad about that, seeing the trouble she took."

He didn't say anything after that. The birds were starting to call, the black of night giving over to lightest gray edged with pink. It was almost sunrise.

"It's not a dream, is it?" Anne said. He could feel tears on his skin. "It's a memory."

They lay in each other's arms and watched the sun come up.

"Yeah," Jack said, holding her tight against the growing light of the new day.

Chapter Twenty-three

The house was just rousing when there was a banging on the front door. Daphne was up and going down those stairs like a trail boss, mumbling her irritation with each step she took. Her temper didn't sweeten when she saw who was parked on her porch.

"Morning, ma'am," Callahan said, stepping over the threshold. "We need to talk to Jack."

"It's too early to receive visitors," she snapped, but she was unable to stop his forward momentum. Gabriel was right behind him.

"Ma'am." He tipped his hat.

They were both covered in dust and had a growth of whiskers sprouting up. They looked like they'd had a hard night.

They had.

Jack came down the stairs, fully dressed and fully armed, as they walked in. There was only one reason for them to be here, one thing he'd asked for them to do while he had his time with Anne: Tucker.

Callahan and Gabe nodded to Jack, ignoring Miss

Daphne as they left her behind, standing at the door with her mouth open and her eyes snapping.

"Morning, Miss Daphne," Jack said cordially. "We need to talk in private, so we'll just go on and use that room you set up for me a few days back." He was walking toward the kitchen as he spoke, with Callahan and Gabriel following. Daphne didn't say a word; he didn't give her the chance to.

When they were in the room, the door closed, Callahan started talking.

"Found Tucker."

"That was quick," Jack said.

"Dead," Gabriel said.

"Dead?" Jack said, his eyes disbelieving.

"Worse than dead; murdered," Callahan said. "Gutted like a fish and with his throat cut open from ear to ear; worst-looking smile you ever saw."

"How long?" Jack asked.

"A day or two, maybe three, no more than that. Found him in an old shack not much above five miles from here. Two horses in, different directions, two out, same direction."

"Met his killer out there and somebody's got a horse more than he did two days ago," Jack concluded. "Met him by accident or on purpose?"

"Hard to say," Callahan said. "From what you said about him, I'd think he was going to a meeting. The place was quiet and tucked away. Not something you'd stumble on out riding."

"Could a woman have done it?"

"Not likely," Gabe said. "He didn't have a bullet hole on him and it'd take a powerful woman to slice a man like that. He had to see it comin'."

"You still figure him for the killer?" Callahan asked.

"I don't know," Jack said, slapping his hat against his thigh as he pondered.

Callahan bit his thumb, thinking out loud, "It could be that he killed them gals and then was killed by someone else; maybe by someone who knew him for the killer and was out for revenge."

"Them gals didn't have much, not a one of them; all from little, hoping for much. Can't think of any family that could have done it. In fact, now that I think on it, there wasn't a one that I found who came from a home with a man in it," Jack said.

"Somebody else then? Two killers running over the same track?" Gabe offered.

"Been known to happen, I guess, but it don't smell like that to me. What do you think?" Jack said.

"No, it don't smell casual," Callahan said. "There was something real personal about the way he was cut up. Guts pulled out and left to lie on his legs. Personal."

"Same killer?" Gabe said. "The one thing you gotta say about them strangled gals is that it seemed damned personal. Who kills a woman if it's not personal?"

"I sure had my sights on Tucker as being the one," Jack mumbled.

"If he was, then the problem is solved. No more murders."

"Yeah, but I don't want to find out we're wrong the hard way," Jack said.

"There's that," Gabe said.

"We brought the body in; laid it out at the doc's," Callahan said.

"You tell Lane?"

"Came looking for you first," Callahan said.

"Let's go get him. He'll need to know one of Abilene's finest citizens has been killed," Jack said, the sarcasm heavy in his voice.

Anne scooted back into the kitchen and hid until they had left the house. She'd heard every word and they hadn't seen her. That was good because she was so pressed by guilt, she was about to fold under the weight. Bill dead. Murdered. And so close to Abilene.

Jack had hated him, believed him capable of killing those women, that had been obvious from what she'd heard. And Jack had been jealous of Bill because she'd made him so, purposely, deliberately, and at every opportunity. Jack was a violent man, given to violent acts. Everybody knew that. He was a bounty hunter. It was a violent life.

She'd pushed him to violence. It was as clear as rainwater. She'd used poor Bill and manipulated Jack and now a man was dead.

All because she'd kissed Jack.

Lane was on his way to the doc's when they found him; the doc had sent one of the Walton kids for him and the kid had given him the message. About half the town knew about the murder already. Jack knew that just by the looks he was getting. Guess he was high on the list of possible suspects and he figured it was a mighty short list besides.

"Didn't need for this to happen," Lane muttered as they joined up with him.

"Never a good time for a murder," Jack said.

"What time did you find him?" Lane asked.

"Last night," Callahan answered, "about an hour or more after moonrise."

"Full moon. Good for tracking," Lane said mildly.

"Yeah, otherwise I don't know as how we'd have found him without daylight. And we did find him. Dead."

Lane nodded. Everyone was a suspect until he had this thing figured out. Murder had come to Abilene, all right, but who'd have thought it'd be Bill Tucker? Not an enemy to his name, except for Jack. Talk was already running that Jack had done it. Couldn't be helped; Bill had been real popular and Jack was a man who made enemies just by showing up. Still, he had two who stood by him now, hard men, used to killing. Was the friendship of the sort that they'd do a killing for a man in need? Lane looked them over as they passed into the doc's office.

Damn, but he hadn't seen this coming.

Bill was laid out on the doc's table, looking as dead as pan-fried steak. Doc Carr was ripping off what was left of Tucker's shirt and laying it aside for his examination.

"Don't take a doctor to see what's killed him," Malcolm snapped. "I didn't become a doctor to stick my fingers into a dead body."

"Then find another line," Jack said, equally sharp. "We need someone who knows what he's doing to check things out."

"He's dead!" Carr stormed.

"How? What went first?" Jack snarled back. "Did the knife get to his heart? Is that how he went? Or was it the gutting itself, did he bleed to death?"

"What does it matter? He's dead," Carr said stonily.

"It's not easy to get the heart, lots of bone in the way. That tells us something. He was gutted, that's for sure, but was his breastbone cut through? Did that knife hack at bone? Takes a strong arm for that. Can you tell which came first, the gut or the throat? Where's there the most blood? It all matters, it all tells us something, maybe something about the killer."

"You seem to know a lot about dead bodies," Malcolm Carr said.

"Yeah, well, I should, I've seen enough of 'em," Jack replied without apology.

The doc closed his mouth with a snap and bent to his "patient."

"Throat first, looks like," Gabe said, bending over Tucker.

"Didn't mar his face," Callahan said.

"What difference does that make? Dead is dead," Carr said.

Claudia Dain

"Whoever did it didn't care that anyone would know it was Tucker that was found," Lane said. "Could have sliced him up and made it tough to know who it was."

"Maybe he wanted us to know," Jack said.

"Throat first," Lane said, "is easier if you have some height. Tucker was a big man."

"So not a woman," Callahan said.

"A woman? Why would a woman—" Carr said.

"Women have their reasons to kill," Gabe said.

"Throat first," Lane said, "so the rest was for sport. Or revenge."

"Them guts laying out," Callahan said, "that tells me it was personal. Doc? Are them guts cut or whole?"

The doctor kept his commentary to himself and examined the cavity. "Whole."

"That means that they were lifted out with hands, not pulled out with a knife. Very personal."

Anne made a special trip to talk to Reverend Holt. He didn't seem surprised to see her. That in itself was plain embarrassing.

"Good day to you, Mrs. Scullard," he said with a smile.

"Good morning, Reverend Holt. I hope I'm not disturbing you?"

"Of course not. I'm always happy to talk to you. How are you faring today?"

"Oh, fine," she said weakly.

"Has anyone yet told you . . . ?"

"Oh, yes, I know about Bill. I feel just terrible about it. So guilty," she said, resisting the need to wring her hands.

"Guilty?" he said. "Sit down, Anne, and you tell me why you would have anything to feel guilty about. You can't mean that you feel responsible for Bill's death?"

Anne settled herself in the upholstered chair that faced the reverend's desk and clasped her hands in her lap; she had the look of a penitent pilgrim.

"I do. I do feel responsible," she gasped out. "Oh, Reverend, you don't know what I did, the awful, sinful things I did."

Holt sat down behind his desk and leaned across it, his big arms almost covering the desktop.

"Tell me. I'll listen."

"I provoked him, provoked him as often as I could."

"Bill?"

"No, not Bill. Jack."

Holt frowned and rubbed a hand across his chin. "What does Jack have to do with it?"

"I kept . . . kissing him," she whispered.

"Bill?" he asked on a high note.

"No, Jack."

"You are saying that you kept kissing Jack and that it provoked . . . Bill?"

"No, Jack," she said on a sigh. This confession was impossible. The reverend didn't seem to be following her at all.

"Why would Jack be provoked by your kissing him? Are you saying that he didn't like it? But that can't be so since he married you. Anne, really, just tell me straight out so I can make sense of what you're saying."

"I liked Jack, but Bill was my beau," she said, feeling like a Jezebel, "so I sort of . . . courted Jack, kissing him and such, and then I used Jack to sort of force Bill off, which made Bill mad and Jack got mad about that, too. I'm sure Jack wouldn't have asked me to marry him if Bill hadn't been about to do it himself. And then Bill and Jack had a fight, which they couldn't help but have what with the way I'd played them against each other, and Jack said he'd kill Bill. And now Bill's dead," she finished in a rush of breath, her eyes pleading for understanding and forgiveness.

"You believe Jack killed Bill?" Holt asked, his own eyes wide with horror. But Anne mistook the cause. "You believed he was capable of it all along, didn't you?"

She nodded, uncertain where the reverend was going.

"Anne Ross Scullard," he thundered, "you willingly married a man you believe capable of cold and ruthless murder?"

Was that what she'd done? She didn't answer because the reverend was building to a fine outrage.

"I would never have married you to any man I thought capable of such a thing. Yes, I know Jack Scullard's reputation and yes, I know the gossip, but killing in the line of duty is one thing and murder is something else again. And I can tell you one thing, if you sort the wheat from the chaff, you'll find that Jack is not a man to resort to murder, no matter how provoked."

"But everyone is saying—"

"Anne, you're a grown woman, or I never would have married you, but you've got to stop turning with the whim of the crowd. Do *you* have evidence of brutality in Jack?"

She thought of last night and all the days before when he'd been gentle and patient and protective. "No," she whispered, "but Miss Daphne always says, 'Lean not on your own understanding.' "

"I know the line well," he said briskly. "Would you like to know what the whole verse says?"

Before she had a chance to answer, his Bible was on his desk, flipped to the page, and pushed over to her. With a finger he pointed to the line while he recited from memory.

"Proverbs, chapter three, verses five and six:

'Trust in the Lord with all thine heart,
And lean not unto thine own understanding.
In all thy ways acknowledge Him,
And He shall direct thy paths.' "

Anne read the lines with him. It was nothing like what she'd been taught all her life. She'd been instructed that she was a foolish child, given to acts of reckless disobedience, and that she had to lean upon the wisdom of her grandmother, not of God. Some days, she thought that God would have been an easier taskmaster.

"Do you understand this verse, Anne?" Reverend Holt asked. "Do you see that what you have been doing *is* leaning on your own understanding? You listen to Powell, to McShay, to Sheriff Lane, to Miss Daphne, but do you listen to God? Have you ever asked Him which path He has for you? He's the only one you can listen to and trust, Anne, because He's the only one who knows everything and who truly has your best interests at heart."

No, she had never thought to ask God . . . for anything. She went to church twice weekly, sat and listened to the sermons, participated in the ladies' circle, and tried not to make anybody mad at her; that's what she did, all of what she did. She had stopped talking to God right after her father had left her; she'd prayed once, hard, for God to bring her daddy back. But God hadn't done it and so she'd stopped asking for anything. Not because she was mad at God, but because she was learning that what she wanted didn't matter and that nothing she did, no matter what prayer she whispered in the dark of her bedroom or how good she was, changed that.

She had never trusted the Lord with all her heart. The only thing she'd done with all her heart was be afraid.

"Anne," he said gently, "do you love Jack? Beyond the passion that God created as surely as He created everything else?"

Did she love Jack? She didn't want to love Jack; loving Jack would make everything all the harder. Why didn't he ask if Jack loved *her*? That would be easier to answer because she knew he didn't. He'd never spoken of love, he'd only spoken of kisses, of passion. She didn't want to love a man who didn't love her. Not again.

"I don't know," she answered.

"Why?"

"I don't think I want to love," she said, lifting her chin and staring into the reverend's large brown eyes. She half expected a rebuke. She got a smile.

"Love is a choice, Anne. Always," he said. "It's not earned, but given, and never to anybody who deserves it."

"I didn't say he didn't deserve it," she said, lifting her brows. Reverend or not, she wasn't going to let him insult Jack.

"No, you didn't." He smiled. "And didn't you vow, just yesterday, to love him all the days of your life, as well as to honor and obey? How's it going?" He had a huge grin on his face. She smiled back and relaxed in her chair.

"A bit rocky," she said.

"Usually is," he said.

"Really? Did you and Constance ever—?"

"All the time." He grinned. "The first year she must have cried once a week and I left the house in a rage just as often."

"You seem so happy now."

"We are. We worked it all out. I'd come back, she'd stop crying, and then we'd start talking."

He'd come back. It all rested on that. But Jack would leave and he wouldn't come back. No matter what anybody said.

"Anne," the reverend said, coming around from his desk and taking her by the hand, " ' . . . love bears all things, believes all things, hopes all things, endures all things. Love never fails.' Honor your marriage vows to Jack; he doesn't deserve any less."

"He'll leave me," she said, not quite aware she had spoken the words out loud.

"You don't know that."

"I do."

"No, you only know that you believe he will. Give him a chance to fulfill the vow he gave you, the vow to love,

336

honor, and cherish. A man doesn't leave someone he cherishes."

But he didn't cherish her, did he? That was the whole trouble; she didn't know. She didn't know what love was supposed to look like in a man. But she wanted to believe that if anyone could show her, it would be Jack. Maybe that was something.

After a tearful hug in the bearlike embrace of Reverend Holt, Anne started home. She had a lot to think about and she wasn't in any hurry to get where she was headed; Miss Daphne always had a pile of work to be done and she just needed some quiet time to ponder all that the reverend had said, especially about that verse, "Lean not unto thine own understanding." She hoped she had the guts to tell Miss Daphne that she knew the *whole* verse now.

She didn't have long to ponder; the streets were busy, everyone sharing the news about the murder. She didn't want to think about the murder anymore, much less talk about it, since it would only force her to defend Jack and she wasn't sure she could do that right now. She was flat exhausted.

"Good morning, Anne Scullard!" Martha O'Shaughnessy called out as she walked toward her from the mercantile. "How does it feel to be a married woman?"

She obviously hadn't heard about Bill's murder or she wouldn't have asked what it felt like to be married to the town's top suspect.

"It feels just fine, Mrs. O'Shaughnessy," Anne said, smiling politely.

"Anne Scullard," Martha repeated under her breath and then her breath caught in her throat and she reached out for Anne.

"Are you all right, Martha?" Anne asked, taking her basket of packages. "Do you need to sit?"

"No," she gasped, then grinned. "I knew that name was familiar. I kept telling Shaughn and he kept waving me off, but I'm not likely to forget that name, now, am I? No, things like that don't happen often, praise the Lord."

"Amen," Anne murmured, completely lost as to Martha's meaning.

"I'm so glad he turned out well after such a bad start. I had my doubts, sending him off like that, had half a mind to keep him for myself, but that wouldn't have been right, his having family and all. Family first, I always say."

"Who are you talking about?"

"Why, little Jacques!" she exclaimed with a huge smile.

"Oh," Anne said blankly. "Perhaps I can walk with you into the Demorest, it's right here and you might want to rest a bit before you go on down to your place," Anne said, seriously frightened for Martha, who had always been the most solid of women. This threadbare conversation was nothing like her.

"Oh, Anne, I'm all right! Don't you understand? Jacques's parents had been killed, murdered for their stock, and the little boy was all alone out there, sitting by the river like the lost child he was. Why, he couldn't have been more than four at the time and no more than a good stone's throw from where his parents lay. Sitting in a square of dirt, huddled and rocking and staring with big blue eyes down at all these lines he'd made. His house, he called it. I'll never forget that. Poor little thing, sitting in the dirt and pretending it was his house."

"You're the woman," Anne said, her face going white. "You're the woman in his dream."

"He dreams about me? Poor lamb, it must be a nightmare if he dreams of that day," Martha said. "I was down in Texas living with my brother. His wife had died and he needed a woman to keep things for him. I wasn't there

338

long since he married again not a year later, but I was there long enough for that murder. Never caught the bandits, not that I ever heard, and of course, I never had any contact with Jacques after he went to New Orleans; his father's sister, I think it was, took him in. I never knew how that turned out, but I just couldn't imagine anyone not taking to that boy. Sweet as sugar with blue eyes that rivaled an angel's and the most polite manners I'd ever seen."

"How did you know?" Anne thought to ask. "How did you finally remember after all these years?"

"Why, it was saying your name." Martha smiled and clasped Anne by the arm. "That was his mother's name— Anne Scullard."

Chapter Twenty-four

Anne didn't even have time to let that knowledge settle before Martha was bustling off, full of excitement. Jack was walking down the street with Sheriff Lane and Callahan and Gabriel. A somber foursome they made, but Martha wouldn't be put off by that, not after years of worrying and wondering.

She reached them in front of her own place, the Mustang Saloon, and stopped them by the very force of her smile.

"I knew your name," she said. "The first time Shaughn told me about you, I knew I knew you but I didn't know how."

She was looking at Jack and it was Jack who responded. "Ma'am?"

Martha reached out and touched his arm, sending him a grin as bright as a hundred candles. "Don't you know me? But I wouldn't expect that you would, being as you were smaller than a jackrabbit and twice as quiet. I declare, I never knew a boy so quiet and composed; please and thank you and not much else came out of his mouth that I ever could tell. My, but your ma was pleased by you; she thought the sun rose and set on you, that's a fact. I'm Martha, Jacques," she urged. "Martha Conner, back then. It was down on the Brazos, with my brother, Pete."

Jack just looked down at his boots and shook his head. "I'm sorry, ma'am, but I don't recall . . . Did you call me Jacques?" he asked, looking at her face.

"Of course, child, Jacques Scullard, and your mama was Anne and your pa Eduard, God rest them both. It's been many a year I've prayed that all went well for you, Jacques, and now, here you are, as handsome and fit as any man has a right to be. Your mama would be so, so pleased," she said brokenly, tears welling in her eyes as she stroked his arm.

Jack looked at her hard, at the lined face and the large-bosomed shape of her; he could see nothing that was familiar, but the sound of her voice as she had spoken, the tears so ready to spring up, stirred something. Her hair was silver brown and she wore it in a coronet of braids. He liked the way that looked and, he remembered, he'd liked it once before. . . .

"You used to borrow flour and salt from my mama," he said softly.

"Yes, and she eggs from me. My brother had five good layers," she sniffed. "She loved to make you pies and crumbles."

Yes, she had. His mother had loved to bake for him, luring him into the house for a treat and a nap. She would watch his every mouthful, a smile wide on her beautiful face. Then she would lay him down and sit on the bed to take off his shoes and he would try to fight the sleepiness that tugged at his body, trying so hard to be like his daddy, who didn't need to take a nap in the heart of the day.

He remembered. He remembered it all.

Jack reached out and laid a hand over Martha's clenching fingers, pressing the touch of her into his arm, this dim and distant connection to all that he had lost in one splintered moment so many years ago.

"You look fine, Jacques," she said, looking up at him, tears welling in her eyes.

Jack smiled down at her and whispered, "Thank you, ma'am. And thank you for the lunch; it lasted me all the way to New Orleans and I savored every bite."

With a small cry of emotion, Martha threw her arms around Jack and embraced him with all the care and affection of a mother. As Jack wrapped his arms around her, he bent his head down and caught her scent; the same. It was just the same as when she'd wrapped her arms around a lost boy and carried him back into the world, buying him new shoes for his trip. It was the last hug he'd known as a boy and was the closest thing to his mother's hug as he was going to get. So he let her hug him. Yeah, he let her, the deep joy of the act enfolding him as surely as her arms did.

"What are you doing, Ma?" Shaughn said, coming out onto the boardwalk.

She pulled away and sniffed and pushed a pin back into her high-bound hair. "I was saying hello and welcome to a man I knew as a boy. This is Jacques Scullard, Shaughn, and I told you that his name sounded familiar!"

"Jacques?" Shaughn asked.

"Of course, Jacques! With a name like Scullard, what else would it be but Jacques? I would have figured out who he was days ago if you'd only given me the right name! Why did you have to keep calling him Jack Skull?"

Jack looked over at Shaughn and said, "Yeah, why'd you tell her my name was Skull?"

Shaughn coughed a few times and then with a sweep of his hand said, "Come on in and have a drink. It's too hot a day to stand around outside."

A Kiss to Die For

It was overcast and breezy, but the whole lot of them went into the saloon.

"You all just sit while I go on back and dish you up some food; I've been aching to feed this boy again for years and it'll be something hot this time, Jacques, and better than a box lunch!"

"Thank you, ma'am," came a round of amused male voices. Callahan and Gabriel were used to it; Jack just seemed to attract this sort of thing from most women. It appeared he'd started young, judging by Martha's comments.

Anne followed Martha to the small room at the back that served as kitchen. The Mustang didn't serve food as a rule, not like the Demorest, but if a customer got hungry and wanted a little something, it seemed a shame to let him walk out the door when Martha could throw together something that would keep him satisfied and spending his money in the Mustang. Why should the Demorest get all the business? It had been Martha's idea and Shaughn hadn't said a word against it, especially as she was doing all of the work.

"How can I help?" Anne asked.

Martha was already pulling out the chicken she'd made that morning; it wasn't quite hot, but she could make a nice gravy and it would only take a few minutes for the corn bread to warm. . . .

"Thank you, Anne, I've almost got this together, but if you'd just divide those chickens into man-sized servings while I stick this corn bread in. And there's a fresh apron hanging behind the door on a hook."

Anne found it and tied it on, then picked up a knife and began dividing the chickens into parts.

"So, you knew Jack's mother and father," Anne said, probing for information the way she was probing the chicken. "What were they like?"

"Oh, nice folks," Martha said, heating up the stock for the gravy. "Such a tragedy."

"What happened?"

"Shot dead, both of them, and their stock stolen; horses mostly. That man had a knack with horses and could get them to do most anything. He had a real eye, too. Folks around there respected him, sought him out when they were looking to buy. And you know the talk about horse dealers, not an honest one in a hundred, but he was that one. Fine man."

"And his wife?"

Martha smiled in memory and stirred in some flour with the heated chicken stock. "Pretty as daylight. Devoted mother. Friendly when you came to call and had a free hand when it came to lending. We shared a cup of coffee a time or two, sitting in that little house. Her table was fine, walnut with scrolled legs; she said it came all the way from Louisiana. That's how it came out about her family being from there. His, too."

"Pretty as daylight? Was she blond?"

"No, hair black as pitch with eyes to match. His hair was lightish and the bluest eyes I ever saw. Jacques takes after his pa more 'n' his ma, I'd say, though there's some of both in him."

"It's strange, isn't it, that he'd marry a woman with the same name as his ma?" Anne asked.

Martha shrugged. "Anne's not so uncommon a name and hers, I think, was Annette, though no one called her that, 'cept maybe her man."

Anne flicked back a curl of her dark hair and pondered. It couldn't be more than coincidence. Martha was right; Anne was a common name. Besides, she'd courted Jack, not the other way around. Of course, he was the one who'd insisted they marry, but a man wouldn't marry a woman just because of her name.

A Kiss to Die For

"Anne, that bread smells done," Martha said, whisking the gravy with a sharp hand.

Anne pulled herself out of her doubts and bent to take the corn bread from the oven. Martha poured gravy over the chicken. Anne cut the corn bread and put it on a platter. Arms full, they carried the food in to the men.

The talking had been quiet, but it stopped when they came in. They must have been talking about Bill's murder.

They had been.

Martha went back to fetch plates and forks and then the eating began. The men were disinclined to talk. Martha wasn't.

"So how was it, growing up in New Orleans? I always wondered how a little boy as used to lonesome as you were would do in a city like that."

Jack finished chewing his chicken and took a long swallow of beer to wash it down before he answered. "I did all right."

"And your folks, they got the letter I sent off?"

"They knew I was coming, yeah." Jack broke off a hunk of corn bread and buttered it heavily.

"So, growing up in the city like that, how'd you end up out West? I wouldn't have thought they'd let you go, especially after what happened to your pa and ma."

"Oh, they let me go all right. Didn't seem to be no problem with that. And I wasn't in Louisiana all that long; I've been back home awhile now." Jack picked up a leg and began chewing on it.

Things didn't seem to have turned out too well with his family in New Orleans. Anne wished Martha would let it lie. Martha kept talking.

"Is that right?" she said, holding the platter for Callahan at the other end of the table. Jack was on his third piece of corn bread and seemed unwilling to pass it down.

"Well, what you been doing with yourself these last years? I suppose you fought."

"Yes, ma'am," he answered, his eyes on his plate.

"Ma, leave him be," Shaughn said from behind the bar. There wasn't a man alive who wanted to talk about the war. He sure didn't want the man who'd stolen up Anne to talk about it, maybe impressing her by his bravery or some such.

"Leave him be? When I only want to know how the sweetest boy in all the world has gotten on?" Martha argued, hands on hips.

Callahan choked on a piece of corn bread.

Gabe slugged him on the back a time or two until Callahan pushed him off.

"You want to know what he's been up to, I'll tell ya, Miz O'Shaughnessy." Callahan grinned.

Jack looked up from his plate with a scowl. He might have even growled. Callahan ignored him.

"I met him in the Texas Rangers, signed up the same day and worked with him more than not during the years before the war. Got disbanded then and it was the biggest mistake that Yank government ever made. Outlaws going wild down there now."

"They'll start it up again," Gabriel said, putting down his beer. "They'll see the need."

"Damn straight they will," Callahan said. "But they'd better get on it quick."

"The Texas Rangers," Martha said. "That's a hard life."

"Hard times need hard remedies, ma'am, and besides, it warn't too much rougher than what he'd been doing," Callahan winked. "Running cattle up and down the country."

"Really? Did you ever come to Abilene before now, Jacques?"

Jack wiped his mouth with the back of his hand. "Yes, ma'am, I did."

"Started cowboying when he was little bigger than a calf, the way I hear it." Callahan grinned broadly. "What were you, Jack, ten, eleven?"

"Shut up, Callahan," Jack said, looking down at his empty plate.

"That's when he met up with Gabe here," Callahan jerked a thumb at Gabriel. "Both of 'em just boys, out running cattle on the range with a quick horse under 'em. A boy's dream."

"It's a dream if you need to eat," Gabriel said. "And we did."

"Just boys . . ." Martha said. "But why would you leave your family?"

"Wanted to come West, ma'am," Jack said. "West is where home is."

"But your family, didn't they mind?"

Jack leaned back on the two rear legs of his chair. "Didn't seem to."

"And what about you, Mr. Gabriel? Did your family know what you were about?"

"No family for me to worry about, ma'am," he said.

Or any family to worry about him. Anne listened and heard all that was not being said by these men who had lived so hard. Jack had seen his parents murdered, been sent to family that didn't know him and clearly hadn't wanted him, made his way West somehow and gotten a dangerous job with long hours and short pay as a cowhand, joined the Texas Rangers, who didn't take just anybody and where the work was more dangerous than any payment could cover, and then fought in the Civil War. And when that was done, he'd started hunting bounty, looking for the worst men the country had to offer to get them behind bars or swinging from a well-deserved rope.

Martha was right. Jack had turned out well.

Jack had been taking care of himself in a callous world for most of his life and there he sat, soft-spoken, self-assured, self-reliant. And alive. He'd grown into a man.

Her life had been nothing like his. She'd been sheltered and protected from all that could have hurt her; she'd had her share of troubles, but she hadn't had to face them alone. In fact, she hadn't had to face much of anything at all. And she suddenly knew why. Miss Daphne. When her grandfather had walked out, the final man in the family to do so, her grandmother had held her head up and forced each of them to do the same. Her grandmother had held them all together. Her grandmother had given them a home when her father had left her and her mother alone for the last time in that small town in Missouri. Her grandmother had seen they had a roof and food and clothes. And pride.

Her grandmother was a hard woman, but she'd seen hard things happen to her children, and no matter what else a person could say about her, and there was a lot, she'd kept her family together and she'd given them a home.

Anne had known a home and family. Jack had known neither, not since the age of four, except in dreams. Unwelcome dreams.

Anne felt a hard, cold knot of silent resentment ease up inside her. She hadn't had it so bad. If nothing else, Miss Daphne had done the best she could and if it wasn't quite what Anne would have wanted for herself, she was going to be grateful for what she had, thankful for the effort that had been put in on her account. That's all a person could do, his best. To want more was asking for misery.

And hadn't she done that, too?

Wanting what no one could give her. Her ma couldn't make her pa come home. No one could do that, not even she.

It was time to grow up.

She was a married woman now. She looked over at Jack,

at the still, quiet strength of Jack, and she let the sight of him fill her up. If he left, he left. She couldn't make him do a thing; the only person she could control was herself and she was none too good at doing that. Jack was here, now, and she was going to enjoy him for as long as he was about. Somehow, she'd find the strength to live when he moved on and moved off. Somehow.

She wasn't going to think about her pa anymore. She wasn't going to wonder if he would come. She wasn't going to wish for anything about that train, either getting on or getting off. She was going to stay where Jack was. She was going to choose to—

The whistle of the noon train from Lawrence pierced the air. Anne jerked in her seat and looked over at Jack. He was looking right back at her.

"Train's late today," Martha said. "It's half past noon at least."

Sheriff Lane was looking at her. Jack was looking at her. Shaughn O'Shaughnessy was looking at her. Callahan and Gabriel ended up looking at her because everyone else was. The train was in. She was supposed to go meet it. They all knew that. It was what she did. She met the train and no explanation was necessary.

It was time to grow up, to leave behind childish dreams of finding her father or uncle or grandfather climbing down off the train, but what harm did it do? It was just a train. It didn't mean much. It was more habit than wish.

Anne rose from her seat and tucked in her chair. Martha's apron was still draped over her and she took that off, laying it over the back of the chair. Jack looked into her eyes, his blue eyes searching, measuring, asking . . . ? She didn't know what; maybe she didn't want to know. It was enough that she had seen the shadow of pain and then the shield of resignation drop down over him. How many times had he had to do that in his life? Face the pain of something he couldn't change and then find the strength to resign himself to it? Too many times. Maybe even one time too many.

But what could she do about it now? Everyone expected her to go.

It was just a train.

Jack looked down into his beer and took a long swallow. Anne left, her boots making a hollow sound on the wood floor, echoing after her when she was gone.

He stayed put and let her face her shadows alone.

Jack drained his glass and let Callahan carry the conversation. He and Lane were talking about the Rangers, with Gabe throwing in his two bits every now and again. He let them talk on around him and without him. He had nothing to say.

Anne had left to go meet the train. Again. Whatever it was that gnawed on her was still chewing and there didn't seem to be a thing he could do about it. Hell, if she wanted to keep meeting the train, looking for the lost men in her life, he could hardly blame her. If he thought his mama or pa might appear on a train coming through someday, he'd meet every damned one. It was the least he would do and he wasn't going to fault Anne for still having the need of them even when she had him lock, stock, and barrel. A gal needed more than a husband in her life to love and fuss over. If she did love him.

She'd never said she loved him.

But a gal would hardly marry a man if she didn't.

Unless that gal was Anne, a woman who said yes every time she ought to be saying no.

Jack scraped his chair getting up. Callahan and Lane ignored him. Gabriel looked up at him, catching his eye; Jack shook his head. Gabriel stayed put and lit a cheroot, nodding as Jack walked out of the Mustang Saloon.

He wasn't going to let it get to him. A woman was allowed to marry a man without his digging through her reasons, not when he figured more than a few would bite him where he was soft. Anne was his wife, that was permanent; she'd figure that out eventually. And love was something that could grow between a man and a woman, if they tried hard enough, and he was going to try. He was going to get what his parents had had between them if it took all his life, and he was going to get it with Anne. Even if the only thing she seemed dead sure of was that he'd leave her someday.

Jack walked away from the depot and toward the cemetery. It wasn't a long stretch of the legs to get there and the day was soft with spring. Still no rain, though there'd been dew on the ground that morning; that should have put a smile on Miss Daphne's face if nothing else would.

The cemetery was on a small rise. Tucker's grave had already been dug; he was due to go in later that day. Jack walked right by that open wound in the soil and went to a small wooden cross planted in fresh-turned ground.

He stood there awhile, ignoring the sound of the train steaming up to go, trying to block out his thoughts about what was happening in the heart of his wife down there at the depot.

A breeze came up sudden and he lifted his face to it. A flock of birds skimmed over the ground in a swarm half a mile off, silent hunters.

The wood on the cross was raw, unweathered, and splintered. He laid his hand on the wood and spoke into the wind.

"I'll come every day I'm in town. That's a promise. You'll not be forgotten, Mary Hyde."

With that simple vow, he was finished. Jack walked off down the rise, leaving the sight of the birds at their hunt behind him. Leaving Mary until tomorrow.

He made his way back into Abilene, thinking about Anne, about his folks, thinking about everything but the killings. It was then, when his thoughts were floating free, that he remembered the horse. He'd seen the tracks of that horse, right in Abilene. Seen it just days ago when he was walking Anne to the train. He knew where that horse was stabled. Powell's.

With long strides, Jack walked into Powell's stable. The old man was sitting on an old chair in the shadows, smoking his pipe. He jumped to his feet when Jack walked up to him.

"What you want?" Powell snapped.

"I want to look over your stock, that's what I want," Jack said.

"I don't need you coming in here—"

"What you need is to shut your mouth and do what I'm telling you," Jack said, past all patience. "You got a horse in here who's heavy on his right rear foot."

Powell just stood there, his pipe hanging from his fingertips, his mouth open.

Jack gave up on getting any help and went to each stall, running his hands over each horse by way of hello. "You got any stock out? They all here?" he asked.

He pulled out the black and led him around. It wasn't the black.

"Anyone use the sorrel besides Mrs. Halloway?" Jack asked. "Answer me, Powell!"

"No," Powell said, tightening his grip on his pipe. "And you got no call to be coming in here and messing with my animals. I got a responsibility—"

"You got that killer's horse in here, that's what you got!" Jack said on a bark of command.

"Hell, no," Powell said. "I ain't got no such."

"Hell, yes; I've seen the tracks."

Jack pulled out the dun and led it around by the halter. The right rear walked heavy. It was the dun. The shoe was a bit off and it was throwing off the gait.

"Who hires the dun?"

Powell just looked at him, his pipe falling from his fingers to land in the dust.

"Who? Who had it last? Who takes it most?"

"The doc. The doc uses the dun," Powell said.

She wasn't quite to the train when he stopped her with a touch on her arm.

"You meeting the train on the day after your wedding, what's that say about your husband?"

She looked up at Doc Carr and felt her spine go stiff. "It doesn't say anything about anything. I always meet the trains. Everybody knows that."

"And everybody knows why. Or at least I do," he said.

It was quiet where they were. The train didn't have anybody on it and was already steaming up to go. The wind was blowing hard and cold; there wasn't anyone outside. Even the Walton kids were gone from the streets.

"I just like to meet the trains," she said, pulling her arm from his.

Doc smiled and took her arm again, light and friendly, and walked her to the tracks. "And you'd just like to find your pa climbing down off one of them one day, wouldn't you? Or maybe you'd like to climb on and leave Abilene. I always thought that's what you wanted. I was so sure you didn't want to stay around here. Married. Settled."

"Really, Doc, I didn't know you spent so much time thinking about me. I'm not that important."

"You're important to me, Anne," he said, smiling down at her.

There was something wrong with this conversation. Everything about it was out of balance. She just couldn't think what to do about it.

"Thank you. I guess that's what makes you a good doctor, your caring about us all."

The train moved off, a loud, dark noise that moved faster as it left Abilene behind. How many times had she wanted to run out of Abilene? Plenty, but she hadn't wanted it enough to make it happen. She saw that now.

She was full of excuses, full of reasons why she couldn't leave Abilene until later, always later. But the truth was, she couldn't leave her family. She loved them. They loved her. Their love was what had kept her from drifting off like the wind, caught up and carried on into the hazy distance of the unknown.

"Oh, but I care about you in a special way, Anne. You must have felt it," he said.

They were alone, in that place where prairie, town, and tracks met. It was a lonely place without the train to fill it. Loneliness was a frightening place with Doc Carr.

"No," she said, pulling her arm free again and keeping herself away from him. "I sure didn't. You have a good day, Doc."

He stood in her way, smiling and pleasant, but still, he stood in her way. She didn't know what to do. If he'd been rude or forceful, she could have fought back, maybe, but he was being nice. What could she do but be nice in return?

"I will. Thank you, Anne. You know, I was almost married once, back in Texas," he said, looking out at the prairie that rolled all around Abilene. She couldn't seem to stop herself. She hesitated and looked out to where he was looking.

"No, I didn't know. What happened?"

"She refused me," he said and then he started to chuckle. "Can you believe that? She turned me down cold."

"I'm sorry, Doc. That must have been hard to take."

She sort of felt like she should pat him on the shoulder or some such thing, to offer comfort somehow. That's what she would have done, if he hadn't said all those strange things about her being special.

"Oh, it was harder for her, all told," he said. "I even offered her my mother's cameo as a token. She laughed, she actually laughed and said she'd never accept me. She didn't want to marry me. She didn't want my children in her."

"Doc—"

This was getting too personal. She didn't need to know all this about Doc Carr's past. She didn't want to know it.

"But, like I said," he interrupted, turning to face her, his eyes lit with amusement, "it ended up hard on her. She should have accepted me. She should have agreed to be my wife."

"Well, but a woman knows her own heart and she'd just have to follow where it led her, wouldn't she? She couldn't marry a man she didn't love, a man she didn't want to live her life with, could she?"

Of course she couldn't. Anne felt like crying, it hit her so plain and so hard. Of course she couldn't. A woman wouldn't marry a man for anything but love and the belief that they would build a life together, day upon day, trouble upon trouble. She hadn't married Jack because he needed her. She'd married him because she needed him. She needed him like air, like sun, like—

"You ain't listening, Anne. And you need to listen. I'm telling you something real important," Doc said.

"I'm sorry, Doc. It's just that, well, I just figured out something that—"

"Here's the cameo." He held it out toward her. It was beautiful, a woman's profile in ivory, her hair pulled up to cascade down around her white shoulders. "You'd take it, wouldn't you, Anne?"

"It's lovely, but I couldn't take it. You give that to your wife. You just need to find the right woman this time."

She really had to get on. She wanted to find Jack. She wanted to get away from Doc and his cameo and his conversation.

Doc laughed. She didn't laugh with him. Something was wrong about that laugh. It was cold and hard, just like the wind blowing her hair into her face. They were too alone. There wasn't any life around them. There wasn't any noise, nothing but the sound of the wind and Doc Carr's laughter.

"I've found her," he said, still holding the cameo out to her. "I've found her more than once, Anne. It's not so hard to find a woman to marry you if you know the right words."

"That's fine, Doc. Well, I need to get on."

"No, Anne. You don't need to get anywhere," he said.

She watched him come to her as if he were coming out of the dust and the wind; hands first and then arms and then eyes. He was still smiling when he put the cameo with its velvet ribbon around her throat. The wind seemed to force him on her. She couldn't seem to push him off. She wasn't even sure she tried.

This wasn't right. He was choking her. The cameo was on too tight. Something wasn't right and she needed to fight. That's what Jack would say. She needed to fight for herself.

Doc was killing her.

She didn't have a gun. It was too heavy and too oily and too ugly with her dress and so she didn't have a gun. Stupid.

And all she'd wanted was to be smart.

All she was going to be was dead.

She reached up and clawed at the cameo, but Doc was too strong. Jack had taught her that lesson; he'd also taught her what to do next. She reached up and dug her thumbs into his eyes. He yelped a little and then pulled the cord tighter while his body backed away from hers, giving her some space, but giving no air.

No air. Just pain. Just panic.

She had lights swimming in her eyes and her head was pounding. She was getting weaker. The wind still blew hard and cold. How long had it been since this started?

A Kiss to Die For

When would the wind stop blowing? How much longer before she stopped feeling it?

A rifle shot ripped through the wind, sending it howling away across the prairie. For once, she didn't jump at the sound. Doc let go, twisted, and fell at her feet, the cameo tangled in his fingers. He was bleeding, shot in the hip, his body shattered. But he was still breathing.

She couldn't see clearly, everything was black and bright lights, but she knew who had saved her. She knew. She tumbled to the ground, unable to stand, but she knew who'd catch her up. She knew who'd cradle her as she lay in the hard dust of Abilene.

She felt him before she heard him. The presence that was Jack. The hard comfort of Jack. She blinked against the pounding in her head and saw him in outline against the sky. He held his gun easily, pointing it down at Doc. Doc was grunting, maybe in pain, maybe in anger; she didn't know. She didn't care.

"Cover your ears, Anne; it's going to be loud," Jack said.

She did it. And she closed her eyes. She knew what was coming. He was Jack Skull. He was going to do his job.

With a single shot, Doc was dead. She heard his breath stop. She didn't look to see where Jack had shot him. She didn't want to live with that memory. And then he was kneeling beside her, the smell of gunpowder strong on him.

"Anne," he said, his voice a whisper against her skin. "Anne, talk to me. Tell me you're all right. Tell me you're alive. Tell me I'm a fool for not keeping you in my sights every minute."

Tell him? She couldn't tell him anything, her wind was cut and her throat felt as if it were pressed down to her spine. She could feel him and she could almost see him through the red haze in her eyes. And she could hear him.

"Anne, I'm a damned fool. I've been a damned, lost

357

fool since I first saw you. I haven't taken a solid step on firm ground since you first looked at me with those eyes of yours. If Callahan knew how far gone I am for you, I'd have to kill him to shut him up. You talk to me, Anne. You tell me you're alive and that you'll stay alive."

She swallowed gingerly and whispered, "You looked . . . at me."

She could see him now. His eyes were full of tears and he was staring at her like she was his sole reason for living. Yeah, she could see that. She could see so much; even through the wind and the dust, she could see that Jack loved her.

He chuckled, rocking her in his arms, and then he laughed, soft and warm. "I'm not taking the blame, Anne. You did the looking. I just tumbled into Abilene, having no idea who the reception committee was."

"And if . . . and if you had known?" she said with a rasp to her voice, looking her fill of him. Letting her eyes just rest on the sight of him gazing down at her, holding her, loving her.

He traced her face, his fingertips gentle on her skin, his eyes drinking her in as if she were the last water for a thousand miles. Like he wanted to drown in her. Like he loved her.

"If I'd known you were waiting for me in Abilene," he said, "I would've arranged to be born here."

He was leaving. Jack was leaving, taking the train to Dodge to deliver Jessup to the marshal there. Jessup was handcuffed to a seat already. She wasn't going to share her good-bye to her husband with Jessup listening at her elbow. She had walked Jack to the train, which was right and natural. She knew he'd be back. He might leave, but he'd always come back. He was Jack Skull and a woman would have to be a fool to think he'd act like any other man. She was no fool. No, she was smart.

It'd been a week since Doc's death. She was still bruised, a long necklace of a bruise around her throat with two vertical lines in the center, where the cameo had been. Her throat hurt when she laughed, but she was all right. Jack had done some scouting and found out some things about Doc Carr.

He'd been a cook for a Texas outfit and he'd been in charge of the chuck wagon on two trips up the Abilene Trail. He wasn't a real doctor. He'd killed seven women that they knew about and Jack was still afraid they'd find one or two more before the story was all told. It sure didn't look like Carr had killed Bill.

That was bad. Bill's killer was still out there somewhere. Of course, some folks still wanted to lay that at Jack's feet, but she didn't care. They were wrong and time would prove it. And if time didn't prove it, she still didn't care.

"You going to kiss me again or you going to make me wait till I get back?" Jack said.

Anne looked up at him, her fingers trailing over his shirt and all the new buttons she'd sewn on. "I'm going to make you wait. You think I'm pretty free with my kisses. I'm going to prove you wrong."

"You sound set and determined," he said, pressing himself against the fullness of her skirts.

"I am. You scared?"

"Yeah, I'm scared," he said. "No man alive wants a determined woman sharing his bed, unless it's that she's determined to put her mouth on his—"

"You shut!" she said, laughing, scandalized. "I'm a proper married woman. You don't talk to me like that. You do, and I'll pull my gun on you."

"Yeah, you'd do that, wouldn't you?" he said, grinning. "You're a fighter. I could tell that by the first look."

She was carrying a gun. She'd been carrying a gun since Doc had attacked her. Now she knew why Jack always wore his. It was a good, safe feeling to be able to take

care of yourself, no matter what came off the prairie
hunting up trouble. She felt the heft of it as it lay quiet
and comforting in her reticule. It was a smaller one than
the one Jack had given her before, a pocket pistol, lighter,
easier to carry, easier to shoot. She was getting used to
the feel of it.

"That's good," she said. "I don't want any trouble from
you."

"Ma'am, you ain't ever gonna have trouble from me."

Trouble? He was all trouble. But she didn't mind. He'd
taken her plans and thrown them to the wind to be blown
off to Canada, and she didn't mind at all. But in the next
instant all thoughts were blown away, even thoughts of
Jack.

A man got off of the train. A man. The man she'd spent
a lifetime waiting for. Her father.

He had changed some in the fifteen years he'd been
gone from her. He was fuller in the jaw, his dark brow
shaggier, his nose thickened, his hair lightened with gray.
But it was he. She would have known him anywhere.

It was her dream come true, everything she'd ever
longed for, every hope realized. And yet it was a nightmare, worse even than Jack's nightmare, because her father, Tim Ross, walked by her with a tip of his hat and
an empty smile. Walked by her and kept going. He didn't
know her.

She'd found a wanted poster years back with his name
and his face and she'd taken it. Wanting something of
him. Wanting some way to etch his face in her mind the
way her longing for him was etched in her heart.

She turned to follow him without a second thought.
He was her father and he'd come back. That's all she
knew. All she needed to know.

Jack pulled her away from following her father and
snapped, "Get on the train. Now!"

He pushed and she took a few steps toward the train, the iron stair rail bumping her shoulder.

No. She wasn't leaving. She wasn't going to leave her father. Not now.

"Anne, get outta here!" Jack said harshly, just before he knelt on the platform and pulled his gun.

When Jack pulled his gun, he meant to pull the trigger. He meant to empty the gun of shells. He meant to kill. And he was pointing the gun at her father.

"No!" she said as loud as she could. It came out a whisper, a whisper that rocked against the wind coming off the prairie, a whisper that slammed against Jack's soul. "He's my father."

Her father pulled his gun at the commotion behind him, dropped to his knee, and fired off a shot. It spat up chunks of wood from the platform. No. This dream was turning all wrong, twisting into something that couldn't be happening. But it was. They'd kill each other, these two men who were hardened by life and used to killing.

Which man could she bear to live without?

No, that wasn't a question she could answer. She had to stop it somehow.

How?

Her voice was frozen in her throat, her breath pressed down into her lungs with the fist of despair. Everything slowed until she could count the beats of her heart, timing them against the breath she wanted to gulp down into her. Jack was the law. Her father stood outside the law.

It didn't matter. Tim Ross was her father.

In the stretched-out eternity of that moment, she saw blood soak through the fabric of Jack's pants from a thrown splinter, saw the tiny dark hairs covering the back of her father's hand, saw the gleam of metal and heard the distinctive clink of the hammer begin thumbed back for another shot.

Which could she live without?

Jack didn't move. His gun was out, but he didn't raise it, didn't have his thumb on the hammer, didn't even duck in the face of that monstrous black barrel facing him.

He was going against every lesson he'd learned to survive, every lesson he'd taught her to survive. He wasn't going to do the one thing he did best: fight. Jack, who slept with his gun by his side, who wasn't comfortable unless he had three hundred rounds of ammunition on his body, who had learned that a gun was his best friend in his fight to stay alive, wasn't going to fight. He was a fighter to the marrow and he wasn't going to fight.

He wasn't going to fire.

Her father fired off his shot. He was too experienced to hesitate when the target was clear and he was too experienced not to miss.

The bullet hit Jack high up on the outside of his right thigh.

Jack flinched as the bullet tore a hole in him; he grunted, but he didn't fire. No, he didn't fire. He looked at Anne over his shoulder, his blue eyes hot with pain and anguish. And resolve. But no regret. Not one ounce of regret. The look in his eyes tore the breath out of her lungs.

Anne felt the breath she had been trying to force rise up in a willing sob as she watched his blood turn his pants dark and wet. He wasn't going to fire. He wasn't going to fire on her pa. She watched Jack lower his gun even more. Never once did his eyes leave hers.

"Go on. Get outta here," he commanded, his voice a growl of loving despair.

He was trying to protect her in every way he could. He didn't want her near when shots were fired, perhaps going wide of the mark, and he didn't want her near, watching as her father killed him, shot by shot. He didn't want her to see him die.

A Kiss to Die For

Jack would die, because he wouldn't be the one to kill her pa.

Understanding exploded in her heart like gunpowder. He wouldn't be the one to take her father from her; not again. He would let himself be shot to death, piece by piece, wound by wound, because he loved her. He'd let himself be killed, because he loved her, and he was trying to give her what she wanted. Even if he died doing it.

Love endures all things.

Yes, love endured all things, even death. Even letting your life bleed out so that the woman you loved could have a father.

Tears ran out of her like water. She couldn't stop them. She couldn't make anything stop.

She couldn't make Jack defend himself.

Did she want him to? Did she want Jack to save himself, risking her father's life?

Her father? Tim Ross had never loved her, not like this. Only Jack loved her enough to die for her, but he wasn't going to. Not on her account. Not if she could stop it.

She had to stop it.

Which could she live without?

The man kneeling in the dirt had never been her father; that knowing burst open like rotten fruit in her hand, sticky and spoiled. Tim Ross had never been a father. He didn't know her. She didn't know him. All she had ever had was the dream of him.

And the dream of Tim Ross was nothing but cloud compared to the solid reality of Jack.

Which could she live without?

She moved then, freed from hesitation and indecision. Never in her life had she felt so free, free of the need to find a place in the world, free of the need to be loved. She was loved. Jack loved her and she loved him and that's all there was to know.

She had the answer. It was a question she could answer, after all.

Anne didn't hesitate. For once, she didn't hesitate. Because it was Jack. Because she could do anything for Jack. She was ready for Tim Ross.

Love bears all things.

A shot rang out, deafening, cracking, rebounding. Tim Ross fell on his face in the dust of Abilene, Kansas, shot by his daughter. She'd killed him with the first shot. She hadn't flinched and she hadn't hesitated. Because it was for Jack.

Jack rose stiffly to his feet, his eyes never leaving Anne. He knew Brazos, Tim Ross, was dead. A shot like that could only kill. Anne had killed her father. That took some doing. He didn't know what she'd do now, if she'd blame him, if she'd regret it and dissolve in tears or rise up in anger. What did a woman do when she'd killed her pa to save her man? He didn't know. He never would have asked it of her. He'd never have pushed her to it, no matter how many bullets had found their way into him. He'd take any bullet to save Anne sorrow and trouble.

She'd waited all her life for her pa to come back. He wasn't going to be the one to take Tim Ross away from her again and for good. He'd lived through that kind of loss. He wasn't going to be the one to do it to her.

"Anne," he said, catching her eye. She was staring at Brazos, watching the blood run out to turn the dust to red mud. She'd shot him right in the head. "Anne, look at me."

"Should I keep firing? Should I empty the gun?" she said. Her voice sounded small, lost.

Damn, but he hadn't wanted anything like this for her. This was his world; he hadn't wanted her stained by it. He'd only wanted to keep her safe, but how could a woman be safe, be clean of the filth of life, with him around? He carried filth and sorrow like a coat on his back.

"No, you can put it away," he said. "Go on."

She hesitated and then slipped the gun into her reticule.

"Anne?"

"Jack? You all right?"

"Am I all right?"

They weren't moving. They seemed frozen in place on the platform. He wanted to run to her, take her up and hold her close. But he couldn't. Because of him, she'd killed a man. Her own pa.

"I'm fine," he said, forcing himself to stand. It wasn't much of a wound, just some blood and some sting. "Anne? Will you look at me?"

She did. She wasn't crying. She wasn't anything. She was just looking.

"Anne, I'm sorry about your pa . . . all this time . . . all that waitin'."

"All that time?" she said, taking a step toward him.

"You were waiting for him. He was all you ever wanted. I know it. I'm sorry," he said.

"Jack," she said, her voice husky and soft. "It was you," she said. "It was you all that time, all those years. I was waiting . . . for you."

Chapter Twenty-five

The killing had drawn a crowd. Seemed the whole town, including Jessup at the train window, just had to see what was going on down at the train platform. It sure had been a busy week in Abilene.

Things like this just seemed to happen naturally when a bounty hunter took up residence.

"What happened?" Lane asked, arriving just ahead of the crowd.

"I shot him," Jack said, holding Anne at his side. He was leaning on her as if she were the rock that held up the world and she looked like she could do it, if pressed.

"You know who you shot?" Lane asked.

"Yeah, Brazos. Reward money on him. I'll take it in cash," Jack said.

Lane looked at Anne, who was looking at Jack. Did she know that the man lying in a red mess at the bottom of the platform was her pa? Probably not. She'd been real little when he took off. No reason for her to remember him. No reason at all for her to know that Tim Ross had been going by the name of Brazos for ten years now.

366

"Sounds fair," Lane said. "Looks like he got you some. Anne? How're you doing?"

"Fine," she said, her voice soft and high. Maybe a bit shaky, but she'd seen a shooting and that was to be expected from a gal as sensitive and sheltered as Anne was. "Jack needs some help, though."

"I'm fine, too," he said, looking down at her, his expression unreadable. "Don't no one need to worry over me."

"I'm going to worry over you and you're going to like it. I get to take care of you some now. Understood?" Anne said, looking up at Jack, her expression fierce with love.

Jack cleared his throat and said softly, "Understood." He kissed the top of her head and said, "You sure got grit, you know that?"

She gripped him hard around the waist and said with a crack in her voice, "I sure do."

The crowd reached them then and, at a look from Charles, the women of Anne's family kept still about the dead man at their feet. Tim Ross was dead, but then, he'd been dead to them for years. And now Nell was free and they both knew it. That was all he needed. Once this was cleaned up, he was making Nell his woman and no one, not even Miss Daphne, was going to get in his way. If Jack could manage that woman, so could he.

It didn't take long to clean up the mess Brazos had made in his dying. Once he was carted off, the crowd disappeared with him. Jack, Anne, Miss Daphne, and Nell went off to the Mustang to get him cleaned and doctored some. If Anne hadn't had such a good hold of Jack, he might have wandered off to avoid the fussing that was sure to come, but she had him good and tight.

Neil McShay watched the crowd that had encircled Tim Ross wander off, the Walton kids the last to go and that after being hounded and snapped at by their mother, and looked back toward where Sarah was standing. He'd never known Sarah Davies to be so still.

"You want to go with them? Jack's been shot up some and I guess Anne could use the help."

"No," she said, "I think she'll be fine." And then she smiled. "Did you see how she stood with Jack? That girl's come of age today."

Neil walked across the street and stepped up on the boardwalk. "She's married, too. Been married a whole week now."

"So she has," Sarah said lightly, her eyes shining with expectation.

"So, I guess that makes you free to set your horse on your own trail."

"Free as wind in the grass." She smiled, not meeting his eyes.

"So," he said, edging up next to her, crowding her against the platform, "want me to tell you how Ida died?"

Sarah smiled and let out her breath. "You gave me a scare, Neil; I would have bet money you were going to show me."

Neil didn't say a word, but his smile was a mile wide.

The saloon was crowded, the old man who usually had himself wedged in a corner was up and drinking, rubbing elbows and listening to the talk. Quiet talk it was; nobody seemed to want to talk out loud about what had just happened. Callahan would have, but Jack had told him to shut up straight out and, for once, Callahan was listening.

"Hurt much?" Anne asked as she tied on the bandage.

"Not much," he said. He'd seen worse.

"I'm not much of a hand with gunshot wounds," she said, straightening up.

"You'll do," he said, smiling.

"I don't want to get any good at it either," she said, frowning down at him.

"You sure are an easy woman to please. All's I got to do is not get shot."

"Yeah, but can you do it?" she said.

The old man at the bar listened to them with a smile and then edged over to the sheriff. Gabe and Callahan were down by the window, Martha and Shaughn were washing up, and Nell was walking Miss Daphne home. What he had to say to the sheriff would be private, at least to begin with; what Lane did later was out of his hands.

"You don't need to hunt over God's creation for the man who killed Bill Tucker. He's standing right next to you."

Charles looked sideways at the man next to him. He wasn't much to look at; lean, old, stooped, and gray. Hardly the kind of man to gut a man like a deer.

"Yeah, I know what you're thinkin', but I was a prime man in my day and I still have the strength I earned all those years riding the range and tossing cattle."

"Why'd you do it?" Lane asked softly. "And why are you telling me? You covered your trail good."

"Thank ye," he said amiably. "I'll tell you who Tucker was and then you won't need to ask why I did it."

"I'm listenin'."

"Tucker was no good. His game was to sweet-talk women out of their land. He took my sister for everything, five years back; she died soon after. I lost his trail and then picked it up again here, in Abilene. I've just been sitting, waiting for him to make his move, wanting to catch him in the act. I thought he was trying it with Anne and her folks; looked like he was, too, until Jack Skull rolled into town. That put an end to him."

"Why'd you kill him?"

"He deserved it."

"What's the rest of it?" Lane pressed.

"I'm dying," the old man said easily. "Couldn't wait no more for Tucker to do something where I could catch

369

him. My time's up and I wasn't leaving the world with him still in it."

Lane studied the man in front of him. There was no reason for him to lie, and what he said fit in with other things he'd been finding out about Tucker and his land deals.

"What was your sister's name?" Lane asked.

"Mary Claire Hancock."

It was a name on his list. It fit.

"You going to string me up?"

The sheriff studied the foam on his beer and thought about it. "How long did you say you have?"

"I'll not make it to summer."

"Hell, I'm not going to waste county money on a trial for you," Charles said. "Besides, there ain't no evidence connecting you with Tucker."

The old man studied the sheriff with bright eyes and murmured, "Thank ye," before he ambled off to his corner of the saloon.

The sheriff bought him a fresh beer before he left.

"You don't tell her that was her pa, that's my advice," Miss Daphne said to her daughter as they walked home.

"I agree. No child needs to see her father killed. I wouldn't burden her with that," Nell said. "It sure is a strange ending though, isn't it?"

"I find much of what goes on in this world more than passing strange," Daphne said, "but the Lord's ways are mysterious. At least to me."

"Why, Ma, you hardly ever talk like this. You all right?"

Miss Daphne took one of Nell's hands and held it in her own. "I'm just sorry that it had to come to this for you. I sure thought the world of Tim Ross when you married him. It's not easy being that far wrong."

"It's so long past now, and we were all wrong," Nell

said. "We couldn't have known how he'd turn. He was a good man once."

"You were right to leave him. He would have ruined Anne," Miss Daphne said. "He would have ruined you." She gave Nell a quick squeeze of her hand.

"Well, not a one of us is ruined and it's mostly because of you."

"That's enough of that kind of talk. I didn't do any more than any mother would and you know that for a fact."

"True enough," Nell said. "But I thank you anyway."

"With you feeling this obliging, you might want to take a bit more advice from me today," Daphne said.

"My, you're asking me to take your advice? You really aren't yourself, are you?" Nell teased.

"You hush," Daphne said, dropping Nell's hand. "You tell Anne that you left Tim. She's old enough to know the truth of that. It might even help her some."

"I think you're right. I'll tell her."

"And another thing."

"Here it comes."

"You tell Charles Lane that I won't have another wedding in my house until I have a better show of flowers. Poor Anne didn't even have daisies."

"You might need to tell him that yourself."

"Then I will," Daphne said as she climbed the porch steps. "Don't think I won't."

"Oh," Nell said with a smile as she followed her mother inside, "I know you will."

"Why did you do it?" Anne asked.

"You know why. There's no need for you to face all that," Jack said.

They were walking out toward the house, Jack limping and taking it slow. It was going to take them a while, but they had plenty of time.

"You didn't need to, you know."

"I surely did. Don't go telling me what my job is, Anne. I'm going to protect you whether you like it or not. I'd advise you to make up your mind to like it." He stopped and leaned against the wall of Powell's livery. "Why did you do it?" he asked softly.

"You know why," she said, looking up into his face. He sure was beautiful. He surely was that sweet-eyed boy Martha O'Shaughnessy remembered. "I wasn't going to stand around and watch you get killed. I'm not going to lose you, you know, just make up your mind to it. I'm keeping you around."

"It was a hard thing you did today. You're going to be living with it a long time."

"Jack," she said, wrapping her arms around his waist and burying her face against his shirtfront, "as long as I'm living with you, I can live with anything. He wasn't worth spit and you . . . you," she said, tears filling her voice and flooding her eyes, "you need to do a better job of taking care of yourself. I can't always be around to fight your battles. You need to learn how to fight back. Some things are worth fighting for, you know."

"Yeah?" he said, wrapping his arms around her, watching the Walton kids playing in the street, smelling the tobacco of Powell's pipe somewhere behind him, hearing the whistle of a train just coming into town. "Like what?"

She lifted her face, her light blue eyes huge and fierce. "Like us."

PAMELA CLARE

MacKinnon's Rangers: They were a band of brothers, their loyalty to one another forged by hardship and battle, the bond between these Highland warriors, rugged colonials, and fierce Native Americans stronger even than blood ties.

UNTAMED

Though forced to fight for the hated British, Morgan MacKinnon would no more betray the men he leads than slit his own throat—not even when he was captured by the French and threatened with an agonizing death by fire at the hands of their Abenaki allies. Only the look of innocent longing in the eyes of a convent-bred French lass could make him question his vow to escape and return to the Rangers. And soon the sweet passion he awoke in Amalie had him cursing the war that forced him to choose between upholding his honor and pledging himself to the woman he loves.

ISBN 13: 978-0-8439-5489-0

To order a book or to request a catalog call:
1-800-481-9191
This book is also available at your local bookstore, or you can check out our Web site **www.dorchesterpub.com** where you can look up your favorite authors, read excerpts, or glance at our discussion forum to see what people have to say about your favorite books.

LAURA DREWRY

Author of *The Devil's Daughter*

"The best of Americana, with the right hint of devilishness." —*Romantic Times BOOKreviews*

HELL HATH NO FURY...

Deacon knew Rhea wouldn't exactly be happy to see him again. But he didn't think she'd shoot him. Right in the shoulder, no less. He'd experienced worse pain in his life, though. Besides, now Rhea would have to let him stay until she could nurse him back to health. Oh, the hardship.

LIKE A WOMAN SCORNED

His convalescence would give Deacon a chance to convince Rhea he'd turned over a new leaf, that he was no longer the son-of-a-devil who up and left her all those years ago in a puff of sulfurous smoke. Now he's a man who knows what he wants. And no matter what kind of trouble Rhea has gotten into while he was away, what he wants more than anything is to win her heart.

DANCING WITH THE DEVIL

ISBN 13: 978-0-8439-6049-5

❏ YES!

Sign me up for the Historical Romance Book Club and send my FREE BOOKS! If I choose to stay in the club, I will pay only $8.50* each month, a savings of $6.48!

NAME: _____

ADDRESS: _____

TELEPHONE: _____

EMAIL: _____

❏ I want to pay by credit card.

❏ VISA   ❏ MasterCard.   ❏ DISCOVER

ACCOUNT #: _____

EXPIRATION DATE: _____

SIGNATURE: _____

Mail this page along with $2.00 shipping and handling to:
Historical Romance Book Club
PO Box 6640
Wayne, PA 19087
Or fax (must include credit card information) to:
610-995-9274
You can also sign up online at **www.dorchesterpub.com**.
*Plus $2.00 for shipping. Offer open to residents of the U.S. and Canada only.
Canadian residents please call 1-800-481-9191 for pricing information.
If under 18, a parent or guardian must sign. Terms, prices and conditions subject to change. Subscription subject to acceptance. Dorchester Publishing reserves the right to reject any order or cancel any subscription.